THE PENGUIN POETS

THE PENGUIN BOOK OF ENGLISH CHRISTIAN VERSE

Peter Levi, a classical scholar, archaeologist and poet, was born in 1931. He has translated two books for the Penguin Classics, Pausanias' *Guide to Greece* (two volumes) and *The Psalms*, as well as a collection of Yevtushenko (with R. Milner-Gulland) for the Penguin Modern Poets, and has edited Johnson's *A Journey to the Western Islands of Scotland* and Boswell's *The Journal of a Tour to the Hebrides* for the Penguin English Library. His book *The Light Garden of the Angel King*, an account of his travels in Afghanistan, is published in the Penguin Travel Library. He is Professor of Poetry in the University of Oxford.

THE PENGUIN BOOK OF
ENGLISH CHRISTIAN VERSE

Edited by Peter Levi

PENGUIN BOOKS

Penguin Books Ltd, Harmondsworth, Middlesex, England
Viking Penguin Inc., 40 West 23rd Street, New York, New York 10010, U.S.A.
Penguin Books Australia Ltd, Ringwood, Victoria, Australia
Penguin Books Canada Ltd, 2801 John Street, Markham, Ontario, Canada L3R 1B4
Penguin Books (N.Z.) Ltd, 182–190 Wairau Road, Auckland 10, New Zealand

First published 1984

Introduction and selection copyright © Peter Levi, 1984

Printed and bound in Great Britain by
Cox & Wyman Ltd, Reading

Set in 9/11 Bembo Linotron

FOR DEIRDRE

CONTENTS

CONTENTS

CONTENTS

CONTENTS

CONTENTS

CONTENTS

CONTENTS

ACKNOWLEDGEMENTS

Thanks are due to the copyright holders of the following poems for permission to reprint them in this volume:

W. H. Auden: 'Precious Five', 'The Shield of Achilles' and 'Law Like Love', from *Collected Poems* by W. H. Auden edited by Edward Mendelson, to Faber & Faber Ltd.

John Betjeman: 'Sunday Morning, King's, Cambridge', from *Collected Poems*, to John Murray (Publishers) Ltd.

Charles Causley: 'I Am the Great Sun', 'Sailor's Carol', 'Timothy Winters' and 'King's College Chapel', from *Collected Poems* published by Macmillan Publishers Ltd, to David Higham Associates Ltd.

T. S. Eliot: 'Landscapes III. Usk' and 'Little Gidding', from *Collected Poems 1909–1962* by T. S. Eliot, to Faber & Faber Ltd.

David Gascoyne: 'Tenebrae' and 'Ecce Homo', from *The Collected Poems of David Gascoyne* copyright © Oxford University Press 1965, to Oxford University Press.

Robert Graves: 'In the Wilderness', from *Collected Poems 1975* published by Cassell Ltd, to Robert Graves and Cassell Ltd.

Geoffrey Hill: 'Genesis' from *For the Unfallen*, to André Deutsch Ltd.

Elizabeth Jennings: 'Teresa of Avila', 'Works of Art' and 'LXXV from The Sonnets of Michelangelo', from *Collected Poems* published by Macmillan Publishers Ltd, to David Higham Associates Ltd.

David Jones: excerpts from the volumes *In Parenthesis* and *The Anathemata*, and part of 'The Hunt' from *The Sleeping Lord*, all by David Jones, to Faber & Faber Ltd.

Nicholas Kilmer: 'Petrarch (1)', to Anvil Press Poetry Ltd.

Philip Larkin: 'The Explosion', from *High Windows*, 'Days' and 'Water' from *The Whitsun Weddings*, both by Philip Larkin, to Faber & Faber Ltd.

D. H. Lawrence: the six poems, from *The Complete Poems of D. H. Lawrence*, to Laurence Pollinger Ltd and the Estate of Mrs Frieda Lawrence Ravagli.

Robert Lowell: 'The Quaker Graveyard in Nantucket', from *Poems 1938–1949* by Robert Lowell, to Faber & Faber Ltd.

Louis MacNeice: 'Whit Monday', 'Goodbye to London', 'Apple Blossom' and 'Belfast', from *The Collected Poems of Louis MacNeice*, to Faber & Faber Ltd.

Edwin Muir: 'The Incarnate One', from *The Collected Poems of Edwin Muir,* to Faber & Faber Ltd.

John Ormond: 'Cathedral Builders', to Christopher Davies (Publishers) Ltd.

Theodore Roethke: 'In a Dark Time', 'The Marrow' and 'The Right Thing', from *The Collected Poems of Theodore Roethke*, to Faber & Faber Ltd.

C. H. Sisson: 'In Autumn', from *In the Trojan Ditch: Collected Poems and Selected Translations*, to Carcanet Press Ltd.

Edith Sitwell: 'Still Falls the Rain', from *Collected Poems* published by Macmillan Publishers Ltd, to David Higham Associates Ltd.

Stevie Smith: 'Scorpion', from *The Collected Poems* published by Allen Lane, to the executor, James MacGibbon.

Dylan Thomas: 'Do Not Go Gentle Into That Good Night', from *Collected Poems* published by J. M. Dent & Sons Ltd, to David Higham Associates Ltd.

R. S. Thomas: 'The Country Clergy', to Granada Publishing Ltd, 'Ann Griffith', from *Laboratories of the Spirit*, to Macmillan Publishers Ltd.

W. B. Yeats: 'Calvary', to Michael B. Yeats and Macmillan London Ltd.

INTRODUCTION

By the vaguest definition, Christian poetry might be any verse written by a Christian, or in a Christian framework or language, in Christian centuries, in a Christian society. By the narrowest, it might be whatever poem had a good angel for a muse, whatever poem purely and deliberately expressed Christianity. But there has never really been a Christian society in the full sense of the word, nor can there be, perhaps. There have been no completely or thoroughly Christian centuries, and English has never quite become a Christian language. Probably only the dead Latin of the Middle Ages, a half-language, did that. More important still, poetry itself is not a precisely Christian activity; it is even doubtful whether there exist any perfectly Christian human beings.

There are touches of paganism and of common humanity in all our languages, including the Greek gospels and the liturgy of the church. Unchristian and prechristian elements of many kinds always survive the baptismal font and the experience of conversion; a poet may easily believe that his own poetry is a perfectly Christian expression, but critics will often find other elements in those same poems, for better or worse. Is *Paradise Lost* the Christian epic we once believed it to be, or something else as well? It has more in common with other baroque epics of the Christian period than it has with the gospels. William Empson has demonstrated that even its dogmatic platform is unlike what most of us accept as a Christian message. It is a nice question whether that increases or decreases its force as poetry.

Surely one ought not to demand from Christian poetry a narrow dogmatic rectitude, at least not in advance, not as a matter of definition. If our definition of Christianity in poems is too severe, we shall be left with an anthology of little more than hymns. Sidney and Shakespeare will be too broad-minded to be called Christian poets, Donne will be too personal, Blake too unorthodox, Tennyson and Browning too riddled with doubt. The most interesting thing that emerges about Christian poetry in English as one tries to classify it is this: that if Christianity is widely defined, we have a vast range of splendid Christian poetry, if narrowly, we have very little, and most of it less

powerful than we imagine; but in either case the high point is the
same, the poetry of George Herbert, in which Christianity and human
nature, language and personal depth and musical skill, most perfectly
coincide.

I have allowed no atheism, but there are a few poems, one by Shel-
ley for instance, over which I hesitated a long time, where the poem
is Christian in spite of itself, that is, in spite of an intention at the top
of the poet's mind. I have also sometimes allowed poems like Milton's,
Christian in intention but less so in their undercurrents. The light
shines in the darkness, and the darkness does not comprehend it, but
poetry and the muses frequent the twilight where light is visible but
darkness is not subdued. It is a forest light, *entre le chien et le loup*, or
so I have come to believe. For the purposes of this collection, a Chris-
tian poem is a poem by any Christian which touches on Christian
themes or implicitly throws a Christian light on some common expe-
rience. My view of what Christian attitudes and Christian poetry are
like has always apparently been more catholic than I realized, but the
task of considering this collection for months and years on end has
brought the paradoxes out into the open.

The 'Lyke-Wake Dirge' was discovered by John Aubrey the anti-
quary. It is obviously a pagan survival that took its half-Christian form
in an early England we can hardly even imagine. But to exclude it
from Christian poetry would be like refusing Christian burial to the
builders of our most ancient churches. And this is a magnificent poem.
On the other hand Alexander Pope was consciously a Christian, and,
I believe, a very great poet. But in his celebration of reason and of
virtue, the tendency away from or beyond or independent of Chris-
tianity is so undeniably strong that I did not feel it decent to claim him
as a Christian poet. I admire him unreservedly, but I felt his poetry
was less Christian, even though it was more orthodox, than Tennyson's
In Memoriam.

Some poets, and some whole ages of poetry, turned out to be
disappointing and surprising from this point of view. There has been
much more splendid and profound Christian poetry written in modern
times in English than one would ever have imagined until one came
to collect it. It is like the baskets full of crumbs when the gospel feast
was over; or else our souls are more Christian than we admit. But in
the wonderful sixteenth century, I could find very little. That is prob-
ably because the reformation and the beginning of modernity had cut
away branches from the medieval tree, and English poetry took time

to find a new religious voice. It may also be because of the flattening bulk of the Bible and the weariness of controversy. The secular imagination of Shakespeare and his generation gave us the greatest poetry this country, or perhaps any other, has ever had. But in all that vast opening of horizons and victorious and intricate flowering, Christianity was a silent condition, it was not the dominant theme.

We have excluded medieval poetry, including Chaucer and Langland, because of the problems of spelling and language. That was a decision I could personally hardly have borne, but I was glad in the end that the publisher had taken it for me; otherwise at least half of this collection would be medieval. It would unreasonably have overshadowed the genuine Christian gestures of later centuries. It would have roamed backwards as far as Beowulf. The medieval world is very different from ours. In the poetry of Dante one can see more or less from end to end of the universe; it is hard for us to feel at home in that strange and clear atmosphere. By contrast, the Christian poetry of the seventeenth century in English, though not in all other European languages, is peculiarly modern. It is about our own doubtful and uncomforted souls.

Earlier Christian anthologies have sometimes contained acres and acres of Browning and Patmore, or else a numerous assortment of the hymns sung in church. It is always difficult to be clear-eyed about the familiar poetry of childhood, and perhaps equally so about poetry set to ennobling and moving music. I hesitated a long time over 'Calvary Mount', which we sang as boys to music by Tallis; also over 'Jerusalem my happy home', which as a child I read and reread during sermons. But in both cases the full version is uneven, the singing version too smooth. I was not brought up on the hymns of the Church of England, though I have learnt to sing them and love them. But the worst fault of any poetry, particularly religious poetry, is a certain falsity, an archaism and formality that pretend to a spirit they are not quite able to summon up. One may be crazy about 'For those in peril on the sea'; it is close to the heart of worship, but that does not make it a great poem. 'Quality', as C. A. Trypanis wrote about the song 'Lili Marlene', 'can be a matter of circumstance'. So after a lot of heart-searching I have excluded the vast majority of hymns, because as poems they are not quite good enough. If I had written them myself, I would still not print them in a book of poems. At their worst they are as Robert Lowell described them in 'Waking Early Sunday Morning':

O Bible chopped and crucified
in hymns we hear but do not read,
none of the milder subtleties
of grace or art will sweeten these
stiff quatrains shovelled out four-square –
they sing of peace, and preach despair;
yet they gave darkness some control,
and left a loophole for the soul.

It would be a mistake to impose on all Christian poetry in English the perfect good manners of the sanest, calmest poems. Some of it is by nature extremely wild. Giles Fletcher, for example, deserves a hearing not only for his influence on Milton. Charles Cotton strikes us nowadays as almost too cheerful to be called Christian at all, but the happy sensuousness of Cotton and Herrick and Fletcher is, after all, a possible Christian attitude.

All things were Adam's, and all things are ours.
Our suns as bright as his, our fruits and flowers
As sweet and good: nought's blasted but our powers . . .

Personally, I find this attitude as Traherne expresses it* preferable to that of the Olney hymns. The Christian ritual drama I have printed by Yeats is wild in another way, but at the same time it is very strong and ought to be better known. Would I have given pleasure by printing some of Christopher Smart's mad poetry? Regretfully I excluded it, because the organizing principle of its wildness and dramatic depth really is mad, and sets it apart from Christianity. Its detail is magnificent only out of context. In a not utterly dissimilar way I found that the sane but tortured extravagance of language in Crashaw and in Robert Southwell ruled out most of their poetry from this collection. Those techniques might be applied to anything whatsoever, like rococo decorations or almost like wallpaper. They are Christian poetry in the sense in which Bavarian churches contain Christian woodwork.

On the other hand, I am disinclined to accept the conclusion of Donald Davie's argument about Christian style in his introduction to the *New Oxford Book of Christian Verse*. His argument is as lucid and coherent as his taste, and the collection is fascinating. It differs widely from this one, though he does quote the same lines of Lowell as I do

* In *Commentaries of Heaven*, a newly discovered manuscript; cf. *Times Literary Supplement*, 9 March 1982.

about hymns. Perhaps it was inevitable to do so; Lowell is hard to forget. The new Oxford anthology is excellent. But I hesitate at Professor Davie's view, perhaps more protestant than mine, perhaps a matter of temperament and background, that for Christian poets the question of style is 'what sort of language is most appropriate when I would speak of, or to, my God? And it is not only the puritans among poets who appear to have decided that the only language proper for such exalted purposes is a language stripped of fripperies and seductive indulgences, the most direct and unswerving English.' The plain style is fine, though rarer in English than at first appears. (I doubt whether George Herbert's style ought to be called plain.) But when one begins to speak of 'exalted purposes' one is lost. The sense of 'exalted purposes' generates not simplicity but the false sublime.

And in fact there are many decent ways of talking about God; early Christian writings offer a variety. As for addressing God, it is hard to see why one tradition is preferable to another, and there are many. The faults and excesses of language that are unacceptable in religious poetry are unacceptable in all personal poetry. The problems of Christian style are only a part of the problem of all poetry. No poem is really a sincere and stuttering outpouring, directly from the heart. Nor does any religious poem quite attain the dimension of silence in which God is most closely approached on earth, although one may suspect that religious poetry at its best is perhaps no more than an introduction to that silence.

Allegory and rhetorical grandeur cannot be banished at this time of day from the resources of Christian poetry. In fact a simple and strong rhetoric has very often been the mark of Christian poetry, from the time of Everyman and the Mystery Plays down to some of the poems of David Gascoyne. It is as if the poetry were a climbing vine that must wreathe itself around scaffolding, God being invisible and offering it no support. As for fripperies, the poetry of Donne and Herbert is full of toys and ornaments. The awfulness of frivolous ornament really begins with poets capable of little else. One of my worst disappointments in making this anthology has been George Wither. I know by heart a few verses by him which I have always greatly admired, but a most laborious search through his thousands and thousands of lines turned out to be time wasted. He is capable of starting a poem, 'Lord, in a public Meeting, I, this day, . . .' and equally of 'My Withered Sprouts were then by thee replanted, / Where they enjoy the nourishment they wanted . . .'. In fact he combines the earnestness

23

of the emerging lower middle class with awkwardly applied fripperies.

Adrienne Rich, in her informative and well considered introduction to the works of Anne Bradstreet (Harvard, 1981), makes the important suggestion that 'the seventeenth-century Puritan reader was not in search of "new voices" in poetry. If its theme was the individual in his experience of God, the final value of a poem lay in its revelation of God and not the individual.' That would go a long way towards explaining the jejuneness, the dryness and the false sublimity of so much Christian verse. She observes also the influence of *La Sepmaine de la Creation* by Du Bartas, translated by Joshua Sylvester as *The Divine Weekes and Works*. In English that influence was pervasive and somewhat deadly, in French it was crushing. In contrast to the awful Du Bartas and the unhappy George Wither, Christian poetry in English is often radical and wild. It is a dramatic soul-language.

Its relation to our history is intimate but indirect. Sometimes a poet does seem to express directly the state of the nation, but it may as likely be William Blake or D. H. Lawrence as John Dryden. I have included part of *Annus Mirabilis* because it is such a magnificent poem, and at a critical point a radically Christian imagination just touches it. Lines like 'The Paraclete in fiery pomp descend' suggest a direction that English life and poetry might have taken in the eighteenth century, had our history been otherwise. By contrast, a poem like Matthew Arnold's 'Rugby Chapel', although it may generate a mood of false optimism and gloomy endeavour, deserves serious consideration because arguably it is the classic statement of what became the prevailing feeling and the best feeling in English Christianity for a hundred years or more. As a poem it is good enough, though not a great masterpiece like 'Dover Beach'. That can be claimed as a Christian poem because of the cirumstances of its composition; otherwise one might call it the first and most moving English expression of agnostic humanism. But Arnold wrote it on his honeymoon on the way to a French monastery; it expresses thoughts and feelings many of us know well and call Christian.

It is even more difficult to defend one's omissions, yet only the same kind of reasoning and redefining is involved. Newman's 'Lead kindly light' is a hymn, moving to most of us by its associations. As a mere poem, I like it less than Tennyson's 'Crossing the Bar', though they have both been hackneyed to death, and in both I deeply distrust the mood that lies behind their tones. Newman's 'Dream of Gerontius' has a stronger claim, but I find it terribly hard to separate that from

Elgar's music, and from the authority of the Victorian views of death our schoolmasters imposed on us. The 'Dream of Gerontius' is wonderful, but is it a wonderful poem? The case of Christina Rossetti is still more distressing. She was a lovely poet, but I am unable to find that she ever wrote a complete poem without serious faults, at least among her Christian poetry. The privacy and subtlety of women's poetry suits religious themes; in these qualities Emily Dickinson is supreme and also typical, although I found her almost impossible to anthologize. We need those intensely personal voices.

After all, there is no liturgical poetry in English, except for the four-square hymns intended for congregational singing. There has been rather little public poetry touching on Christian themes at all except for epitaphs, which are as private as they are public. Dryden's *Annus Mirabilis* is one of very few exceptions. The curious wildness of Christian poets has been an inner wildness. By wildness I do not mean madness. The private madnesses of Collins and Smart and John Clare are surely the result of their financial and social circumstances; the wild quality of Blake is personal, visionary, inspired more by God than by the muses. A respectable academic lady from Oxbridge recently wrote, in a book which was well reviewed, that 'the true author of Blake's lyric poetry was ... the revolutionary British lower middle class'. It may be that Christian poetry throws light on class conflict, or on the role of an unregarded class, but, to put it mildly, Blake was the author of his own lyric poems; they are intensely personal. His roots were deeper than Milton's, as deep as Shakespeare's, very much deeper than class roots.

Another wild and beautiful Christian poet is Thomas Wyatt, but here the problem was different, and more clearly historical. I did not find his translations of the psalms quite good enough to use; moving as they are now and again, they should possibly be classed with Milton's Latin verse version. It was a popular enterprise in the reform movement and in early protestantism to translate the psalms. It was for translating the psalms that Marot had to flee to Geneva in 1543; but Marot's French psalms are very much more remarkable than Wyatt's. It would have been more tempting to print a piece of Wyatt's satires, but wherever possible I have tried to avoid fragments of poems, so that I chose in the end a poem which for some reason most of Wyatt's editors reject. It is a ballad in traditional form, and it has the gravity of Villon and of the Middle Ages. It was certainly written by a courtier and by a great poet, and apparently by someone in the

Tower at the time when Anne Boleyn's lovers were beheaded. There is no reason at all why it should not be by Wyatt; I cannot see who else could have written it.

Compared to the strangeness and gravity of Wyatt, Skelton's voice, a few years earlier, is lighter and more embittered. But from such a fine poet one must have something, and he is a witness not only to his theme but to the name and nature of poetry. His skill, his humour and his detachment are his most intimate ingredients; it is not possible to have a Christian poet without having a poet first. (That mistake was made by those who over-valued Keble.) Skelton illustrates very well that there is no pure Christian poetry and very little pure Christianity. One must use the language that there is and the forms that come to hand. Much of what is conveyed will be only the musings and voices of our common language, the inevitable atmosphere of the forms we handle. A Catholic and a protestant flute concerto composed in 1765 will not differ very much. Chaucer's universality is preferable to the sectarian ghettos of later Christianity.

Probably Christian poetry is purest when it is anonymous, and among anonymous poems in the merest touches and allusions. There is no epic poetry in modern English; the period of illiterate, traditional composition before Shakespeare was too short. Could there have been Christian epic poems, a true epic in our language? The *Chanson de Roland*, and even Beowulf, suggest that there could, if the Norman conquest had not set back English language and poetry so badly, or if the Middle Ages had lasted longer. But the Bible in English when it came took the place of epic poetry. The people took to the Bible, and it stifled as much as it nourished. Theologians swarmed around it like mosquitoes, and poets translated bits and pieces of it into depressing verse. The future of genuine Christian poetry lay with what was individual and radically personal, or else with Milton. But things had once been otherwise. The Robin Hood poems never came together at the right temperatue and pressure to produce a true epic, yet they were not far off from one when the world altered. The few lines I have taken from a ballad were chosen only as one might pick a blackberry from the hedge of a green lane. They must serve as a mere taste, a mere symbol of the quality of Christian feeling in those poems. The Robin Hood ballads speak, as all anonymous, traditional poetry always has done, for unknown people and older generations to whom we owe much more than we realize of our thoughts and our feelings and whatever else goes to make poetry.

The famous disruption of Christian tradition that took place later was just a part of a more vast disruption that we can trace now through centuries. Christian poetry has not been marked by a recent original sin or a historical fall from grace; there really were never any Christian centuries, only a light shining in darkness. The disruptions that we sense at the enlightenment or the reformation or the industrial revolution were part of a longer historical process. We ought not, therefore, to be surprised at the persistence of religious poetry and of Christianity itself into the present century. Nor is the passionate unorthodoxy of poetry confined to modern poets like Blake or D. H. Lawrence. Individual intensity has increased not because faith has decayed, but because the moral world we must all inhabit has become intolerable, and freedom of spirit a rare possession.

To say that is not to underestimate the quiet old work-horse of the Church of England jogging along from year to year. It has its poetry, and the admirable tribute of R. S. Thomas to the country clergy does not differ from a long tradition of similar thoughts and feelings except by its sharpness as language, its excellence as a poem. Yet I am conscious of my inadequacy in dealing with such material as the Olney hymns. Cowper is a poet of despair, and also of quiet recreation, of long walks in winter. I do not believe the hymns were his true vein. I have a sense that they were a drug against suicide, and even as a drug pernicious and ineffective. In those days the quiet and genuine notes of the Church of England went almost unnoticed, or they were everywhere, like church bells. Reading the poetry of the eighteenth century, one might almost believe that the greatest Christian poet was Virgil in his *Georgics*. I admit I would have some sympathy with that paradox.

In a way, English Christian poetry is curiously limited by being so extremely personal. There has been no intellect at work in it so sharp and probing or so deadly serious as Dante's. It can boast nothing so strong, long and passionately eloquent as the Byzantine hymns of Romanos. It has never created a poem as frightening or as grand as the Latin *Dies Irae*. There is a certain lack of space in English Christian poetry. This is a matter of period; English is a modern language. But we should admit that there have been curiously few Christian poems of merit on a great scale. In Milton's *Paradise Lost*, the scale and construction are one of the least Christian elements in the poem, though Milton is a poet so magnificent that it would be folly to wish him otherwise. After Milton we have one long celebration by Christopher Smart, and Tennyson's *In Memoriam*, and T. S. Eliot's *Four Quartets*.

Smart's classic praises, humming with private truth and idiosyncrasy long before his madness, were already appearing late in the day; his was a structure the Victorians might envy but could not imitate. The only Victorian Christian poem that has a comparable range, and inside which the human spirit has room to breathe, is *In Memoriam*. It is a long series of roughly connected thoughts and recurring feelings. Behind Cambridge stands the Rectory of Tennyson's childhood. In spite of its weaknesses of argument, the poetry succeeds overwhelmingly because of being so genuine; and at the same time the work of so great a poet, so brilliant a reviser of his own poems. It is not 'about' Christianity; no poem so personal and so wide-ranging is 'about' anything so precise. I do not find it at all a comforting poem, but I find its discomfort thrilling and its disquiet nourishing.

The *Four Quartets* are one of the great and classic works of modernism. Dame Helen Gardner has written so well and with such full information about them that I have no ambition to add anything here. They are not easy poems, and they are certainly complicated in their levels of meaning. I have been through stages of distrusting them for one reason or another, but they were always victorious at every rereading. I think now that they are profoundly personal and as profoundly Christian. I am not so sure of their apparently impersonal authority; they are not a scripture, they are more subjective than appears at once, but they are surely powerful and beautiful poems.

The *Four Quartets* are sometimes gnomic, even sybilline. They recapture lost tones of religious poetry, but always with a difference. It is as if God were very difficult to address or to speak about in the modern world, or as if the attempt demanded an integrity close to that of genius. This is really a problem of sensibility and of poetry, a problem of intellectuals, not a universal problem of modern man or of all Christians. The difficulty of the wizard-like writings of David Jones has a similar and similarly conscious cause. The works of David Jones and T. S. Eliot are, among other things, a continual pondering of integrity and purity in poetry. In both cases the most moving passages in their poems are in the end simple: it is as if a forest had to exist for the sake of a leaf.

It is curious that in most English Christian poetry God is not an active character in any drama but that of the Bible, and the biblical character of Christ is like a fact of nature. These are the verses by Wither I was unable to verify:

> Keep thou the morning of his incarnation,
> the burning noontide of his bitter passion,
> the night of his descending, and the height
> of his ascension ever in my sight.

But in a few poems God is a contemporary character, dramatic and almost unpredictable. That is one of the advantages of George Herbert and John Donne; in Henry Vaughan only the soul is dramatic. One cannot imagine Tennyson's or Matthew Arnold's God doing anything unexpected, or their souls either. In T. S. Eliot's *Four Quartets* God is once again a dramatic character, but the procedure of heavenly grace is vast and inevitable, like that of the seasons or of music. It looks as if these differences are not precisely choices made by poets; they are already present in the religious traditions that nourish personal poetry. A poet must write as he can; his God is the God of his world or his theology. In the earlier religious poetry, not only of the pagan Greeks but also of the severe Jews, God was most vigorously active. We celebrate in English those 'who rolled the psalm to wintery skies', but we are far from the days when the God of the psalms dressed himself for judgement simply in sandals, a sword-belt and a cloak; he was not in Hebrew a quiet and sublime principle, scarcely an all-father. God has been tranquillized by the rule of law and too many church services. Christian poetry is terribly personal because individuals must rediscover a God. The renewed vigour of T. S. Eliot's God is a projection of his own intellectual activity.

I have not reproduced the best translations of Hebrew poetry into English in this book for several reasons. The first is that the psalms are not exactly Christian. But in general only those translations are eligible here which are poems of great merit in English, and the psalms and prophecies in English make good prose and bad poetry, or so it seems. There must be an exception for Villon, partly because of the representative interest of his poem, which reaches back in Synge's translation from yesterday's Ireland into the Middle Ages, and partly because this really is in English a wonderful prose poem. It was on the edge of being eligible, and rules were made to be broken when necessary.

Alas that in English we have no native equivalent of John of the

Cross. Even Roy Campbell's swiftly and lightly moving version is different from the fire and grace of the Spanish. The uniqueness of the verse writings of John of the Cross is not so much a matter of sanctity or mysticism as it is of his passionate and profound nature. His language is as intoxicated by the earliest invasion of renaissance metre and pastoral convention into Spanish, which happened when he was a young man, as it is by the apprehension of the Spirit of God. The long prose commentaries that he wrote on his own poems, with their theological formality and their scholastic precision, coexist as strangely with his verse as the very different elements in Thomas Browne's *Religio Medici*. What John of the Cross has in common with the only other great saint who was also a great poet, Francis of Assisi, is lightness, fire, the whisper of the Spirit, a complete inward liberty.

Of all our poets Henry Vaughan is closest to those, but his thoughts are often painful, and he very seldom sustains through a whole poem the simple raptures of a few lines. The one lyric poet in English whose verses are morally Christian, and who wrote often as a Christian, yet whose numerous poems are very often as perfect as snowflakes, is William Blake. But Blake is a moral writer; he is a visionary and a prophetic poet with the same moral fire in his veins as the Hebrew prophets had. He is not a mystic thirsting for God and in love with God in the same sense as John of the Cross and Francis of Assisi and maybe Henry Vaughan. And he is not a man of the renaissance; on the contrary, he is rather puzzled by the enlightenment, not at all the same situation.

The 'divided tongues as it were of fire', which descended on the heads of the apostles at Pentecost, have run wild through many centuries. Christian poetry is a wildfire, it is not to be found always in the same direction. If it has any value as a witness to Christianity itself, that is because the act of poetry, the coming together of everything that goes into a good poem, or a great poem, confirms the moral seriousness, the human decency, of what is said. The poet speaks to us directly, and at once we take him seriously. That is not magic, it is the effect of a poem. It is in the discipline that every poet must undertake, that he should be taken seriously. In the romantic movement that discipline was well understood, although the poetry of Wordsworth is not always successful and not usually Christian. It may be that the *Hyperion* of Keats, with its Christ-like suffering Apollo, would have been a great and profound Christian poem if it had been finished, an English equivalent to Hölderlin. As it is, we have among all the great poems of the romantics in English, unless Blake was a romantic, only the *Rime of the Ancient Mariner*, one of the most unexpected and most fascinating of all Christian poems. It cannot be denied even by literary critics that love is the greatest of the Christian virtues.

★

Longer time might have produced a fuller book, but this one has taken long enough. I would like to acknowledge the constant help and advice of Eirian Wain in putting together the collection. Her remarkable range and almost more remarkable patience, her flair for the genuine wherever it was to be found, and her detestation of whatever was false or unattractive, made her help invaluable. It goes without saying that the mistakes I will be found to have made were my own, and made against her advice. If I could have added two more pieces at the last moment, they would have been 'Gabriel Dressing', from Cowley's *Davideis*, for its youthful high spirits, and perhaps Book One of Dryden's *Hind and the Panther*, where his wit and ability nearly outweigh one's distaste for *odium theologicum*.

The other anthologies of Christian verse that I have used in the past or consulted recently have been by David Cecil (Oxford), R. S. Thomas (Penguin), Helen Gardner (Faber), Elizabeth Jennings (Batsford), and Donald Davie (Oxford), and one called *Hymns as Poetry*, which I have lost and the names of whose editors I forget. But that is the fate of anthologies.

ANONYMOUS

A Lyke-Wake Dirge

This ae nighte, this ae nighte,
  – Every nighte and alle,
Fire and fleet and candle-lighte,
  And Christe receive thy saule.

When thou from hence away art past,
  – Every nighte and alle,
To Whinny-muir thou com'st at last;
  And Christe receive thy saule.

If ever thou gavest hosen and shoon,
  – Every nighte and alle,
Sit thee down and put them on;
  And Christe receive thy saule.

If hosen and shoon thou ne'er gav'st nane
  – Every nighte and alle,
The whinnes sall prick thee to the bare bane;
  And Christe receive thy saule.

From Whinny-muir when thou mayst pass,
  – Every nighte and alle,
To Brig o' Dread thou com'st at last;
  And Christe receive thy saule.

From Brig o' Dread when thou mayst pass,
  – Every nighte and alle,
To Purgatory fire thou com'st at last;
  And Christe receive thy saule.

If ever thou gavest meat or drink,
  – Every nighte and alle,
The fire sall never make thee shrink;
  And Christe receive thy saule.

If meat or drink thou ne'er gav'st nane,
  – Every nighte and alle,
The fire will burn thee to the bare bane;
  And Christe receive thy saule.

This ae nighte, this ae nighte,
  – *Every nighte and alle,*
Fire and fleet and candle-lighte,
  And Christe receive thy saule.

The Holly and the Ivy

The holly and the ivy,
  When they are both full grown,
Of all the trees that are in the wood,
  The holly bears the crown.
The rising of the sun
  And the running of the deer,
The playing of the merry organ,
  Sweet singing in the choir.

The holly bears a blossom
  As white as lily flower,
And Mary bore sweet Jesus Christ
  To be our sweet saviour.

The holly bears a berry
  As red as any blood,
And Mary bore sweet Jesus Christ
  To do poor sinners good.

The holly bears a prickle
  As sharp as any thorn,
And Mary bore sweet Jesus Christ
  On Christmas day in the morn.

The holly bears a bark
  As bitter as any gall,
And Mary bore sweet Jesus Christ
  For to redeem us all.

The holly and the ivy,
  When they are both full grown,
Of all the trees that are in the wood
  The holly bears the crown.

The Cherry-tree Carol

Joseph was an old man,
  And an old man was he,
When he wedded Mary
  In the land of Galilee.

Joseph and Mary walked
  Through an orchard good,
Where was cherries and berries
  So red as any blood.

Joseph and Mary walked
  Through an orchard green,
Where was berries and cherries
  As thick as might be seen.

O then bespoke Mary
  So meek and so mild:
Pluck me one cherry, Joseph,
  For I am with child.

O then bespoke Joseph
  With words most unkind:
Let him pluck thee a cherry
  That brought thee with child.

O then bespoke the Babe
  Within his Mother's womb:
Bow down then the tallest tree
  For my Mother to have some.

Then bowed down the highest tree
  Unto his Mother's hand;
Then she cried, See, Joseph,
  I have cherries at command.

O then bespake Joseph:
  I have done Mary wrong;
But cheer up, my dearest,
  And be not cast down.

Then Mary plucked a cherry
    As red as the blood,
Then Mary went home
    With her heavy load.

Then Mary took her Babe
    And sat him on her knee,
Saying, My dear Son, tell me
    What this world will be.

O I shall be as dead, Mother,
    As the stones in the wall;
O the stones in the streets, Mother,
    Shall mourn for me all.

Upon Easter-day, Mother,
    My uprising shall be;
O the sun and the moon, Mother,
    Shall both rise with me.

from *A Gest of Robyn Hode*

They toke togyder theyr counsell
    Robyn Hode for to sle,
And how they myght best do that dede
    His banis for to be.

Than bespake good Robyn
    In place where as he stode:
To morow I muste to Kyrke[s]ly
    Craftely to be leten blode.

Syr Roger of Donkestere
    By the pryoresse he lay,
And there they betrayed good Robyn Hode
    Through theyr false playe.

Cryst have mercy on his soule
   That dyed on the rode;
For he was a good outlawe
   And dyde pore men moch god[e].

JOHN SKELTON
(1460/4–1529)

from *The Manner of the World Nowadays*

So many cloisters closed,
And priests at large loosed,
Being so evil deposed,
     Saw I never.
God save our sovereign lord the King
And all his royal spring,
For so noble a prince reigning,
     Saw I never.

So many Easterlings,
Lombards and Flemings,
To bear away our winnings,
     Saw I never.
By their subtle ways
All England decays,
For such false Januays,
     Saw I never.

Sometime we sang of mirth and play,
But now our joy is gone away,
For so many fall in decay,
     Saw I never:
Whither is the wealth of England gone?
The spiritual saith they have none,
And so many wrongfully undone,
     Saw I never.

It is great pity that every day
So many bribers go by the way,
And so many extortioners in each countrey,
　　Saw I never:
To thee, Lord, I make my moan,
For thou mayst help us every one:
Alas, the people is so woe-begone,
　　Worst was it never!

Amendment
Were convenient,
But it may not be:
We have exiled verity.
God is neither dead nor sick;
He may amend all yet,
And trow ye so indeed,
As ye believe ye shall have meed.
After better I hope ever,
For worse was it never.

Januays: Genoese

SIR THOMAS WYATT
(?1503–1542)

from *Unpublished Poems by Thomas Wyatt and his Circle*

from the Blage Manuscript,
edited by K. Muir, Liverpool, 1961

Written May 1536. The Blage Manuscript is from Archbishop Ussher's Library, in Trinity College Dublin. Geo. Blage M.P. died in 1551 but was nearly burned for heresy in 1546. He was a close friend of Wyatt and Surrey.

No. XXVII

In mourning wise since daily I increase
Thus should I cloak the cause of all my grief,
So pensive mind with tongue to hold his peace,
My reason saith there can be no relief:
Wherefore give ear, I humble you require,
The affects to know that thus doeth make me moan.
The cause is great of all my doleful cheer,
For those that were, and now be dead and gone.

What though to death desert be now their call,
As by their faults it doeth appear right plain,
Of force I must lament that such a fall
Should light on those that so wealthy did reign;
Though some perchance will say of cruel heart,
A traitor's death why should we thus bemoan?
But I, alas, set this offence apart,
Must needs bewail the death of some begone.

As for them all I do not thus lament,
But as of right my reason doeth me bind;
But as the most do all their deaths repent
Even so do I by force of mourning mind.
Some say: Rocheford, hadst thou been not so proud,
For thy great wit each man would thee bemoan;
Since as it is so, many cry aloud:
It is great loss that thou art dead and gone.

Ah Norris, Norris, my tears begin to run
To think what hap did thee so lead or guide,
Whereby thou hast both thee and thine undone.
That is bewailed in court of every side,
In place also where thou hast never been
Both man and child do piteously thee moan.
They say: Alas thou art far over seen
By their offence to be thus dead and gone.

Ah Weston, Weston, that pleasant was and young;
In active things who might with thee compare?
All words accept that thou didst speak with tongue;
So well esteemed with each where thou didst fare.
And we that now in court do lead our life
Most part in mind do thee lament and moan;
But that thy faults we daily hear so rife,
All we should weep that thou art dead and gone.

Brewton, farewell, as one that least I knew.
Great was thy love with divers as I hear;
But common voice doeth not so sore thee rue
As other twain that doeth before appear.
But yet no doubt but thy friends lament ye,
And others hear their piteous cry and moan,
So doeth each heart for thee likewise relent
That thou gavest cause thus to be dead and gone.

Ah Mark, what moan should I for thee make more,
Since that thy death thou hast deserved best,
Save only that mine eye is forced sore
With piteous plaint to moan thee with the rest?
A time thou hadst above thy poor degree
The fall whereof thy friends may well bemoan.
A rotten twig upon so high a tree
Hath slipped thy hold and thou art dead and gone.

And thus farewell each one in hearty wise!
The axe is home, your heads be in the street;
The trickling tear do fall so from my eyes,
I scarce may write, my paper is so wet.
But what can help when death hath played his part,
Though nature's course will thus lament and moan?
Leave sobs therefore, and every christian heart
Pray for the souls of those be dead and gone.

HENRY HOWARD, EARL OF SURREY
(c. 1517–1547)

Tribute to Wyatt

Wyatt resteth here, that quick could never rest:
Whose heavenly gifts increased by disdain;
And virtue sank the deeper in his breast:
Such profit he by envy could obtain.

A head where wisdom mysteries did frame;
Whose hammers beat still in that lively brain
As on a stithe, where that some work of fame
Was daily wrought, to turn to Britain's gain.

A visage stern and mild, where both did grow,
Vice to contemn, in virtue to rejoice:
Amid great storms, whom grace assurèd so,
To live upright, and smile at fortune's choice.

A hand that taught what might be said in rhyme:
That reft Chaucer the glory of his wit.
A mark the which (unperfected, for time)
Some may approach but never none shall hit.

A tongue that served in foreign realms his king;
Whose courteous talk to virtue did inflame
Each noble heart; a worthy guide to bring
Our English youth by travail unto fame.

An eye whose judgment none affect could blind,
Friends to allure, and foes to reconcile;
Whose piercing look did represent a mind
With virtue fraught, reposèd, void of guile.

A heart where dread was never so imprest
To hide the thought that might the truth advance;
In neither fortune lost, nor yet represt,
To swell in wealth, or yield unto mischance.

A valiant corse where force and beauty met,
Happy, alas, too happy, but for foes,
Lived, and ran the race that nature set;
Of manhood's shape, where she the mould did lose.

But to the heavens that simple soul is fled,
Which left, with such as covet Christ to know,
Witness of faith that never shall be dead;
Sent for our health but not received so.

Thus, for our guilt, this jewel have we lost;
The earth his bones, the heavens possess his ghost.

SIR WALTER RALEGH
(c. 1552–1618)

The Passionate Man's Pilgrimage

Supposed to be written by one at the point of death

Give me my scallop-shell of quiet,
My staff of faith to walk upon,
My scrip of joy, immortal diet,
My bottle of salvation,
My gown of glory, hope's true gage,
And thus I'll take my pilgrimage.

Blood must be my body's balmer,
No other balm will there be given,
Whilst my soul like a white palmer
Travels to the land of heaven,
Over the silver mountains,
Where spring the nectar fountains;
And there I'll kiss
The bowl of bliss,
And drink my eternal fill
On every milken hill.
My Soul will be a-dry before,
But after it will ne'er thirst more.

And by the happy blissful way
More peaceful pilgrims I shall see,
That have shook off their gowns of clay
And go apparelled fresh like me.
I'll bring them first
To slake their thirst,
And then to taste those nectar suckets
At the clear wells
Where sweetness dwells,
Drawn up by saints in crystal buckets.

And when our bottles and all we
Are filled with immortality,
Then the holy paths we'll travel,
Strewed with rubies thick as gravel,
Ceilings of diamonds, sapphire floors,
High walls of coral and pearl bowers.

From thence to heaven's bribeless hall
Where no corrupted voices brawl,
No conscience molten into gold,
Nor forged accusers bought and sold,
No cause deferred, nor vain-spent journey,
For there Christ is the King's Attorney,
Who pleads for all without degrees,
And he hath angels, but no fees.

When the grand twelve million jury
Of our sins with sinful fury
'Gainst our souls black verdicts give,
Christ pleads his death, and then we live.
Be thou my speaker, taintless pleader,
Unblotted lawyer, true proceeder;
Thou mov'st salvation even for alms,
Not with a bribed lawyer's palms.

And this is my eternal plea
To him that made heaven, earth and sea:
Seeing my flesh must die so soon,
And want a head to dine next noon,
Just at the stroke when my veins start and spread,
Set on my soul an everlasting head.
Then am I ready, like a palmer fit,
To tread those blest paths which before I writ.

Epitaph

Even such is Time, which takes in trust
Our youth, our joys, and all we have,
And pays us but with age and dust;
Who in the dark and silent grave,
When we have wandered all our ways,
Shuts up the story of our days:
And from which earth, and grave, and dust,
The Lord shall raise me up, I trust.

FULKE GREVILLE, LORD BROOKE
(1554–1628)

from *Caelica*

SONNET CX

Sion lies waste, and Thy Jerusalem,
O Lord, is fall'n to utter desolation;
Against Thy prophets and Thy holy men,
The sin hath wrought a fatal combination;
   Profan'd Thy name, Thy worship overthrown,
   And made Thee living Lord, a God Unknown.

Thy powerful laws, Thy wonders of creation,
Thy word incarnate, glorious heaven, dark hell,
Lie shadowed under Man's degeneration;
Thy Christ still crucifi'd for doing well;
   Impiety, O Lord, sits on Thy throne,
   Which makes Thee living Lord, a God unknown.

Man's superstition hath Thy truths entombed,
His atheism again her pomps defaceth,
That sensual unsatiable vast womb
Of Thy seen Church, Thy unseen Church disgraceth;
   There lives no truth with them that seem Thine own,
   Which makes Thee living Lord, a God unknown.

Yet unto Thee Lord – mirror transgression –
We who for earthly idols have forsaken,
Thy heavenly image – sinless, pure impression –
And so in nets of vanity lie taken,
   All desolate implore that to Thine own,
   Lord, Thou no longer live a God unknown.

Yet Lord let Israel's plagues not be eternal,
Nor sin for ever cloud Thy sacred mountains,
Nor with false flames spiritual but infernal,
Dry up Thy Mercy's ever springing fountains:
   Rather, sweet Jesus, fill up time and come,
   To yield the sin her everlasting doom.

ANONYMOUS
(16th century)

Hierusalem

Hierusalem, my happy home,
    When shall I come to thee?
When shall my sorrows have an end,
    Thy joys when shall I see?

O happy harbour of the saints,
    O sweet and pleasant soil,
In thee no sorrow may be found,
    No grief, no care, no toil.

There lust and lucre cannot dwell,
    There envy bears no sway;
There is no hunger, heat, nor cold,
    But pleasure every way.

Thy walls are made of precious stones,
    Thy bulwarks diamonds square;
Thy gates are of right orient pearl,
    Exceeding rich and rare.

Thy turrets and thy pinnacles
    With carbuncles do shine;
Thy very streets are paved with gold,
    Surpassing clear and fine.

Ah, my sweet home, Hierusalem,
    Would God I were in thee!
Would God my woes were at an end,
    Thy joys that I might see!

Thy gardens and thy gallant walks
    Continually are green;
There grows such sweet and pleasant flowers
    As nowhere else are seen.

Quite through the streets, with silver sound,
    The flood of life doth flow;
Upon whose banks on every side
    The wood of life doth grow.

There trees for evermore bear fruit,
    And evermore do spring;
There evermore the angels sit,
    And evermore do sing.

Our Lady sings *Magnificat*
    With tune surpassing sweet;
And all the virgins bear their part,
    Sitting about her feet.

Hierusalem, my happy home,
    Would God I were in thee!
Would God my woes were at an end,
    Thy joys that I might see!

SIR HENRY WOTTON (?)
(1568–1639)

Adaptation of Horace, Odes IX, 3, Donec gratus eram tibi

Soul.   Whilst my soul's eye beheld no light
          But what streamed from thy gracious sight,
          To me the world's greatest King
          Seemed but some little vulgar thing.

God.   Whilst thou provedst pure, and that in thee
          I could glass all my Deity,
          How glad did I from heaven depart
          To find a lodging in thy heart.

Soul.   Now fame and greatness bear the sway
          (Tis they that hold my prison's key)
          For whom my soul would die, might she
          Leave them her immortality.

God. I and some few pure souls conspire
      And burn in a mutual fire,
      For whom I'll die once more, ere they
      Should miss of heaven's eternal day.

Soul. But Lord, what if I turn again
      And with an adamantine chain
      Lock me to thee? What if I chase
      The world away to give thee place?

God. Then, though these souls in whom I joy
      Are seraphims, thou but a toy,
      A foolish toy, yet once more I
      Would with thee live and for thee die.

EDMUND SPENSER
(1552–1599)

Easter

Most glorious Lord of lyfe, that on this day,
  Didst make thy triumph over death and sin:
And having harrowd hell, didst bring away
  Captivity thence captive us to win:
  This joyous day, deare Lord, with joy begin,
And grant that we, for whom thou diddest dye,
  Being with thy deare blood clene washt from sin,
May live for ever in felicity.
And that thy love we weighing worthily,
  May likewise love thee for the same againe:
And for thy sake that all lyke deare didst buy,
  With love may one another entertayne.
      So let us love, deare love, lyke as we ought,
      Love is the lesson which the Lord us taught.

An Hymne of Heavenly Beautie

Rapt with the rage of mine own ravisht thought,
Through contemplation of those goodly sights,
And glorious images in heaven wrought,
Whose wondrous beauty breathing sweet delights,
Do kindle love in high conceipted sprights:
I faine to tell the things that I behold,
But feele my wits to faile, and tongue to fold.

Vouchsafe then, O thou most almightie Spright,
From whom all guifts of wit and knowledge flow,
To shed into my breast some sparkling light
Of thine eternall Truth, that I may show
Some litle beames to mortall eyes below,
Of that immortall beautie, there with thee,
Which in my weake distraughted mynd I see.

That with the glorie of so goodly sight,
The hearts of men, which fondly here admyre
Faire seeming shewes, and feed on vaine delight,
Transported with celestiall desyre
Of those faire formes, may lift themselves up hyer,
And learne to love with zealous humble dewty
Th'eternall fountaine of that heavenly beauty.

Beginning then below, with th' easie vew
Of this base world, subject to fleshly eye,
From thence to mount aloft by order dew,
To contemplation of th' immortall sky,
Of the soare faulcon so I learne to fly,
That flags awhile her fluttering wings beneath,
Till she her selfe for stronger flight can breath.

Then looke who list, thy gazefull eyes to feed
With sight of that is faire, looke on the frame
Of this wyde *universe*, and therein reed
The endlesse kinds of creatures, which by name
Thou canst not count, much lesse their natures aime:
All which are made with wondrous wise respect,
And all with admirable beautie deckt.

First th' Earth, on adamantine pillers founded,
Amid the Sea engirt with brasen bands;
Then th' Aire still flitting, but yet firmely bounded
On everie side, with pyles of flaming brands,
Never consum'd nor quencht with mortall hands;
And last, that mightie shining christall wall,
Wherewith he hath encompassed this All.

By view whereof, it plainly may appeare,
That still as every thing doth upward tend,
And further is from earth, so still more cleare
And faire it growes, till to his perfect end
Of purest beautie, it at last ascend:
Ayre more then water, fire much more then ayre,
And heaven then fire appeares more pure and fayre.

Looke thou no further, but affixe thine eye
On that bright shynie round still moving Masse,
The house of blessed Gods, which men call *Skye*,
All sowd with glistring stars more thicke then grasse,
Whereof each other doth in brightnesse passe;
But those two most, which ruling night and day,
As King and Queene, the heavens Empire sway.

And tell me then, what hast thou ever seene,
That to their beautie may compared bee,
Or can the sight that is most sharpe and keene,
Endure their Captains flaming head to see?
How much lesse those, much higher in degree,
And so much fairer, and much more then these,
As these are fairer then the land and seas?

For farre above these heavens which here we see,
Be others farre exceeding these in light,
Not bounded, not corrupt, as these same bee,
But infinite in largenesse and in hight,
Unmoving, uncorrupt, and spotlesse bright,
That need no Sunne t'illuminate their spheres,
But their owne native light farre passing theirs.

And as these heavens still by degrees arize,
Untill they come to their first Movers bound,
That in his mightie compasse doth comprize,
And carrie all the rest with him around,
So those likewise doe by degrees redound,
And rise more faire, till they at last arive
To the most faire, whereto they all do strive.

Faire is the heaven, where happy soules have place,
In full enjoyment of felicitie,
Whence they doe still behold the glorious face
Of the divine eternall Majestie;
More faire is that, where those *Idees* on hie,
Enraunged be, which *Plato* so admyred,
And pure *Intelligences* from God inspyred.

Yet fairer is that heaven, in which doe raine
The soveraine *Powres* and mightie *Potentates*,
Which in their high protections doe containe
All mortall Princes, and imperiall States;
And fayrer yet, whereas the royall Seates
And heavenly *Dominations* are set,
From whom all earthly governance is fet.

Yet farre more faire be those bright *Cherubins*,
Which all with golden wings are overdight,
And those eternall burning *Seraphins*,
Which from their faces dart out fierie light;
Yet fairer then they both, and much more bright
Be th' Angels and Archangels, which attend
On Gods owne person, without rest or end.

These thus in faire each other farre excelling,
As to the Highest they approch more neare,
Yet is that Highest farre beyond all telling,
Fairer then all the rest which there appeare,
Though all their beauties joynd together were:
How then can mortall tongue hope to expresse,
The image of such endlesse perfectnesse?

Cease then my tongue, and lend unto my mynd
Leave to bethinke how great that beautie is,
Whose utmost parts so beautifull I fynd:
How much more those essentiall parts of his,
His truth, his love, his wisedome, and his blis,
His grace, his doome, his mercy and his might,
By which he lends us of himselfe a sight.

Those unto all he daily doth display,
And shew himselfe in th' image of his grace,
As in a looking glasse, through which he may
Be seene, of all his creatures vile and base,
That are unable else to see his face,
His glorious face which glistereth else so bright,
That th' Angels selves can not endure his sight.

But we fraile wights, whose sight cannot sustaine
The Suns bright beames, when he on us doth shyne,
But that their points rebutted backe againe
Are duld, how can we see with feeble eyne,
The glory of that Majestie divine,
In sight of whom both Sun and Moone are darke,
Compared to his least resplendent sparke?

The meanes therefore which unto us is lent,
Him to behold, is on his workes to looke,
Which he hath made in beauty excellent,
And in the same, as in a brasen booke,
To reade enregistred in every nooke
His goodnesse, which his beautie doth declare.
For all thats good, is beautifull and faire.

Thence gathering plumes of perfect speculation,
To impe the wings of thy high flying mynd,
Mount up aloft through heavenly contemplation,
From this darke world, whose damps the soule do blynd,
And like the native brood of Eagles kynd,
On that bright Sunne of glorie fixe thine eyes,
Clear'd from grosse mists of fraile infirmities.

Humbled with feare and awfull reverence,
Before the footestoole of his Majestie,
Throw thy selfe downe with trembling innocence,
Ne dare looke up with corruptible eye
On the dred face of that great *Deity*,
For feare, lest if he chaunce to looke on thee,
Thou turne to nought, and quite confounded be.

But lowly fall before his mercie seate,
Close covered with the Lambes integrity,
From the just wrath of his avengefull threate,
That sits upon the righteous throne on hy:
His throne is built upon Eternity,
More firme and durable then steele or brasse,
Or the hard diamond, which them both doth passe.

His scepter is the rod of Righteousnesse,
With which he bruseth all his foes to dust,
And the great Dragon strongly doth represse,
Under the rigour of his judgement just;
His seate is Truth, to which the faithfull trust;
From whence proceed her beames so pure and bright,
That all about him sheddeth glorious light.

Light farre exceeding that bright blazing sparke,
Which darted is from *Titans* flaming head,
That with his beames enlumineth the darke
And dampish aire, wherby al things are red:
Whose nature yet so much is marvelled
Of mortall wits, that it doth much amaze
The greatest wisards, which thereon do gaze.

But that immortall light which there doth shine,
Is many thousand times more bright, more cleare,
More excellent, more glorious, more divine,
Through which to God all mortall actions here,
And even the thoughts of men, do plaine appeare
For from th' eternall Truth it doth proceed,
Through heavenly vertue, which her beames doe breed.

With the great glorie of that wondrous light,
His throne is all encompassed around,
And hid in his owne brightnesse from the sight
Of all that looke thereon with eyes unsound:
And underneath his feet are to be found
Thunder, and lightning, and tempestuous fyre,
The instruments of his avenging yre.

There in his bosome *Sapience* doth sit,
The soveraine dearling of the *Deity*,
Clad like a Queene in royall robes, most fit
For so great powre and peerelesse majesty.
And all with gemmes and jewels gorgeously
Adornd, that brighter then the starres appeare,
And make her native brightnes seem more cleare.

And on her head a crowne of purest gold
Is set, in signe of highest soveraignty,
And in her hand a scepter she doth hold,
With which she rules the house of God on hy,
And menageth the ever-moving sky,
And in the same these lower creatures all,
Subjected to her powre imperiall.

Both heaven and earth obey unto her will,
And all the creatures which they both containe:
For of her fulnesse which the world doth fill,
They all partake, and do in state remaine,
As their great Maker did at first ordaine,
Through observation of her high beheast,
By which they first were made, and still increast.

The fairenesse of her face no tongue can tell,
For she the daughters of all wemens race,
And Angels eke, in beautie doth excell,
Sparkled on her from Gods owne glorious face,
And more increast by her owne goodly grace,
That it doth farre exceed all humane thought,
Ne can on earth compared be to ought.

Ne could that Painter (had he lived yet)
Which pictured *Venus* with so curious quill,
That all posteritie admyred it,
Have purtrayd this, for all his maistring skill;
Ne she her selfe, had she remained still,
And were as faire, as fabling wits do fayne,
Could once come neare this beauty soverayne.

But had those wits the wonders of their dayes
Or that sweete *Teian* Poet which did spend
His plenteous vaine in setting forth her prayse,
Seene but a glims of this, which I pretend,
How wondrously would he her face commend,
Above that Idole of his fayning thought,
That all the world shold with his rimes be fraught?

How then dare I, the novice of his Art,
Presume to picture so divine a wight,
Or hope t'expresse her least perfections part,
Whose beautie filles the heavens with her light,
And darkes the earth with shadow of her sight?
Ah gentle Muse thou art too weake and faint,
The pourtraict of so heavenly hew to paint.

Let Angels which her goodly face behold
And see at will, her soveraigne praises sing,
And those most sacred mysteries unfold,
Of that faire love of mightie heavens king.
Enough is me t'admyre so heavenly thing,
And being thus with her huge love possest,
In th' only wonder of her selfe to rest.

But who so may, thrise happie man him hold,
Of all on earth, whom God so much doth grace,
And lets his owne Beloved to behold:
For in the view of her celestiall face,
All joy, all blisse, all happinesse have place,
Ne ought on earth can want unto the wight,
Who of her selfe can win the wishfull sight.

For she out of her secret threasury,
Plentie of riches forth on him will powre,
Even heavenly riches, which there hidden ly
Within the closet of her chastest bowre,
Th' eternall portion of her precious dowre,
Which mighty God hath given to her free,
And to all those which thereof worthy bee.

None thereof worthy be, but those whom shee
Vouchsafeth to her presence to receave,
And letteth them her lovely face to see,
Wherof such wondrous pleasures they conceave,
And sweete contentment, that it doth bereave,
Their soule of sense, through infinite delight,
And them transport from flesh into the spright.

In which they see such admirable things,
As carries them into an extasy,
And heare such heavenly notes, and carolings,
Of Gods high praise, that filles the brasen sky,
And feele such joy and pleasure inwardly,
That maketh them all worldly cares forget,
And onely thinke on that before them set.

Ne from thenceforth doth any fleshly sense,
Or idle thought of earthly things remaine:
But all that earst seemd sweet, seemes now offense,
And all that pleased earst, now seemes to paine.
Their joy, their comfort, their desire, their gaine,
Is fixed all on that which now they see,
All other sights but fayned shadowes bee.

And that faire lampe, which useth to enflame
The hearts of men with selfe consuming fyre,
Thenceforth seemes fowle, and full of sinfull blame;
And all that pompe, to which proud minds aspyre
By name of honor, and so much desyre,
Seemes to them basenesse, and all riches drosse,
And all mirth sadnesse, and all lucre losse.

So full their eyes are of that glorious sight,
And senses fraught with such satietie,
That in nought else on earth they can delight,
But in th' aspect of that felicitie,
Which they have written in their inward ey;
On which they feed, and in their fastened mynd
All happie joy and full contentment fynd.

Ah then my hungry soule, which long hast fed
On idle fancies of thy foolish thought,
And with false beauties flattring bait misled,
Hast after vaine deceiptfull shadowes sought,
Which all are fled, and now have left thee nought,
But late repentance through thy follies prief;
Ah ceasse to gaze on matter of thy grief.

And looke at last up to that soveraine light,
From whose pure beams al perfect beauty springs,
That kindleth love in every godly spright,
Even the love of God, which loathing brings
Of this vile world, and these gay seeming things;
With whose sweete pleasures being so possest,
Thy straying thoughts henceforth for ever rest.

GEORGE CHAPMAN
(? 1559–1634)

A Hymn to Our Saviour on the Cross

Hail great Redeemer, man, and God, all hail,
Whose fervent agony tore the temple's veil,
Let sacrifices out, dark Prophesies
And miracles: and let in, for all these,
A simple piety, a naked heart,
And humble spirit, that no less impart,
And prove thy Godhead to us, being as rare,
And in all sacred power, as circular.

Water and blood mix'd, were not sweat from thee
With deadlier hardness: more divinity
Of supportation, thou through flesh and blood,
Good doctrine is diffus'd and life as good.
O open to me then, (like thy spread arms
That East and West reach) all those mystic charms
That hold us in thy life and discipline
Thy merits in thy love so thrice divine;
It made thee, being our God, assume our man;
And like our champion olympian,
Come to the field against Satan, and our sin:
Wrestle with torments, and the garland win
From death and hell; which cannot crown our brows
But blood must follow: thorns mix with thy boughs
Of conquering laurel, fast nailed to thy cross,
Are all the glories we can here engross
Prove then to those, that in vain glories place
Their happiness here: they hold not by thy grace,
To those whose powers proudly oppose thy laws,
Oppressing Virtue, giving Vice applause:
They never manage just authority,
But thee in thy dear members crucify.
    Thou couldst have come in glory past them all,
With power to force thy pleasure, and empale
Thy Church with brass, and Adamant, that no swine,
Nor thieves, nor hypocrites, nor fiends divine
Could have broke in, or rooted, or put on
Vestments of Piety, when their hearts had none:
Or rapt to ruin with pretext, to save:
Would pomp and radiance, rather not out brave
Thy naked truth, than clothe, or countenance it
With grace, and such sincerness as is fit:
But since true piety wears her pearls within,
And outward paintings only prank up sin:
Since bodies strengthened, souls go to the wall;
Since God we cannot serve, and Belial;
Therefore thou put'st on, Earth's most abject plight,
Hid'st thee in humbless, underwent'st despite,
Mockery, detraction, shame, blows, vilest death –
These, thou, thy soldiers taught'st to fight beneath:

Mad'st a commanding President of these,
Perfect, perpetual: bearing all the keys
To holiness, and heaven. To these, such laws
Thou in thy blood writ'st: that were no more cause
T'enflame our loves, and fervent faiths in thee,
Than in them, truth's divine simplicity,
'Twere full enough; for therein we may well
See thy white finger furrowing blackest hell,
In turning up the errors that our sense
And sensual powers, incur by negligence
Of our eternal truth-exploring soul.
All Churches' powers, thy writ word doth control;
And mixed it with the fabulous Alchoran,
A man might bolt it out, as flow from bran;
Easily discerning it, a heavenly birth,
Brake it but now out, and but crept on earth.
Yet (as if God lacked man's election
And shadows were creators of the Sun)
Men must authorise it: antiquities
Must be explored, to spirit, and give it thies,
And controversies, thick as flies at Spring,
Must be maintained about th' ingenuous meaning;
When no style can express itself so clear,
Nor holds so even, and firm a character –
Those mysteries that are not to be reached,
Still to be strived with, make them more impeached:
And as the Mill fares with an ill picked grist,
When any stone, the stones is got betwist,
Rumbling together, fill the grain with grit;
Offends the ear, sets teeth an [sic?] edge with it:
Blunts the picked quarry so, 'twill grind no more,
Spoils bread, and scouts the Miller's custom'd store.
So in the Church, when controversy falls,
It mars her music, shakes her battered walls,
Grates tender consciences, and weakens faith;
The bread of life taints, and makes work for Death;
Darkens truth's light, with her perplexed Abysms,
And dustlike grinds men into sects and schisms.
And what's the cause? the word's deficiency?
In volume, matter, perspecuity?

GEORGE CHAPMAN

Ambition, lust, and damned avarice,
Pervert, and each the sacred word applies
To his profane ends; all to profit given,
And pursuets lay to catch the joys of heaven.
  Since truth, and real worth, men seldom seize,
  Impostors most, and slightest learnings please.
And, where the true Church, like the nest should be
Of chaste, and provident Alcione:
(To which is only one strait orifice,
Which is so strictly fitted to her size.
That no bird bigger than herself, or less,
Can pierce and keep it, or discern th' access:
Nor which the sea itself, on which 'tis made,
Can ever overflow, or once invade;)
Now ways so many to her Altars are,
So easy, so profane, and popular:
That torrents charged with weeds, and sin-drowned beasts,
Break, load, crack them: sensual joys and feasts
Corrupt their pure fumes: and the slenderest flash
Of lust, or profit, makes a standing plash
Of sin about them, which men will not pass.
Look (Lord) upon them, build them walls of brass,
To keep profane feet off: do not thou
In wounds and anguish ever overflow,
And suffer such in ease, and sensuality,
Dare to reject thy rules of humble life:
The mind's true peace, and turn their zeals to strife,
For objects earthly, and corporeal.
A trick of humbless, now they practise all,
Confess their no deserts, habilities none:
Profess all frailties, and amend not one:
As if a privilege they meant to claim
In sinning by acknowledging the maim
Sin gave in Adam: Nor the surplussage
Of thy redemption, seem to put in gage
For his transgression: that thy virtuous pains
(Dear Lord) have eat out all their former stains;
That thy most mighty innocence had power
To cleanse their guilts: that the unvalued dower
Thou madest the Church thy spouse, in piety,

And (to endure pains impious) constancy,
Will and alacrity (if they invoke)
To bear the sweet load, and the easy yoke
Of thy injunctions, in diffusing these
(In thy perfection) through her faculties:
In every finer, suffering to her use,
And perfecting the form thou didst infuse
In man's creation: made him clear as then
Of all the frailties, since defiling men.
And as a runner at th' Olympian games,
With all the luggage he can lay on, frames
His whole powers to the race, bags, pockets, greaves
Stuffed full of sand he wears, then when he leaves,
And doth his other weighty weeds uncover,
With which half smothered, he is wrapped all over:
Then seems he light, and fresh as morning air;
Girds him with silks, swaddles with rollers fair
His lightsome body, and away he scours
So swift, and light, he scarce treads down the flowers:
So to our fame proposed, of endless joy
(Before thy dear death, when we did employ
Our tainted powers; we felt them clogged and chained
With sin and bondage, which did rust, and reigned
In our most mortal bodies: but when thou
Strip'dst us of these bands, and from foot to brow
Girt, rolled and trimmed us up in thy deserts:
Free were our feet, and hands; and sprightly hearts
Leapt in our bosoms; and (ascribing still
All to thy merits; both our power and will
To every thought of goodness, wrought by thee;
That divine scarlet, in which didst dye
Our cleansed consistence; lasting still in power
T'enable acts in us, as the next hour
To thy most saving, glorious sufferance)
We may make all our manly powers advance
Up to thy Image; and these forms of earth,
Beauties and mockeries, matched in beastly birth:
We may despise, with still aspiring spirits
To thy high graces, in thy still fresh merits:
Not touching at this base and spongy mould,

For any springs of lust, or mines of gold.
  For else (mild Saviour, pardon me to speak)
How did thy foot, the Serpent's forehead break?
How hath the nectar of thy virtuous blood,
The sink of Adam's forfeit overflowed;
How doth it set us free, if we still stand
(For all thy sufferings) bound both foot and hand
Vassals to Satan? Didst thou only die,
Thine own divine deserts to glorify,
And show thou could'st do this? O were not those
Given to our use in power? If we shall lose
By damn'd relapse, grace to enact that power:
And basely give up our redemption's tower
Before we try our strengths, built all on thine,
And with a humbless [sic], false, and asinine,
Flattering our senses, lay upon our souls
The burthen of their conquests, and like moles
Grovel in earth still, being advanced to heaven:
Cows that we are) in herds how are we driven
To Satan's shambles? Wherein stand we for
Thy heavenly image, Hell's great Conqueror?
Didst thou not offer, to restore our fall
Thy sacrifice, full once, and one for all?
If we be still down, how then can we rise
Again with thee, and seek crowns in the skies?
But we excuse this; saying, We are but men,
And must err, must fall: what thou didst sustain
To free our beastly frailties, never can
With all thy grace, by any power in man
Make good thy rise to us: O blasphemy
In hypocritical humility!
As we are men, we death and hell control,
Since thou createdst man a living soul:
As every hour we sin, we do like beasts:
Herdless, and wilful, murdering in our breasts
Thy saved image, out of which, one calls
Our human souls, mortal celestials:
When casting off a good life's godlike grace,
We fall from God; and then make good our place
When we return to him: and so are said

To live: when life like his true form we lead,
And die (as much as can immortal creature:)
Not that we utterly can cease to be,
But that we fall from life's best quality.

   But we are tossed out of our human Throne
By pied and Protean opinion;
We vouch thee only, for pretext and fashion,
And are not inward with thy death and passion.
We slavishly renounce thy royalty
With which thou crown'st us in thy victory:
Spend all our manhoods in the fiend's defence,
And drown thy right, in beastly negligence.

   God never is deceived so, to respect,
His shade in Angels' beauties, to neglect
His own most clear and rapting loveliness:
Nor Angels dote so on the species
And grace given to our soul (which is their shade)
That therefore they will let their own forms fade.
And yet our soul (which most deserves our woe,
And that from which our whole mishap doth flow)
So softened is, and rapt (as with a storm)
With flatteries of our base corporeal form,
(Which is her shadow) that she quite forsakes
Her proper nobless, and for nothing takes
The beauties that for her love, thou putt'st on;
In torments rarefied far past the Sun.

   Hence came the cruel fate that Orpheus
Sings of Narcissus: who being amorous
Of his shade in the water (which denotes
Beauty in bodies, that like water floats)
Despised himself, his soul, and so let fade
His substance for a never-purchased shade.
Since souls of their use, ignorant are still,
With this vile body's use, men never fill.

   And, as the Sun's light, in streams ne'er so fair
Is but a shadow, to his light in air,
His splendour that in air we so admire,
Is but a shadow to his beams in fire:
In fire his brightness, but a shadow is
To radiance fired, in that pure breast of his:

So as the subject on which thy grace shines,
Is thick, or clear; to earth or heaven inclines;
So that truth's light shows; so thy passion takes;
With which, who inward is, and thy breast makes
Bulwark to his breast, against all the darts
The foe still shoots more, more his late blow smarts,
And sea-like raves most, where 'tis most withstood.
He tastes the strength and virtue of thy blood:
He knows that when flesh is most soothed and graced,
Admired and magnified, adored, and placed
In height of all the blood's Idolatry,
And fed with all the spirits of Luxury,
One thought of joy, in any soul that knows
Her own true strength, and thereon doth repose;
Bringing her body's organs to attend
Chiefly her powers, to her eternal end;
Makes all things outward; and the sweetest sin,
That ravisheth the beastly flesh within;
All but a fiend, pranked in an Angel's plume:
A shade, a fraud, before the wind a fume.
  Hail then divine Redeemer, still all hail,
All glory, gratitude, and all avail,
Be given thy all deserving agony;
Whose vinegar thou Nectar mak'st in me,
Whose goodness freely all my ill turns good:
Since thou being crushed, and strained through flesh and blood:
Each nerve and artery needs must taste of thee,
What odour burned in airs that noisome be,
Leaves not his scent there? O then how much more
Must thou, whose sweetness sweat eternal odour,
Stick where it breathed, and for whom thy sweet breath,
Thou freely gav'st up, to revive his death?
Let those that shrink then as their conscience loads,
That fight in Satan's right, and not in God's
Still count them slaves to Satan. I am none:
Thy fight hath freed me, thine thou mak'st mine own.

Invocatio

O then (my sweetest and my only life)
Confirm this comfort, purchased with thy grief,
And my despised soul of the world, love thou:
No thought to any other joy I vow.
Order these last steps of my abject state,
Straight on the mark a man should level at:
And grant that while I strive to form in me,
Thy sacred image, no adversity
May make me draw one limb, or line amiss:
Let no vile fashion wrest my faculties
From what becomes that Image. Quiet so
My body's powers, that neither weal nor woe,
May stir one thought up, against thy freest will.
Grant, that in me, my mind's waves may be still.
The world for no extreme may use her voice;
Nor Fortune treading reeds, make any noise.

Amen.

WILLIAM KETHE
(*c.* 1560)

Psalm 100. 'O be joyful in the Lord, all ye lands'

All people that on earth do dwell,
  Sing to the Lord with cheerful voice;
Him serve with mirth, his praise forth tell,
  Come ye before him, and rejoice.

The Lord, ye know, is God indeed;
  Without our aid he did us make;
We are his folk, he doth us feed,
  And for his sheep he doth us take.

Oh enter then his gates with praise,
   Approach with joy his courts unto;
Praise, laud, and bless his name always.
   For it is seemly so to do.

For why, the Lord our God is good;
   His mercy is for ever sure;
His truth at all times firmly stood,
   And shall from age to age endure.

ROBERT SOUTHWELL
(1561–1595)

A Child My Choice

Let folly praise that fancy loves, I praise and love that child,
Whose heart no thought: whose tongue, no word: whose hand no
   deed defiled.
I praise him most, I love him best, all praise and love is his:
While him I love, in him I live, and cannot live amiss.

Love's sweetest mark, Laud's highest theme, man's most desired
   light:
To love him, life: to leave him, death: to live in him delight.
He mine, by gift: I his, by debt: thus each, to other due:
First friend he was: best friend he is, all times will try him true.

Though young, yet wise: though small, yet strong: though man, yet
   God he is:
As wise, he knows: as strong, he can: as God, he loves to bliss.
His knowledge rules: his strength, defends; his love, doth cherish
   all:
His birth, our Joy: his life, our light: his death, our end of thrall.

Alas, he weeps, he sighs, he pants, yet do his Angels sing:
Out of his tears, his sighs and throbs, doth bud a joyful spring.
Almighty babe, whose tender arms can force all foes to fly:
Correct my faults, protect my life, direct me when I die.

WILLIAM SHAKESPEARE
(1564–1616)

The Phoenix and the Turtle

Let the bird of loudest lay,
On the sole Arabian tree,
Herald sad and trumpet be,
To whose sound chaste wings obey.

But thou shrieking harbinger,
Foul precurrer of the fiend,
Augur of the fever's end,
To this troop come thou not near!

From this session interdict
Every fowl of tyrant wing,
Save the eagle, feath'red king:
Keep the obsequy so strict.

Let the priest in surplice white,
That defunctive music can,
Be the death-divining swan,
Lest the requiem lack his right.

And thou treble-dated crow,
That thy sable gender mak'st
With the breath thou giv'st and tak'st,
'Mongst our mourners shalt thou go.

Here the anthem doth commence:
Love and constancy is dead;
Phoenix and the turtle fled
In a mutual flame from hence.

So they loved, as love in twain
Had the essence but in one;
Two distincts, division none:
Number there in love was slain.

Hearts remote, yet not asunder;
Distance, and no space was seen
'Twixt this turtle and his queen:
But in them it were a wonder.

So between them love did shine,
That the turtle saw his right
Flaming in the phoenix' sight;
Either was the other's mine.

Property was thus appalléd,
That the self was not the same;
Single nature's double name
Neither two nor one was calléd.

Reason, in itself confounded,
Saw division grow togcthcr,
To themselves yet either neither,
Simple were so well compounded;

That it cried, How true a twain
Seemeth this concordant one!
Love hath reason, reason none,
If what parts can so remain.

Whereupon it made this threne
To the phoenix and the dove,
Co-supremes and stars of love,
As chorus to their tragic scene.

Threnos
Beauty, truth, and rarity,
Grace in all simplicity,
Here enclosed, in cinders lie.

Death is now the phoenix' nest;
And the turtle's loyal breast
To eternity doth rest.

Leaving no posterity,
'Twas not their infirmity,
It was married chastity.

Truth may seem, but cannot be;
Beauty brag, but 'tis not she;
Truth and beauty buried be.

To this urn let those repair
That are either true or fair;
For these dead birds sigh a prayer.

from *Hamlet*

Marcellus. It faded on the crowing of the cock.
 Some say that ever 'gainst that season comes
 Wherein our Saviour's birth is celebrated,
 The bird of dawning singeth all night long:
 And then, they say, no spirit dare stir abroad,
 The nights are wholesome, then no planets strike,
 No fairy takes nor witch hath power to charm,
 So hallow'd and so gracious is the time.

Horatio. So have I heard and do in part believe it.

CHRISTOPHER MARLOWE
(1564–1593)

from *Dr Faustus*

Faustus. Ah, Faustus,
Now hast thou but one bare hour to live,
And then thou must be damned perpetually!
Stand still, you ever-moving spheres of Heaven,
That time may cease, and midnight never come;
Fair Nature's eye, rise, rise again and make
Perpetual day; or let this hour be but
A year, a month, a week, a natural day,
That Faustus may repent and save his soul!
O lente, lente, currite noctis equi!
The stars move still, time runs, the clock will strike,
The Devil will come, and Faustus must be damned.
O, I'll leap up to my God! Who pulls me down?
See, see where Christ's blood streams in the firmament!
One drop would save my soul – half a drop: ah, my Christ!
Ah, rend not my heart for naming of my Christ!
Yet will I call on him: O spare me, Lucifer! –
Where is it now? 'tis gone; and see where God
Stretcheth out his arm, and bends his ireful brows!
Mountain and hills come, come and fall on me,
And hide me from the heavy wrath of God!
No! no!
Then will I headlong run into the earth;
Earth gape! O no, it will not harbour me!
You stars that reigned at my nativity,
Whose influence hath allotted death and hell,
Now draw up Faustus like a foggy mist
Into the entrails of yon labouring clouds,
That when they vomit forth into the air,
My limbs may issue from their smoky mouths,
So that my soul may but ascend to Heaven.
                    [*The clock strikes the half hour.*]
Ah, half the hour is past! 'twill all be past anon!
O God!
If thou wilt not have mercy on my soul,

Yet for Christ's sake whose blood hath ransomed me,
Impose some end to my incessant pain;
Let Faustus live in hell a thousand years –
A hundred thousand, and – at last – be saved!
O, no end is limited to damnèd souls!
Why wert thou not a creature wanting soul?
Or why is this immortal that thou hast?
Ah, Pythagoras' metempsychosis! were that true,
This soul should fly from me, and I be changed
Unto some brutish beast! all beasts are happy,
For, when they die,
Their souls are soon dissolved in elements;
But mine must live, still to be plagued in hell.
Curst be the parents that engendered me!
No, Faustus: curse thyself: curse Lucifer
That hath deprived thee of the joys of Heaven.
                         [*The clock strikes twelve.*]
O, it strikes, it strikes! Now, body, turn to air,
Or Lucifer will bear thee quick to hell.
                         [*Thunder and lightning.*]
O soul, be changed into little water-drops,
And fall into the ocean – ne'er be found.
                         [*Enter Devils*]
My God! my God! look not so fierce on me!
Adders and serpents, let me breathe awhile!
Ugly hell, gape not! come not, Lucifer!
I'll burn my books! – Ah Mephistophilis!
                         [*Exeunt Devils with Faustus.*]

THOMAS NASHE
(1567–1601)

In Time of Pestilence

Adieu, farewell earth's bliss,
This world uncertain is;
Fond are life's lustful joys,
Death proves them all but toys,
None from his darts can fly.
I am sick, I must die.
　　Lord, have mercy on us!

Rich men, trust not in wealth,
Gold cannot buy you health;
Physic himself must fade,
All things to end are made.
The plague full swift goes by.
I am sick, I must die.
　　Lord, have mercy on us!

Beauty is but a flower
Which wrinkles will devour;
Brightness falls from the air,
Queens have died young and fair,
Dust hath closed Helen's eye.
I am sick, I must die.
　　Lord, have mercy on us!

Strength stoops unto the grave,
Worms feed on Hector brave,
Swords may not fight with fate,
Earth still holds ope her gate.
Come! come! the bells do cry.
I am sick, I must die.
　　Lord, have mercy on us!

Wit with his wantonness
Tasteth death's bitterness;
Hell's executioner
Hath no ears for to hear
What vain art can reply.
I am sick, I must die.
     Lord, have mercy on us!

Haste, therefore, each degree,
To welcome destiny.
Heaven is our heritage,
Earth but a player's stage;
Mount we unto the sky.
I am sick, I must die.
     Lord, have mercy on us!

THOMAS CAMPION
(1567–1620)

'To Music bent is my retirèd mind'

To Music bent is my retirèd mind.
  And fain would I some song of pleasure sing,
But in vain joys no comfort now I find;
  From heavenly thoughts all true delight doth spring.
Thy power, O God, thy mercies, to record,
Will sweeten every note and every word.

All earthly pomp or beauty to express
  Is but to carve in snow, on waves to write.
Celestial things, though men conceive them less,
  Yet fullest are they in themselves of light;
Such beams they yield as know no means to die,
Such heat they cast as lifts the Spirit high.

SIR JOHN DAVIES
(1569–1626)

from *Orchestra*

'What eye doth see the heaven but doth admire
When it the movings of the heavens doth see?
Myself, if I to heaven may once aspire,
If that be dancing, will a dancer be;
But as for this, your frantic jollity,
How it began or whence you did it learn
I never could with reason's eye discern.'

Antinous answered: 'Jewel of the earth,
Worthy you are that heavenly dance to lead,
But, for you think our Dancing base of birth
And newly born but of a brain-sick head,
I will forthwith his antique gentry read,
And, for I love him, will his herald be,
And blaze his arms, and draw his pedigree.

'When Love had shaped this world, this great fair wight
That all wights else in this wide womb contains,
And had instructed it to dance aright
A thousand measures with a thousand strains
Which it should practise with delightful pains
Until that fatal instant should revolve
When all to nothing should again resolve,

'The comely order and proportion fair
On every side did please his wandering eye,
Till glancing through the thin transparent air
A rude disordered rout he did espy
Of men and women that most spitefully
Did one another throng and crowd so sore,
That his kind eye in pity wept therefore.

'And swifter than the lightning down he came,
Another shapeless chaos to digest:
He will begin another world to frame,
For Love, till all be well, will never rest.
Then with such words as cannot be exprest
He cuts the troops, that all asunder fling,
And ere they wist he casts them in a ring.'

★

'"For lo, the sea that fleets about the land
And like a girdle clips her solid waist
Music and measure both doth understand,
For his great crystal eye is always cast
Up to the moon and on her fixèd fast,
And as she danceth in her pallid sphere,
So danceth he about the centre here.

'"Sometimes his proud green waves in order set,
One after other, flow unto the shore;
Which when they have with many kisses wet
They ebb away in order, as before;
And to make known his courtly love the more
He oft doth lay aside his three-fork'd mace
And with his arms the timorous earth embrace.

'"Only the earth doth stand forever still:
Her rocks remove not, nor her mountains meet,
Although some wits enrich'd with learning's skill
Say heaven stands firm and that the earth doth fleet
And swiftly turneth underneath their feet;
Yet, though the earth is ever steadfast seen,
On her broad breast hath dancing ever been.

'"For those blue veins that through her body spread,
Those sapphire streams which from great hills do spring,
The earth's great dugs, for every wight is fed
With sweet fresh moisture from them issuing,
Observe a dance in their wild wandering;
And still their dance begets a murmur sweet,
And still the murmur with the dance doth meet.

'"Of all their ways, I love Meander's path,
Which, to the tunes of dying swans, doth dance
Such winding sleights. Such turns and tricks he hath,
Such creeks, such wrenches, and such dalliance,
That, whether it be hap or heedless chance,
In his indented course and wriggling play
He seems to dance a perfect cunning hay.

'"But wherefore do these streams forever run?
To keep themselves forever sweet and clear.
For, let their everlasting course be done,
They straight corrupt and foul with mud appear.
O ye sweet nymphs, that beauty's loss do fear,
Contemn the drugs that physic doth devise
And learn of Love this dainty exercise."'

JOHN DONNE
(1573–1631)

To the Countess of Salisbury
August, 1614

Fair, great, and good, since seeing you, we see
What Heaven can do, and what any Earth can be:
Since now your beauty shines, now when the Sun
Grown stale, is to so low a value run,
That his dishevell'd beams and scattered fires
Serve but for Ladies' Periwigs and Tires
In lovers' Sonnets: you come to repair
God's book of creatures, teaching what is fair.
Since now, when all is withered, shrunk, and dried,
All Virtues ebb'd out to a dead low tide,
All the world's frame being crumbled into sand,
Where every man thinks by himself to stand,
Integrity, friendship, and confidence,
(Cements of greatness) being vapour'd hence,
And narrow man being fill'd with little shares,

Court, City, Church, are all shops of small-wares,
All having blown to sparks their noble fire,
And drawn their sound gold-ingot into wire;
All trying by a love of littleness
To make abridgments, and to draw to less
Even that nothing, which at first we were;
Since in these times, your greatness doth appear,
And that we learn by it, that man to get
Towards him that's infinite, must first be great.
Since in an age so ill, as none is fit
So much as to accuse, much less mend it,
(For who can judge, or witness of those times
Where all alike are guilty of the crimes?)
Where he that would be good, is thought by all
A monster, or at best fantastical:
Since now you durst be good, and that I do
Discern, by daring to contemplate you,
That there may be degrees of fair, great, good,
Through your light, largeness, virtue understood;
If in this sacrifice of mine, be shown
Any small spark of these, call it your own.
And if things like these, have been said by me
Of others; call not that Idolatry.
For had God made man first, and man had seen
The third day's fruits, and flowers, and various green,
He might have said the best that he could say
Of those fair creatures, which were made that day;
And when next day, he had admir'd the birth
Of Sun, Moon, Stars, fairer than late-prais'd earth,
He might have said the best that he could say,
And not be chid for praising yesterday:
So though some things are not together true
As, that another's worthiest, and, that you:
Yet, to say so, doth not condemn a man.
If when he spoke them, they were both true then.
How fair a proof of this, in our soul grows?
We first have souls of growth, and sense, and those,
When our last soul, our soul immortal came,
Were swallowed into it, and have no name.
Nor doth he injure those souls, which doth cast,

The power and praise of both them, on the last;
No more do I wrong any; I adore
The same things now, which I ador'd before,
The subject chang'd, and measure; the same thing
In a low constable, and in the King
I reverence; His power to work on me:
So did I humbly reverence each degree
Of fair, great, good; but more, now I am come
From having found their *walks*, to find their *home*.
And as I owe my first souls thanks, that they
For my last soul did fit and mould my clay,
So am I debtor unto them, whose worth,
Enabled me to profit, and take forth
This new great lesson, thus to study you;
Which none, not reading others, first, could do.
Nor lack I light to read this book, though I
In a dark Cave, yea in a Grave do lie;
For as your fellow-Angels, so you do
Illustrate them who come to study you.
The first whom we in Histories do find
To have profess'd all Arts, was one born blind:
He lack'd those eyes beasts have as well as we,
Not those, by which Angels are seen and see;
So, though I'm born without those eyes to live,
Which fortune, who hath none herself, doth give,
Which are, fit means to see bright courts and you,
Yet may I see you thus, as now I do;
I shall by that, all goodness have discern'd,
And though I burn my library, be learn'd.

Sonnets
VII

At the round earth's imagin'd corners, blow
Your trumpets, Angels, and arise, arise
From death, you numberless infinities
Of souls, and to your scatter'd bodies go,
All whom the flood did, and fire shall o'erthrow,
All whom war, dearth, age, agues, tyrannies,
Despair, law, chance, hath slain, and you whose eyes,
Shall behold God, and never taste death's woe.
But let them sleep, Lord, and me mourn a space,
For, if above all these, my sins abound,
'Tis late to ask abundance of Thy grace,
When we are there; here on this lowly ground,
Teach me how to repent; for that's as good
As if Thou hadst seal'd my pardon, with Thy blood.

X

Death be not proud, though some have called thee
Mighty and dreadful, for, thou art not so,
For, those, whom thou think'st, thou dost overthrow,
Die not, poor death, nor yet canst thou kill me.
From rest and sleep, which but thy pictures be,
Much pleasure, then from thee, much more must flow,
And soonest our best men with thee do go,
Rest of their bones, and soul's delivery.
Thou art slave to Fate, Chance, kings, and desperate men,
And dost with poison, war, and sickness dwell,
And poppy, or charms can make us sleep as well,
And better than thy stroke; why swell'st thou then?
One short sleep past, we wake eternally,
And death shall be no more; death, thou shalt die.

XIII

What if this present were the world's last night?
Mark in my heart, O Soul, where thou dost dwell,
The picture of Christ crucified, and tell
Whether that countenance can thee affright,
Tears in His eyes quench the amazing light,
Blood fills His frowns, which from His pierc'd head fell.
And can that tongue adjudge thee unto hell,
Which pray'd forgiveness for His foes' fierce spite?
No, no; but as in my idolatry·
I said to all my profane mistresses,
Beauty, of pity, foulness only is
A sign of rigour: So I say to thee,
To wicked spirits are horrid shapes assign'd,
This beauteous form assures a piteous mind.

XIV

Batter my heart, three-person'd God; for, you
As yet but knock, breathe, shine, and seek to mend;
That I may rise, and stand, o'erthrow me, and bend
Your force, to break, blow, burn and make me new.
I, like an usurp'd town, to another due,
Labour to admit you, but Oh, to no end,
Reason your viceroy in me, me should defend,
But is captiv'd, and proves weak or untrue.
Yet dearly I love you, and would be loved fain,
But am betroth'd unto your enemy:
Divorce me, untie, or break that knot again,
Take me to you, imprison me, for I
Except you enthral me, never shall be free,
Nor ever chaste, except you ravish me.

XVIII

Show me, dear Christ, Thy Spouse, so bright and clear.
What! is it She, which on the other shore
Goes richly painted? or which rob'd and tore
Laments and mourns in Germany and here?
Sleeps she a thousand, then peeps up one year?
Is she self truth and errs? now new, now outwore?
Doth she, and did she, and shall she evermore
On one, on seven, or on no hill appear?
Dwells she with us, or like adventuring knights
First travail we to seek and then make Love?
Betray kind husband thy spouse to our sights,
And let mine amorous soul court thy mild Dove,
Who is most true, and pleasing to thee, then
When she is embrac'd and open to most men.

Good Friday, 1613. Riding Westward

Let man's Soul be a Sphere, and then, in this,
The intelligence that moves, devotion is,
And as the other Spheres, by being grown
Subject to foreign motions, lose their own,
And being by others hurried every day,
Scarce in a year their natural form obey:
Pleasure or business, so, our Souls admit
For their first mover, and are whirl'd by it.
Hence is't, that I am carried towards the West
This day, when my Soul's form bends toward the East.
There I should see a Sun, by rising set,
And by that setting endless day beget;
But that Christ on this Cross, did rise and fall,
Sin had eternally benighted all.
Yet dare I almost be glad, I do not see
That spectacle of too much weight for me.
Who sees God's face, that is self life, must die;
What a death were it then to see God die?

It made His own Lieutenant Nature shrink,
It made His footstool crack, and the Sun wink.
Could I behold those hands which span the Poles,
And turn all spheres at once, pierced with those holes?
Could I behold that endless height which is
Zenith to us, and our Antipodes,
Humbled below us? or that blood which is
The seat of all our Souls, if not of His,
Made dirt of dust, or that flesh which was worn,
By God, for His apparel, rag'd, and torn?
If on these things I durst not look, durst I
Upon his miserable mother cast mine eye,
Who was God's partner here, and furnish'd thus
Half of that Sacrifice, which ransom'd us?
Though these things, as I ride, be from mine eye,
They're present yet unto my memory,
For that looks towards them; and Thou look'st towards me
O Saviour, as Thou hang'st upon the tree;
I turn my back to Thee, but to receive
Corrections, till Thy mercies bid Thee leave.
O think me worth Thine anger, punish me,
Burn off my rusts, and my deformity,
Restore Thine Image, so much, by Thy grace,
That Thou may'st know me, and I'll turn my face.

A Hymn to Christ

At the author's last going into Germany

In what torn ship soever I embark,
That ship shall be my emblem of Thy Ark;
What sea soever swallow me, that flood
Shall be to me an emblem of Thy blood;
Though Thou with clouds of anger do disguise
Thy face; yet through that mask I know those eyes,
  Which, though they turn away sometimes,
    They never will despise.

I sacrifice this Island unto Thee,
And all whom I lov'd there, and who lov'd me;
When I have put our seas 'twixt them and me,
Put thou Thy sea betwixt my sins and Thee.
As the tree's sap doth seek the root below
In winter, in my winter now I go,
   Where none but Thee, th' Eternal root
     Of true Love I may know.

Nor Thou nor Thy religion dost control,
The amorousness of an harmonious Soul,
But thou would'st have that love Thyself: as Thou
Art jealous, Lord, so I am jealous now,
Thou lov'st not, till from loving more, Thou free
My soul: who ever gives, takes liberty:
   O, if Thou car'st not whom I love
     Alas, Thou lov'st not me.

Seal then this bill of my Divorce to All,
On whom those fainter beams of love did fall;
Marry those loves, which in youth scattered be
On Fame, Wit, Hopes (false mistresses) to Thee.
Churches are best for Prayer, that have least light:
To see God only, I go out of sight:
   And to 'scape stormy days, I choose
     An Everlasting night.

A Hymn to God the Father

I

Wilt Thou forgive that sin where I begun,
   Which is my sin, though it were done before?
Wilt Thou forgive that sin, through which I run,
   And do run still: though still I do deplore?
     When Thou hast done, Thou hast not done,
       For, I have more.

II

Wilt Thou forgive that sin by which I have won
  Others to sin? and, made my sin their door?
Wilt Thou forgive that sin which I did shun
  A year, or two: but wallowed in, a score?
    When Thou hast done, Thou hast not done,
      For I have more.

III

I have a sin of fear, that when I have spun
  My last thread, I shall perish on the shore;
Swear by Thyself, that at my death Thy son
  Shall shine as He shines now, and heretofore;
    And, having done that, Thou hast done,
      I fear no more.

GILES FLETCHER
(1585/6–1623)

from *Christ's Victorie on Earth*

3

Seemèd that Man had them devourèd all,
Whome to devoure the beasts had made pretence;
But Him their salvage thirst did nought appall,
Though weapons none He had for His defence:
What armes for Innocence, but innocence?
  For when they saw their Lord's bright cognizance
  Shine in His face, soone did they disadvaunce
And some unto Him kneele, and some about Him daunce.

4

Downe fell the lordly lion's angrie mood,
And he himselfe fell downe in congies lowe;
Bidding Him welcome to his wastfull wood;
Sometime he kist the grasse whear He did goe,
And, as to wash His feete he well did knowe,
   With fauning tongue he lickt away the dust;
   And every one would neerest to Him thrust,
And every one, with new, forgot his former lust.

5

Unmindfull of himselfe, to minde his Lord,
The lamb stood gazing by the tyger's side,
As though betweene them they had made accord;
And on the lion's back the goate did ride,
Forgetfull of the roughnes of the hide:
   If He stood still, their eyes upon Him bayted,
   If walkt, they all in order on Him wayted,
And when He slept, they as His watch themselves conceited.

7

Upon a grassie hillock He was laid,
With woodie primroses befreckelèd;
Over His head the wanton shadowes plaid
Of a wilde olive, that her bowghs so spread,
As with her leavs she seem'd to crowne His head,
   And her greene armes to embrace the Prince of Peace;
   The sunne so neere, needs must the Winter cease,
The sunne so neere, another Spring seem'd to increase.

8

His haire was blacke, and in small curls did twine,
As though it wear the shadowe of some light;
And underneath, His face, as day did shine –
But sure the day shinèd not halfe so bright,
Nor the sunne's shadowe made so darke a night.
  Under His lovely locks, her head to shroude,
  Did make Humilitie her selfe growe proude: –
Hither, to light their lamps, did all the Graces croude.

9

One of ten thousand soules I am, and more,
That of His eyes, and their sweete wounds complaine:
Sweete are the wounds of Love, never so sore –
Ah! might He often slaie me so againe!
He never lives that thus is never slaine.
  What boots it watch? those eyes for all my art,
  Mine owne eyes looking on, have stole my heart:
In them Love bends his bowe, and dips his burning dart.

10

As when the sunne, caught in an adverse clowde,
Flies crosse the world, and thear a-new begets
The watry picture of his beautie proude:
Throwes all abroad his sparkling spangelets,
And the whole world in dire amazement sets,
  To see two dayes abroad at once; and all
  Doubt whether nowe he rise, or nowe will fall:
So flam'd the Godly flesh, proude of his heav'nly thrall.

11

His cheekes as snowie apples, sop't in wine,
Had their red roses quencht with lillies white,
And like to garden strawberries did shine,
Wash't in a bowle of milk, or rose-buds bright
Unbosoming their brests against the light:
  Here love-sick soules did eat, thear dranke, and made
  Sweete-smelling posies, that could never fade, –
But worldly eyes Him thought more like some living shade.

12

For Laughter never look't upon His browe,
Though in His face all smilling joyes did bide:
No silken banners did about Him flowe –
Fooles make their fetters ensignes of their pride:
He was the best cloath'd when naked was His side.
  A Lambe He was, and wollen fleece He bore,
  Wove with one thread: His feete low sandalls wore;
But barèd were his legges, – so went the times of yore.

13

As two white marble pillars that uphold
God's holy place, whear He in glorie sets,
And rise with goodly grace and courage bold,
To beare his temple on their ample jetts,
Vein'd every whear with azure rivulets:
  Whom all the people on some holy morne,
  With boughs and flowrie garlands doe adorne –
Of such, though fairer farre, this temple was upborne.

14

Twice had Diana bent her golden bowe,
And shot from heav'n her silver shafts, to rouse
The sluggish salvages, that den belowe,
And all the day in lazie couvert drouze,
Since Him the silent wildernesse did house:
    The heav'n His roofe and arbour harbour was,
    The ground His bed, and His moist pillowe, grasse;
But fruit thear none did growe, nor rivers none did passe.

15

At length an aged Syre farre off He sawe
Come slowely footing; everie step he guest
One of his feete he from the grave did drawe;
Three legges he had – the wooden was the best;
And all the waie he went, he ever blest
    With benedicities, and prayers' store;
    But the bad ground was blessèd ne'r the more;
And all his head with snowe of age was waxen hore.

16

A good old hermit he might seeme to be,
That for devotion had the world forsaken,
And now was travailing some Saint to see,
Since to his beads he had himselfe betaken,
Whear all his former sinnes he might awaken,
    And them might wash away with dropping brine,
    And almes, and fasts, and churche's discipline;
And dead, might rest his bones under the holy shrine.

★

PHINEAS FLETCHER
(1582–1650)

A Hymn

Drop, drop, slow tears
  and bathe those beauteous feet,
Which brought from heaven
  the news and Prince of peace:
Cease not, wet eyes,
  his mercies to entreat;
To cry for vengeance
  sin doth never cease:
In your deep floods
  drown all my faults and fears;
Nor let his eye
  see sin, but through my tears.

ROBERT HERRICK
(1591–1674)

The Argument of His Book

I sing of brooks, of blossoms, birds and bowers,
Of April, May, of June and July-flowers;
I sing of May-poles, hock-carts, wassails, wakes,
Of bridegrooms, brides and of their bridal cakes;
I write of youth, of love, and have access
By these to sing of cleanly wantonness;
I sing of dews, of rains, and piece by piece
Of balm, of oil, of spice and ambergris;
I sing of times trans-shifting, and I write
How roses first came red and lilies white;
I write of groves, of twilights, and I sing
The Court of Mab, and of the Fairy King;
I write of hell; I sing (and ever shall)
Of heaven, and hope to have it after all.

His Litany to the Holy Spirit

In the hour of my distress,
When temptations me oppress,
And when I my sins confess,
      Sweet Spirit, comfort me!

When I lie within my bed,
Sick in heart and sick in head,
And with doubts discomforted,
      Sweet Spirit, comfort me!

When the house doth sigh and weep,
And the world is drown'd in sleep,
Yet mine eyes the watch do keep,
      Sweet Spirit, comfort me!

When the artless doctor sees
No one hope, but of his fees,
And his skill runs on the lees,
      Sweet Spirit, comfort me!

When his potion and his pill
Has, or none, or little skill,
Meet for nothing, but to kill;
      Sweet Spirit, comfort me!

When the passing bell doth toll,
And the furies in a shoal
Come to fright a parting soul,
      Sweet Spirit, comfort me!

When the tapers now burn blue,
And the comforters are few,
And that number more than true,
      Sweet Spirit, comfort me!

When the priest his last hath prayed,
And I nod to what is said,
'Cause my speech is now decayed,
      Sweet Spirit, comfort me!

When, God knows, I'm toss'd about,
Either with despair, or doubt;
Yet before the glass be out,
      Sweet Spirit, comfort me!

When the tempter me pursu'th
With the sins of all my youth,
And half damns me with untruth,
      Sweet Spirit, comfort me!

When the flames and hellish cries
Fright mine ears, and fright mine eyes,
And all terrors me surprise,
      Sweet Spirit, comfort me!

When the judgment is reveal'd,
And that open'd which was seal'd,
When to Thee I have appeal'd,
      Sweet Spirit, comfort me!

A Thanksgiving to God for His House

Lord, Thou hast given me a cell
      Wherein to dwell;
A little house, whose humble roof
      Is weather-proof;
Under the spars of which I lie
      Both soft and dry;
Where Thou my chamber for to ward
      Hast set a guard
Of harmless thoughts, to watch and keep
      Me, while I sleep.
Low is my porch, as is my fate,
      Both void of state;
And yet the threshold of my door
      Is worn by th' poor,
Who thither come, and freely get
      Good words or meat;

Like as my parlour, so my hall
      And kitchen's small;
A little buttery, and therein
      A little bin
Which keeps my little loaf of bread
      Unclipt, unflead.
Some brittle sticks of thorn or briar
      Make me a fire,
Close by whose living coal I sit,
      And glow like it.
Lord, I confess, too, when I dine,
      The pulse is Thine,
And all those other bits, that be
      There placed by Thee;
The worts, the purslain, and the mess
      Of water-cress,
Which of Thy kindness Thou hast sent;
      And my content
Makes those, and my beloved beet,
      To be more sweet.
'Tis Thou that crown'st my glittering hearth
      With guiltless mirth;
And giv'st me wassail bowls to drink,
      Spiced to the brink.
Lord, 'tis Thy plenty-dropping hand,
      That soils my land;
And giv'st me for my bushel sown,
      Twice ten for one.
Thou mak'st my teeming hen to lay
      Her egg each day;
Besides my healthful ewes to bear
      Me twins each year,
The while the conduits of my kine
      Run cream for wine.
All these, and better Thou dost send
      Me, to this end,
That I should render, for my part,
      A thankful heart;

    Which, fired with incense, I resign,
        As wholly Thine;
    But the acceptance, that must be,
        My Christ, by Thee.

To His Saviour, a Child: A Present by a Child

Go, pretty child, and bear this flower
Unto thy little Saviour;
And tell Him, by that bud now blown,
He is the Rose of Sharon known.
When thou hast said so, stick it there
Upon His bib or stomacher;
And tell Him, for good handsel too,
That thou hast brought a whistle new,
Made of a clean strait oaten reed,
To charm His cries at time of need.
Tell Him, for coral, thou hast none,
But if thou hadst, He should have one;
But poor thou art, and known to be
Even as moneyless as He.
Lastly, if thou canst win a kiss
From those mellifluous lips of His;
Then never take a second on,
To spoil the first impression.

---

handsel: first instalment of future gifts

FRANCIS QUARLES
(1592–1644)

from *Pentelogia*

SONNET I

Can he be fair that withers at a blast?
Or he be strong, that airy breath can cast?
Can he be wise, that knows not how to live?
Or he be rich, that nothing hath to give?
Can he be young, that's feeble, weak, and wan?
  So fair, strong, wise, so rich, so young is man:
So fair is man, that death (a parting blast)
Blasts his fair flow'r, and makes him earth at last;
So strong is man, that with a gasping breath
He totters, and bequeaths his strength to death;
So wise is man, that if with death he strive,
His wisdom cannot teach him how to live;
So rich is man, that (all his debts being paid)
His wealth's the winding-sheet wherein he's laid:
So young is man, that (broke with care and sorrow)
He's old enough to-day, to die to-morrow:
Why brag'st thou then, thou worm of five foot long?
Th'art neither fair, nor strong, nor wise, nor rich, nor young.

from *Divine Fancies*

BOOK I: 18

ON THE LIFE OF MAN

Our life's the model of a winter's day;
Our soul's the sun, whose faint and feeble ray
Gives our earth light; a light but weak, at strongest,
But low, at highest; very short, at longest:
The childish tears, that from our eyes do pass,
Is like the dew that pearls the morning grass:

Whereas our sun is but an hour high,
We go to school, to learn; are whipped and cry:
We truant up and down; we make a spoil
Of previous time, and sport in our own toil:
Our bed's the quiet grave; wherein we lay
Our weary bodies, tired with the day:
The early trumpet, like the morning bell,
Calls to account; where they that have learned well
Shall find reward; and such as have mis-spent
Their time, shall reap an earnèd punishment:
So loath to go to bed; so loth to rise.

BOOK II: 25

ON GOD'S FAVOUR

God's favour like the sun, whose beams appear
To all that dwell in the world's hemisphere,
Though not to all, alike: To some, they express
Themselves more radiant, and to others, less;
To some, they rise more early; and they fall
More late to others giving day to all:
Some soil's more gross, and breathing more impure
And earthy vapours forth, whose fogs obscure
The darkened medium of the moister air;
Whilst other soils, more perfect, yield more rare
And purer fumes; whereby, those beams appear,
To some, less glorious; and to some, more clear:
It would be ever day; day, always bright,
Did not our interposèd earth make night:
The sun shines always strenuous and fair,
But, ah, our sins, our clouds benight the air;
Lord, drain the fens of this my boggy soul,
Whose grosser vapours make my day so foul;
The Son hath strength enough to chase away
These rising fogs, and make a glorious day:
Rise, and shine always clear; but, most of all
Let me behold thy glory, in thy fall;

That being set, poor I (my flesh being hurled
From this) may meet thee, in another world.

BOOK II: 41

ON DEATH

Why should we not, as well, desire death,
As sleep? No difference, but a little breath:
'Tis all but rest; 'tis all but a releasing
Our tired limbs; why then not alike pleasing?
Being burthened with the sorrows of the day,
We wish for night; which, being come, we lay
Our bodies down; yet when our very breath
Is irksome to us, we're afraid of death:
Our sleep is oft accompanied with frights,
Distracting dreams and dangers of the nights;
When in the sheets of death, our bodies sure
From all such evils, and we sleep secure:
What matter, down, or earth? what boots it whether?
Alas, our body's sensible of neither:
Things that are senseless, feel nor pains nor ease;
Tell me; and why not worms as well as fleas?
In sleep, we know not whether our closed eyes
Shall ever wake; from death we're sure to rise:
Aye, but 'tis long first; O, is that our fears?
Dare we trust God for nights? and not for years?

BOOK IV: 10

ON OUR SAVIOUR'S PASSION

The earth did tremble; and heaven's closed eye
Was loath to see the Lord of Glory die:
The skies were clad in mourning, and the Spheres
Forgot their harmony; the clouds dropped tears;

Th' ambitious dead arose to give him room;
And every grave did gape to be His tomb;
Th' affrighted heavens sent down elegious thunder;
The world's foundation loosed, to lose their founder;
Th' impatient temple rent her veil in two,
To teach our hearts what our sad hearts should do:
Shall senseless things do this, and shall not I
Melt one poor drop to see my Saviour die?
Drill forth my tears; and trickle one by one,
Till you have pierced this heart of mine, this stone.

HENRY KING
(1592–1669)

Exequy upon His Wife

Accept, thou shrine of my dead saint,
Instead of dirges this complaint;
And for sweet flowers to crown thy hearse,
Receive a strew of weeping verse
From thy grieved friend, whom thou mightst see
Quite melted into tears for thee.
  Dear loss! since thy untimely fate
My task hath been to meditate
On thee, on thee! Thou art the book,
The library, whereon I look
Though almost blind. For thee, loved clay,
I languish out, not live, the day,
Using no other exercise
But what I practise with mine eyes.
By which wet glasses I find out
How lazily time creeps about
To one that mourns. This, only this,
My exercise and business is:
So I compute the weary hours
With sighs dissolvèd into showers.

Nor wonder if my time go thus
Backward and most preposterous:
Thou hast benighted me. Thy set
This eve of blackness did beget,
Who wast my day (though overcast
Before thou hadst thy noon-tide past)
And I remember must in tears
Thou scarce hadst seen so many years
As day tells hours. By thy clear sun
My love and fortune first did run;
But thou wilt never more appear
Folded within my hemisphere,
Since both thy light and motion,
Like a fled star, is fallen and gone,
And 'twixt me and my soul's dear wish
The earth now interposèd is,
Which such a strange eclipse doth make
As ne'er was read in almanac.
    I could allow thee for a time
To darken me and my sad clime;
Were it a month, a year, or ten,
I would thy exile live till then;
And all that space my mirth adjourn,
So thou wouldst promise to return
And, putting off thy ashy shroud,
At length disperse this sorrow's cloud.
    But woe is me! the longest date
Too narrow is to calculate
These empty hopes. Never shall I
Be so much blest as to descry
A glimpse of thee, till that day come
Which shall the earth to cinders doom,
And a fierce fever must calcine
The body of this world, like thine,
My little world! That fit of fire
Once off, our bodies shall aspire
To our souls' bliss: then we shall rise,
And view ourselves with clearer eyes
In that calm region where no night
Can hide us from each other's sight.

Meantime thou hast her, Earth: much good
May my harm do thee. Since it stood
With Heaven's will I might not call
Her longer mine, I give thee all
My short-lived right and interest
In her, whom living I loved best:
With a most free and bounteous grief,
I give thee what I could not keep.
Be kind to her, and prithee look
Thou write into thy Doomsday book
Each parcel of this rarity,
Which in thy casket shrined doth lie.
See that thou make thy reckoning straight,
And yield her back again by weight;
For thou must audit on thy trust
Each grain and atom of this dust,
As thou wilt answer him that lent,
Not gave thee, my dear monument.
  So close the ground, and 'bout her shade
Black curtains draw: my bride is laid.
  Sleep on, my Love, in thy cold bed
Never to be disquieted.
My last good night! Thou wilt not wake
Till I thy fate shall overtake:
Till age, or grief, or sickness must
Marry my body to that dust
It so much loves; and fill the room
My heart keeps empty in thy tomb.
Stay for me there: I will not fail
To meet thee in that hollow vale.
And think not much of my delay;
I am already on the way,
And follow thee with all the speed
Desire can make, or sorrows breed.
Each minute is a short degree
And every hour a step towards thee.
At night when I betake to rest,
Next morn I rise nearer my west
Of life, almost by eight hours sail
Than when sleep breathed his drowsy gale.

Thus from the sun my bottom steers,
And my day's compass downward bears.
Nor labour I to stem the tide
Through which to thee I swiftly glide.
　'Tis true, with shame and grief I yield;
Thou, like the van, first took'st the field
And gotten hast the victory
In thus adventuring to die
Before me, whose more years might crave
A just precedence in the grave.
But hark! my pulse, like a soft drum,
Beats my approach, tells thee I come;
And slow howe'er my marches be
I shall at last sit down by thee.
　The thought of this bids me go on
And wait my dissolution
With hope and comfort. Dear, (forgive
The crime) I am content to live
Divided, with but half a heart,
Till we shall meet and never part.

GEORGE HERBERT
(1593–1633)

Redemption

Having been tenant long to a rich Lord,
　Not thriving, I resolved to be bold,
　And make a suit unto him, to afford
A new small-rented lease, and cancell th' old.

In heaven at his manour I him sought:
　They told me there, that he was lately gone
　About some land, which he had dearly bought
Long since on earth, to take possession.

I straight return'd, and knowing his great birth,
  Sought him accordingly in great resorts;
  In cities, theatres, gardens, parks, and courts:
At length I heard a ragged noise and mirth

  Of theeves and murderers: there I him espied,
  Who straight, *Your suit is granted*, said, and died.

Easter

Rise heart; thy Lord is risen. Sing his praise
                Without delayes,
Who takes thee by the hand, that thou likewise
                With him mayst rise:
That, as his death calcined thee to dust,
His life may make thee gold, and much more just.

Awake, my lute, and struggle for thy part
                With all thy art.
The crosse taught all wood to resound his name,
                Who bore the same.
His streched sinews taught all strings, what key
Is best to celebrate this most high day.

Consort both heart and lute, and twist a song
                Pleasant and long:
Or since all musick is but three parts vied
                And multiplied;
O let thy blessed Spirit bear a part,
And make up our defects with his sweet art.

I got me flowers to straw thy way;
I got me boughs off many a tree:
But thou wast up by break of day,
And brought'st thy sweets along with thee.

The Sunne arising in the East,
Though he give light, and th' East perfume;
If they should offer to contest
With thy arising, they presume.

Can there be any day but this,
Though many sunnes to shine endeavour?
We count three hundred, but we misse:
There is but one, and that one ever.

Prayer (1)

Prayer the Churches banquet, Angels age,
   Gods breath in man returning to his birth,
   The soul in paraphrase, heart in pilgrimage,
The Christian plummet sounding heav'n and earth;

Engine against th' Almightie, sinners towre,
   Reversed thunder, Christ-side-piercing spear,
   The six-daies world-transposing in an houre,
A kinde of tune, which all things heare and fear;

Softnesse, and peace, and joy, and love, and blisse,
   Exalted Manna, gladnesse of the best,
   Heaven in ordinarie, man well drest,
The milkie way, the bird of Paradise,

   Church-bels beyond the starres heard, the souls bloud,
   The land of spices; something understood.

Antiphon (1)

Chorus. Let all the world in ev'ry corner sing,
        My God and King.

Verse. The heav'ns are not too high,
      His praise may thither flie:
      The earth is not too low,
      His praises there may grow.

Chorus. Let all the world in ev'ry corner sing,
        My God and King.

Verse. The church with psalms must shout,
      No doore can keep them out:
      But above all, the heart
      Must bear the longest part.

Chorus. Let all the world in ev'ry corner sing,
        My God and King.

Jordan (1)

Who sayes that fictions onely and false hair
Become a verse? Is there in truth no beautie?
Is all good structure in a winding stair?
May no lines passe, except they do their dutie
  Not to a true, but painted chair?

Is it no verse, except enchanted groves
And sudden arbours shadow course-spunne lines?
Must purling streams refresh a lovers loves?
Must all be vail'd, while he that reades, divines,
  Catching the sense at two removes?

Shepherds are honest people; let them sing:
Riddle who list, for me, and pull for Prime:
I envie no mans nightingale or spring;
Nor let them punish me with losse of rime,
  Who plainly say, *My God, My King.*

GEORGE HERBERT

The Church-floore

Mark you the floore? that square and speckled stone,
   Which looks so firm and strong,
      Is *Patience*:

And th' other black and grave, wherewith each one
   Is checker'd all along,
      Humilitie:

The gentle rising, which on either hand
   Leads to the Quire above,
      Is *Confidence*:

But the sweet cement, which in one sure band
   Ties the whole frame, is *Love*
      And *Charitie*.

   Hither sometimes Sinne steals, and stains
   The marbles neat and curious veins:
But all is cleansed when the marble weeps.
   Sometimes Death, puffing at the doore,
   Blows all the dust about the floore:
But while he thinks to spoil the room, he sweeps.
   Blest be the *Architect*, whose art
   Could build so strong in a weak heart.

The Windows

   Lord, how can man preach thy eternall word?
      He is a brittle crazie glasse:
   Yet in thy temple thou dost him afford
         This glorious and transcendent place,
         To be a window, through thy grace.

But when thou dost anneal in glasse thy storie,
    Making thy life to shine within
The holy Preachers; then the light and glorie
      More rev'rend grows, and more doth win:
      Which else shows watrish, bleak, and thin.

Doctrine and life, colours and light, in one
    When they combine and mingle, bring
A strong regard and aw: but speech alone
      Doth vanish like a flaring thing,
      And in the eare, not conscience ring.

The Starre

Bright spark, shot from a brighter place,
    Where beams surround my Saviours face,
      Canst thou be any where
      So well as there?

Yet, if thou wilt from thence depart,
    Take a bad lodging in my heart;
      For thou canst make a debter,
      And make it better.

First with thy fire-work burn to dust
    Folly, and worse then folly, lust:
      Then with thy light refine,
      And make it shine:

So disengag'd from sinne and sicknesse,
    Touch it with thy celestiall quicknesse,
      That it may hang and move
      After thy love.

Then with our trinitie of light,
    Motion, and heat, let's take our flight
      Unto the place where thou
      Before didst bow.

Get me a standing there, and place
  Among the beams, which crown the face
    Of him, who dy'd to part
     Sinne and my heart:

That so among the rest I may
  Glitter, and curle, and winde as they:
    That winding is their fashion
     Of adoration.

Sure thou wilt joy, by gaining me
  To flie home like a laden bee
    Unto that hive of beams
     And garland-streams.

Sunday

    O day most calm, most bright,
The fruit of this, the next worlds bud,
Th' indorsement of supreme delight,
Writ by a friend, and with his bloud;
The couch of time; cares balm and bay:
The week were dark, but for thy light:
    Thy torch doth show the way.

    The other dayes and thou
Make up one man; whose face thou art,
Knocking at heaven with thy brow:
The worky-daies are the back-part;
The burden of the week lies there,
Making the whole to stoup and bow,
    Till thy release appeare.

    Man had straight forward gone
To endlesse death: but thou dost pull
And turn us round to look on one,
Whom if we were not very dull,
We could not choose but look on still;
Since there is no place so alone,
    The which he doth not fill.

GEORGE HERBERT

Sundaies the pillars are,
On which heav'ns palace arched lies:
The other dayes fill up the spare
And hollow room with vanities.
They are the fruitfull beds and borders
In Gods rich garden: that is bare,
      Which parts their ranks and orders.

The Sundaies of mans life,
Thredded together on times string,
Make bracelets to adorn the wife
Of the eternall glorious King.
On Sunday heavens gate stands ope;
Blessings are plentifull and rife,
      More plentifull then hope.

This day my Saviour rose,
And did inclose this light for his:
That, as each beast his manger knows,
Man might not of his fodder misse.
Christ hath took in this piece of ground,
And made a garden there for those
      Who want herbs for their wound.

The rest of our Creation
Our great Redeemer did remove
With the same shake, which at his passion
Did th' earth and all things with it move.
As Samson bore the doores away,
Christs hands, though nail'd, wrought our salvation,
      And did unhinge that day.

The brightnesse of that day
We sullied by our foul offence:
Wherefore that robe we cast away,
Having a new at his expence,
Whose drops of bloud paid the full price,
That was requir'd to make us gay,
      And fit for Paradise.

Thou art a day of mirth:
  And where the week-dayes trail on ground,
  Thy flight is higher, as thy birth.
  O let me take thee at the bound,
  Leaping with thee from sev'n to sev'n,
  Till that we both, being toss'd from earth,
      Flie hand in hand to heav'n!

Christmas

All after pleasures as I rid one day,
  My horse and I, both tir'd, bodie and minde,
  With full crie of affections, quite astray;
I took up in the next inne I could finde.

There when I came, whom found I but my deare,
  My dearest Lord, expecting till the grief
  Of pleasures brought me to him, readie there
To be all passengers most sweet relief?

O Thou, whose glorious, yet contracted light,
  Wrapt in nights mantle, stole into a manger;
  Since my dark soul and brutish is thy right,
To Man of all beasts be not thou a stranger:

  Furnish and deck my soul, that thou mayst have
  A better lodging, then a rack, or grave.

The shepherds sing; and shall I silent be?
        My God, no hymne for thee?
My soul's a shepherd too; a flock it feeds
        Of thoughts, and words, and deeds.
The pasture is thy word: the streams, thy grace
        Enriching all the place.
Shepherd and flock shall sing, and all my powers
        Out-sing the day-light houres.
Then we will chide the sunne for letting night
        Take up his place and right:

We sing one common Lord; wherefore he should
   Himself the candle hold.
I will go searching, till I finde a sunne
   Shall stay, till we have done;
A willing shiner, that shall shine as gladly,
   As frost-nipt sunnes look sadly.
Then we will sing, and shine all our own day,
   And one another pay:
His beams shall cheer my breast, and both so twine,
Till ev'n his beams sing, and my musick shine.

Vertue

 Sweet day, so cool, so calm, so bright,
 The bridall of the earth and skie:
 The dew shall weep thy fall to night;
   For thou must die.

 Sweet rose, whose hue angrie and brave
 Bids the rash gazer wipe his eye:
 Thy root is ever in its grave,
   And thou must die.

 Sweet spring, full of sweet dayes and roses,
 A box where sweets compacted lie;
 My musick shows ye have your closes,
   And all must die.

 Onely a sweet and vertuous soul,
 Like season'd timber, never gives;
 But though the whole world turn to coal,
   Then chiefly lives.

The British Church

I joy, deare Mother, when I view
Thy perfect lineaments, and hue
            Both sweet and bright.

Beautie in thee takes up her place,
And dates her letters from thy face,
            When she doth write.

A fine aspect in fit aray,
Neither too mean, nor yet too gay,
            Shows who is best.

Outlandish looks may not compare:
For all they either painted are,
            Or else undrest.

She on the hills, which wantonly
Allureth all in hope to be
            By her preferr'd,

Hath kiss'd so long her painted shrines,
That ev'n her face by kissing shines,
            For her reward.

She in the valley is so shie
Of dressing, that her hair doth lie
            About her eares:

While she avoids her neighbours pride,
She wholly goes on th' other side,
            And nothing wears.

But dearest Mother, (what those misse)
The mean thy praise and glorie is,
            And long may be.

Blessed be God, whose love it was
To double-moat thee with his grace,
            And none but thee.

The Sonne

Let forrain nations of their language boast,
What fine varietie each tongue affords:
I like our language, as our men and coast:
Who cannot dresse it well, want wit, not words.
How neatly doe we give one onely name
To parents issue and the sunnes bright starre!
A sonne is light and fruit; a fruitfull flame
Chasing the fathers dimnesse, carri'd farre
From the first man in th' East, to fresh and new
Western discov'ries of posteritie.
So in one word our Lords humilitie
We turn upon him in a sense must true:
    For what Christ once in humblenesse began,
    We him in glorie call, *The Sonne of Man.*

Aaron

Holinesse on the head,
    Light and perfections on the breast,
Harmonious bells below, raising the dead
    To leade them unto life and rest.
        Thus are true Aarons drest.

Profanenesse in my head,
    Defects and darknesse in my breast,
A noise of passions ringing me for dead
    Unto a place where is no rest.
        Poore priest thus am I drest.

Onely another head
    I have, another heart and breast,
Another musick, making live not dead,
    Without whom I could have no rest:
        In him I am well drest.

Christ is my onely head,
My alone onely heart and breast,
My onely musick, striking me ev'n dead;
That to the old man I may rest,
And be in him new drest.

So holy in my head,
Perfect and light in my deare breast,
My doctrine tun'd by Christ, (who is not dead,
But lives in me while I do rest)
Come people; Aaron's drest.

Love

Thou art too hard for me in Love:
There is no dealing with thee in that Art:
 That is thy Master-peece I see
 When I contrive and plott to prove
Something that may be conquest on my part
 Thou still, O Lord, outstrippest mee.

Sometimes, when as I wash, I say
And shrodely, as I think Lord wash my soule
 More spotted then my flesh can bee.
 But then there comes into my way
Thy ancient baptism which when I was foule
 And knew it not, yet cleansed mee.

I took a time when thou didst sleep
Great waves of trouble combating my brest:
 I thought it brave to praise thee then,
 Yet then I found, that thou didst creep
Into my hart with joye, giving more rest
 Then flesh did lend thee, back agen,

Let mee but once the conquest have
Upon the matter 'twill thy conquest prove:
   If thou subdue mortalitie
   Thou do'st no more, then doth the grave:
Whereas if I orecome thee and thy Love
   Hell, Death and Divel come short of mee.

THOMAS CAREW
(?1595–1640)

'And here the precious dust is laid'

And here the precious dust is laid,
Whose purely-temper'd clay was made
So fine, that it the guest betray'd.

Else, the soul grew so fast within
It broke the outward shell of sin,
And so was hatch'd a Cherubin.

In height it soar'd to God above;
In depth it did to knowledge move,
And spread in breadth to general love.

Before, a pious duty shined
To parents; courtesy behind;
On either side, an equal mind.

Good to the poor, to kindred dear,
To servants kind, to friendship clear:
To nothing but herself severe.

So, though a virgin, yet a bride
To every grace, she justified
A chaste polygamy, and died.

Learn from hence, Reader, what small trust
We owe this world, where virtue must,
Frail as our flesh, crumble to dust.

JAMES SHIRLEY
(1596–1666)

'The glories of our blood and state'

The glories of our blood and state,
   Are shadows, not substantial things,
There is no armour against fate,
   Death lays his icy hand on Kings,
      Scepter and Crown,
      Must tumble down,
And in the dust be equal made,
With the poor crooked sithe and spade.

Some men with swords may reap the field,
   And plant fresh laurels where they kill,
But their strong nerves at last must yield,
   They tame but one another still;
      Early or late,
      They stoop to fate,
And must give up the murmuring breath,
When they pale Captives creep to death.

The Garlands wither on your brow,
   Then boast no more your mighty deeds,
Upon Deaths purple Altar now,
   See where the Victor-victim bleeds,
      Your heads must come
      To the cold Tomb;
Onely the actions of the just
Smell sweet, and blossom in their dust.

EDMUND WALLER
(1606–1687)

Of the Last Verses in the Book

When we for Age could neither read nor write,
The Subject made us able to indite.
The Soul with Nobler Resolutions deckt,
The Body stooping, does Herself erect:
No Mortal Parts are requisite to raise
Her, that Unbody'd can her Maker praise.

The Seas are quiet, when the Winds give o're;
So calm are we, when Passions are no more:
For then we know how vain it was to boast
Of fleeting Things, so certain to be lost.
Clouds of Affection from our younger Eyes
Conceal that emptiness, which Age descries.

The Soul's dark Cottage, batter'd and decay'd,
Lets in new Light thro chinks that time has made.
Stronger by weakness, wiser Men become
As they draw near to their Eternal home:
Leaving the Old, both Worlds at once they view,
That stand upon the Threshold of the New.

JOHN MILTON
(1608–1674)

from *Paradise Lost*

from BOOK I

Of Mans First Disobedience, and the Fruit
Of that Forbidden Tree, whose mortal taste
Brought Death into the World, and all our woe,
With loss of *Eden*, till one greater Man
Restore us, and regain the blissful Seat,
Sing Heav'nly Muse, that on the secret top

Of *Oreb*, or of *Sinai*, didst inspire
That Shepherd, who first taught the chosen Seed,
In the Beginning how the Heav'ns and Earth
Rose out of *Chaos*: Or if *Sion* Hill
Delight thee more, and *Siloa's* Brook that flowd
Fast by the Oracle of God; I thence
Invoke thy aid to my adventrous Song,
That with no middle flight intends to soar
Above th' *Aonian* Mount, while it persues
Things unattempted yet in Prose or Rime.
And chiefly Thou O Spirit, that dost preferr
Before all Temples th' upright heart and pure,
Instruct me, for Thou knowst; Thou from the first
Wast present, and with mighty wings outspred
Dove-like satst brooding on the vast Abyss
And mad'st it pregnant: What in me is dark
Illumin, what is low raise and support;
That to the highth of this great Argument
I may assert Eternal Providence,
And justifie the wayes of God to men.

from BOOK III

　　Hail holy Light, offspring of Heav'n first-born,
Or of th' Eternal Coeternal beam
May I express thee unblam'd? since God is Light,
And never but in unapproached Light
Dwelt from Eternitie, dwelt then in thee,
Bright effluence of bright essence increate.
Or hear'st thou rather pure Ethereal stream,
Whose Fountain who shall tell? before the Sun,
Before the Heav'ns thou wert, and at the voice
Of God, as with a Mantle didst invest
The rising world of waters dark and deep,
Won from the void and formless infinite.
Thee I revisit now with bolder wing,
Escap't the *Stygian* Pool, though long detain
In that obscure sojourn, while in my flight
Through utter and through middle darkness borne

JOHN MILTON

With other notes than to th' *Orphean* Lyre
I sung of *Chaos* and *Eternal Night*,
Taught by the heav'nly Muse to venture down
The dark descent, and up to reascend,
Though hard and rare: thee I revisit safe,
And feel thy sovran vital Lamp; but thou
Revisitst not these eyes, that roul in vain
To find thy piercing ray, and find no dawn;
So thick a drop serene hath quencht thir Orbs,
Or dim suffusion veild. Yet not the more
Cease I to wander where the Muses haunt
Clear Spring, or shadie Grove, or Sunnie Hill,
Smit with the love of sacred song; but chief
Thee *Sion* and the flowrie Brooks beneath
That wash thy hallowd feet, and warbling flow,
Nightly I visit: nor somtimes forget
Those other two equald with me in Fate,
So were I equald with them in renown,
Blind *Thamyris* and blind *Mœonides*,
And *Tiresias* and *Phineus* Prophets old.
Then feed on thoughts, that voluntarie move
Harmonious numbers; as the wakeful Bird
Sings darkling, and in shadiest Covert hid
Tunes her nocturnal Note. Thus with the Year
Seasons return, but not to me returns
Day, or the sweet approach of Ev'n or Morn,
Or sight of vernal bloom, or Summers Rose,
Or flocks, or herds, or human face divine;
But cloud in stead, and ever-during dark
Surrounds me, from the cheerful ways of men
Cut off, and for the Book of knowledge fair
Presented with a Universal blanc
Of Natures works to mee expung'd and ras'd,
And wisdom at one entrance quite shut out.
So much the rather thou Celestial Light
Shine inward, and the mind through all her powers
Irradiate, there plant eyes, all mist from thence
Purge and disperse, that I may see and tell
Of things invisible to mortal sight.

Now had th' Almighty Father from above,
From the pure Empyrean where he sits
High Thron'd above all highth, bent down his eye,
His own works and their works at once to view:
About him all the Sanctities of Heaven
Stood thick as Starrs, and from his sight receiv'd
Beatitude past utterance; on his right
The radiant image of his Glory sat
His onely Son: On Earth he first beheld
Our two first Parents, yet the onely two
Of mankind, in the happie Garden plac't,
Reaping immortal fruits of joy and love,
Uninterrupted joy, unrivald love
In blissful solitude;

from BOOK IV

                              Thus was this place,
A happy rural seat of various view;
Groves whose rich Trees wept odorous Gumms and Baum,
Others whose fruit burnisht with Golden Rinde
Hung amiable, *Hesperian* Fables true,
If true, here only, and of delicious taste:
Betwixt them Lawns or level Downs, and Flocks
Grazing the tender herb, were interpos'd,
Or palmie hillock, or the flowrie lap
Of som irriguous Valley spred her store,
Flowrs of all hue, and without Thorn the Rose:
Another side, umbrageous Grots and Caves
Of cool recess, ore which the mantling Vine
Lays forth her purple Grape; and gently creeps
Luxuriant; mean while murmuring waters fall
Down the slope hills, disperst or in a Lake,
That to the fringed Bank with Myrtle crownd
Her crystal mirror holds, unite thir streams.
The Birds thir quire apply; airs, vernal airs,
Breathing the smell of field and grove, attune
The trembling leaves, while Universal *Pan*
Knit with the *Graces* and the *Hours* in dance
Led on th' Eternal Spring. Not that fair field
Of *Enna*, where *Proserpin* gathring flowrs

Her self a fairer Flowre by gloomie *Dis*
Was gatherd, which cost *Ceres* all that pain
To seek her through the world; nor that sweet Grove
Of *Daphne* by *Orontes*, and th' inspir'd
Castalian Spring, might with this Paradise
Of *Eden* strive;

*

Two of far nobler shape erect and tall,
Godlike erect, with native Honour clad
In naked Majestie seemd Lords of all,
And worthie seemd, for in thir looks Divine
The image of thir glorious Maker shon,
Truth, Wisdom, Sanctitude severe and pure,
Severe, but in true filial freedom plac't;
Whence true autoritie in men; though both
Not equal, as thir sex not equal seemd;
For contemplation hee and valour formd,
For softness shee and sweet attractive Grace,
Hee for God only, shee for God in him:

*

So passd they naked on, nor shunnd the sight
Of God or Angel, for they thought no ill:
So hand in hand they passd, the lovliest pair
That ever since in loves imbraces met,
Adam the goodliest man of men since born
His Sons, the fairest of her Daughters *Eve*.
Under a tuft of shade that on a green
Stood whispering soft, by a fresh Fountain side
They sat them down, and after no more toil
Of thir sweet Gardning labour than suffic'd
To recommend cool *Zephyr*, and made ease
More easie, wholsom thirst and appetite
More grateful, to thir Supper Fruits they fell,
Nectarine Fruits which the compliant boughes
Yielded them, side-long as they sat recline
On the soft downie Bank damaskt with flowrs:

*

Now came still Ev'ning on, and Twilight gray
Had in her sober Liverie all things clad;
Silence accompanied, for Beast and Bird,
They to thir grassie Couch, these to thir Nests
Were slunk, all but the wakeful Nightingale;
Shee all night long her amorous descant sung;
Silence was pleas'd: now glowd the Firmament
With living Saphirs: *Hesperus* that led
The starrie Host, rode brightest, till the Moon
Rising in clouded Majestie, at length
Apparent Queen unveild her peerless light,
And o'er the dark her Silver Mantle threw.
    When *Adam* thus to *Eve*: Fair Consort, th' hour
Of night, and all things now retir'd to rest
Mind us of like repose, since God hath set
Labour and rest, as day and night to men
Successive, and the timely dew of sleep
Now falling with soft slumbrous weight inclines
Our eye-lids; other Creatures all day long
Rove idle unimployd, and less need rest;
Man hath his daily work of body or mind
Appointed, which declares his Dignitie,
And the regard of Heav'n on all his ways;
While other Animals unactive range,
And of thir doings God takes no account.
To morrow ere fresh Morning streak the East
With first approach of light, we must be ris'n,
And at our pleasant labour, to reform
Yon flowrie Arbors, yonder Allies green,
Our walk at noon, with branches overgrown,
That mock our scant manuring, and require
More hands than ours to lop thir wanton growth:
Those Blossoms also, and those dropping Gumms,
That lie bestrowne unsightly and unsmooth,
Ask riddance, if we mean to tread with ease;
Mean while, as Nature wills, Night bids us rest.
    To whom thus *Eve* with perfet beauty adornd.
My Author and Disposer, what thou bidst
Unargu'd I obey; so God ordains,
God is thy Law; thou mine: to know no more

Is womans happiest knowledge and her praise.
With thee conversing I forget all time,
All seasons and thir change, all please alike.
Sweet is the breath of morn, her rising sweet,
With charm of earliest Birds; pleasant the Sun
When first on this delightful Land he spreads
His orient Beams, on herb, tree, fruit, and flowr,
Glistring with dew; fragrant the fertil earth
After soft showers; and sweet the coming on
Of grateful Ev'ning mild, then silent Night
With this her solemn Bird and this fair Moon,
And these the Gemms of Heav'n, her starrie train:
But neither breath of Morn when she ascends
With charm of earliest Birds, nor rising Sun
On this delightful land, not herb, fruit, flowr,
Glistring with dew, not fragrance after showers,
Nor grateful Ev'ning mild, nor silent Night
With this her solemn Bird, nor walk by Moon,
Or glittering Starr-light without thee is sweet.
But wherfore all night long shine these, for whom
This glorious sight, when sleep hath shut all eyes?
   To whom our general Ancestor repli'd.
Daughter of God and Man, accomplisht *Eve*,
Those have thir course to finish, round the Earth,
By morrow Ev'ning, and from Land to Land
In order, though to Nations yet unborn,
Ministring light prepar'd, they set and rise;
Lest total darkness should by Night regain
Her old possession, and extinguish life
In Nature and all things, which these soft fires
Not only enlighten, but with kindly heat
Of various influence foment and warm,
Temper or nourish, or in part shed down
Thir stellar vertue on all kinds that grow
On Earth, made hereby apter to receive
Perfection from the Suns more potent Ray.
These then, though unbeheld in deep of night,
Shine not in vain, nor think, though men were none,
That Heav'n would want spectators, God want praise;
Millions of spiritual Creatures walk the Earth

Unseen, both when we wake, and when we sleep:
All these with ceaseless praise his works behold
Both day and night: how often from the steep
Of echoing Hill or Thicket have we heard
Celestial voices to the midnight air,
Sole, or responsive each to others note
Singing thir great Creator: oft in bands
While they keep watch, or nightly rounding walk
With Heav'nly touch of instrumental sounds
In full harmonic number joind, thir songs
Divide the night, and lift our thoughts to Heaven.

from BOOK V

At once on th' Eastern cliff of Paradise
He lights, and to his proper shape returns
A Seraph wingd; six wings he wore, to shade
His lineaments Divine; the pair that clad
Each shoulder broad, came mantling ore his brest
With regal Ornament; the middle pair
Girt like a Starrie Zone his waist, and round
Skirted his loins and thighes with downie Gold
And colours dipt in Heav'n; the third his feet
Shaddowd from either heele with featherd maile
Skie-tinctur'd grain. Like *Maia's* son he stood,
And shook his Plumes, that Heav'nly fragrance filld
The circuit wide. Straight knew him all the Bands
Of Angels under watch; and to his state,
And to his message high in honour rise;
For on som message high they guessd him bound.

from BOOK VII

Thus God the Heav'n created, thus the Earth,
Matter unformd and void: Darkness profound
Coverd th' Abyss: but on the watrie Calm
His brooding wings the Spirit of God outspred,
And vital vertue infus'd, and vital warmth
Throughout the fluid Mass, but downward purg'd
The black tartareous cold Infernal dregs

Adverse to life: then founded, then conglob'd
Like things to like, the rest to several place
Disparted, and between spun out the Air,
And Earth self-ballanc't on her Center hung.

from BOOK X

                  Such was thir song,
While the Creator calling forth by name
His mightie Angels gave them several charge,
As sorted best with present things. The Sun
Had first his precept so to move, so shine,
As might affect the Earth with cold and heat
Scarce tollerable, and from the North to call
Decrepit Winter, from the South to bring
Solstitial summers heat. To the blanc Moon
Her office they prescrib'd, to th' other five
Thir planetarie motions and aspects
In *Sextile, Square,* and *Trine,* and *Opposite,*
Of noxious efficacie, and when to join
In Synod unbenign, and taught the fixt
Thir influence malignant when to showr,
Which of them rising with the Sun, or falling,
Should prove tempestuous: To the Winds they set
Thir corners, when with bluster to confound
Sea, Air, and Shore, the Thunder when to roul
With terror through the dark Aëreal Hall.
Some say he bid his Angels turn askance
The Poles of Earth twice ten degrees and more
From the Suns Axle; they with labour pushd
Oblique the Centric Globe: Some say the Sun
Was bid turn Reines from th' Equinoctial Road
Like distant bredth to *Taurus* with the Sev'n
Atlantic Sisters, and the *Spartan* Twins
Up to the *Tropic* Crab; thence down amain
By *Leo* and the *Virgin* and the *Scales,*
As deep as *Capricorn,* to bring in change
Of Seasons to each Clime; else had the Spring
Perpetual smil'd on Earth with vernant Flowrs,
Equal in Days and Nights, except to those

Beyond the Polar Circles; to them Day
Had unbenighted shon, while the low Sun
To recompense his distance, in thir sight
Had rounded still th' Horizon, and not known
Or East or West, which had forbid the Snow
From cold *Estotiland,* and South as farr
Beneath *Magellan.* At that tasted Fruit
The Sun, as from *Thyestean* Banquet, turnd
His course intended; else how had the World
Inhabited, though sinless, more than now
Avoided pinching cold and scorching heat?

from BOOK XI

To whom the Father, without Cloud, serene.
All they request for Man, accepted Son,
Obtain, all thy request was my Decree:
But longer in that Paradise to dwell,
The Law I gave to Nature him forbids:
Those pure immortal Elements that know
No gross, no unharmoneous mixture foul,
Eject him tainted now, and purge him off
As a distemper, gross to aire as gross,
And mortal food, as may dispose him best
For dissolution wrought by Sin, that first
Distemperd all things, and of incorrupt
Corrupted. I at first with two fair gifts
Created him endowd, with Happiness
And Immortalitie: that fondly lost,
This other serv'd but to eternize wo;
Till I provided Death; so Death becomes
His final remedie, and after Life
Tri'd in sharp tribulation, and refin'd
By Faith and faithful works, to second Life,
Wak't in the renovation of the just,
Resigns him up with Heav'n and Earth renewd.

★

This most afflicts me, that departing hence,
As from his face I shall be hid, depriv'd
His blessed count'nance; here I could frequent,
With worship, place by place where he voutsaf'd
Presence Divine, and to my Sons relate:
On this Mount he appear'd, under this Tree
Stood visible, among these Pines his voice
I heard, here with him at this Fountain talkd:
So many grateful Altars I would reare
Of grassie Terf, and pile up every Stone
Of lustre from the brook, in memorie
Or monument to Ages, and thereon
Offer sweet smelling Gumms and Fruits and Flowrs:
In yonder nether World where shall I seek
His bright appearances, or footstep trace?
For though I fled him angrie, yet recalld
To life prolongd and promis'd Race, I now
Gladly behold though but his utmost skirts
Of glory, and farr off his steps adore.

from BOOK XII

To whom thus also th' Angel last repli'd:
This having learnt, thou hast attaind the summ
Of wisdom; hope no higher, though all the Starrs
Thou knewst by name, and all th' ethereal Powers,
All secrets of the Deep, all Natures works,
Or works of God in Heav'n, Air, Earth or Sea,
And all the riches of this World enjoydst,
And all the rule, one Empire; only add
Deeds to thy knowledge answerable, add Faith,
Add Vertue, Patience, Temperance, add Love,
By name to come calld Charitie, the soul
Of all the rest: then wilt thou not be loath
To leave this Paradise, but shalt possess
A paradise within thee, happier farr.
Let us descend now therefore from this top
Of Speculation; for the hour precise
Exacts our parting hence; and see, the Guards,
By mee encampt on yonder Hill, expect

Thir motion, at whose Front a flaming Sword,
In signal of remove, waves fiercely round;
We may no longer stay: go waken *Eve*;
Her also I with gentle Dreams have calmd
Portending good, and all her spirits compos'd
To meek submission: thou at season fit
Let her with thee partake what thou hast heard,
Chiefly what may concern her Faith to know,
The great deliverance by her Seed to come
(For by the Womans Seed) on all Mankind.
That ye may live, which will be many days,
Both in one Faith unanimous though sad,
With cause for evils past, yet much more cheerd
With meditation on the happie end.

  He ended, and they both descend the Hill;
Descended, *Adam* to the Bowre where *Eve*
Lay sleeping ran before, but found her wak't;
And thus with words not sad she him receiv'd.

  Whence thou returnst, and whither wentst, I know;
For God is also in sleep, and Dreams advise,
Which he hath sent propitious, som great good
Presaging, since with sorrow and hearts distress
Wearied I fell asleep: but now lead on;
In mee is no delay; with thee to goe
Is to stay here; without thee here to staye
Is to go hence unwilling; thou to mee
Art all things under Heav'n, all places thou,
Who for my wilful crime art banisht hence.
This further consolation yet secure
I carry hence; though all by mee is lost,
Such favour I unworthie am voutsaf't,
By mee the Promis'd Seed shall all restore.
  So spake our Mother *Eve*, and *Adam* heard
Well pleas'd, but answered not; for now too nigh
Th' Archangel stood, and from the other Hill
To thir fixt Station, all in bright array
The Cherubim descended; on the ground
Gliding meteorous, as Ev'ning Mist
Ris'n from a River o'er the marish glides,
And gathers ground fast at the Labourers heel

Homeward returning. High in Front advanc't,
The brandisht Sword of God before them blaz'd
Fierce as a Comet; which with torrid heat,
And vapour as the *Libyan* Air adust,
Began to parch that temperat Clime; whereat
In either hand the hastning Angel caught
Our lingring Parents, and to th' Eastern Gate
Led them direct, and down the Cliff as fast
To the subjected Plain; then disappear'd.
They looking back, all th' Eastern side beheld
Of Paradise, so late thir happie seat,
Wav'd over by that flaming Brand, the Gate
With dreadful Faces throngd and fierie Arms:
Som natural tears they dropd, but wip'd them soon;
The World was all before them, where to choose
Thir place of rest, and Providence thir guide:
They hand in hand with wandring steps and slow,
Through *Eden* took their solitarie way.

from *Paradise Regain'd*

from BOOK I

I who erewhile the happy Garden sung,
By one mans disobedience lost, now sing
Recoverd Paradise to all mankind,
By one mans firm obedience fully tri'd
Through all temptation, and the Tempter foild
In all his wiles, defeated and repulst,
And *Eden* rais'd in the waste Wilderness.

*

So they in Heav'n thir Odes and Vigils tun'd:
Mean while the Son of God, who yet som days
Lodg'd in *Bethabara* where *John* baptiz'd,
Musing and much revolving in his brest,
How best the mighty work he might begin

Of Saviour to mankind, and which way first
Publish his God-like office now mature,
One day forth walkd alone, the Spirit leading
And his deep thoughts, the better to converse
With solitude, till far from track of men,
Thought following thought, and step by step led on,
He enterd now the bordering Desert wild,
And with dark shades and rocks environd round,
His holy Meditations thus persu'd.

*

  So spake our Morning Star then in his rise,
And looking round on every side beheld
A pathless Desert, dusk with horrid shades;
The way he came not having markt, return
Was difficult, by human steps untrod;
And he still on was led, but with such thoughts
Accompanied of things past and to come
Lodg'd in his brest, as well might recommend
Such Solitude before choicest Society.
Full forty days he passd, whether on hill
Somtimes, anon in shady vale, each night
Under the covert of som ancient Oak
Or Cedar, to defend him from the dew,
Or harbourd in som Cave, is not reveal'd;
Nor tasted human food, nor hunger felt
Till those days ended, hungerd then at last
Among wild Beasts: they at his sight grew mild,
Nor sleeping him nor waking harmd, his walk
The fiery Serpent fled, and noxious Worm,
The Lion and fierce Tiger glar'd aloof.
But now an aged man in rural weeds,
Following, as seemd, the quest of some stray Ewe,
Or witherd sticks to gather, which might serve
Against a Winters day when winds blow keen
To warm him wet returnd from field at Eve,
He saw approach; who first with curious eye
Perus'd him, then with words thus utterd spake.

   Sir what ill chance hath brought thee to this place
So far from path or road of men, who pass
In Troop or Caravan? for single none
Durst ever, who returnd, and dropd not here
His Carcass, pin'd with hunger and with drouth.

from BOOK II

Somtimes they thought he might be only shewn,
And for a time caught up to God, as once
Moses was in the Mount, and missing long;
And the great *Thisbite* who on fiery wheels
Rode up to Heaven, yet once again to come.
Therefore as those young Prophets then with care
Sought lost *Elijah*, so in each place these
Nigh to *Bethabara*; in *Jerico*
The City of Palms, *Ænon*, and *Salem* Old,
Machærus and each Town or City walld
On this side the broad lake *Genezaret*,
Or in *Perea*; but returnd in vain.
Then on the bank of *Jordan*, by a Creek
Where winds with Reeds and Osiers whisp'ring play,
Plain Fishermen, no greater men them call,
Close in a Cottage low together got,
Thir unexpected loss and plaints outbreath'd.

*

   Set women in his eye and in his walk,
Among daughters of men the fairest found;
Many are in each Region passing fair
As the noon Skie; more like to Goddesses
Than Mortal Creatures, graceful and discreet,
Expert in amorous Arts, enchanting tongues
Persuasive, Virgin majesty with mild
And sweet allayd, yet terrible to approach,
Skilld to retire, and in retiring draw
Hearts after them tangl'd in Amorous Nets.

*

It was the hour of night, when thus the Son
Commun'd in silent walk, then laid him down
Under the hospitable covert nigh
Of Trees thick interwoven; there he slept,
And dream'd, as appetite is wont to dream,
Of meats and drinks, Natures refreshment sweet;
Him thought, he by the Brook of *Cherith* stood
And saw the Ravens with thir horny beaks
Food to *Elijah* bringing Ev'n and Morn,
Though ravenous, taught to abstain from what they brought:
He saw the Prophet also how he fled
Into the Desert, and how there he slept
Under a Juniper; then how awak't
He found his Supper on the coals prepar'd,
And by the Angel was bid rise and eat,
And eat the second time after repose,
The strength whereof suffic'd him forty days:
Somtimes that with *Elijah* he partook,
Or as a guest with *Daniel* at his pulse.
Thus wore out night; and now the Herald Lark
Left his ground-nest, high touring to descry
The morns approach, and greet her with his Song:
As lightly from his grassy Couch up rose
Our Saviour, and found all was but a dream;
Fasting he went to sleep, and fasting wak'd.
Up to a hill anon his steps he rear'd,
From whose high top to ken the prospect round,
If Cottage were in view, Sheep-cote or Herd;
But Cottage, Herd or Sheep-cote none he saw,
Onely in a bottom saw a pleasant Grove,
With chaunt of tuneful Birds resounding loud;

from BOOK IV

To whom the Fiend with fear abasht repli'd.
Be not so sore offended, Son of God;
Though Sons of God both Angels are and Men,
If I to try whether in higher sort
Than these thou bear'st that title, have propos'd
What both from Men and Angels I receive,
Tetrarchs of fire, air, flood, and on the earth

Nations besides from all the quarterd winds,
God of this World invok't and World beneath:

*

Look once more ere we leave this specular Mount
Westward, much nearer by Southwest, behold
Where on the *Ægean* shore a City stands
Built nobly, pure the air, and light the soil,
Athens the eye of *Greece*, Mother of Arts
And Eloquence, native to famous wits
Or hospitable, in her sweet recess,
City or Suburban, studious walks and shades.
See there the Olive Grove of *Academe*,
Plato's retirement, where the *Attic* Bird
Trills her thick-warbl'd notes the summer long;
There flowrie hill *Hymettus* with the sound
Of Bees industrious murmur oft invites
To studious musing; there *Ilissus* rouls
His whispering stream. Within the walls then view
The schools of ancient Sages; his who bred
Great *Alexander* to subdue the world,
Lyceum there, and painted *Stoa* next:
There thou shalt hear and learn the secret power
Of harmony in tones and numbers hit
By voice or hand, and various-measurd verse,
Æolian charms and *Dorian Lyric* Odes,
And his who gave them breath, but higher sung,
Blind *Melesigenes* thence *Homer*, calld,
Whose Poem *Phœbus* challeng'd for his own.
Thence what the lofty grave Tragœdians taught
In *Chorus* or *Iambic*, teachers best
Of moral prudence, with delight receiv'd
In brief sententious precepts, while they treat
Of fate and chance and change in human life;
High actions and high passions best describing.
Thence to the famous Orators repair,
Those ancient, whose resistless eloquence
Wielded at will that fierce Democratie,
Shook th' Arsenal and fulmind over *Greece*
To *Macedon*, and *Artaxerxes* Throne.

*

Or if I would delight my privat hours
With Music or with Poem, where so soon
As in our native Language can I find
That solace? All our Law and Story strewd
With Hymns, our Psalms with artful terms inscrib'd,
Our Hebrew Songs and Harps in *Babylon*,
That pleas'd so well our Victors ear, declare
That rather *Greece* from us these Arts deriv'd;
Ill imitated, while they loudest sing
The vices of thir Deities, and thir own
In Fable, Hymn or Song, so personating
Thir Gods ridicullous, and themselves past shame.
Remove thir swelling Epithetes thick laid
As varnish on a Harlots cheek, the rest,
Thin sown with aught of profit or delight,
Will far be found unworthy to compare
With *Sions* songs, to all true tastes excelling,
Where God is prais'd aright, and Godlike men,
The Holiest of Holies, and his Saints.

Sonnets

XXIII
To Mr Cyriack Skinner *upon his Blindness*

Cyriack, this three years day these eyes, though clear
  To outward view of blemish or of spot,
  Bereft of light thir seeing have forgot,
  Nor to thir idle orbs doth sight appear
Of Sun or Moon or Starr throughout the year,
  Or man or woman. Yet I argue not
  Against heav'ns hand or will, nor bate a jot
  Of heart or hope; but still bear up and steer
Right onward. What supports me, dost thou ask?
  The conscience, Friend, to have lost them overpli'd
  In libertys defence, my noble task,
Of which all *Europe* talks from side to side.
  This thought might lead me through the worlds vain mask
  Content though blind, had I no better guide.

XXIV

Methought I saw my late espoused Saint
  Brought to me like *Alcestis* from the grave,
  Whom *Joves* great Son to her glad Husband gave,
  Rescu'd from death by force though pale and faint.
Mine as whom washt from spot of child-bed taint
  Purification in the old Law did save,
  And such as yet once more I trust to have
  Full sight of her in Heav'n without restraint,
Came vested all in white, pure as her mind:
  Her face was veild, yet to my fancied sight
  Love, sweetness, goodness in her person shin'd
So clear, as in no face with more delight
  But O as to embrace me she enclin'd
  I wak'd, she fled, and day brought back my night.

from *Lycidas*

  Return *Alpheus*, the dread voice is past
That shrunk thy streams; Return *Sicilian* Muse,
And call the Vales, and bid them hither cast
Their Bells, and Flowrets of a thousand hues.
Ye valleys low where the milde whispers use
Of shades and wanton winds and gushing brooks,
On whose fresh lap the swart Star sparely looks,
Throw hither all your quaint enameld eyes,
That on the green terf suck the honied showrs,
And purple all the ground with vernal flowrs.
Bring the rathe Primrose that forsaken dies,
The tufted Crow-toe, and pale Gessamine,
The white Pink, and the Pansie freak't with jet,
The glowing Violet,
The Musk-rose, and the well attir'd Woodbine,
With Cowslips wan that hang the pensive hed,
And every flowr that sad embroidery wears:
Bid *Amarantus* all his beauty shed,

And Daffadillies fill their cups with tears,
To strew the Laureat Herse where *Lycid* lies.
For so to interpose a little ease,
Let our frail thoughts dally with false surmise.
Ay me! Whilst thee the shores and sounding Seas
Wash far away, where e're thy bones are hurld,
Whether beyond the stormy *Hebrides*,
Where thou perhaps under the whelming tide
Visitst the bottom of the monstrous world;
Or whether thou to our moist vows deni'd,
Sleepst by the fable of *Bellerus* old,
Where the great vision of the guarded Mount
Looks toward *Namancos* and *Bayona's* hold;
Look homeward Angel now, and melt with ruth.
And, O ye *Dolphins*, waft the hapless youth.

  Weep no more, woeful Shepherds weep no more,
For *Lycidas* your sorrow is not dead,
Sunk though he be beneath the watry floore,
So sinks the day-star in the Ocean bed,
And yet anon repairs his drooping head,
And tricks his beams, and with new spangl'd Ore
Flames in the forhead of the morning sky:
So *Lycidas* sunk low, but mounted high
Through the dear might of him that walkd the waves;
Where other groves, and other streams along,
With *Nectar* pure his oozy Locks he laves.
And hears the unexpressive nuptial Song,
In the blest Kingdoms meek of joy and love.
There entertain him all the Saints above
In solemn troops and sweet Societies
That sing, and singing in their glory move,
And wipe the tears for ever from his eyes.
Now *Lycidas* the Shepherds weep no more;
Hence forth thou art the Genius of the shore
In thy large recompense, and shalt be good
To all that wander in that perilous flood.

  Thus sang the uncouth Swain to th' oaks and rills
While the still morn went out with Sandals gray;
He touchd the tender stops of various Quills,
With eager thought warbling his *Doric* lay:

And now the Sun had stretcht out all the hills,
And now was dropt into the Western bay;
At last he rose, and twitchd his Mantle blew:
Tomorrow to fresh Woods and Pastures new.

SIDNEY GODOLPHIN
(1610–1643)

Hymn

Lord when the wise men came from farr,
Led to thy Cradle by a Starr,
Then did the shepheards too rejoyce,
Instructed by thy Angells voyce:
Blest were the wisemen in their skill,
And shepheards in their harmlesse will.

Wisemen in tracing Natures lawes
Ascend unto the highest cause,
Shepheards with humble fearefulnesse
Walke safely, though their light be lesse:
Though wisemen better know the way
It seemes noe honest heart can stray.

Ther is noe merrit in the wise
But love, (the shepheards sacrifice).
Wisemen all wayes of knowledge past,
To th' shepheards wonder come at last:
To know, can only wonder breede,
And not to know, is wonders seede.

A wiseman at the Altar bowes
And offers up his studied vowes
And is received; may not the teares,
Which spring too from a shepheards feares,
And sighs upon his fraylty spent,
Though not distinct, be eloquent?

'Tis true, the object sanctifies
All passions which within us rise,
But since noe creature comprehends
The cause of causes, end of ends,
Hee who himselfe vouchsafes to know
Best pleases his creator soe.

When then our sorrowes wee applye
To our owne wantes and poverty,
When wee looke up in all distresse
And our owne misery confesse,
Sending both thankes and prayers above,
Then though we doe not know, we love.

RICHARD CRASHAW
(c. 1612–1649)

The Howres for the Hour of Matines

The Versicle
Lord, by thy Sweet and Saving SIGN,

The Responsory
Defend us from our foes and Thine.

V. Thou shalt open my lippes, O LORD.
R. And my mouth shall shew forth thy Prayse.
V. O GOD make speed to save me.
R. O LORD make hast to help me.
GLORY be to the FATHER,
        and to the SON,
        and to the H. GHOST.
  As it was in the beginning, is now, and ever shall be, world
without end.   Amen.

THE HYMN

The wakefull Matines hast to sing
The unknown sorrows of our king,
The FATHER'S word and wisdom, made
MAN, for man, by man's betraid;
The world's price sett to sale, and by the bold
Merchants of Death and sin, is bought and sold.
Of his Best Freinds (yea of himself) forsaken,
By his worst foes (because he would) beseig'd and taken.

The Antiphona
All hail, fair TREE.
Whose Fruit we be.
What song shall raise
Thy seemly praise.
Who broughtst to light
Life out of death, Day out of night.

The Versicle
Lo, we adore thee,
Dread LAMB! And bow thus low before thee,

The Responsor
'Cause, by the covenant of thy CROSSE,
Thou'hast sav'd at once the whole world's losse.

The Prayer
O Lord JESU-CHRIST, son of the living GOD! interpose, I pray thee,
thine own pretious death, thy CROSSE and Passion, betwixt my soul
and thy judgment, now and in the hour of my death. And vouchsafe
to graunt unto me thy grace and mercy; unto all quick and dead,
remission and rest; to thy church peace and concord; to us sinners life
and glory ever-lasting. Who livest and reignest with the FATHER, in
the unity of the HOLY GHOST, one GOD, world without end. Amen.

ANNE BRADSTREET
(?1612–1672)

Before the Birth of One of Her Children

All things within this fading world hath end,
Adversity doth still our joys attend;
No ties so strong, no friends so dear and sweet,
But with death's parting blow is sure to meet.
The sentence past is most irrevocable,
A common thing, yet oh inevitable.
How soon, my Dear, death may my steps attend,
How soon't may be thy Lot to lose thy friend,
We are both ignorant, yet love bids me
These farewell lines to recommend to thee,
That when that knot's untied that made us one,
I may seem thine, who in effect am none.
And if I see not half my dayes that's due,
What nature would, God grant to yours and you;
The many faults that well you know I have
Let be interr'd in my oblivious grave;
If any worth or virtue were in me,
Let that live freshly in thy memory
And when thou feel'st no grief, as I no harms,
Yet love thy dead, who long lay in thine arms.
And when thy loss shall be repaid with gains
Look to my little babes[,] my dear remains.
And if thou love thyself, or loved'st me[,]
These o protect from step Dames injury.
And if chance to thine eyes shall bring this verse,
With some sad sighs honour my absent Herse;
And kiss this paper for thy loves dear sake,
Who with salt tears this last Farewel did take.

JOHN CLEVELAND
(1613–1658)

Epitaph on the Earl of Strafford

Here lies wise and valiant dust,
Huddled up 'twixt fit and just,
Strafford, who was hurried hence
'Twixt treason and convenience.
He spent his time here in a mist,
A Papist, yet a Calvinist;
His Prince's nearest joy and grief,
He had, yet wanted, all relief;
The prop and ruin of the State,
The peoples' violent love and hate;
One in extremes loved and abhorred.
Riddles lie here, or in a word,
Here lies blood, and let it lie
Speechless still, and never cry.

HENRY VAUGHAN
(1621–1695)

To the Best, and Most Accomplished Couple

Blessings as rich and fragrant crown your heads
    As the mild heaven on *roses* sheds,
      When at their cheeks (like pearls) they wear
      The clouds that court them in a tear,
    And may they be fed from above
    By him which first ordained your love!

Fresh as the *hours* may all your pleasures be,
    And healthful as *eternity*!
      Sweet as the flowers' *first breath*, and close
      As the *unseen spreadings* of the rose,
    When he unfolds his curtained head,
    And makes his bosom the *Sun's* bed.

Soft as *your selves* run your whole lives, and clear
 As your own *glass*, or *what shines* there;
 Smooth as heaven's *face*, and bright as he
 When without *mask*, or *tiffany*,
 In all your time not one *jar* meet
 But peace as silent as his *feet*.

Like the day's *warmth* may all your comforts be,
 Untoiled for, and *serene* as he,
 Yet free and full as is that *sheaf*
 Of sun-beams gilding every leaf,
 When now the *tyrant-heat* expires
 And his cooled locks breath milder fires.

And as those *parcelled glories* he doth shed
 Are the *fair issues* of his head,
 Which ne'er so distant are soon known
 By the *heat* and *lustre* for his own,
 So may each branch of yours we see
 Your *copies*, and our *wonders* be!

And when no more on earth you must remain
 Invited hence to heaven again,
 Then may your virtuous, virgin-flames
 Shine in those *heirs* of your fair names,
 And teach the world that mystery
 Your selves in your posterity!

So you to both worlds shall *rich presents* bring,
And *gathered* up to heaven, leave here a *spring*.

Religion

My God, when I walk in those groves,
And leaves thy spirit doth still fan,
I see in each shade that there grows
An Angel talking with a man.

Under a *juniper*, some house,
Or the cool *myrtle's* canopy,
Others beneath an oak's green boughs,
Or at some *fountain's* bubbling eye;

Here *Jacob* dreams, and wrestles; there
Elias by a raven is fed,
Another time by the Angel, where
He brings him water with his bread;

In *Abraham's* tent the winged guests
(O how familiar then was heaven!)
Eat, drink, discourse, sit down, and rest
Until the cool, and shady *even*;

Nay thou thy self, my God, in *fire*,
Whirl-winds, and *clouds*, and the *soft voice*
Speak'st there so much, that I admire
We have no conference in these days;

Is the truce broke? or 'cause we have
A mediator now with thee,
Dost thou therefore old treaties waive
And by appeals from him decree?

Or is't so, as some green heads say
That now all miracles must cease?
Though thou hast promised they should stay
The tokens of the Church, and peace;

No, no; Religion is a spring
That from some secret, golden mine
Derives her birth, and thence doth bring
Cordials in every drop, and wine;

But in her long, and hidden course
Passing through the earth's dark veins,
Grows still from better unto worse,
And both her taste, and colour stains,

Then drilling on, learns to increase
False *echoes*, and confused sounds,
And unawares doth often seize
On veins of *sulphur* under ground;

So poisoned, breaks forth in some clime,
And at first sight doth many please,
But drunk, is puddle, or mere slime
And 'stead of physic, a disease;

Just such a tainted sink we have
Like that *Samaritan's* dead *well*,
Nor must we for the kernel crave
Because most voices like the *shell*.

Heal then these waters, Lord; or bring thy flock,
Since these are troubled, to the springing rock,
Look down great Master of the feast; O shine,
And turn once more our *Water* into *Wine*!

Song of Solomon, iv, 12
*My sister, my spouse is as a garden enclosed, as a spring shut
up, and a fountain sealed up.*

The British Church

I

Ah! he is fled!
And while these here their *mists*, and *shadows* hatch,
My glorious head
Doth on those hills of myrrh, and incense watch.
Haste, haste my dear,
The soldiers here
Cast in their lots again,
That seamless coat
The Jews touched not,
These dare divide, and stain.

2

O get thee wings!
Or if as yet (until these clouds depart,
    And the day springs,)
Thou think'st it good to tarry where thou art,
    Write in thy books
    My ravished looks
  Slain flock, and pillaged fleeces,
    And haste thee so
    As a young roe
  Upon the mounts of spices.

O Rosa Campi! O lilium Convallium! quomodò nunc facta es pabulum Aprorum!

The Retreat

Happy those early days! when I
Shined in my Angel-infancy.
Before I understood this place
Appointed for my second race,
Or taught my soul to fancy aught
But a white, celestial thought,
When yet I had not walked above
A mile, or two, from my first love,
And looking back (at that short space,)
Could see a glimpse of his bright-face;
When on some *gilded cloud*, or *flower*
My gazing soul would dwell an hour,
And in those weaker glories spy
Some shadows of eternity;
Before I taught my tongue to wound
My conscience with a sinful sound,
Or had the black art to dispense
A several sin to every sense,
But felt through all this fleshly dress
Bright *shoots* of everlastingness.

O how I long to travel back
And tread again that ancient track!
That I might once more reach that plain,
Where first I left my glorious train,
From whence the enlightened spirit sees
That shady city of palm trees;
But (ah!) my soul with too much stay
Is drunk, and staggers in the way.
Some men a' forward motion love,
But I by backward steps would move,
And when this dust falls to the urn
In that state I came return.

The Morning-Watch

O joys! Infinite sweetness! with what flowers,
And shoots of glory, my soul breaks, and buds!
     All the long hours
     Of night, and rest
     Through the still shrouds
     Of sleep, and clouds,
   This dew fell on my breast;
     O how it *bloods*,
And *spirits* all my earth! hark! In what rings,
And *hymning circulations* the quick world
     Awakes, and sings;
     The rising winds,
     And falling springs,
     Birds, beasts, all things
   Adore him in their kinds.
     Thus all is hurled

In sacred *hymns*, and *order*, the great *chime*
And *symphony* of nature. Prayer is
       The world in tune,
       A spirit-voice,
       And vocal joys
     Whose *echo is* heaven's bliss.
       O let me climb
When I lie down! The pious soul by night
Is like a clouded star, whose beams though said
       To shed their light
       Under some cloud
       Yet are above,
       And shine, and move
     Beyond that misty shroud.
       So in my bed
That curtained grave, though sleep, like ashes, hide
My lamp, and life, both shall in thee abide.

Easter-Day

Thou, whose sad heart, and weeping head lies low,
    Whose cloudy breast cold damps invade,
Who never feel'st the sun, nor smooth'st thy brow,
    But sitt'st oppressed in the shade,
        Awake, awake,
And in his Resurrection partake,
    Who on this day (that thou might'st rise as he,)
    Rose up, and cancelled two deaths due to thee.

Awake, awake; and, like the sun, disperse
    All mists that would usurp this day;
Where are thy palms, thy branches, and thy verse?
    Hosanna! hark; why dost thou stay?
        Arise, arise,
And with his healing blood anoint thine eyes,
    Thy inward eyes; his blood will cure thy mind,
    Whose spittle only could restore the blind.

The World (I)

1

I saw Eternity the other night
Like a great *Ring* of pure and endless light,
   All calm, as it was bright,
And round beneath it, Time in hours, days, years
     Driven by the spheres
Like a vast shadow moved, in which the world
   And all her train were hurled;
The doting lover in his quaintest strain
     Did there complain,
Near him, his lute, his fancy, and his flights,
     Wit's sour delights,
With gloves, and knots the silly snares of pleasure
     Yet his dear treasure
All scattered lay, while he his eyes did pour
     Upon a flower.

2

The darksome states-man hung with weights and woe
Like a thick midnight-fog moved there so slow
   He did nor stay, nor go;
Condemning thoughts (like sad eclipses) scowl
     Upon his soul,
And clouds of crying witnesses without
   Pursued him with one shout.
Yet digged the mole, and lest his ways be found
     Worked under ground,
Where he did clutch his prey, but one did see
     That policy,
Churches and altars fed him, perjuries
     Were gnats and flies,
It rained about him blood and tears, but he
     Drank them as free.

3

The fearful miser on a heap of rust
Sat pining all his life there, did scarce trust
  His own hands with the dust,
Yet would not place one piece above, but lives
    In fear of thieves.
Thousands there were as frantic as himself
    And hugged each one his pelf,
The down-right epicure placed heaven in sense
    And scorned pretence
While others slipped into a wide excess
    Said little less;
The weaker sort slight, trivial wares enslave
    Who think them brave,
And poor, despised truth sat counting by
    Their victory.

4

Yet some, who all this while did weep and sing,
And sing, and weep, soared up into the *Ring*,
  But most would use no wing.
O fools (said I,) thus to prefer dark night
    Before true light,
To live in grots, and caves, and hate the day
  Because it shows the way,
The way which from this dead and dark abode
    Leads up to God,
A way where you might tread the Sun, and be
    More bright than he.
But as I did their madness so discuss
    One whispered thus,
This ring the bride-groom did for none provide
    But for his bride.

John, ii, 16–17
All that is in the world, the lust of the flesh, the lust of the eyes, and the pride of life, is not of the father but is of the world.
   And the world passeth away, and the lusts thereof, but he that doth the will of God abideth for ever.

'They are all gone into the world of light!'

They are all gone into the world of light!
   And I alone sit ling'ring here;
Their very memory is fair and bright,
    And my sad thoughts doth clear.

It glows and glitters in my cloudy breast
   Like stars upon some gloomy grove,
Or those faint beams in which this hill is dressed,
    After the sun's remove.

I see them walking in an air of glory,
   Whose light doth trample on my days:
My days, which are at best but dull and hoary,
    Mere glimmering and decays.

O holy hope! and high humility,
   High as the Heavens above!
These are your walks, and you have showed them me
    To kindle my cold love,

Dear, beauteous death! the jewel of the just,
   Shining nowhere, but in the dark;
What mysteries do lie beyond thy dust;
    Could man outlook that mark!

He that hath found some fledged bird's nest, may know
   At first sight, if the bird be flown;
But what fair well, or grove he sings in now,
    That is to him unknown.

And yet, as Angels in some brighter dreams
   Call to the soul, when man doth sleep:
So some strange thoughts transcend our wonted themes,
    And into glory peep.

If a star were confined into a tomb
   Her captive flames must needs burn there;
But when the hand that locked her up, gives room,
    She'll shine through all the sphere.

O Father of eternal life, and all
   Created glories under thee!
Resume thy spirit from this world of thrall
     Into true liberty.

Either disperse these mists, which blot and fill
   My perspective (still) as they pass,
Or else remove me hence unto that hill,
     Where I shall need no glass.

The Dwelling-Place

John, i, 38, 39

    What happy, secret fountain,
      Fair shade, or mountain,
Whose undiscovered virgin glory
Boasts it this day, though not in story,
Was then thy dwelling? did some cloud
Fixed to a tent, descend and shroud
My distressed Lord? or did a star
Beckoned by thee, though high and far,
In sparkling smiles haste gladly down
To lodge light, and increase her own?
My dear, dear God! I do not know
What lodged thee then, nor where, nor how;
But I am sure, thou dost now come
Oft to a narrow, homely room,
Where thou too hast but the least part,
My God, I mean *my sinful heart*.

To the Pious Memory of C. W. Esquire who Finished His Course Here, and Made His Entrance into Immortality upon the 13 of September, in the Year of Redemption 1653

Now, that the public sorrow doth subside,
And those slight tears which *custom* springs, are dried;
While all the rich and *outside mourners* pass
Home from thy *dust* to empty their own *glass*:
I (who the throng affect not, nor their state:)
Steal to thy grave undressed, to meditate
On our sad loss, accompanied by none,
An obscure mourner that would weep alone.

    So when the world's great luminary sets,
Some scarce known star into the *zenith* gets,
Twinkles and curls a weak but willing spark:
As glow-worms here do glitter in the dark.
Yet, since the dimmest flame that kindles there,
An humble love unto the light doth bear,
And true devotion from an hermit's cell
Will Heaven's kind King as soon reach and as well
As that which from rich shrines and altars flies
Led by ascending incense to the skies:
'Tis no malicious rudeness, if the might
Of love makes dark things wait upon the bright,
And from my sad retirements calls me forth
The just recorder of thy death and worth.

    Long didst thou live (if length be measured by
The tedious reign of our calamity:)
And counter to all storms and changes still
Kept'st the same temper, and the self same will.
Though trials came as duly as the day,
And in such mists, that none could see his way:
Yet thee I found still virtuous, and saw
The sun give clouds: and *Charles* give both the law.
When private interest did all hearts bend
And wild dissents the public peace did rend:
Thou neither won, nor worn wert still thy self;
Not awed by force, nor basely bribed with pelf.

    What the insuperable stream of times
Did dash thee with, those *sufferings* were, not *crimes*.

So the bright *sun* eclipses bears; and we
Because then passive, blame him not; should he
For inforced shades, and the *moon's* ruder veil
Much nearer us, than him, be judged to fail?
Who traduce thee, so err. As poisons by
Correction are made antidotes, so thy
Just soul did turn even hurtful things to good;
Used bad laws so, they drew not tears, nor blood.
Heav'n was thy aim, and thy great rare design
Was not to lord it here, but there to shine.
Earth nothing had, could tempt thee. All that e'r
Thou pray'dst for here, was *peace*; and *glory* there.
For though thy course in time's long progress fell
On a sad age, when war and opened hell
Licensed all arts and sects, and made it free
To thrive by fraud and blood and blasphemy:
Yet thou thy just inheritance didst by
No sacrilege, nor pillage multiply;
No rapine swelled thy state: no bribes, nor fees
Our new oppressors' best annuities.
Such clean, pure hands hadst thou! And for thy heart
Man's secret region and his noblest part;
Since I was privy to't, and had the key
Of that fair room, where thy bright spirit lay:
I must affirm, it did as much surpass
Most I have known, as the clear sky doth glass.
Constant and kind, and plain and meek and mild
It was, and with no new conceits defiled.
Busy, but sacred thoughts (like *bees*) did still
Within it stir, and strive unto that hill,
Where redeemed spirits evermore alive
After their work is done, ascend and *hive*.
No outward tumults reached this inward place,
'Twas holy ground: where peace, and love and grace
Kept house: where the immortal restless life
In a most dutiful and pious strife
Like a fixed *watch*, moved all in order, still;
The *will* served God, and every *sense* the will!
  In this safe state death met thee. Death which is
But a kind usher of the good to bliss.

Therefore to weep because thy course is run,
Or droop like flowers, which lately lost the *sun*:
I cannot yield, since faith will not permit,
A *tenure* got by *conquest* to the *pit*.
For the great Victor fought for us, and He
Counts every dust, that is laid up of thee.
Besides, Death now grows decrepit and hath
Spent the most part both of its time and wrath.
That thick, black night which mankind feared, is torn
By *troops* of stars, and the bright day's *forlorn*.
The next glad news (most glad unto the just!)
Will be the Trumpet's summons from the dust.
Then I'll not grieve; nay more, I'll not allow
My soul should think thee absent from me now.
Some bid their dead *good night!* but I will say
Good morrow to dear Charles! for it is day.

ANDREW MARVELL
(1621–1678)

Bermudas

Where the remote Bermudas ride
In the ocean's bosom unespied,
From a small boat, that rowed along,
The listening winds received this song.

  'What should we do but sing his praise
That led us through the watery maze,
Unto an isle so long unknown,
And yet far kinder than our own?

Where he the huge sea-monsters wracks,
That lift the deep upon their backs,
He lands us on a grassy stage,
Safe from the storms, and prelate's rage.

He gave us this eternal spring,
Which here enamels everything,
And sends the fowl to us in care,
On daily visits through the air.

He hangs in shades the orange bright,
Like golden lamps in a green night,
And does in the pom'granates close
Jewels more rich than Ormus shows.

He makes the figs our mouths to meet,
And throws the melons at our feet,
But apples plants of such a price,
No tree could ever bear them twice.

With cedars, chosen by his hand,
From Lebanon, he stores the land,
And makes the hollow seas, that roar,
Proclaim the ambergris on shore.

He cast (of which we rather boast)
The gospel's pearl upon our coast,
And in these rocks for us did frame
A temple, where to sound his name.

Oh let our voice his praise exalt,
Till it arrive at heaven's vault:
Which thence (perhaps) rebounding, may
Echo beyond the Mexique Bay.'

   Thus sung they, in the English boat,
An holy and a cheerful note,
And all the way, to guide their chime,
With falling oars they kept the time.

CHARLES COTTON
(1630–1687)

The Morning Quatrains

The Cock has crow'd an hour ago,
'Tis time we now dull sleep forgo;
Tir'd Nature is by sleep redress'd,
And Labour's overcome by Rest.

We have out-done the work of Night,
'Tis time we rise t'attend the Light,
And e'er he shall his Beams display,
To plot new bus'ness for the day.

None but the slothfull, or unsound,
Are by the Sun in Feathers found,
Nor, without rising with the Sun,
Can the World's bus'ness e'er be done.

Hark! Hark! the watchfull Chanticler,
Tells us the day's bright Harbinger
Peeps o'er the Eastern Hills, to awe
And warn night's sov'reign to withdraw.

The Morning Curtains now are drawn,
And now appears the blushing dawn;
Aurora has her Roses shed,
To strew the way *Sol's* steeds must tread.

Xanthus and *Æthon* harness'd are,
To roll away the burning Carr,
And, snorting flame, impatient bear
The dressing of the Chariotier.

The sable Cheeks of sullen Night
Are streak'd with Rosie streams of light,
Whilst she retires away in fear,
To shade the other Hemisphere.

The merry Lark now takes her wings,
And long'd-for day's loud wellcome sings,

Mounting her body out of sight,
As if she meant to meet the light.

Now doors and windows are unbar'd,
Each-where are chearfull voices heard,
And round about Good-morrows fly
As if Day taught Humanity.

The Chimnies now to smoke begin,
And the old Wife sits down to spin,
Whilst *Kate*, taking her Pail, does trip
Mull's swoln and stradl'ing Paps to strip.

Vulcan now makes his Anvil ring,
Dick whistles loud, and *Maud* doth sing,
And *Silvio* with his Bugle Horn
Winds an Imprime unto the Morn.

Now through the morning doors behold
Phœbus array'd in burning Gold,
Lashing his fiery Steeds, displays
His warm and all enlight'ning Rays.

Now each one to his work prepares,
All that have hands are Labourers,
And Manufactures of each trade
By op'ning Shops are open laid.

Hob yokes his Oxen to the Team,
The Angler goes unto the stream,
The Wood-man to the Purlews highs,
And lab'ring Bees to load their thighs.

Fair *Amarillis* drives her Flocks,
All night safe folded from the Fox,
To flow'ry Downs, where *Collin* stays,
To court her with his Roundelays.

The Traveller now leaves his Inn
A new day's Journey to begin,
As he would post it with the day,
And early rising makes good way.

The slick-fac'd School-boy Sachel takes,
And with slow pace small riddance makes;
For why, the haste we make, you know,
To Knowledge and to Vertue's slow.

The Fore-horse gingles on the Road,
The Waggoner lugs on his Load,
The Field with busie people snies;
And City rings with various cries.

The World is now a busie swarm,
All doing good, or doing harm;
But let's take heed our Acts be true,
For Heaven's eye sees all we doe.

None can that piercing sight evade,
It penetrates the darkest shade,
And sin, though it could scape the eye,
Would be discover'd by the Cry.

JOHN DRYDEN
(1631–1700)

from *Annus Mirabilis*

Yet *London*, Empress of the Northern Clime,
By an high Fate thou greatly didst expire:
Great as the Worlds, which, at the death of time,
Must fall, and rise a nobler frame by fire.

As when some dire Usurper Heav'n provides
To scourge his Country with a lawless sway:
His birth perhaps some petty Village hides,
And sets his Cradle out of Fortune's way.

Till fully ripe his swelling Fate breaks out,
And hurries him to mighty Mischiefs on:
His Prince, surpriz'd at first, no ill could doubt,
And wants the pow'r to meet it when 'tis known.

Such was the Rise of his prodigious fire,
Which in mean Buildings first obscurely bred,
From thence did soon to open Streets aspire,
And straight to Palaces and Temples spread.

The diligence of Trades and noiseful Gain,
And luxury, more late, asleep were laid:
All was the nights, and in her silent reign
No sound the rest of Nature did invade.

In this deep quiet, from what source unknown,
Those seeds of Fire their fatal Birth disclose;
And first, few scatt'ring Sparks about were blown,
Big with the flames that to our Ruin rose.

Then, in some close-pent Room it crept along,
And, smouldring as it went, in silence fed;
Till th' infant Monster, with devouring strong,
Walk'd boldly upright with exalted head.

Now like some rich or mighty Murderer,
Too great for Prison, which he breaks with Gold,
Who fresher for new Mischiefs does appear
And dares the World to tax him with the old:

So scapes th' insulting Fire his narrow Jail
And makes small out-lets into open air:
There the fierce Winds his tender Force assail,
And beat him down-ward to his first repair.

The Winds, like crafty Courtezans, withheld
His Flames from burning, but to blow them more:
And every fresh attempt he is repell'd
With faint Denials, weaker than before.

And now, no longer letted of his Prey,
He leaps up at it with inrag'd desire:
O'relooks the Neighbours with a wide survey,
And nods at every House his threatening Fire.

The Ghosts of Traitors from the *Bridge* descend,
With bold Fanatick Spectres to rejoyce:
About the fire into a Dance they bend,
And sing their Sabbath Notes with feeble voice.

Our Guardian Angel saw them where he sate
Above the Palace of our slumbring King;
He sigh'd, abandoning his charge to Fate,
And, drooping, oft lookt back upon the wing.

At length the crackling noise and dreadful blaze
Call'd up some waking Lover to the sight;
And long it was ere he the rest could raise,
Whose heavy Eye-lids yet were full of Night.

The next to Danger, hot persu'd by Fate,
Half-cloth'd, half-naked, hastily retire:
And frighted Mothers strike their Breasts, too late,
For helpless Infants left amidst the Fire.

Their Cries soon waken all the Dwellers near;
Now murmuring Noises rise in every Street;
The more remote run stumbling with their fear,
And, in the dark, Men justle as they meet.

So weary Bees in little Cells repose;
But if Night-robbers lift the well-stor'd Hive,
An humming through their waxen City grows,
And out upon each others wings they drive.

Now Streets grow throng'd and busie as by day:
Some run for Buckets to the hallow'd Quire:
Some cut the Pipes, and some the Engines play;
And some more bold mount Ladders to the fire.

In vain: For from the East a *Belgian* wind
His hostile Breath through the dry Rafters sent;
The Flames impell'd soon left their Foes behind
And forward, with a wanton fury went.

A Key of Fire ran all along the Shore,
And lighten'd all the River with a blaze:
The waken'd Tides began again to roar,
And wond'ring Fish in shining waters gaze.

Old Father Thames rais'd up his reverend head,
But fear'd the fate of *Simoeis* would return:
Deep in his *Ooze* he sought his sedgy Bed,
And shrunk his Waters back into his Urn.

The Fire, mean time walks in a broader gross;
To either hand his Wings he opens wide:
He wades the Streets, and streight he reaches cross,
And plays his longing Flames on th' other side.

At first they warm, then scorch, and then they take;
Now with long Necks from side to side they feed:
At length, grown strong, their Mother-fire forsake,
And a new Colony of Flames succeed.

To every nobler Portion of the Town
The curling Billows roll their restless Tide:
In parties now they straggle up and down,
As Armies, unoppos'd, for Prey divide.

One mighty Squadron with a Side-wind sped,
Through narrow Lanes his cumber'd Fire does haste:
By pow'rful charms of Gold and Silver led,
The *Lombard* Banquers and the *Change* to waste.

Another backward to the *Tow'r* would go,
And slowly eats his way against the Wind:
But the main body of the marching Foe
Against th' Imperial Palace is design'd.

Now Day appears, and with the day the King,
Whose early Care had robb'd him of his rest:
Far off the Cracks of Falling houses ring,
And Shrieks of Subjects pierce his tender Breast.

Near as he draws, thick harbingers of Smoke
With gloomy Pillars cover all the place:
Whose little intervals of Night are broke
By Sparks, that drive against his Sacred Face.

More than his Guards his Sorrows made him known,
And pious Tears, which down his Cheeks did show'r:
The Wretched in his Grief forgot their own;
(So much the Pity of a King has pow'r.)

He wept the Flames of what he lov'd so well
And what so well had merited his love:
For never Prince in Grace did more excel,
Or Royal City more in Duty strove.

Nor with an idle Care did he behold:
(Subjects may grieve, but Monarchs must redress;)
He chears the Fearful and commends the Bold,
And makes Despairers hope for good Success.

Himself directs what first is to be done,
And orders all the Succours which they bring:
The Helpful and the Good about him run,
And form an Army worthy such a King.

He sees the dire Contagion spread so fast
That where it seizes, all Relief is vain:
And therefore must unwillingly lay waste
That Country, which would, else, the Foe maintain.

The Powder blows up all before the Fire:
Th' amazed flames stand gather'd on a heap;
And from the precipices-brink retire,
Afraid to venture on so large a leap.

Thus fighting Fires a while themselves consume,
But streight like *Turks*, forc'd on to win or die,
They first lay tender Bridges of their fume,
And o're the Breach in unctuous vapours flie.

Part stays for Passage, 'till a gust of wind
Ships o're their Forces in a shining Sheet:
Part, creeping under ground, their Journey blind,
And, climbing from below, their Fellows meet.

Thus to some desert Plain, or old Wood-side,
Dire Night-hags come from far to dance their round:
And o're broad rivers, on their Fiends, they ride,
Or sweep in Clouds above the blasted ground.

No help avails: for, *Hydra*-like, the Fire
Lifts up his Hundred heads to aim his way:
And scarce the wealthy can one half retire,
Before he rushes in to share the Prey.

The Rich grow suppliant, and the Poor grow proud:
Those offer mighty gain, and these ask more;
So void of pity is th' ignoble Crowd,
When others Ruin may increase their Store.

As those who live by Shores with joy behold
Some wealthy Vessel split or stranded nigh;
And from the Rocks leap down for shipwrack'd Gold,
And seek the Tempest which the others flie:

So these but wait the Owners last despair,
And what's permitted to the flames invade:
Ev'n from their Jaws they hungry morsels tear,
And, on their backs, the Spoils of *Vulcan* lade.

The days were all in this lost labour spent;
And when the weary King gave place to Night,
His Beams he to his Royal Brother lent,
And so shone still in his reflective Light.

Night came, but without darkness or repose,
A dismal Picture of the gen'ral Doom;
Where Souls distracted when the Trumpet blows,
And half unready with their Bodies come.

Those who have Homes, when Home they do repair,
To a last Lodging call their wand'ring Friends:
Their short uneasie Sleeps are broke with Care,
To look how near their own Destruction tends.

Those who have none, sit round where once it was,
And with full Eyes each wonted Room require:
Haunting the yet warm Ashes of the place,
As murder'd Men walk where they did expire.

Some stir up Coals, and watch the Vestal fire,
Others in vain from sight of Ruin run;
And, while through burning Lab'rinths they retire,
With loathing Eyes repeat what they would shun.

The most in Feilds like herded Beasts lie down,
To Dews obnoxious on the grassie Floor;
And while their Babes in Sleep their Sorrows drown,
Sad Parents watch the remnants of their Store.

While by the Motion of the Flames they guess
What Streets are burning now, and what are near,
An infant waking to the Paps would press,
And meets, instead of Milk, a falling Tear.

No thought can ease them but their Sovereign's Care,
Whose Praise th' afflicted as their Comfort sing;
Ev'n those, whom Want might drive to just despair,
Think Life a Blessing under such a King.

Mean time he sadly suffers in their Grief,
Out-weeps an Hermite, and out-prays a Saint:
All the long night he studies their relief,
How they may be suppli'd, and he may want.

O God, said he, thou Patron of my Days,
Guide of my Youth in Exile and Distress!
Who me unfriended brought'st by wondrous ways,
The Kingdom of my Fathers to possess:

Be thou my Judge, with what unwearied Care
I since have labour'd for my People's good;
To bind the Bruises of a Civil War,
And stop the Issues of their wasting Blood.

Thou, who has taught me to forgive the Ill,
And recompense, as Friends, the Good misled:
If Mercy be a Precept of thy Will,
Return that Mercy on thy Servants head.

Or, if my heedless Youth has stept astray,
Too soon forgetful of thy gracious hand;
On me alone thy just Displeasure lay,
But take thy Judgments from this mourning Land.

We all have sinn'd, and thou hast laid us low,
As humble Earth from whence at first we came:
Like flying Shades before the Clouds we shew,
And shrink like Parchment in consuming Flame.

O let it be enough what thou hast done;
When spotted Deaths ran arm'd thro' every Street,
With poison'd Darts which not the Good could shun,
The Speedy could out-flie, or Valiant meet.

The living few, and frequent Funerals then,
Proclaim'd thy Wrath on this forsaken place:
And now those few, who are return'd agen,
Thy searching Judgments to their dwellings trace.

O pass not, Lord, an absolute Decree,
Or bind thy Sentence unconditional:
But in thy Sentence our Remorse foresee,
And, in that foresight, this thy Doom recall.

Thy Threatings, Lord, as thine thou maist revoke:
But, if immutable and fix'd they stand,
Continue still thy self to give the stroke,
And let not Foreign-foes oppress Thy Land.

Th' Eternal heard, and from the Heav'nly Quire
Chose out the Cherub with the flaming Sword:
And bad him swiftly drive th' approaching Fire
From where our Naval Magazines were stor'd.

The blessed Minister his Wings displai'd,
And like a shooting Star he cleft the night;
He charg'd the Flames, and those that disobey'd
He lash'd to duty with his Sword of light.

The fugitive Flames, chastis'd, went forth to prey
On pious Structures, by our Fathers rear'd;
By which to Heav'n they did affect the way,
Ere Faith in Church-men without Works was heard.

The wanting Orphans saw with watry Eyes
Their Founders Charity in Dust laid low,
And sent to God their ever-answer'd cries,
(For he protects the Poor, who made them so.)

Nor could thy Fabrick, *Paul's*, defend thee long,
Though thou wert Sacred to thy Makers praise:
Though made Immortal by a Poet's Song,
And Poets Songs the *Theban* walls could raise.

The daring Flames peep't in, and saw from far
The awful Beauties of the Sacred Quire:
But, since it was prophan'd by Civil War,
Heav'n thought it fit to have it purg'd by fire.

Now down the narrow Streets it swiftly came,
And, widely opening, did on both sides prey:
This benefit we sadly owe the Flame,
If only Ruin must enlarge our way.

And now four days the Sun had seen our Woes;
Four nights the Moon beheld th' incessant fire;
It seem'd as if the Stars more sickly rose,
And farther from the feav'rish North retire.

In th' Empyrean Heav'n (the Bless'd abode),
The Thrones and the Dominions prostrate lie.
Not daring to behold their angry God:
And an hush'd silence damps the tuneful Sky.

At length th' Almighty cast a pitying Eye,
And Mercy softly touch'd his melting Breast:
He saw the Towns one half in Rubbish lie,
And eager flames drive on to storm the rest.

An hollow chrystal Pyramid he takes,
In firmamental Waters dipt above;
Of it a broad Extinguisher he makes
And hoods the Flames that to their quarry strove.

The vanquish'd Fires withdraw from every place,
Or, full with feeding, sink into a sleep:
Each household Genius shows again his face,
And, from the hearths, the little Lares creep.

Our King this more than natural change beholds;
With sober Joy his heart and eyes abound:
To the All-good his lifted hands he folds,
And thanks him low on his redeemed ground.

As when sharp Frosts had long constrain'd the earth,
A kindly Thaw unlocks it with mild Rain,
And first the tender Blade peeps up to birth,
And streight the Green fields laugh with promis'd grain:

By such degrees the spreading Gladness grew
In every heart, which Fear had froze before:
The standing Streets with so much joy they view,
That with less grief the Perish'd they deplore.

The Father of the People open'd wide
His stores, and all the Poor with Plenty fed;
Thus God's Anointed God's own place suppli'd,
And fill'd the Empty with his daily Bread.

Alexander's Feast

or, The Power of Music; an Ode in Honour of St Cecilia's Day

I

'Twas at the royal feast, for Persia won
    By Philip's warlike son:
  Aloft in awful state
  The godlike hero sate
    On his imperial throne:
  His valiant peers were placed around;
Their brows with roses and with myrtles bound:
  (So should desert in arms be crowned).
The lovely Thais, by his side,
Sate like a blooming Eastern bride
In flow'r of youth and beauty's pride.
    Happy, happy, happy pair!
    None but the brave,
    None but the brave,
    None but the brave deserves the fair.

CHORUS

Happy, happy, happy pair!
None but the brave,
None but the brave,
None but the brave deserves the fair.

II

Timotheus, placed on high
    Amid the tuneful choir,
    With flying fingers touched the lyre:
The trembling notes ascend the sky,
    And heav'nly joys inspire.
The song began from Jove,
Who left his blissful seats above,
(Such is the pow'r of mighty love).
A dragon's fiery form belied the god:
Sublime on radiant spires he rode,
    When he to fair Olympia pressed;
    And while he sought her snowy breast:

Then, round her slender waist he curled,
And stamped an image of himself, a sov'reign of the world.
The list'ning crowd admire the lofty sound:
'A present deity,' they shout around;
'A present deity,' the vaulted roofs rebound.
       With ravished ears
       The monarch hears,
       Assumes the god,
       Affects to nod,
   And seems to shake the spheres.

CHORUS

*   With ravished ears*
*   The monarch hears,*
*   Assumes the god,*
*   Affects to nod,*
And seems to shake the spheres.

III

  The praise of Bacchus then the sweet musician sung,
    Of Bacchus ever fair and ever young:
       The jolly god in triumph comes;
       Sound the trumpets; beat the drums;
         Flushed with a purple grace
         He shows his honest face:

Now gives the hautboys breath; he comes, he comes.
  Bacchus, ever fair and young,
     Drinking joys did first ordain;
  Bacchus' blessings are a treasure,
  Drinking is a soldier's pleasure;
       Rich the treasure,
       Sweet the pleasure,
      Sweet is pleasure after pain.

Bacchus' blessings are a treasure,
Drinking is the soldier's pleasure;
Rich the treasure,
Sweet the pleasure,
Sweet is pleasure after pain.

IV

Soothed with the sound, the king grew vain;
　　Fought all his battles o'er again;
And thrice he routed all his foes; and thrice he slew the slain.
　　　　The master saw the madness rise;
　　　　His glowing cheeks, his ardent eyes;
　　　　And, while he heav'n and earth defied,
　　　　Changed his hand, and checked his pride.
　　　　　He chose a mournful Muse,
　　　　　　Soft pity to infuse:
　　　　He sung Darius great and good,
　　　　　　By too severe a fate,
　　　Fallen, fallen, fallen, fallen,
　　　　　Fallen from his high estate,
　　　And welt'ring in his blood;
Deserted at his utmost need,
By those his former bounty fed;
On the bare earth exposed he lies,
With not a friend to close his eyes.

With downcast looks the joyless victor sate,
　　Revolving in his altered soul
　　　　The various turns of chance below;
　　And, now and then, a sigh he stole,
　　　　And tears began to flow.

Revolving in his altered soul
　　The various turns of chance below;
And, now and then, a sigh he stole,
　　And tears began to flow.

V

The mighty master smiled to see
That love was in the next degree:
'Twas but a kindred sound to move,
For pity melts the mind to love.
      Softly sweet, in Lydian measures,
   Soon he soothed his soul to pleasures.
  'War,' he sung, 'is toil and trouble;
  Honour, but an empty bubble.
      Never ending, still beginning,
  Fighting still, and still destroying:
    If the world be worth thy winning,
  Think, O think it worth enjoying.
      Lovely Thais sits beside thee,
      Take the good the gods provide thee.'

The many rend the skies with loud applause;
So Love was crowned, but Music won the cause.
  The prince, unable to conceal his pain,
      Gazed on the fair
      Who caused his care,
  And sighed and looked, sighed and looked,
Sighed and looked, and sighed again:
At length, with love and wine at once oppressed,
The vanquished victor sunk upon her breast.

CHORUS

* The prince, unable to conceal his pain,*
*   Gazed on the fair*
*   Who caused his care,*
* And sighed and looked, sighed and looked,*
Sighed and looked, and sighed again:
At length, with love and wine at once oppressed,
The vanquished victor sunk upon her breast.

VI

Now strike the golden lyre again:
A louder yet, and yet a louder strain.
Break his bands of sleep asunder,
And arouse him, like a rattling peal of thunder.
   Hark, hark, the horrid sound
    Has raised up his head:
    As awaked from the dead,
    And amazed, he stares around.
'Revenge, revenge!' Timotheus cries,
   'See the Furies arise!
   See the snakes that they rear,
   How they hiss in their hair,
 And the sparkles that flash from their eyes!
   Behold a ghastly band,
   Each a torch in his hand!
Those are Grecian ghosts, that in battle were slain,
    And unburied remain
    Inglorious on the plain:
   Give the vengeance due
   To the valiant crew.
Behold how they toss their torches on high,
 How they point to the Persian abodes,
And glitt'ring temples of their hostile gods!'
The princes applaud, with a furious joy;
And the king seized a flambeau with zeal to destroy;
   Thais led the way,
   To light him to his prey,
And, like another Helen, fired another Troy.

CHORUS

And the king seized a flambeau with zeal to destroy;
   Thais led the way,
   To light him to his prey,
And, like another Helen, fired another Troy.

VII

Thus, long ago,
Ere heaving bellows learned to blow,
While organs yet were mute;
Timotheus, to his breathing flute,
And sounding lyre,
Could swell the soul to rage, or kindle soft desire.
At last, divine Cecilia came,
Inventress of the vocal frame;
The sweet enthusiast, from her sacred store,
Enlarged the former narrow bounds,
And added length to solemn sounds,
With nature's mother wit, and arts unknown before.
Let old Timotheus yield the prize,
Or both divide the crown:
He raised a mortal to the skies;
She drew an angel down.

GRAND CHORUS

At last, divine Cecilia came,
Inventress of the vocal frame;
The sweet enthusiast, from her sacred store,
Enlarged the former narrow bounds,
And added length to solemn sounds,
With nature's mother wit, and arts unknown before.
Let old Timotheus yield the prize,
Or both divide the crown:
He raised a mortal to the skies;
She drew an angel down.

THOMAS TRAHERNE
(1637–1674)

The Bible

That! That! There I was told
That I *the Son of God* am made,
His Image. O Divine! And that fine Gold,
    With all the Joys that here do fade,
Are but a Toy, compared to the Bliss
Which Hev'nly, God-like, and Eternal is.
    That We on earth are Kings;
    And, tho we're cloath'd with mortal Skin,
Are Inward Cherubins; hav Angels Wings;
    Affections, Thoughts, and Minds within,
Can soar throu all the Coasts of Hev'n and Earth;
And shall be sated with Celestial Mirth.

EDWARD TAYLOR
(?1644–1729)

Upon a Spider Catching a Fly

Thou sorrow, venom Elfe.
  Is this thy play,
To spin a web out of thyselfe
  To Catch a Fly?
    For Why?

I saw a pettish wasp
  Fall foule therein.
Whom yet thy Whorle pins did not clasp
  Lest he should fling
    His sting.

But as affraid, remote
  Didst stand hereat
And with thy little fingers stroke
  And gently tap
    His back.

Thus gently him didst treate
  Lest he should pet,
And in a froppish, waspish heate
  Should greatly fret
    Thy net.

Whereas the silly Fly,
  Caught by its leg
Thou by the throate tookst hastily
  And 'hinde the head
    Bite Dead.

This goes to pot, that not
  Nature doth call.
Strive not above what strength hath got
  Lest in the brawle
    Thou fall.

This Frey seems thus to us.
  Hells Spider gets
His intrails spun to whip Cords thus
  And wove to nets
    And sets.

To tangle Adams race
  In's stratigems
To their Destructions, spoil'd, made base
  By venom things
    Damn'd Sins.

But mighty, Gracious Lord
  Communicate
Thy Grace to breake the Cord, afford
  Us Glorys Gate
    And State.

We'l Nightingaile sing like
  When pearcht on high
In Glories Cage, thy glory, bright,
  And thankfully,
    For joy.

ISAAC WATTS
(1674–1748)

Crucifixion to the World by the Cross of Christ
(Galatians 6:14)

When I survey the wondrous Cross
Where the young Prince of Glory died,
My richest gain I count but loss,
And pour contempt on all my pride.

Forbid it, Lord, that I should boast
Save in the death of Christ, my God;
All the vain things that charm me most,
I sacrifice them to his blood.

See from his head, his hands, his feet,
Sorrow and love flow mingled down;
Did e'er such love and sorrow meet?
Or thorns compose so rich a crown?

His dying crimson like a robe
Spreads o'er his body on the Tree,
Then am I dead to all the globe,
And all the globe is dead to me.

Were the whole realm of nature mine,
That were a present far too small;
Love so amazing, so divine,
Demands my soul, my life, my all.

The Church the Garden of Christ

We are a Garden wall'd around,
Chosen and made peculiar Ground;
A little Spot inclos'd by Grace
Out of the World's wide Wilderness.

Like Trees of Myrrh and Spice we stand,
Planted by God the Father's Hand;
And all his Springs in Sion flow,
To make the young Plantation grow.

Awake, O heavenly Wind, and come,
Blow on this garden of Perfume;
Spirit Divine, descend and breathe
A gracious Gale on Plants beneath.

Make our best Spices flow abroad
To entertain our Saviour-God:
And faith, and Love, and Joy appear,
And every Grace be active here.

Let my Beloved come, and taste
His pleasant Fruits at his own Feast.
I come, my Spouse, I come, he cries,
With Love and Pleasure in his Eyes.

Our Lord into his Garden comes,
Well pleas'd to smell our poor Perfumes,
And calls us to a Feast divine,
Sweeter than Honey, Milk, or Wine.

Eat of the Tree of life, my Friends,
The Blessings that my Father sends;
Your Taste shall all my Dainties prove,
And drink abundance of my Love.

Jesus, we will frequent thy Board,
And sing the Bounties of our Lord:
But the rich Food on which we live
Demands more Praise than Tongues can give.

A Prospect of Heaven Makes Death Easy

There is a land of pure delight
  Where saints immortal reign;
Infinite day excludes the night,
  And pleasures banish pain.

There everlasting spring abides,
  And never-withering flowers:
Death like a narrow sea divides
  This heavenly land from ours.

Sweet fields beyond the swelling flood
  Stand dressed in living green:
So to the Jews old Canaan stood,
  While Jordan rolled between.

But timorous mortals start and shrink
  To cross this narrow sea,
And linger shivering on the brink
  And fear to launch away.

O could we make our doubts remove,
  These gloomy doubts that rise,
And see the Canaan that we love
  With unbeclouded eyes,

Could we but climb where Moses stood,
  And view the landscape o'er,
Not Jordan's stream, nor Death's cold flood,
  Should fright us from the shore.

CHARLES WESLEY
(1707–1788)

Wrestling Jacob

Come, O thou Traveller unknown,
  Whom still I hold, but cannot see,
My company before is gone,
  And I am left alone with thee,
With thee all night I mean to stay,
And wrestle till the break of day.

I need not tell thee who I am,
  My misery, or sin declare,
Thyself hast called me by my name,
  Look on thy hands, and read it there,
But who, I ask thee, who art thou?
Tell me thy name, and tell me now.

In vain thou strugglest to get free,
  I never will unloose my hold:
Art thou the Man that died for me?
  The secret of thy love unfold.
Wrestling I will not let thee go,
Till I thy name, thy nature know.

Wilt thou not yet to me reveal
  Thy new, unutterable name?
Tell me, I still beseech thee, tell;
  To know it now resolved I am.
Wrestling I will not let thee go,
Till I thy name, thy nature know.

'Tis all in vain to hold thy tongue,
  Or touch the hollow of my thigh:
Though every sinew be unstrung,
  Out of my arms thou shalt not fly.
Wrestling I will not let thee go,
Till I thy name, thy nature know.

What though my shrinking flesh complain,
   And murmur to contend so long,
I rise superior to my pain,
   When I am weak then I am strong,
And when my all of strength shall fail,
I shall with the God-Man prevail.

My strength is gone, my nature dies,
   I sink beneath thy weighty hand,
Faint to revive, and fall to rise;
   I fall, and yet by faith I stand,
I stand, and will not let thee go,
Till I thy name, thy nature know.

Yield to me now – for I am weak;
   But confident in self-despair:
Speak to my heart, in blessings speak,
   Be conquered by my instant prayer,
Speak, or thou never hence shalt move,
And tell me, if thy name is Love.

'Tis Love, 'tis Love! Thou diedst for me,
   I hear thy whisper in my heart.
The morning breaks, the shadows flee:
   Pure Universal Love thou art;
To me, to all, thy bowels move,
Thy nature and thy name is Love.

My prayer hath power with God; the Grace
   Unspeakable I now receive,
Through Faith I see thee face to face,
   I see thee face to face, and live:
In vain I have not wept, and strove,
Thy nature and thy name is Love.

I know thee, Saviour, who thou art,
   Jesus, the feeble sinner's friend;
Nor wilt thou with the night depart,
   But stay, and love me to the end;
Thy mercies never shall remove,
Thy nature and thy name is Love.

The Sun of Righteousness on me
   Hath rose with healing in his wings,
Withered my nature's strength; from thee
   My soul its life and succour brings,
My help is all laid up above;
Thy nature and thy name is Love.

Contented now upon my thigh
   I halt, till life's short journey end;
All helplessness, all weakness I,
   On thee alone for strength depend,
Nor have I power, from thee, to move;
Thy nature and thy name is Love.

Lame as I am, I take the prey,
   Hell, earth, and sin with ease o'ercome;
I leap for joy, pursue my way,
   And as a bounding hart fly home,
Through all eternity to prove
Thy nature and thy name is Love.

SAMUEL JOHNSON
(1709–1784)

On the Death of Mr Robert Levet

A Practiser in Physic

Condemned to Hope's delusive mine,
As on we toil from day to day,
By sudden blasts, or slow decline,
Our social comforts drop away.

Well tried through many a varying year,
See Levet to the ground descend;
Officious, innocent, sincere,
Of every friendless name the friend.

Yet still he fills affection's eye,
Obscurely wise, and coarsely kind;
Nor, lettered arrogance, deny
Thy praise to merit unrefined.

When fainting nature called for aid,
And hovering death prepared the blow,
His vigorous remedy displayed
The power of art without the show.

In misery's darkest caverns known,
His useful care was ever nigh,
Where hopeless anguish poured his groan,
And lonely want retired to die.

No summons mocked by chill delay,
No petty gain disdained by pride,
The modest wants of every day
The toil of every day supplied.

His virtues walked their narrow round,
Nor made a house, nor left a void;
And sure the Eternal Master found
The single talent well employed.

The busy day, the peaceful night,
Unfelt, uncounted, glided by;
His frame was firm, his powers were bright,
Though now his eightieth year was nigh,

Then with no fiery throbbing pain,
No cold gradations of decay,
Death broke at once the vital chain,
And freed his soul the nearest way.

WILLIAM COWPER
(1731–1800)

Walking with God

Oh! for a closer walk with God,
   A calm and heavenly frame;
A light to shine upon the road
   That leads me to the Lamb!

Where is the blessedness I knew
   When first I saw the Lord?
Where is the soul-refreshing view
   Of Jesus and his word?

What peaceful hours I once enjoyed!
   How sweet their memory still!
But they have left an aching void
   The world can never fill.

Return, O holy Dove, return,
   Sweet messenger of rest;
I hate the sins that made thee mourn,
   And drove thee from my breast.

The dearest idol I have known,
   Whate'er that idol be,
Help me to tear it from thy throne,
   And worship only Thee.

So shall my walk be close with God,
   Calm and serene my frame;
So purer light shall mark the road
   That leads me to the Lamb.

WILLIAM BLAKE
(1757–1827)

Song

Fresh from the dewy hill, the merry year
Smiles on my head, and mounts his flaming car;
Round my young brows the laurel wreathes a shade,
And rising glories beam around my head.

My feet are wing'd, while o'er the dewy lawn,
I meet my maiden, risen like the morn:
Oh bless those holy feet, like angels' feet;
Oh bless those limbs, beaming with heav'nly light!

Like as an angel glitt'ring in the sky,
In times of innocence, and holy joy;
The joyful shepherd stops his grateful song,
To hear the music of an angel's tongue.

So when she speaks, the voice of Heaven I hear
So when we walk, nothing impure comes near;
Each field seems Eden, and each calm retreat;
Each village seems the haunt of holy feet.

But that sweet village where my black-ey'd maid,
Closes her eyes in sleep beneath night's shade:
Whene'er I enter, more than mortal fire
Burns in my soul, and does my song inspire.

The Divine Image

To Mercy Pity Peace and Love,
All pray in their distress:
And to these virtues of delight
Return their thankfulness.

For Mercy Pity Peace and Love,
Is God our father dear:
And Mercy Pity Peace and Love,
Is Man his child and care.

For Mercy has a human heart
Pity, a human face:
And Love, the human form divine,
And Peace, the human dress.

Then every man of every clime,
That prays in his distress,
Prays to the human form divine
Love Mercy Pity Peace.

And all must love the human form,
In heathen, turk or jew.
Where Mercy, Love & Pity dwell
There God is dwelling too.

Holy Thursday

Twas on a Holy Thursday their innocent faces clean
The children walking two & two in red & blue & green
Grey headed beadles walkd before with wands as white as snow
Till into the high dome of Pauls they like Thames waters flow

O what a multitude they seemd these flowers of London town
Seated in companies they sit with radiance all their own
The hum of multitudes was there but multitudes of lambs
Thousands of little boys & girls raising their innocent hands

Now like a mighty wind they raise to heaven the voice of song
Or like harmonious thunderings the seats of heaven among
Beneath them sit the aged men wise guardians of the poor
Then cherish pity, lest you drive an angel from your door

The Little Black Boy

My mother bore me in the southern wild,
And I am black, but O! my soul is white;
White as an angel is the English child:
But I am black as if bereav'd of light.

My mother taught me underneath a tree
And sitting down before the heat of day,
She took me on her lap and kissed me,
And pointing to the east began to say.

Look on the rising sun: there God does live
And gives his light, and gives his heat away.
And flowers and trees and beasts and men receive
Comfort in morning joy in the noon day.

And we are put on earth a little space,
That we may learn to bear the beams of love,
And these black bodies and this sun-burnt face
Is but a cloud, and like a shady grove.

For when our souls have learn'd the heat to bear
The cloud will vanish we shall hear his voice.
Saying: come out from the grove my love & care,
And round my golden tent like lambs rejoice.

Thus did my mother say and kissed me,
And thus I say to little English boy.
When I from black and he from white cloud free,
And round the tent of God like lambs we joy:

Ill shade him from the heat till he can bear,
To lean in joy upon our fathers knee.
And then I'll stand and stroke his silver hair,
And be like him and he will then love me.

The Tyger

Tyger Tyger, burning bright,
In the forests of the night:
What immortal hand or eye,
Could frame thy fearful symmetry?

In what distant deeps or skies
Burnt the fire of thine eyes!
On what wings dare he aspire?
What the hand, dare seize the fire?

And what shoulder, & what art,
Could twist the sinews of thy heart?
And when thy heart began to beat,
What dread hand? & what dread feet?

What the hammer? what the chain,
In what furnace was thy brain?
What the anvil? what dread grasp,
Dare its deadly terrors clasp?

When the stars threw down their spears
And water'd heaven with their tears:
Did he smile his work to see?
Did he who made the Lamb make thee?

Tyger, Tyger burning bright,
In the forests of the night:
What immortal hand or eye,
Dare frame thy fearful symmetry?

A Little Boy Lost

Nought loves another as itself
Nor venerates another so.
Nor is it possible to Thought
A greater than itself to know:

And Father, how can I love you,
Or any of my brothers more?
I love you like the little bird
That picks up crumbs around the door.

The Priest sat by and heard the child.
In trembling zeal he seiz'd his hair:
He led him by his little coat:
And all admir'd the Priestly care.

And standing on the altar high,
Lo what a fiend is here! said he:
One who sets reason up for judge
Of our most holy Mystery.

The weeping child could not be heard.
The weeping parents wept in vain:
They strip'd him to his little shirt.
And bound him in an iron chain.

And burn'd him in a holy place,
Where many had been burn'd before:
The weeping parents wept in vain.
Are such things done on Albions shore.

'Mock on Mock on Voltaire Rousseau'

Mock on Mock on Voltaire Rousseau
Mock on Mock on tis all in vain
You throw the sand against the wind
And the wind blows it back again

And every sand becomes a Gem
Reflected in the beams divine
Blown back they blind the mocking Eye
But still in Israels paths they shine

The Atoms of Democritus
And Newtons Particles of light
Are sands upon the Red sea shore
Where Israels tents do shine so bright

The Grey Monk

I die I die the Mother said
My Children die for lack of Bread
What more has the merciless Tyrant said
The Monk sat down on the Stony Bed

The blood red ran from the Grey Monks side
His hands & feet were wounded wide
His Body bent his arms & knees
Like to the roots of ancient trees

His eye was dry no tear could flow
A hollow groan first spoke his woe
He trembled & shudderd upon the Bed
At length with a feeble cry he said

When God commanded this hand to write
In the studious hours of deep midnight
He told me the writing I wrote should prove
The Bane of all that on Earth I lovd

My Brother starvd between two Walls
His Childrens Cry my Soul appalls
I mockd at the wrack & griding chain
My bent body mocks their torturing pain

Thy Father drew his sword in the North
With his thousands strong he marched forth
Thy Brother has armd himself in Steel
To avenge the wrongs thy Children feel

But vain the Sword & vain the Bow
They never can work Wars overthrow
The Hermits Prayer & the Widows tear
Alone can free the World from fear

For a Tear is an Intellectual Thing
And a Sigh is the Sword of an Angel King
And the bitter groan of the Martyrs woe
Is an Arrow from the Almighties Bow

The hand of Vengeance found the Bed
To which the Purple Tyrant fled
The iron hand crushd the Tyrants head
And became a Tyrant in his stead

Auguries of Innocence

To see a World in a Grain of Sand
And a Heaven in a Wild Flower
Hold Infinity in the palm of your hand
And Eternity in an hour
A Robin Red breast in a Cage
Puts all Heaven in a Rage
A dove house filld with doves & Pigeons
Shudders Hell thro all its regions
A dog starvd at his Masters Gate
Predicts the ruin of the State
A Horse misusd upon the Road
Calls to Heaven for Human blood
Each outcry of the hunted Hare
A fibre from the Brain does tear
A Skylark wounded in the wing
A Cherubim does cease to sing
The Game Cock clipd & armd for fight
Does the Rising Sun affright
Every Wolfs & Lions howl
Raises from Hell a Human Soul

The wild deer wandring here & there
Keeps the Human Soul from Care
The Lamb misusd breeds Public strife
And yet forgives the Butchers Knife
The Bat that flits at close of Eve
Has left the Brain that wont Believe
The Owl that calls upon the Night
Speaks the Unbelievers fright
He who shall hurt the little Wren
Shall never be belovd by Men
He who the Ox to wrath has movd
Shall never be by Woman lovd
The wanton Boy that kills the Fly
Shall feel the Spiders enmity
He who torments the Chafers sprite
Weaves a Bower in endless Night
The Catterpiller on the Leaf
Repeats to thee thy Mothers grief
Kill not the Moth nor Butterfly
For the Last Judgment draweth nigh
He who shall train the Horse to War
Shall never pass the Polar Bar
The Beggers Dog & Widows Cat
Feed them & thou wilt grow fat
The Gnat that sings his Summers song
Poison gets from Slanders tongue
The poison of the Snake & Newt
Is the sweat of Envys Foot
The Poison of the Honey Bee
Is the Artists Jealousy
The Princes Robes & Beggars Rags
Are Toadstools on the Misers Bags
A truth thats told with bad intent
Beats all the Lies you can invent
It is right it should be so
Man was made for Joy & Woe
And when this we rightly know
Thro the World we safely go
Joy & Woe are woven fine
A Clothing for the Soul divine

Under every grief & pine
Runs a joy with silken twine
The Babe is more than swadling Bands
Throughout all these Human Lands
Tools were made & Born were hands
Every Farmer Understands
Every Tear from Every Eye
Becomes a Babe in Eternity
This is caught by Females bright
And returnd to its own delight
The Bleat the Bark Bellow & Roar
Are Waves that Beat on Heavens Shore
The Babe that weeps the Rod beneath
Writes Revenge in realms of death
The Beggars Rags fluttering in Air
Does to Rags the Heavens tear
The Soldier armd with Sword & Gun
Palsied strikes the Summers Sun
The poor Mans Farthing is worth more
Than all the Gold on Africs Shore
One Mite wrung from the Labrers hands
Shall buy & sell the Misers Lands
Or if protected from on high
Does that whole Nation sell & buy
He who mocks the Infants Faith
Shall be mock'd in Age & Death
He who shall teach the Child to Doubt
The rotting Grave shall neer get out
He who respects the Infants faith
Triumphs over Hell & Death
The Childs Toys & the Old Mans Reasons
Are the Fruits of the Two seasons
The Questioner who sits so sly
Shall never know how to Reply
He who replies to words of Doubt
Doth put the Light of Knowledge out
The Strongest Poison ever known
Came from Caesars Laurel Crown
Nought can deform the Human Race
Like to the Armours iron brace

When Gold & Gems adorn the Plow
To peaceful Arts shall Envy Bow
A Riddle or the Crickets Cry
Is to Doubt a fit Reply
The Emmets Inch & Eagles Mile
Make Lame Philosophy to smile
He who Doubts from what he sees
Will neer Believe do what you Please
If the Sun & Moon should doubt
Theyd immediately Go out
To be in a Passion you Good may do
But no Good if a Passion is in you
The Whore & Gambler by the State
Licencd build that Nations Fate
The Harlots cry from Street to Street
Shall weave Old Englands winding Sheet
The Winners Shout the Losers Curse
Dance before dead Englands Hearse
Every Night & every Morn
Some to Misery are Born
Every Morn & every Night
Some are Born to sweet delight
Some are Born to sweet delight
Some are Born to Endless Night
We are led to Believe a Lie
When we see [*with*] not Thro the Eye
Which was Born in a Night to perish in a Night
When the Soul Slept in Beams of Light
God Appears & God is Light
To those poor Souls who dwell in Night
But does a Human Form Display
To those who Dwell in Realms of day

'And did those feet in ancient time'

And did those feet in ancient time.
Walk upon Englands mountains green:
And was the holy Lamb of God,
On Englands pleasant pastures seen!

And did the Countenance Divine,
Shine forth upon our clouded hills?
And was Jerusalem builded here,
Among these dark Satanic Mills?

Bring me my Bow of burning gold:
Bring me my Arrows of desire:
Bring me my Spear: O clouds unfold!
Bring me my Chariot of fire!

I will not cease from Mental Fight,
Nor shall my Sword sleep in my hand:
Till we have built Jerusalem,
In Englands green & pleasant Land.

Would to God that all the Lords people were Prophets.
Numbers XI. ch 29 v.

from *Milton*

BOOK THE FIRST

Daughters of Beulah! Muses who inspire the Poets Song
Record the journey of immortal Milton thro' your Realms
Of terror & mild moony lustre, in soft sexual delusions
Of varied beauty, to delight the wanderer and repose
His burning thirst & freezing hunger! Come into my hand
By your mild power; descending down the Nerves of my right arm
From out the Portals of my Brain, where by your ministry
The Eternal Great Humanity Divine, planted his Paradise,

And in it caus'd the Spectres of the Dead to take sweet forms
In likeness of himself. Tell also of the False Tongue! vegetated
Beneath your land of shadows: of its sacrifices. and
Its offerings; even till Jesus, the image of the Invisible God
Became its prey; a curse, an offering. and an atonement,
For Death Eternal in the heavens of Albion, & before the Gates
Of Jerusalem his Emanation, in the heavens beneath Beulah

Say first! what mov'd Milton, who walkd about in Eternity
One hundred years, pondring the intricate mazes of Providence
Unhappy tho in heav'n, he obey'd, he murmur'd not. he was silent
Viewing his Sixfold Emanation scatter'd thro' the deep
In torment! To go into the deep her to redeem & himself perish?
What cause at length mov'd Milton to this unexampled deed?
A Bards prophetic Song! for sitting at eternal tables,
Terrific among the Sons of Albion in chorus solemn & loud
A Bard broke forth! all sat attentive to the awful man.
Mark well my words! they are of your eternal salvation:

[Epilogue]
To the Accuser Who is the God of This World

Truly My Satan thou art but a Dunce
And dost not know the Garment from the Man
Every Harlot was a Virgin once
Nor canst thou ever change Kate into Nan

Tho thou art Worshipd by the Names Divine
Of Jesus & Jehovah: thou art still
The Son of Morn in weary Nights decline
The lost Travellers Dream under the Hill

WILLIAM WORDSWORTH
(1770–1850)

from *The Prelude*

BOOK THIRTEENTH

CONCLUSION

In one of these excursions, travelling then
Through Wales on foot, and with a youthful Friend,
I left Bethhelert's huts at couching-time,
And westward took my way to see the sun
Rise from the top of Snowdon. Having reach'd
The Cottage at the Mountain's foot, we there
Rouz'd up the Shepherd, who by ancient right
Of office is the Stranger's usual guide;
And after short refreshment sallied forth.

  It was a Summer's night, a close warm night,
Wan, dull and glaring, with a dripping mist
Low-hung and thick that cover'd all the sky,
Half threatening storm and rain; but on we went
Uncheck'd, being full of heart and having faith
In our tried Pilot. Little could we see
Hemm'd round on every side with fog and damp,
And, after ordinary travellers' chat
With our Conductor, silently we sank
Each into commerce with his private thoughts:
Thus did we breast the ascent, and by myself
Was nothing either seen or heard the while
Which took me from my musings, save that once
The Shepherd's Cur did to his own great joy
Unearth a hedgehog in the mountain crags
Round which he made a barking turbulent.
This small adventure, for even such it seemed
In that wild place and at the dead of night,
Being over and forgotten, on we wound
In silence as before. With forehead bent
Earthward, as if in opposition set
Against an enemy, I panted up

With eager pace, and no less eager thoughts.
Thus might we wear perhaps an hour away,
Ascending at loose distance each from each,
And I, as chanced, the foremost of the Band;
When at my feet the ground appear'd to brighten,
And with a step or two seem'd brighter still;
Nor had I time to ask the cause of this,
For instantly a Light upon the turf
Fell like a flash: I looked about, and lo!
The Moon stood naked in the Heavens, at height
Immense above my head, and on the shore
I found myself of a huge sea of mist,
Which, meek and silent, rested at my feet:
A hundred hills their dusky backs upheaved
All over this still Ocean, and beyond,
Far, far beyond, the vapours shot themselves,
In headlands, tongues, and promontory shapes,
Into the Sea, the real Sea, that seem'd
To dwindle, and give up its majesty,
Usurp'd upon as far as sight could reach.
Meanwhile, the Moon look'd down upon this shew
In single glory, and we stood, the mist
Touching our very feet; and from the shore
At distance not the third part of a mile
Was a blue chasm; a fracture in the vapour,
A deep and gloomy breathing-place through which
Mounted the roar of waters, torrents, streams
Innumerable, roaring with one voice.
The universal spectacle throughout
Was shaped for admiration and delight,
Grand in itself alone, but in that breach
Through which the homeless voice of waters rose,
That dark deep thoroughfare had Nature lodg'd
The Soul, the Imagination of the whole.

A meditation rose in me that night
Upon the lonely Mountain when the scene
Had pass'd away, and it appear'd to me
The perfect image of a mighty Mind,
Of one that feeds upon infinity,

That is exalted by an underpresence,
The sense of God, or whatsoe'er is dim
Or vast in its own being, above all
One function of such mind had Nature there
Exhibited by putting forth, and that
With circumstance most awful and sublime,
That domination which she oftentimes
Exerts upon the outward face of things,
So moulds them, and endues, abstracts, combines,
Or by abrupt and unhabitual influence
Doth make one object so impress itself
Upon all others, and pervade them so
That even the grossest minds must see and hear
And cannot chuse but feel. The Power which these
Acknowledge when thus moved, which Nature thus
Thrusts forth upon the senses, is the express
Resemblance, in the fulness of its strength
Made visible, a genuine Counterpart
And Brother of the glorious faculty
Which higher minds bear with them as their own.
That is the very spirit in which they deal
With all the objects of the universe;
They from their native selves can send abroad
Like transformations, for themselves create
A like existence, and, whene'er it is
Created for them, catch it by an instinct;
Them the enduring and the transient both
Serve to exalt; they build up greatest things
From least suggestions, ever on the watch,
Willing to work and to be wrought upon,
They need not extraordinary calls
To rouze them, in a world of life they live,
By sensible impressions not enthrall'd,
But quicken'd, rouz'd, and made thereby more apt
To hold communion with the invisible world.
Such minds are truly from the Deity,
For they are Powers; and hence the highest bliss
That can be known is theirs, the consciousness
Of whom they are habitually infused
Through every image, and through every thought,

And all impressions; hence religion, faith,
And endless occupation for the soul
Whether discursive or intuitive;
Hence sovereignty within and peace at will
Emotion which best foresight need not fear
Most worthy then of trust when most intense.
Hence chearfulness in every act of life
Hence truth in moral judgements and delight
That fails not in the external universe.

SAMUEL TAYLOR COLERIDGE
(1772–1834)

The Rime of the Ancient Mariner

IN SEVEN PARTS

Facile credo, plures esse Naturas invisibiles quam visibiles in rerum universitate. Sed horum omnium familiam quis nobis enarrabit? et gradus et cognationes et discrimina et singulorum munera? Quid agunt? quae loca habitant? Harum rerum notitiam semper ambivit ingenium humanum, nunquam attigit. Juvat, interea, non diffiteor, quandoque in animo, tanquam in Tabulâ, majoris et melioris mundi imaginem contemplari: ne mens assuefacta hodiernae vitae minutiis se contrahat nimis, et tota subsidat in pusillas cogitationes. Sed veritati interea invigilandum est, modusque servandus, ut certa ab incertis, diem a nocte, distinguamis. – T. BURNET, *Archaeol. Phil.* p. 68.

ARGUMENT

How a Ship having passed the Line was driven by storms to the cold Country towards the South Pole; and how from thence she made her course to the tropical Latitude of the Great Pacific Ocean; and of the strange things that befell; and in what manner the Ancyent Marinere came back to his own Country.

PART I

An ancient
Mariner meeteth
three Gallants
bidden to a wedd-
ing-feast, and
detaineth one.

It is an ancient Mariner,
And he stoppeth one of three.
'By thy long grey beard and glittering eye,
Now wherefore stopp'st thou me?

The Bridegroom's doors are opened wide,
And I am next of kin;
The guests are met, the feast is set:
May'st hear the merry din.'

He holds him with his skinny hand,
'There was a ship,' quoth he.
'Hold off! unhand me, greybeard loon!'
Eftsoons his hand dropt he.

The Wedding-
Guest is spell-
bound by the eye
of the old sea-
faring man, and
constrained to
hear his tale.

He holds him with his glittering eye –
The Wedding-Guest stood still,
And listens like a three years' child:
The Mariner hath his will.

The Wedding-Guest sat on a stone:
He cannot choose but hear;
And thus spake on that ancient man,
The bright-eyed Mariner.

'The ship was cheered, the harbour cleared,
Merrily did we drop
Below the kirk, below the hill,
Below the light house top.

The Mariner tells
how the ship
sailed southward
with a good wind
and fair weather,
till it reached the
Line.

The Sun came up upon the left,
Out of the sea came he!
And he shone bright, and on the right
Went down into the sea.

Higher and higher every day,
Till over the mast at noon –'
The Wedding-Guest here beat his breast,
For he heard the loud bassoon.

The Wedding-
Guest heareth
the bridal music;
but the Mariner
continueth his
tale.

The bride hath paced into the hall,
Red as a rose is she;
Nodding their heads before her goes
The merry minstrelsy.

The Wedding-Guest he beat his breast,
Yet he cannot choose but hear;
And thus spake on that ancient man,
The bright-eyed Mariner.

The ship drawn
by a storm
toward the south
pole.

'And now the STORM-BLAST came, and he
Was tyrannous and strong:
He struck with his o'ertaking wings,
And chased us south along.

With sloping masts and dipping prow,
As who pursued with yell and blow
Still treads the shadow of his foe,
And forward bends his head,
The ship drove fast, loud roared the blast,
And southward aye we fled

And now there came both mist and snow,
And it grew wondrous cold:
And ice, mast-high, came floating by,
As green as emerald.

The land of ice,
and of fearful
sounds where no
living thing was
to be seen.

And through the drifts the snowy clifts
Did send a dismal sheen:
Nor shapes of men nor beasts we ken –
The ice was all between.

The ice was here, the ice was there,
The ice was all around:
It cracked and growled, and roared and howled,
Like noises in a swound!

Till a great sea-
bird, called the
Albatross, came
through the
snow-fog, and
was received
with great joy
and hospitality.

At length did cross an Albatross,
Thorough the fog it came;
As if it had been a Christian soul,
We hailed it in God's name.

It ate the food it ne'er had eat,
And round and round it flew.
The ice did split with a thunder-fit;
The helmsman steered us through!

And a good south wind sprung up behind;
The Albatross did follow,
And every day, for food or play.
Came to the mariner's hollo!

In mist or cloud, on mast or shroud,
It perched for vespers nine;
Whiles all the night, through fog-smoke white,
Glimmered the white Moon-shine.'

'God save thee, ancient Mariner!
From the fiends, that plague thee thus! –
Why look'st thou so?' – With my cross-bow
I shot the ALBATROSS.

And lo! the Albatross proveth a bird of good omen, and followeth the ship as it returned northward through fog and floating ice.

The ancient Mariner inhospitably killeth the pious bird of good omen.

PART II

The Sun now rose upon the right:
Out of the sea came he,
Still hid in mist, and on the left
Went down into the sea.

And the good south wind still blew behind,
But no sweet bird did follow,
Nor any day for food or play
Came to the mariners' hollo!

His shipmates cry out against the ancient Mariner, for killing the bird of good luck.

And I had done a hellish thing,
And it would work 'em woe:
For all averred, I had killed the bird
That made the breeze to blow.
Ah wretch! said they, the bird to slay,
That made the breeze to blow!

But when the
fog cleared off,
they justify the
same, and thus
make themselves
accomplices in
the crime.

Nor dim nor red, like God's own head,
The glorious Sun uprist:
Then all averred, I had killed the bird
That brought the fog and mist.
'Twas right, said they, such birds to slay,
That bring the fog and mist.

The fair breeze
continues; the
ship enters the
Pacific Ocean,
and sails north-
ward, even till it
reaches the Line.

The fair breeze blew, the white foam flew,
The furrow followed free;
We were the first that ever burst
Into that silent sea.

The ship hath
been suddenly
becalmed.

Down dropt the breeze, the sails dropt down,
'Twas sad as sad could be;
And we did speak only to break
The silence of the sea!

All in a hot and copper sky,
The bloody Sun, at noon,
Right up above the mast did stand,
No bigger than the Moon.

Day after day, day after day,
We stuck, nor breath nor motion;
As idle as a painted ship
Upon a painted ocean.

And the Alba-
tross begins to be
avenged.

Water, water, every where,
And all the boards did shrink;
Water, water, every where,
Nor any drop to drink.

The very deep did rot: O Christ!
That ever this should be!
Yea, slimy things did crawl with legs
Upon the slimy sea.

About, about, in reel and rout
The death-fires danced at night;
The water, like a witch's oils,
Burnt green, and blue and white.

A Spirit had followed them; one of the invisible inhabitants of this

And some in dreams assurèd were
Of the Spirit that plagued us so;
Nine fathom deep he had followed us
From the land of mist and snow.

planet, neither departed souls nor angels; concerning whom the learned Jew, Josephus, and the Platonic Constantinopolitan, Michael Psellus, may be consulted. They are very numerous, and there is no climate or element without one or more.

And every tongue, through utter drought,
Was withered at the root;
We could not speak, no more than if
We had been choked with soot.

The shipmates, in their sore distress, would fain throw the whole guilt on the ancient Mariner: in sign whereof they hang the dead sea-bird round his neck.

Ah! well a-day! what evil looks
Had I from old and young!
Instead of the cross, the Albatross
About my neck was hung.

PART III

There passed a weary time. Each throat
Was parched, and glazed each eye.
A weary time! a weary time!
How glazed each weary eye,
The ancient Mariner beholdeth a sign in the element afar off.
When looking westward, I beheld
A something in the sky.

At first it seemed a little speck,
And then it seemed a mist;
It moved and moved, and took at last
A certain shape, I wist.

A speck, a mist, a shape, I wist!
And still it neared and neared:
As if it dodged a water-sprite,
It plunged and tacked and veered.

At its nearer approach, it seemeth him to be a ship; and at a dear ransom he freeth his speech from the bonds of thirst.

With throats unslaked, with black lips baked,
We could nor laugh nor wail;
Through utter drought all dumb we stood!
I bit my arm, I sucked the blood,
And cried, A sail! a sail!

With throats unslaked, with black lips baked,
Agape they heard me call:

A flash of joy;

Gramercy! they for joy did grin,
And all at once their breath drew in,
As they were drinking all.

And horror follows. For can it be a ship that comes onward without wind or tide?

See! see! (I cried) she tacks no more!
Hither to work us weal;
Without a breeze, without a tide,
She steadies with upright keel!

The western wave was all a-flame.
The day was well nigh done!
Almost upon the western wave
Rested the broad bright Sun;
When that strange shape drove suddenly
Betwixt us and the Sun.

It seemeth him but the skeleton of a ship.

And straight the Sun was flecked with bars,
(Heaven's Mother send us grace!)
As if through a dungeon-grate he peered
With broad and burning face.

Alas! (thought I, and my heart beat loud)
How fast she nears and nears!
Are those *her* sails that glance in the Sun,
Like restless gossameres?

And its ribs are seen as bars on the face of the setting Sun. The Spectre-Woman and her Death-mate, and no other on board the skeleton ship. Like vessel, like crew!

Are those *her* ribs through which the Sun
Did peer, as through a grate?
And is that Woman all her crew?
Is that a DEATH? and are there two?
Is DEATH that woman's mate?

Her lips were red, *her* looks were free,
Her locks were yellow as gold:
Her skin was as white as leprosy,
The Night-mare LIFE-IN-DEATH was she,
Who thicks man's blood with cold.

Death and
Life-in-Death
have diced for the
ship's crew, and
she (the latter)
winneth the
ancient Mariner.

The naked hulk alongside came,
And the twain were casting dice;
'The game is done! I've won! I've won!'
Quoth she, and whistles thrice.

No twilight
within the courts
of the Sun.

The Sun's rim dips; the stars rush out:
At one stride comes the dark;
With far-heard whisper, o'er the sea,
Off shot the spectre-bark.

At the rising of
the Moon,

We listened and looked sideways up!
Fear at my heart, as at a cup,
My life-blood seemed to sip!
The stars were dim, and thick the night,
The steersman's face by his lamp gleamed white;
From the sails the dew did drip –
Till clomb above the eastern bar
The hornèd Moon, with one bright star
Within the nether tip.

One after
another,

One after one, by the star-dogged Moon,
Too quick for groan or sigh,
Each turned his face with a ghastly pang,
And cursed me with his eye.

His shipmates
drop down dead.

Four times fifty living men,
(And I heard nor sigh nor groan)
With heavy thump, a lifeless lump,
They dropped down one by one.

But Life-in-Death
begins her work
on the ancient
Mariner.

The souls did from their bodies fly, –
They fled to bliss or woe!
And every soul, it passed me by,
Like the whizz of my cross-bow!

PART IV

The
Wedding-Guest
feareth that a
Spirit is talking to
him;

'I fear thee, ancient Mariner!
I fear thy skinny hand!
And thou art long, and lank, and brown,
As is the ribbed sea-sand.

I fear thee and thy glittering eye,
And thy skinny hand, so brown.' –
Fear not, fear not, thou Wedding-Guest!
This body dropt not down.

Alone, alone, all, all alone,
Alone on a wide wide sea!
And never a saint took pity on
My soul in agony.

The many men, so beautiful!
And they all dead did lie:
And a thousand thousand slimy things
Lived on; and so did I.

I looked upon the rotting sea,
And drew my eyes away;
I looked upon the rotting deck,
And there the dead men lay.

I looked to heaven, and tried to pray;
But or ever a prayer had gusht,
A wicked whisper came, and made
My heart as dry as dust.

I closed my lids, and kept them close,
And the balls like pulses beat;
For the sky and the sea, and the sea and the sky
Lay like a load on my weary eye,
And the dead were at my feet.

The cold sweat melted from their limbs,
Nor rot nor reek did they:
The look with which they looked on me
Had never passed away.

An orphan's curse would drag to hell
A spirit from on high;
But oh! more horrible than that
Is the curse in a dead man's eye!
Seven days, seven nights, I saw that curse,
And yet I could not die.

In his loneliness
and fixedness he
yearneth towards
the journeying
Moon, and the

The moving Moon went up the sky,
And no where did abide:
Softly she was going up,
And a star or two beside –

stars that still sojourn, yet still move onward; and every where the blue sky belongs to
them, and is their appointed rest, and their native country and their own natural homes,
which they enter unannounced, as lords that are certainly expected and yet there is a silent
joy at their arrival.

Her beams bemocked the sultry main,
Like April hoar-frost spread;
But where the ship's huge shadow lay,
The charmèd water burnt alway
A still and awful red.

By the light of the
Moon he
beholdeth God's
creatures of the
great calm.

Beyond the shadow of the ship,
I watched the water-snakes:
They moved in tracks of shining white,
And when they reared, the elfish light
Fell off in hoary flakes.

Within the shadow of the ship
I watched their rich attire:
Blue, glossy green, and velvet black,
They coiled and swam; and every track
Was a flash of golden fire.

Their beauty and
their happiness.

O happy living things! no tongue
Their beauty might declare:
A spring of love gushed from my heart,

He blesseth them
in his heart.

And I blessed them unaware:
Sure my kind saint took pity on me,
And I blessed them unaware.

The spell begins
to break.

The self-same moment I could pray;
And from my neck so free
The Albatross fell off, and sank
Like lead into the sea.

PART V

Oh sleep! it is a gentle thing,
Beloved from pole to pole!
To Mary Queen the praise be given!
She sent the gentle sleep from Heaven,
That slid into my soul.

*By grace of the
holy Mother, the
ancient Mariner is
refreshed with
rain.*

The silly buckets on the deck,
That had so long remained,
I dreamt that they were filled with dew;
And when I awoke, it rained.

My lips were wet, my throat was cold,
My garments all were dank;
Sure I had drunken in my dreams,
And still my body drank.

I moved, and could not feel my limbs:
I was so light – almost
I thought that I had died in sleep,
And was a blessèd ghost.

*He heareth
sounds and seeth
strange sights and
commotions in
the sky and the
element.*

And soon I heard a roaring wind:
It did not come anear;
But with its sound it shook the sails,
That were so thin and sere.

The upper air burst into life!
And a hundred fire-flags sheen,
To and fro they were hurried about!
And to and fro, and in and out,
The wan stars danced between.

And the coming wind did roar more loud,
And the sails did sigh like sedge;
And the rain poured down from one black cloud;
The Moon was at its edge.

The thick black cloud was cleft, and still
The Moon was at its side:
Like waters shot from some high crag,
The lightning fell with never a jag,
A river steep and wide.

The bodies of the
ship's crew are
inspirited, and the
ship moves on:

The loud wind never reached the ship,
Yet now the ship moved on!
Beneath the lightning and the Moon
The dead men gave a groan.

They groaned, they stirred, they all uprose,
Nor spake, nor moved their eyes;
It had been strange, even in a dream,
To have seen those dead men rise.

The helmsman steered, the ship moved on;
Yet never a breeze up-blew;
The mariners all 'gan work the ropes,
Where they were wont to do;
They raised their limbs like lifeless tools –
We were a ghastly crew.

The body of my brother's son
Stood by me, knee to knee:
The body and I pulled at one rope,
But he said naught to me.

But not by the
souls of the men,
nor by dœmons of
earth or middle
air, but by a
blessed troop of
angelic spirits,
sent down by the
invocation of the
guardian saint.

'I fear thee, ancient Mariner!'
Be calm, thou Wedding-Guest!
'Twas not those souls that fled in pain,
Which to their corses came again,
But a troop of spirits blest:

For when it dawned – they dropped their arms,
And clustered round the mast;
Sweet sounds rose slowly through their mouths,
And from their bodies passed.

Around, around, flew each sweet sound,
Then darted to the Sun;
Slowly the sounds came back again,
Now mixed, now one by one.

Sometimes a-dropping from the sky
I heard the sky-lark sing;
Sometimes all little birds that are,
How they seemed to fill the sea and air
With their sweet jargoning!

And now 'twas like all instruments,
Now like a lonely flute;
And now it is an angel's song,
That makes the heavens be mute.

It ceased; yet still the sails made on
A pleasant noise till noon,
A noise like of a hidden brook
In the leafy month of June,
That to the sleeping woods all night
Singeth a quiet tune.

Till noon we quietly sailed on,
Yet never a breeze did breathe:
Slowly and smoothly went the ship,
Moved onward from beneath.

The lonesome Spirit from the south pole carries on the ship as far as the Line, in obedience to the angelic troop, but still requireth vengeance.

Under the keel nine fathom deep,
From the land of mist and snow,
The spirit slid: and it was he
That made the ship to go.
The sails at noon left off their tune,
And the ship stood still also.

The Sun, right up above the mast,
Had fixed her to the ocean:
But in a minute she 'gan stir,
With a short uneasy motion –
Backwards and forwards half her length
With a short uneasy motion.

Then like a pawing horse let go,
She made a sudden bound:
It flung the blood into my head,
And I fell down in a swound.

The Polar Spirit's fellow-dæmons, the invisible inhabitants of the element, take part in his wrong; and two of them relate, one to the

How long in that same fit I lay,
I have not to declare;
But ere my living life returned,
I heard, and in my soul discerned
TWO VOICES in the air.

other, that
penance long and
heavy for the
ancient Mariner
hath been
accorded to the
Polar Spirit, who
returneth
southward.

'Is it he?' quoth one. 'Is this the man?
By him who died on cross,
With his cruel bow he laid full low
The harmless Albatross.

The spirit who bideth by himself
In the land of mist and snow,
He loved the bird that loved the man
Who shot him with his bow.'

The other was a softer voice,
As soft as honey-dew:
Quoth he, 'The man hath penance done,
And penance more will do.'

PART VI

FIRST VOICE

'But tell me, tell me! speak again,
Thy soft response renewing –
What makes that ship drive on so fast?
What is the ocean doing?'

SECOND VOICE

'Still as a slave before his lord,
The ocean hath no blast;
His great bright eye most silently
Up to the Moon is cast –

If he may know which way to go;
For she guides him smooth or grim.
See, brother, see! how graciously
She looketh down on him.'

FIRST VOICE

The Mariner hath
been cast into a
trance; for the
angelic power

'But why drives on that ship so fast,
Without or wave or wind?'

causeth the vessel to drive northward faster than human life could endure.

SECOND VOICE

'The air is cut away before,
And closes from behind.

Fly, brother, fly! more high, more high!
Or we shall be belated:
For slow and slow that ship will go,
When the Mariner's trance is abated.'

The supernatural
motion is
retarded; the
Mariner awakes,
and his penance
begins anew.

I woke, and we were sailing on
As in a gentle weather:
'Twas night, calm night, the moon was high;
The dead men stood together.

All stood together on the deck,
For a charnel-dungeon fitter:
All fixed on me their stony eyes,
That in the Moon did glitter.

The pang, the curse, with which they died,
Had never passed away:
I could not draw my eyes from theirs,
Nor turn them up to pray.

The curse is
finally expiated.

And now this spell was snapt: once more
I viewed the ocean green,
And looked far forth, yet little saw
Of what had else been seen –

Like one, that on a lonesome road
Doth walk in fear and dread,
And having once turned round walks on,
And turns no more his head;
Because he knows, a frightful fiend
Doth close behind him tread.

But soon there breathed a wind on me,
Nor sound nor motion made:
Its path was not upon the sea,
In ripple or in shade.

It raised my hair, it fanned my cheek
Like a meadow-gale of spring –
It mingled strangely with my fears,
Yet it felt like a welcoming.

Swiftly, swiftly flew the ship,
Yet she sailed softly too:
Sweetly, sweetly blew the breeze –
On me alone it blew.

And the ancient Mariner beholdeth his native country.

Oh! dream of joy! is this indeed
The lighthouse top I see?
Is this the hill? is this the kirk?
Is this mine own countree?

We drifted o'er the harbour-bar,
And I with sobs did pray –
O let me be awake, my God!
Or let me sleep alway.

The harbour-bay was clear as glass,
So smoothly it was strewn!
And on the bay the moonlight lay,
And the shadow of the Moon.

The rock shone bright, the kirk no less,
That stands above the rock:
The moonlight steeped in silentness
The steady weathercock.

The angelic spirits leave the dead bodies,

And the bay was white with silent light,
Till rising from the same,
Full many shapes, that shadows were,
In crimson colours came.

And appear in their own forms of light.

A little distance from the prow
Those crimson shadows were:
I turned my eyes upon the deck –
Oh, Christ! what saw I there!

Each corse lay flat, lifeless and flat,
And, by the holy rood!
A man all light, a seraph-man,
On every corse there stood.

This seraph-band, each waved his hand:
It was a heavenly sight!
They stood as signals to the land,
Each one a lovely light;

This seraph-band, each waved his hand,
No voice did they impart –
No voice; but oh! the silence sank
Like music on my heart.

But soon I heard the dash of oars,
I heard the Pilot's cheer;
My head was turned perforce away,
And I saw a boat appear.

The Pilot and the Pilot's boy,
I heard them coming fast:
Dear Lord in Heaven! it was a joy
The dead men could not blast.

I saw a third – I heard his voice:
It is the Hermit good!
He singeth loud his godly hymns
That he makes in the wood.
He'll shrieve my soul, he'll wash away
The Albatross's blood.

PART VII

The Hermit of the Wood.

This Hermit good lives in that wood
Which slopes down to the sea.
How loudly his sweet voice he rears!
He loves to talk with marineres
That come from a far countree.

He kneels at morn, and noon, and eve –
He hath a cushion plump:
It is the moss that wholly hides
The rotted old oak-stump.

The skiff-boat neared: I heard them talk,
'Why, this is strange, I trow!
Where are those lights so many and fair,
That signal made but now?'

Approacheth the
ship with
wonder.

'Strange, by my faith!' the Hermit said –
'And they answered not our cheer!
The planks looked warped! and see those sails,
How thin they are and sere!
I never saw aught like to them,
Unless perchance it were

Brown skeletons of leaves that lag
My forest-brook along;
When the ivy-tod is heavy with snow,
And the owlet whoops to the wolf below,
That eats the she-wolf's young.'

'Dear Lord! it hath a fiendish look –
(The Pilot made reply)
I am a-feared' – 'Push on, push on!'
Said the Hermit cheerily.

The boat came closer to the ship,
But I nor spake nor stirred;
The boat came close beneath the ship,
And straight a sound was heard.

The ship
suddenly sinketh.

Under the water it rumbled on,
Still louder and more dread:
It reached the ship, it split the bay;
The ship went down like lead.

The ancient
Mariner is saved
in the Pilot's
boat.

Stunned by that loud and dreadful sound,
Which sky and ocean smote,
Like one that hath been seven days drowned
My body lay afloat;
But swift as dreams, myself I found
Within the Pilot's boat.

Upon the whirl, where sank the ship,
The boat spun round and round;
And all was still, save that the hill
Was telling of the sound.

I moved my lips – the Pilot shrieked
And fell down in a fit;
The holy Hermit raised his eyes,
And prayed where he did sit.

I took the oars: the Pilot's boy,
Who now doth crazy go,
Laughed loud and long, and all the while
His eyes went to and fro.
'Ha! ha!' quoth he, 'full plain I see,
The Devil knows how to row.'

And now, all in my own countree,
I stood on the firm land!
The Hermit stepped forth from the boat,
And scarcely he could stand.

The ancient Mariner earnestly entreateth the Hermit to shrieve him; and the penance of life falls on him.

'O shrieve me, shrieve me, holy man!'
The Hermit crossed his brow.
'Say quick,' quoth he, 'I bid thee say –
What manner of man art thou?'

Forthwith this frame of mine was wrenched
With a woful agony,
Which forced me to begin my tale;
And then it left me free.

And ever and anon throughout his future life an agony constraineth him to travel from land to land.

Since then, at an uncertain hour,
The agony returns:
And till my ghastly tale is told,
This heart within me burns.

I pass, like night, from land to land;
I have strange power of speech;
That moment that his face I see,
I know the man that must hear me:
To him my tale I teach.

What loud uproar bursts from that door!
The wedding-guests are there:
But in the garden-bower the bride
And bride-maids singing are:
And hark the little vesper bell,
Which biddeth me to prayer!

O Wedding-Guest! this soul hath been
Alone on a wide wide sea:
So lonely 'twas, that God himself
Scarce seemèd there to be.

O sweeter than the marriage-feast,
'Tis sweeter far to me,
To walk together to the kirk
With a goodly company! –

To walk together to the kirk,
And all together pray,
While each to his great Father bends,
Old men, and babes, and loving friends
And youths and maidens gay!

And to teach, by his own example, love and reverence to all things that God made and loveth.

Farewell, farewell! but this I tell
To thee, thou Wedding-Guest!
He prayeth well, who loveth well
Both man and bird and beast.

He prayeth best, who loveth best
All things both great and small;
For the dear God who loveth us,
He made and loveth all.'

The Mariner, whose eye is bright,
Whose beard with age is hoar,
Is gone: and now the Wedding-Guest
Turned from the bridegroom's door.

He went like one that hath been stunned,
And is of sense forlorn:
A sadder and a wiser man,
He rose the morrow morn.

An Invocation

from Remorse, *Act iii, Scene i, ll. 69–82*

Hear, sweet spirit, hear the spell,
Lest a blacker charm compel!
So shall the midnight breezes swell
With thy deep long-lingering knell.

And at evening evermore,
In a Chapel on the shore,
Shall the Chaunters sad and saintly,
Yellow tapers burning faintly,
Doleful Masses chaunt for thee,
    Miserere Domine!

Hush! the cadence dies away
    On the quiet moonlight sea:
The boatmen rest their oars and say,
    Miserere Domine!

Epitaph

Stop, Christian passer-by! – Stop, child of God,
And read with gentle breast. Beneath this sod
A poet lies, or that which once seem'd he. –
O, lift one thought in prayer for S. T. C.;
That he who many a year with toil of breath
Found death in life, may here find life in death!
Mercy for praise – to be forgiven for fame
He ask'd, and hoped, through Christ. Do thou the same!

P. B. SHELLEY
(1792–1822)

Ode to the West Wind

I

O Wild West Wind, thou breath of Autumn's being,
Thou, from whose unseen presence the leaves dead
Are driven, like ghosts from an enchanter fleeing,

Yellow, and black, and pale, and hectic red,
Pestilence-stricken multitudes: O thou,
Who chariotest to their dark wintry bed

The wingèd seeds, where they lie cold and low,
Each like a corpse within its grave, until
Thine azure sister of the Spring shall blow

Her clarion o'er the dreaming earth, and fill
(Driving sweet buds like flocks to feed in air)
With living hues and odours plain and hill:

Wild Spirit, which art moving everywhere;
Destroyer and preserver; hear, oh, hear!

II

Thou on whose stream, 'mid the steep sky's commotion,
Loose clouds like earth's decaying leaves are shed,
Shook from the tangled boughs of Heaven and Ocean,

Angels of rain and lightning: there are spread
On the blue surface of thine aery surge,
Like the bright hair uplifted from the head

Of some fierce Maenad, even from the dim verge
Of the horizon to the zenith's height,
The locks of the approaching storm. Thou dirge

Of the dying year, to which this closing night
Will be the dome of a vast sepulchre,
Vaulted with all thy congregated might

Of vapours, from whose solid atmosphere
Black rain, and fire, and hail will burst: oh, hear!

III

Thou who didst waken from his summer dreams
The blue Mediterranean, where he lay,
Lulled by the coil of his crystalline streams,

Beside a pumice isle in Baiae's bay,
And saw in sleep old palaces and towers
Quivering within the wave's intenser day,

All overgrown with azure moss and flowers
So sweet, the sense faints picturing them! Thou
For whose path the Atlantic's level powers

Cleave themselves into chasms, while far below
The sea-blooms and the oozy woods which wear
The sapless foliage of the ocean, know

Thy voice, and suddenly grow gray with fear,
And tremble and despoil themselves: oh, hear!

IV

If I were a dead leaf thou mightest bear;
If I were a swift cloud to fly with thee;
A wave to pant beneath thy power, and share

The impulse of thy strength, only less free
Than thou, O uncontrollable! If even
I were as in my boyhood, and could be

The comrade of thy wanderings over Heaven,
As then, when to outstrip thy skiey speed
Scarce seemed a vision; I would ne'er have striven

As thus with thee in prayer in my sore need.
Oh, lift me as a wave, a leaf, a cloud!
I fall upon the thorns of life! I bleed!

A heavy weight of hours has chained and bowed
One too like thee: tameless, and swift, and proud.

V

Make me thy lyre, even as the forest is:
What if my leaves are falling like its own!
The tumult of thy mighty harmonies

Will take from both a deep, autumnal tone,
Sweet though in sadness. Be thou, Spirit fierce,
My spirit! Be thou me, impetuous one!

Drive my dead thoughts over the universe
Like withered leaves to quicken a new birth!
And, by the incantation of this verse,

Scatter, as from an unextinguished hearth
Ashes and sparks, my words among mankind!
Be through my lips to unawakened earth

The trumpet of a prophecy! O, Wind,
If Winter comes, can Spring be far behind?

from Prometheus Unbound

Demogorgon

Thou, Earth, calm empire of a happy soul,
   Sphere of divinest shapes and harmonies,
Beautiful orb! gathering as thou dost roll
   The love which paves thy path along the skies:

The Earth

I hear: I am as a drop of dew that dies.

Demogorgon

Thou, Moon, which gazest on the nightly Earth
   With wonder, as it gazes upon thee;
Whilst each to men, and beast, and the swift birth
   Of birds, is beauty, love, calm, harmony:

The Moon

I hear: I am a leaf shaken by thee!

Demogorgon

Ye Kings of suns and stars, Daemons and Gods,
    Aetherial Dominations, who possess
Elysian, windless, fortunate abodes
    Beyond Heaven's constellated wilderness:

A Voice from above

Our great Republic hears, we are blest, and bless.

Demorgorgon

Ye Happy Dead, whom beams of brightest verse
    Are clouds to hide, not colours to portray,
Whether your nature is that universe
    Which once ye saw and suffered –

A Voice from beneath

                    Or as they
Whom we have left, we change and pass away.

Demogorgon

Ye elemental Genii, who have homes
    From man's high mind even to the central stone
Of sullen lead; from heaven's star-fretted domes
    To the dull weed some sea-worm battens on:

A confused Voice

We hear: thy words waken oblivion.

Demogorgon

Spirits, whose homes are flesh: ye beasts and birds,
  Ye worms, and fish; ye living leaves and buds;
Lightning and wind; and ye untameable herds,
  Meteors and mists, which throng air's solitudes: –

A Voice

  Thy voice to us is wind among still woods.

Demogorgon

Man who wert once a despot and a slave;
  A dupe and a deceiver; a decay;
A traveller from the cradle to the grave
  Through the dim night of this immortal day:

All

  Speak: thy strong words may never pass away.

Demogorgon

This is the day, which down the void abysm
At the Earth-born's spell yawns for Heaven's despotism.
  And Conquest is dragged captive through the deep:
Love, from its awful throne of patient power
In the wise heart, from the last giddy hour
  Of dread endurance, from the slippery, steep,
And narrow verge of crag-like agony, springs
And folds over the world its healing wings.

Gentleness, Virtue, Wisdom, and Endurance,
These are the seals of that most firm assurance
  Which bars the pit over Destruction's strength;
And if, with infirm hand, Eternity,
Mother of many acts and hours, should free
  The serpent that would clasp her with his length;
These are the spells by which to reassume
An empire o'er the disentangled doom.

To suffer woes which Hope thinks infinite;
To forgive wrongs darker than death or night;
   To defy Power, which seems omnipotent;
To love, and bear; to hope till Hope creates
From its own wreck the thing it contemplates;
   Neither to change, nor falter, nor repent;
This, like thy glory, Titan, is to be
Good, great and joyous, beautiful and free;
This is alone Life, Joy, Empire, and Victory.

JOHN CLARE
(1793–1864)

I Am

I am: yet what I am none cares or knows,
   My friends forsake me like a memory lost;
I am the self-consumer of my woes,
   They rise and vanish in oblivious host,
Like shades in love and death's oblivion lost;
And yet I am, and live with shadows tost

Into the nothingness of scorn and noise,
   Into the living sea of waking dreams,
Where there is neither sense of life nor joys,
   But the vast shipwreck of my life's esteems;
And e'en the dearest – that I loved the best –
Are strange – nay, rather stranger than the rest.

I long for scenes where man has never trod,
   A place where woman never smiled or wept;
There to abide with my Creator, God,
   And sleep as I in childhood sweetly slept:
Untroubling and untroubled where I lie,
The grass below – above the vaulted sky.

RALPH WALDO EMERSON
(1803–1882)

Concord Hymn

Sung at the completion of the Battle Monument, 4 July 1837

By the rude bridge that arched the flood,
  Their flag to April's breeze unfurled,
Here once the embattled farmers stood
  And fired the shot heard round the world.

The foe long since in silence slept;
  Alike the conqueror silent sleeps;
And Time the ruined bridge has swept
  Down the dark stream which seaward creeps.

On this green bank, by this soft stream,
  We set today a votive stone;
That memory may their deed redeem,
  When, like our sires, our sons are gone.

Spirit, that made those heroes dare
  To die, and leave their children free,
Bid Time and Nature gently spare
  The shaft we raise to them and thee.

ALFRED, LORD TENNYSON
(1809–1892)

The Kraken

Below the thunders of the upper deep;
Far, far beneath in the abysmal sea,
His ancient, dreamless, uninvaded sleep
The Kraken sleepeth: faintest sunlights flee
About his shadowy sides: above him swell
Huge sponges of millennial growth and height;
And far away into the sickly light,

223

From many a wondrous grot and secret cell
Unnumbered and enormous polypi
Winnow with giant arms the slumbering green.
There hath he lain for ages and will lie
Battening upon huge seaworms in his sleep,
Until the latter fire shall heat the deep;
Then once by man and angels to be seen,
In roaring he shall rise and on the surface die.

from *The Passing of Arthur*

And answer made King Arthur, breathing hard:
'My end draws nigh; 'tis time that I were gone.
Make broad thy shoulders to receive my weight,
And bear me to the margin; yet I fear
My wound hath taken cold, and I shall die.'

So saying, from the pavement he half rose,
Slowly, with pain, reclining on his arm,
And looking wistfully with wide blue eyes
As in a picture. Him Sir Bedivere
Remorsefully regarded through his tears,
And would have spoken, but he found not words,
Then took with care, and kneeling on one knee,
O'er both his shoulders drew the languid hands,
And rising bore him through the place of tombs.

But, as he walked, King Arthur panted hard,
Like one that feels a nightmare on his bed
When all the house is mute. So sighed the King,
Muttering and murmuring at his ear, 'Quick, quick!
I fear it is too late, and I shall die.'
But the other swiftly strode from ridge to ridge,
Clothed with his breath, and looking, as he walked,
Larger than human on the frozen hills.
He heard the deep behind him, and a cry
Before. His own thought drove him, like a goad.
Dry clashed his harness in the icy caves

And barren chasms, and all to left and right
The bare black cliff clanged round him, as he based
His feet on juts of slippery crag that rang
Sharp-smitten with the dint of armèd heels –
And on a sudden, lo! the level lake,
And the long glories of the winter moon.

　　Then saw they how there hove a dusky barge,
Dark as a funeral scarf from stem to stern,
Beneath them; and descending they were ware
That all the decks were dense with stately forms
Black-stoled, black-hooded, like a dream – by these
Three Queens with crowns of gold – and from them rose
A cry that shivered to the tingling stars,
And, as it were one voice, an agony
Of lamentation, like a wind, that shrills
All night in a waste land, where no one comes,
Or hath come, since the making of the world.

　　Then murmured Arthur, 'Place me in the barge,'
And to the barge they came. There those three Queens
Put forth their hands, and took the King, and wept.
But she, that rose the tallest of them all
And fairest, laid his head upon her lap,
And loosed the shattered casque, and chafed his hands,
And called him by his name, complaining loud,
And dropping bitter tears against his brow
Striped with dark blood: for all his face was white
And colourless, and like the withered moon
Smote by the fresh beam of the springing east;
And all his greaves and cuisses dashed with drops
Of onset; and the light and lustrous curls –
That made his forehead like a rising sun
High from the dais-throne – were parched with dust;
Or, clotted into points and hanging loose,
Mixed with the knightly growth that fringed his lips.
So like a shattered column lay the King;
Not like that Arthur who, with lance in rest,
From spur to plume a star of tournament,
Shot through the lists at Camelot, and charged
Before the eyes of ladies and of kings.

Then loudly cried the bold Sir Bedivere,
'Ah! my Lord Arthur, whither shall I go?
Where shall I hide my forehead and my eyes?
For now I see the true old times are dead,
When every morning brought a noble chance,
And every chance brought out a noble knight.
Such times have been not since the light that led
The holy Elders with the gift of myrrh.
But now the whole ROUND TABLE is dissolved
Which was an image of the mighty world;
And I, the last, go forth companionless,
And the days darken round me, and the years,
Among new men, strange faces, other minds.'

And slowly answered Arthur from the barge:
'The old order changeth, yielding place to new,
And God fulfils Himself in many ways,
Lest one good custom should corrupt the world.
Comfort thyself: what comfort is in me?
I have lived my life, and that which I have done
May He within Himself make pure! but thou,
If thou shouldst never see my face again,
Pray for my soul. More things are wrought by prayer
Than this world dreams of. Wherefore, let thy voice
Rise like a fountain for me night and day.
For what are men better than sheep or goats
That nourish a blind life within the brain,
If, knowing God, they lift not hands of prayer
Both for themselves and those who call them friend?
For so the whole round earth is every way
Bound by gold chains about the feet of God.
But now farewell. I am going a long way
With these thou seëst – if indeed I go –
(For all my mind is clouded with a doubt)
To the island-valley of Avilion;
Where falls not hail, or rain, or any snow,
Nor ever wind blows loudly; but it lies
Deep-meadowed, happy, fair with orchard-lawns
And bowery hollows crowned with summer sea,
Where I will heal me of my grievous wound.'

So said he, and the barge with oar and sail
Moved from the brink, like some full-breasted swan
That, fluting a wild carol ere her death,
Ruffles her pure cold plume, and takes the flood
With swarthy webs. Long stood Sir Bedivere
Revolving many memories, till the hull
Looked one black dot against the verge of dawn,
And on the mere the wailing died away.

from *In Memoriam*

V

I sometimes hold it half a sin
    To put in words the grief I feel;
    For words, like Nature, half reveal
And half conceal the Soul within.

But, for the unquiet heart and brain,
    A use in measured language lies;
    The sad mechanic exercise,
Like dull narcotics, numbing pain.

In words, like weeds, I'll wrap me o'er,
    Like coarsest clothes against the cold:
    But that large grief which these enfold
Is given in outline and no more.

XI

Calm is the morn without a sound,
    Calm as to suit a calmer grief,
    And only through the faded leaf
The chestnut pattering to the ground:

Calm and deep peace on this high wold,
    And on these dews that drench the furze,
    And all the silvery gossamers
That twinkle into green and gold:

Calm and still light on yon great plain
  That sweeps with all its autumn bowers,
  And crowded farms and lessening towers,
To mingle with the bounding main:

Calm and deep peace in this wide air,
  These leaves that redden to the fall;
  And in my heart, if calm at all,
If any calm, a calm despair:

Calm on the seas, and silver sleep,
  And waves that sway themselves in rest,
  And dead calm in that noble breast
Which heaves but with the heaving deep.

XV

Tonight the winds begin to rise
  And roar from yonder dropping day:
  The last red leaf is whirled away,
The rooks are blown about the skies;

The forest cracked, the waters curled,
  The cattle huddled on the lea;
  And wildly dashed on tower and tree
The sunbeam strikes along the world:

And but for fancies, which aver
  That all thy motions gently pass
  Athwart a plane of molten glass,
I scarce could brook the strain and stir

That makes the barren branches loud;
  And but for fear it is not so,
  The wild unrest that lives in woe
Would dote and pore on yonder cloud

That rises upward always higher,
  And onward drags a labouring breast,
  And topples round the dreary west,
A looming bastion fringed with fire.

XVII

Thou comest, much wept for: such a breeze
   Compelled thy canvas, and my prayer
   Was as the whisper of an air
To breathe thee over lonely seas.

For I in spirit saw thee move
   Through circles of the bounding sky,
   Week after week: the days go by:
Come quick, thou bringest all I love.

Henceforth, wherever thou mayst roam,
   My blessing, like a line of light,
   Is on the waters day and night,
And like a beacon guards thee home.

So may whatever tempest mars
   Mid-ocean, spare thee, sacred bark;
   And balmy drops in summer dark
Slide from the bosom of the stars.

So kind an office hath been done,
   Such precious relics brought by thee;
   The dust of him I shall not see
Till all my widowed race be run.

XXII

The path by which we twain did go,
   Which led by tracts that pleased us well,
   Through four sweet years arose and fell,
From flower to flower, from snow to snow:

And we with singing cheered the way,
   And, crowned with all the season lent,
   From April on to April went,
And glad at heart from May to May:

But where the path we walked began
   To slant the fifth autumnal slope,
   As we descended following Hope,
There sat the Shadow feared of man;

Who broke our fair companionship,
   And spread his mantle dark and cold,
   And wrapt thee formless in the fold,
And dulled the murmur on thy lip,

And bore thee where I could not see
   Nor follow, though I walk in haste,
   And think, that somewhere in the waste
The Shadow sits and waits for me.

XXXI

When Lazarus left his charnel-cave
   And home to Mary's house returned,
   Was this demanded – if he yearned
To hear her weeping by his grave?

'Where wert thou, brother, those four days?'
   There lives no record of reply,
   Which telling what it is to die
Had surely added praise to praise.

From every house the neighbours met,
   The streets were filled with joyful sound,
   A solemn gladness even crowned
The purple brows of Olivet.

Behold a man raised up by Christ!
   The rest remaineth unrevealed;
   He told it not; or something sealed
The lips of that Evangelist.

XXXIII

O thou that after toil and storm
   Mayst seem to have reached a purer air,
   Whose faith has centre everywhere,
Nor cares to fix itself to form,

Leave thou thy sister when she prays,
   Her early Heaven, her happy views;
   Nor thou with shadowed hint confuse
A life that leads melodious days.

Her faith through form is pure as thine,
  Her hands are quicker unto good:
  Oh, sacred be the flesh and blood
To which she links a truth divine!

See thou, that countest reason ripe
  In holding by the law within,
  Thou fail not in a world of sin,
And even for want of such a type.

XXXIX

Old warder of these buried bones,
  And answering now my random stroke
  With fruitful cloud and living smoke,
Dark yew, that graspest at the stones

And dippest toward the dreamless head,
  To thee too comes the golden hour
  When flower is feeling after flower;
But Sorrow – fixt upon the dead,

And darkening the dark graves of men, –
  What whispered from her lying lips?
  Thy gloom is kindled at the tips,
And passes into gloom again.

XLIII

If Sleep and Death be truly one,
  And every spirit's folded bloom
  Through all its intervital gloom
In some long trance should slumber on;

Unconscious of the sliding hour,
  Bare of the body, might it last,
  And silent traces of the past
Be all the colour of the flower:

So then were nothing lost to man;
  So that still garden of the souls
  In many a figured leaf enrolls
The total world since life began;

And love will last as pure and whole
  As when he loved me here in Time,
  And at the spiritual prime
Rewaken with the dawning soul.

L

 Be near me when my light is low,
  When the blood creeps, and the nerves prick
  And tingle; and the heart is sick,
And all the wheels of Being slow.

Be near me when the sensuous frame
  Is racked with pangs that conquer trust;
  And Time, a maniac scattering dust,
And Life, a Fury slinging flame.

Be near me when my faith is dry,
  And men the flies of latter spring,
  That lay their eggs, and sting and sing
And weave their petty cells and die.

Be near me when I fade away,
  To point the term of human strife,
  And on the low dark verge of life
The twilight of eternal day.

LIV

Oh yet we trust that somehow good
  Will be the final goal of ill,
  To pangs of nature, sins of will,
Defects of doubt, and taints of blood;

That nothing walks with aimless feet;
  That not one life shall be destroyed,
  Or cast as rubbish to the void,
When God hath made the pile complete;

That not a worm is cloven in vain;
  That not a moth with vain desire
  Is shrivelled in a fruitless fire,
Or but subserves another's gain.

Behold, we know not anything;
   I can but trust that good shall fall
   At last – far off – at last, to all,
And every winter change to spring.

So runs my dream: but what am I?
   An infant crying in the night:
   An infant crying for the light:
And with no language but a cry.

LXVII

When on my bed the moonlight falls,
   I know that in thy place of rest
   By that broad water of the west,
There comes a glory on the walls;

Thy marble bright in dark appears,
   As slowly steals a silver flame
   Along the letters of thy name,
And o'er the number of thy years.

The mystic glory swims away;
   From off my bed the moonlight dies;
   And closing eaves of wearied eyes
I sleep till dusk is dipt in gray:

And then I know the mist is drawn
   A lucid veil from coast to coast,
   And in the dark church like a ghost
Thy tablet glimmers to the dawn.

LXXII

Risest thou thus, dim dawn, again,
   And howlest, issuing out of night,
   With blasts that blow the poplar white,
And lash with storm the streaming pane?

Day, when my crowned estate begun
   To pine in that reverse of doom,
   Which sickened every living bloom,
And blurred the splendour of the sun;

Who usherest in the dolorous hour
    With thy quick tears that make the rose
    Pull sideways, and the daisy close
Her crimson fringes to the shower;

Who might'st have heaved a windless flame
    Up the deep East, or, whispering, played
    A chequer-work of beam and shade
Along the hills, yet looked the same.

As wan, as chill, as wild as now;
    Day, marked as with some hideous crime,
    When the dark hand struck down through time,
And cancelled nature's best: but thou,

Lift as thou mayst thy burthened brows
    Through clouds that drench the morning star,
    And whirl the ungarnered sheaf afar,
And sow the sky with flying boughs,

And up thy vault with roaring sound
    Climb thy thick noon, disastrous day;
    Touch thy dull goal of joyless gray,
And hide thy shame beneath the ground.

LXXVIII

Again at Christmas did we weave
    The holly round the Christmas hearth;
    The silent snow possessed the earth,
And calmly fell our Christmas-eve:

The yule-clog sparkled keen with frost,
    No wing of wind the region swept,
    But over all things brooding slept
The quiet sense of something lost.

As in the winters left behind,
    Again our ancient games had place,
    The mimic picture's breathing grace,
And dance and song and hoodman-blind.

Who showed a token of distress?
   No single tear, no mark of pain:
   O sorrow, then can sorrow wane?
O grief, can grief be changed to less?

O last regret, regret can die!
   No – mixt with all this mystic frame,
   Her deep relations are the same,
But with long use her tears are dry.

XCV

By night we lingered on the lawn,
   For underfoot the herb was dry;
   And genial warmth; and o'er the sky
The silvery haze of summer drawn;

And calm that let the tapers burn
   Unwavering: not a cricket chirred:
   The brook alone far-off was heard,
And on the board the fluttering urn:

And bats went round in fragrant skies,
   And wheeled or lit the filmy shapes
   That haunt the dusk, with ermine capes
And woolly breasts and beaded eyes;

While now we sang old songs that pealed
   From knoll to knoll, where, couched at ease,
   The white kine glimmered, and the trees
Laid their dark arms about the field.

But when those others, one by one,
   Withdrew themselves from me and night,
   And in the house light after light
Went out, and I was all alone,

A hunger seized my heart; I read
   Of that glad year which once had been,
   In those fallen leaves which kept their green,
The noble letters of the dead:

And strangely on the silence broke
   The silent-speaking words, and strange
   Was love's dumb cry defying change
To test his worth; and strangely spoke

The faith, the vigour, bold to dwell
   On doubts that drive the coward back,
   And keen through wordy snares to track
Suggestion to her inmost cell.

So word by word, and line by line,
   The dead man touched me from the past,
   And all at once it seemed at last
The living soul was flashed on mine,

And mine in this was wound, and whirled
   About empyreal heights of thought,
   And came on that which is, and caught
The deep pulsations of the world,

Aeonian music measuring out
   The steps of Time – the shocks of Chance –
   The blows of Death. At length my trance
Was cancelled, stricken through with doubt.

Vague words! but ah, how hard to frame
   In matter-moulded forms of speech,
   Or even for intellect to reach
Through memory that which I became:

Till now the doubtful dusk revealed
   The knolls once more where, couched at ease,
   The white kine glimmered, and the trees
Laid their dark arms about the field:

And sucked from out the distant gloom
   A breeze began to tremble o'er
   The large leaves of the sycamore,
And fluctuate all the still perfume,

And gathering freshlier overhead,
   Rocked the full-foliaged elms, and swung
   The heavy-folded rose, and flung
The lilies to and fro, and said

'The dawn, the dawn,' and died away;
   And East and West, without a breath,
   Mixt their dim lights, like life and death,
To broaden into boundless day.

CI

Unwatched, the garden bough shall sway,
   The tender blossom flutter down,
   Unloved, that beech will gather brown,
This maple burn itself away;

Unloved, the sun-flower, shining fair,
     Ray round with flames her disk of seed,
   And many a rose-carnation feed
With summer spice the humming air;

Unloved, by many a sandy bar,
   The brook shall babble down the plain,
   At noon or when the lesser wain
Is twisting round the polar star;

Uncared for, gird the windy grove,
   And flood the haunts of hern and crake;
   Or into silver arrows break
The sailing moon in creek and cove;

Till from the garden and the wild
   A fresh association blow,
   And year by year the landscape grow
Familiar to the stranger's child;

As year by year the labourer tills
   His wonted glebe, or lops the glades;
   And year by year our memory fades
From all the circle of the hills.

CVI

Ring out, wild bells, to the wild sky,
   The flying cloud, the frosty light:
   The year is dying in the night;
Ring out, wild bells, and let him die.

Ring out the old, ring in the new,
   Ring, happy bells, across the snow:
   The year is going, let him go;
Ring out the false, ring in the true.

Ring out the grief that saps the mind,
   For those that here we see no more;
   Ring out the feud of rich and poor,
Ring in redress to all mankind.

Ring out a slowly dying cause,
   And ancient forms of party strife;
   Ring in the nobler modes of life,
With sweeter manners, purer laws.

Ring out the want, the care, the sin,
   The faithless coldness of the times;
   Ring out, ring out my mournful rhymes,
But ring the fuller minstrel in.

Ring out false pride in place and blood,
   The civic slander and the spite;
   Ring in the love of truth and right,
Ring in the common love of good.

Ring out old shapes of foul disease;
   Ring out the narrowing lust of gold;
   Ring out the thousand wars of old,
Ring in the thousand years of peace.

Ring in the valiant man and free,
   The larger heart, the kindlier hand;
   Ring out the darkness of the land,
Ring in the Christ that is to be.

CXVII

O days and hours, your work is this
   To hold me from my proper place,
   A little while from his embrace,
For fuller gain of after bliss:

That out of distance might ensue
   Desire of nearness doubly sweet;
   And unto meeting when we meet,
Delight a hundredfold accrue,

For every grain of sand that runs,
   And every span of shade that steals,
   And every kiss of toothèd wheels,
And all the courses of the suns.

CXXVI

Love is and was my Lord and King,
   And in his presence I attend
   To hear the tidings of my friend,
Which every hour his couriers bring.

Love is and was my King and Lord,
   And will be, though as yet I keep
   Within his court on earth, and sleep
Encompassed by his faithful guard,

And hear at times a sentinel
   Who moves about from place to place,
   And whispers to the worlds of space,
In the deep night, that all is well.

To the Rev. F. D. Maurice

Come, when no graver cares employ,
Godfather, come and see your boy:
   Your presence will be sun in winter,
Making the little one leap for joy.

For, being of that honest few,
Who give the Fiend himself his due,
   Should eighty-thousand college-councils
Thunder 'Anathema,' friend, at you;

Should all our churchmen foam in spite
At you, so careful of the right,
   Yet one lay-hearth would give you welcome
(Take it and come) to the Isle of Wight;

Where, far from noise and smoke of town,
I watch the twilight falling brown
   All round a careless-ordered garden
Close to the ridge of a noble down.

You'll have no scandal while you dine,
But honest talk and wholesome wine,
   And only hear the magpie gossip
Garrulous under a roof of pine:

For groves of pine on either hand,
To break the blast of winter, stand;
   And further on, the hoary Channel
Tumbles a billow on chalk and sand;

Where, if below the milky steep
Some ship of battle slowly creep,
   And on through zones of light and shadow
Glimmer away to the lonely deep,

We might discuss the Northern sin
Which made a selfish war begin;
   Dispute the claims, arrange the chances;
Emperor, Ottoman, which shall win:

Or whether war's avenging rod
Shall lash all Europe into blood;
   Till you should turn to dearer matters,
Dear to the man that is dear to God;

How best to help the slender store,
How mend the dwellings, of the poor;
   How gain in life, as life advances,
Valour and charity more and more.

Come, Maurice, come: the lawn as yet
Is hoar with rime, or spongy-wet;
   But when the wreath of March has blossomed,
Crocus, anemone, violet,

Or later, pay one visit here,
For those are few we hold as dear;
 Nor pay but one, but come for many,
Many and many a happy year.

Milton

ALCAICS

O mighty-mouthed inventor of harmonies,
O skilled to sing of Time or Eternity,
 God-gifted organ-voice of England,
  Milton, a name to resound for ages;
Whose Titan angels, Gabriel, Abdiel,
Starred from Jehovah's gorgeous armouries,
 Tower, as the deep-domed empyrëan
  Rings to the roar of an angel onset –
Me rather all that bowery loneliness,
The brooks of Eden mazily murmuring,
 And bloom profuse and cedar arches
  Charm, as a wanderer out in ocean,
Where some refulgent sunset of India
Streams o'er a rich ambrosial ocean isle,
 And crimson-hued the stately palm-woods
  Whisper in odorous heights of even.

Crossing the Bar

Sunset and evening star,
 And one clear call for me!
And may there be no moaning of the bar,
 When I put out to sea,

But such a tide as moving seems asleep,
    Too full for sound and foam,
When that which drew from out the boundless deep
    Turns again home.

Twilight and evening bell,
    And after that the dark!
And may there be no sadness of farewell,
    When I embark;

For though from out our bourne of Time and Place
    The flood may bear me far,
I hope to see my Pilot face to face
    When I have crost the bar.

ROBERT BROWNING
(1812–1889)

The Guardian-Angel
A PICTURE AT FANO

Dear and great Angel, wouldst thou only leave
    That child, when thou hast done with him, for me!
Let me sit all the day here, that when eve
    Shall find performed thy special ministry
And time come for departure, thou, suspending
Thy flight, mayst see another child for tending,
    Another still, to quiet and retrieve.

Then I shall feel thee step one step, no more,
    From where thou standest now, to where I gaze,
And suddenly my head be covered o'er
    With those wings, white above the child who prays
Now on that tomb – and I shall feel thee guarding
Me, out of all the world! for me, discarding
    Yon heaven thy home, that waits and opes its door!

I would not look up thither past thy head
  Because the door opes, like that child, I know,
For I should have thy gracious face instead,
  Thou bird of God! And wilt thou bend me low
Like him, and lay, like his, my hands together,
And lift them up to pray, and gently tether
  Me, as thy lamb there, with thy garment's spread?

If this was ever granted, I would rest
  My head beneath thine, while thy healing hands
Close-covered both my eyes beside thy breast,
  Pressing the brain, which too much thought expands
Back to its proper size again, and smoothing
Distortion down till every nerve had soothing,
  And all lay quiet, happy and supprest.

How soon all worldly wrong would be repaired!
  I think how I should view the earth and skies
And sea, when once again my brow was bared
  After thy healing, with such different eyes.
O, world, as God has made it! all is beauty:
And knowing this, is love, and love is duty.
  What further may be sought for or declared?

Guercino drew this angel I saw teach
  (Alfred, dear friend) – that little child to pray,
Holding the little hands up, each to each
  Pressed gently, – with his own head turned away
Over the earth where so much lay before him
Of work to do, though heaven was opening o'er him,
  And he was left at Fano by the beach.

We were at Fano, and three times we went
  To sit and see him in his chapel there,
And drink his beauty to our soul's content
  – My angel with me too: and since I care
For dear Guercino's fame, (to which in power
And glory comes this picture for a dower,
  Fraught with a pathos so magnificent)

And since he did not work so earnestly
 At all times, and has else endured some wrong, –
I took one thought his picture struck from me,
 And spread it out, translating it to song.
My love is here. Where are you, dear old friend?
How rolls the Wairoa at your world's far end?
 This is Ancona, yonder is the sea.

A Grammarian's Funeral

Let us begin and carry up this corpse,
 Singing together.
Leave we the common crofts, the vulgar thorpes,
 Each in its tether
Sleeping safe on the bosom of the plain,
 Cared-for till cock-crow.
Look out if yonder's not the day again
 Rimming the rock-row!
That's the appropriate country – there, man's thought,
 Rarer, intenser,
Self-gathered for an outbreak, as it ought,
 Chafes in the censer!
Leave we the unlettered plain its herd and crop;
 Seek we sepulture
On a tall mountain, citied to the top,
 Crowded with culture!
All the peaks soar, but one the rest excels;
 Clouds overcome it;
No, yonder sparkle is the citadel's
 Circling its summit!
Thither our path lies – wind we up the heights –
 Wait ye the warning?
Our low life was the level's and the night's;
 He's for the morning!
Step to a tune, square chests, erect the head,
 'Ware the beholders!

This is our master, famous, calm, and dead,
    Borne on our shoulders.
Sleep, crop and herd! sleep, darkling thorpe and croft,
    Safe from the weather!
He, whom we convey to his grave aloft,
    Singing together,
He was a man born with thy face and throat,
    Lyric Apollo!
Long he lived nameless: how should spring take note
    Winter would follow?
Till lo, the little touch, and youth was gone!
    Cramped and diminished,
Moaned he, 'New measures, other feet anon!
    My dance is finished?'
No, that's the world's way! (keep the mountain-side,
    Make for the city.)
He knew the signal, and stepped on with pride
    Over men's pity;
Left play for work, and grappled with the world
    Bent on escaping:
'What's in the scroll,' quoth he, 'thou keepest furled?
    Show me their shaping,
Theirs, who most studied man, the bard and sage, –
    Give!' – So he gowned him,
Straight got by heart that book to its last page:
    Learned, we found him!
Yea, but we found him bald too – eyes like lead,
    Accents uncertain:
'Time to taste life,' another would have said,
    'Up with the curtain!'
This man said rather, 'Actual life comes next?
    Patience a moment!
Grant I have mastered learning's crabbed text,
    Still, there's the comment.
Let me know all. Prate not of most or least,
    Painful or easy:
Even to the crumbs I'd fain eat up the feast,
    Ay, nor feel queasy!'
Oh, such a life as he resolved to live,
    When he had learned it,

When he had gathered all books had to give;
      Sooner, he spurned it!
Image the whole, then execute the parts –
      Fancy the fabric
Quite, ere you build, ere steel strike fire from quartz,
      Ere mortar dab brick!
(Here's the town-gate reached: there's the market-place
      Gaping before us.)
Yea, this in him was the peculiar grace
      (Hearten our chorus)
Still before living he'd learn how to live –
      No end to learning.
Earn the means first – God surely will contrive
      Use for our earning.
Others mistrust and say – 'But time escapes, –
      Live now or never!'
He said, 'What's Time? leave Now for dogs and apes!
      Man has For ever.'
Back to his book then: deeper drooped his head;
      Calculus racked him:
Leaden before, his eyes grew dross of lead;
      Tussis attacked him.
'Now, Master, take a little rest!' – not he!
      (Caution redoubled!
Step two a-breast, the way winds narrowly.)
      Not a whit troubled,
Back to his studies, fresher than at first,
      Fierce as a dragon
He, (soul-hydroptic with a sacred thirst)
      Sucked at the flagon.
Oh, if we draw a circle premature,
      Heedless of far gain,
Greedy for quick returns of profit, sure,
      Bad is our bargain!
Was it not great? did not he throw on God,
      (He loves the burthen) –
God's task to make the heavenly period
      Perfect the earthen?
Did not he magnify the mind, shew clear
      Just what it all meant?

He would not discount life, as fools do here,
  Paid by instalment!
He ventured neck or nothing – heaven's success
  Found, or earth's failure:
'Wilt thou trust death or not?' he answered 'Yes.
  Hence with life's pale lure!'
That low man seeks a little thing to do,
  Sees it and does it:
This high man, with a great thing to pursue,
  Dies ere he knows it.
That low man goes on adding one to one,
  His hundred's soon hit:
This high man, aiming at a million,
  Misses an unit.
That, has the world here – should he need the next,
  Let the world mind him!
This, throws himself on God, and unperplext
  Seeking shall find Him.
So, with the throttling hands of Death at strife,
  Ground he at grammar;
Still, thro' the rattle, parts of speech were rife.
  While he could stammer
He settled *Hoti's* business – let it be! –
  Properly based *Oun* –
Gave us the doctrine of the enclitic *De,*
  Dead from the waist down.
Well, here's the platform, here's the proper place.
  Hail to your purlieus
All ye highfliers of the feathered race,
  Swallows and curlews!
Here's the top-peak! the multitude below
  Live, for they can there.
This man decided not to Live but Know –
  Bury this man there?
Here – here's his place, where meteors shoot, clouds form,
  Lightnings are loosened,
Stars come and go! let joy break with the storm –
  Peace let the dew send!
Lofty designs must close in like effects:
  Loftily lying,

Leave him – still loftier than the world suspects,
    Living and dying.

ARTHUR HUGH CLOUGH
(1819–1861)

The Latest Decalogue

Thou shalt have one God only; who
Would be at the expense of two?
No graven images may be
Worshipped, except the currency:
Swear not at all; for, for thy curse
Thine enemy is none the worse:
At church on Sunday to attend
Will serve to keep the world thy friend:
Honour thy parents; that is, all
From whom advancement may befall:
Thou shalt not kill; but need'st not strive
Officiously to keep alive:
Do not adultery commit;
Advantage rarely comes of it:
Thou shalt not steal; an empty feat,
When it's so lucrative to cheat:
Bear not false witness; let the lie
Have time on its own wings to fly:
Thou shalt not covet; but tradition
Approves all forms of competition.

The sum of all is, thou shalt love,
If anybody, God above:
At any rate shall never labour
More than thyself to love thy neighbour.

MATTHEW ARNOLD
(1822–1888)

Rugby Chapel
November, 1857

Coldly, sadly descends
The autumn evening. The Field
Strewn with its dank yellow drifts
Of wither'd leaves, and the elms,
Fade into dimness apace,
Silent; – hardly a shout
From a few boys late at their play!
The lights come out in the street,
In the school-room windows; but cold,
Solemn, unlighted, austere,
Through the gathering darkness, arise
The Chapel walls, in whose bound
Thou, my father! art laid.

There thou dost lie, in the gloom
Of the autumn evening. But ah!
That word, *gloom,* to my mind
Brings thee back in the light
Of thy radiant vigour again!
In the gloom of November we pass'd
Days not of gloom at thy side;
Seasons impair'd not the ray
Of thine even cheerfulness clear.
Such thou wast; and I stand
In the autumn evening, and think
Of bygone autumns with thee.

Fifteen years have gone round
Since thou arosest to tread,
In the summer morning, the road
Of death, at a call unforeseen,
Sudden. For fifteen years,
We who till then in thy shade
Rested as under the boughs
Of a mighty oak, have endured
Sunshine and rain as we might,
Bare, unshaded, alone,
Lacking the shelter of thee.

O strong soul, by what shore
Tarriest thou now? For that force,
Surely, has not been left vain!
Somewhere, surely, afar,
In the sounding labour-house vast
Of being, is practised that strength,
Zealous, beneficent, firm!

Yes, in some far-shining sphere,
Conscious or not of the past,
Still thou performest the word
Of the Spirit in whom thou dost live,
Prompt, unwearied, as here!
Still thou upraisest with zeal
The humble good from the ground,
Sternly repressest the bad.
Still, like a trumpet, dost rouse
Those who with half-open eyes
Tread the border-land dim
'Twixt vice and virtue; reviv'st,
Succourest; – this was thy work,
This was thy life upon earth.

What is the course of the life
Of mortal men on the earth? –
Most men eddy about
Here and there – eat and drink,
Chatter and love and hate,
Gather and squander, are raised

Aloft, are hurl'd in the dust,
Striving blindly, achieving
Nothing; and, then they die –
Perish ; and no one asks
Who or what they have been,
More than he asks what waves
In the moonlit solitudes mild
Of the midmost Ocean, have swell'd,
Foam'd for a moment, and gone.

And there are some, whom a thirst
Ardent, unquenchable, fires,
Not with the crowd to be spent,
Not without aim to go round
In an eddy of purposeless dust,
Effort unmeaning and vain.
Ah yes, some of us strive
Not without action to die
Fruitless, but something to snatch
From dull oblivion, nor all
Glut the devouring grave!
We, we have chosen our path –
Path to a clear-purposed goal,
Path of advance! but it leads
A long, steep journey, through sunk
Gorges, o'er mountains in snow!
Cheerful, with friends, we set forth;
Then, on the height, comes the storm!
Thunder crashes from rock
To rock, the cataracts reply;
Lightnings dazzle our eyes;
Roaring torrents have breach'd
The track, the stream-bed descends
In the place where the wayfarer once
Planted his footstep – the spray
Boils o'er its borders; aloft,
The unseen snow-beds dislodge
Their hanging ruin; – alas,
Havoc is made in our train!
Friends who set forth at our side

Falter, are lost in the storm!
We, we only, are left!
With frowning foreheads, with lips
Sternly compress'd, we strain on,
On – and at nightfall, at last,
Come to the end of our way,
To the lonely inn 'mid the rocks;
Where the gaunt and taciturn Host
Stands on the threshold, the wind
Shaking his thin white hairs –
Holds his lantern to scan
Our storm-beat figures, and asks:
Whom in our party we bring?
Whom we have left in the snow?

Sadly we answer: We bring
Only ourselves; we lost
Sight of the rest in the storm.
Hardly ourselves we fought through,
Stripp'd, without friends, as we are.
Friends, companions, and train
The avalanche swept from our side.

But thou would'st not *alone*
Be saved, my father! *alone*
Conquer and come to thy goal,
Leaving the rest in the wild.
We were weary, and we
Fearful, and we, in our march,
Fain to drop down and to die.
Still thou turnedst, and still
Beckonedst the trembler, and still
Gavest the weary thy hand!
If, in the paths of the world,
Stones might have wounded thy feet,
Toil or dejection have tried
Thy spirit, of that we saw
Nothing! to us thou wert still
Cheerful, and helpful, and firm.
Therefore to thee it was given

Many to save with thyself;
And, at the end of thy day,
O faithful shepherd! to come,
Bringing thy sheep in thy hand.

And through thee I believe
In the noble and great who are gone;
Pure souls honour'd and blest
By former ages, who else –
Such, so soulless, so poor,
Is the ace of men whom I see –
Seem'd but a dream of the heart,
Seem'd but a cry of desire.
Yes! I believe that there lived
Others like thee in the past,
Not like the men of the crowd
Who all round me to-day
Bluster or cringe, and make life
Hideous, and arid, and vile;
But souls temper'd with fire,
Fervent, heroic, and good,
Helpers and friends of mankind.

Servants of God! – or sons
Shall I not call you? because
Not as servants ye knew
Your Father's innermost mind,
His, who unwillingly sees
One of his little ones lost –
Yours is the praise, if mankind
Hath not as yet in its march
Fainted, and fallen, and died!

See! in the rocks of the world
Marches the host of mankind,
A feeble, wavering line.
Where are they tending? – A God
Marshall'd them, gave them their goal –
Ah, but the way is so long!
Years they have been in the wild!
Sore thirst plagues them; the rocks,

Rising all round, overawe.
Factions divide them; their host
Threatens to break, to dissolve.
Ah, keep, keep them combined!
Else, of the myriads who fill
That army, not one shall arrive!
Sole they shall stray; in the rocks
Labour for ever in vain,
Die one by one in the waste.

Then, in such hour of need
Of your fainting, dispirited race,
Ye, like angels, appear,
Radiant with ardour divine.
Beacons of hope, ye appear!
Languor is not in your heart,
Weakness is not in your word,
Weariness not on your brow.

Ye alight in our van; at your voice,
Panic, despair, flee away.
Ye move through the ranks, recall
The stragglers, refresh the outworn,
Praise, re-inspire the brave.
Order, courage, return.
Eyes rekindling, and prayers,
Follow your steps as ye go.
Ye fill up the gaps in our files,
Strengthen the wavering line,
Stablish, continue our march,
On, to the bound of the waste,
On, to the City of God.

Dover Beach

The sea is calm to-night,
The tide is full, the moon lies fair
Upon the Straits ; – on the French coast, the light
Gleams, and is gone; the cliffs of England stand,
Glimmering and vast, out in the tranquil bay.
Come to the window, sweet is the night air!
Only, from the long line of spray
Where the ebb meets the moon-blanch'd sand,
Listen! you hear the grating roar
Of pebbles which the waves suck back, and fling,
At their return, up the high strand,
Begin, and cease, and then again begin,
With tremulous cadence slow, and bring
The eternal note of sadness in.

   Sophocles long ago
Heard it on the Aegean, and it brought
Into his mind the turbid ebb and flow
Of human misery; we
Find also in the sound a thought,
Hearing it by this distant northern sea.

The sea of faith
Was once, too, at the full, and round earth's shore
Lay like the folds of a bright girdle furl'd;
But now I only hear
Its melancholy, long, withdrawing roar,
Retreating to the breath
Of the night-wind down the vast edges drear
And naked shingles of the world.

Ah, love, let us be true
To one another! for the world, which seems
To lie before us like a land of dreams,
So various, so beautiful, so new,
Hath really neither joy, nor love, nor light,
Nor certitude, nor peace, nor help for pain;
And we are here as on a darkling plain
Swept with confused alarms of struggle and flight,
Where ignorant armies clash by night.

THOMAS HARDY
(1839–1928)

The Choirmaster's Burial

He often would ask us
That, when he died,
After playing so many
To their last rest,
If out of us any
Should here abide,
And it would not task us,
We would with our lutes
Play over him
By his grave-brim
The psalm he liked best –
The one whose sense suits
'Mount Ephraim' –
And perhaps we should seem
To him, in Death's dream,
Like the seraphim.

As soon as I knew
That his spirit was gone
I thought this his due,
And spoke thereupon.
'I think,' said the vicar,
'A read service quicker
Than viols out-of-doors
In these frosts and hoars.
That old-fashioned way
Requires a fine day,
And it seems to me
It had better not be.'

Hence, that afternoon,
Though never knew he
That his wish could not be,
To get through it faster
They buried the master
Without any tune.

But 'twas said that, when
At the dead of next night
The vicar looked out,
There struck on his ken
Thronged roundabout,
Where the frost was graying
The headstoned grass,
A band all in white
Like the saints in church-glass,
Singing and playing
The ancient stave
By the choirmaster's grave.

Such the tenor man told
When he had grown old.

A Church Romance

(Mellstock: circa 1835)

She turned in the high pew, until her sight
Swept the west gallery, and caught its row
Of music-men with viol, book, and bow
Against the sinking sad tower-window light.

She turned again; and in her pride's despite
One strenuous viol's inspirer seemed to throw
A message from his string to her below,
Which said: 'I claim thee as my own forthright!'

Thus their hearts' bond began, in due time signed.
And long years thence, when Age had scared Romance,
At some old attitude of his or glance

That gallery-scene would break upon her mind,
With him as minstrel, ardent, young, and trim,
Bowing 'New Sabbath' or 'Mount Ephraim'.

Afternoon Service at Mellstock

(circa 1850)

On afternoons of drowsy calm
    We stood in the panelled pew,
Singing one-voiced a Tate-and-Brady psalm
    To the tune of 'Cambridge New'.

We watched the elms, we watched the rooks,
    The clouds upon the breeze,
Between the whiles of glancing at our books,
    And swaying like the trees.

So mindless were those outpourings! –
    Though I am not aware
That I have gained by subtle thought on things
    Since we stood psalming there.

The Oxen

Christmas Eve, and twelve of the clock.
    'Now they are all on their knees,'
An elder said as we sat in a flock
    By the embers in hearthside ease.

We pictured the meek mild creatures where
    They dwelt in their strawy pen,
Nor did it occur to one of us there
    To doubt they were kneeling then.

So fair a fancy few would weave
    In these years! Yet, I feel,
If someone said on Christmas Eve,
    'Come; see the oxen kneel

'In the lonely barton by yonder coomb
    Our childhood used to know,'
I should go with him in the gloom,
    Hoping it might be so.

1915

Channel Firing

That night your great guns, unawares,
Shook all our coffins as we lay,
And broke the chancel window-squares,
We thought it was the Judgment-day

And sat upright. While drearisome
Arose the howl of wakened hounds:
The mouse let fall the altar-crumb,
The worms drew back into the mounds,

The glebe cow drooled. Till God called, 'No;
It's gunnery practice out at sea
Just as before you went below;
The world is as it used to be:

'All nations striving strong to make
Red war yet redder. Mad as hatters
They do no more for Christès sake
Than you who are helpless in such matters.

'That this is not the judgment-hour
For some of them's a blessed thing,
For if it were they'd have to scour
Hell's floor for so much threatening . . .

'Ha, ha. It will be warmer when
I blow the trumpet (if indeed
I ever do; for you are men,
And rest eternal sorely need).'

So down we lay again. 'I wonder,
Will the world ever saner be,'
Said one, 'than when He sent us under
In our indifferent century!'

And many a skeleton shook his head.
'Instead of preaching forty year,'
My neighbour Parson Thirdly said,
'I wish I had stuck to pipes and beer.'

Again the guns disturbed the hour,
Roaring their readiness to avenge,
As far inland as Stourton Tower,
And Camelot, and starlit Stonehenge.

April 1914

G. M. HOPKINS
(1844–1889)

Heaven-Haven

A nun takes the veil

I have desired to go
    Where springs not fail,
To fields where flies no sharp and sided hail
    And a few lilies blow.

And I have asked to be
    Where no storms come,
Where the green swell is in the havens dumb,
    And out of the swing of the sea.

The Wreck of the Deutschland

To the
happy memory of five Franciscan nuns
exiles by the Falck Laws
drowned between midnight and morning of
Dec. 7th, 1875

PART THE FIRST

1

Thou mastering me
God! giver of breath and bread;
World's strand, sway of the sea;
Lord of living and dead;
Thou hast bound bones and veins in me, fastened me flesh,
And after it almost unmade, what with dread,
Thy doing: and dost thou touch me afresh?
Over again I feel thy finger and find thee.

2

I did say yes
O at lightning and lashed rod;
Thou heardst me truer than tongue confess
Thy terror, O Christ, O God;
Thou knowest the walls, altar and hour and night:
The swoon of a heart that the sweep and the hurl of thee trod
Hard down with a horror of height:
And the midriff astrain with leaning of, laced with fire of stress.

3

The frown of his face
Before me, the hurtle of hell
Behind, where, where was a, where was a place?
I whirled out wings that spell
And fled with a fling of the heart to the heart of the Host.
My heart, but you were dovewinged, I can tell,
Carrier-witted, I am bold to boast,
To flash from the flame to the flame then, tower from the grace to the
grace.

4

I am soft sift
In an hourglass — at the wall
Fast, but mined with a motion, a drift,
And it crowds and it combs to the fall;
I steady as a water in a well, to a poise, to a pane,
But roped with, always, all the way down from the tall
Fells or flanks of the voel, a vein
Of the gospel proffer, a pressure, a principle, Christ's gift.

5

I kiss my hand
To the stars, lovely-asunder
Starlight, wafting him out of it; and
Glow, glory in thunder;
Kiss my hand to the dappled-with-damson west:
Since, tho' he is under the world's splendour and wonder,
His mystery must be instressed, stressed;
For I greet him the days I meet him, and bless when I understand.

6

Not out of his bliss
Springs the stress felt
Nor first from heaven (and few know this)
Swings the stroke dealt —
Stroke and a stress that stars and storms deliver,
That guilt is hushed by, hearts are flushed by and melt —
But it rides time like riding a river
(And here the faithful waver, the faithless fable and miss).

7

It dates from day
Of his going in Galilee;
Warm-laid grave of a womb-life grey;
Manger, maiden's knee;
The dense and the driven Passion, and frightful sweat:
Thence the discharge of it, there its swelling to be,
Though felt before, though in high flood yet —
What none would have known of it, only the heart, being hard at bay,

8

Is out with it! Oh,
We lash with the best or worst
Word last! How a lush-kept plush-capped sloe
Will, mouthed to flesh-burst,
Gush! – flush the man, the being with it, sour or sweet,
Brim, in a flash, full! – Hither then, last or first,
To hero of Calvary, Christ,'s feet –
Never ask if meaning it, wanting it, warned of it – men go.

9

Be adored among men,
God, three-numberèd form;
Wring thy rebel, dogged in den,
Man's malice, with wrecking and storm.
Beyond saying sweet, past telling of tongue,
Thou art lightning and love, I found it, a winter and warm;
Father and fondler of heart thou hast wrung:
Hast thy dark descending and most art merciful then.

10

With an anvil-ding
And with fire in him forge thy will
Or rather, rather then, stealing as Spring
Through him, melt him but master him still:
Whether at once, as once at a crash Paul,
Or as Austin, a lingering-out swéet skíll,
Make mercy in all of us, out of us all
Mastery, but be adored, but be adored King.

PART THE SECOND

11

'Some find me a sword; some
        The flange and the rail; flame,
Fang, or flood' goes Death on drum,
        And storms bugle his fame.
But wé dream we are rooted in earth – Dust!
Flesh falls within sight of us, we, though our flower the same,
        Wave with the meadow, forget that there must
The sour scythe cringe, and the blear share come.

12

On Saturday sailed from Bremen,
        American-outward-bound,
Take settler and seamen, tell men with women,
        Two hundred souls in the round –
O Father, not under thy feathers nor ever as guessing
The goal was a shoal, of a fourth the doom to be drowned;
        Yet did the dark side of the bay of thy blessing
Not vault them, the million of rounds of thy mercy not reeve even
    them in?

13

Into the snows she sweeps,
        Hurling the haven behind,
The Deutschland, on Sunday; and so the sky keeps,
        For the infinite air is unkind,
And the sea flint-flake, black-backed in the regular blow,
Sitting Eastnortheast, in cursed quarter, the wind;
        Wiry and white-fiery and whirlwind-swivellèd snow
Spins to the widow-making unchilding unfathering deeps.

14

She drove in the dark to leeward,
    She struck – not a reef or a rock
  But the combs of a smother of sand: night drew her
    Dead to the Kentish Knock;
And she beat the bank down with her bows and the ride of her
    keel;
The breakers rolled on her beam with ruinous shock;
    And canvas and compass, the whorl and the wheel
Idle for ever to waft her or wind her with, these she endured.

15

Hope had grown grey hairs,
    Hope had mourning on,
  Trenched with tears, carved with cares,
    Hope was twelve hours gone;
And frightful a nightfall folded rueful a day
Nor rescue, only rocket and lightship, shone,
    And lives at last were washing away:
To the shrouds they took, – they shook in the hurling and horrible
    airs.

16

One stirred from the rigging to save
    The wild woman-kind below,
  With a rope's end round the man, handy and brave –
    He was pitched to his death at a blow,
For all his dreadnought breast and braids of thew:
They could tell him for hours, dandled the to and fro
    Through the cobbled foam-fleece. What could he do
With the burl of the fountains of air, buck and the flood of the wave?

17

They fought with God's cold –
And they could not and fell to the deck
(Crushed them) or water (and drowned them) or rolled
With the sea-romp over the wreck.
Night roared, with the heart-break hearing a heart-broke rabble,
The woman's wailing, the crying of child without check –
Till a lioness arose breasting the babble,
A prophetess towered in the tumult, a virginal tongue told.

18

Ah, touched in your bower of bone,
Are you! turned for an exquisite smart,
Have you! make words break from me here all alone,
Do you! – mother of being in me, heart.
O unteachably after evil, but uttering truth,
Why, tears! is it? tears; such a melting, a madrigal start!
Never-eldering revel and river of youth,
What can it be, this glee? the good you have there of your own?

19

Sister, a sister calling
A master, her master and mine! –
And the inboard seas run swirling and hawling;
The rash smart sloggering brine
Blinds her; but she that weather sees one thing, one;
Has one fetch in her: she rears herself to divine
Ears, and the call of the tall nun
To the men in the tops and the tackle rode over the storm's brawling.

20

She was first of a five and came
Of a coifèd sisterhood.
(O Deutschland, double a desperate name!
O world wide of its good!
But Gertrude, lily, and Luther, are two of a town,
Christ's lily and beast of the waste wood:
From life's dawn it is drawn down,
Abel is Cain's brother and breasts they have sucked the same.)

21

Loathed for a love men knew in them,
Banned by the land of their birth,
Rhine refused them, Thames would ruin them;
Surf, snow, river and earth
Gnashed: but thou art above, thou Orion of light;
Thy unchancelling poising palms were weighing the worth,
Thou martyr-master: in thy sight
Storm flakes were scroll-leaved flowers, lily showers – sweet heaven
was astrew in them.

22

Five! the finding and sake
And cipher of suffering Christ.
Mark, the mark is of man's make
And the word of it Sacrificed.
But he scores it in scarlet himself on his own bespoken,
Before-time-taken, dearest prizèd and priced –
Stigma, signal, cinquefoil token
For lettering of the lamb's fleece, ruddying of the rose-flake.

23

Joy fall to thee, father Francis,
Drawn to the Life that died;
With the gnarls of the nails in them, niche of the lance, his
Lovescape crucified
And seal of his seraph-arrival! and these thy daughters
And five-livèd and leavèd favour and pride,
Are sisterly sealed in wild waters,
To bathe in his fall-gold mercies, to breathe in his all-fire glances.

24

Away in the loveable west,
On a pastoral forehead of Wales,
I was under a roof here, I was at rest,
And they the prey of the gales;
She to the black-about air, to the breaker, the thickly
Falling flakes, to the throng that catches and quails
Was calling 'O Christ, Christ, come quickly':
The cross to her she calls Christ to her, christens her wild-worst Best.

25

The majesty! what did she mean?
Breathe, arch and original Breath.
Is it love in her of the being as her lover had been?
Breathe, body of lovely Death.
They were else-minded then, altogether, the men
Woke thee with a *We are perishing* in the weather of
Gennesareth.
Or is that she cried for the crown then,
The keener to come at the comfort for feeling the combating keen?

26

For how to the heart's cheering
The down-dugged ground-hugged grey
Hovers off, the jay-blue heavens appearing
Of pied and peeled May!
Blue-beating and hoary-glow height; or night, still higher,
With belled fire and the moth-soft Milky Way,
What by your measure is the heaven of desire,
The treasure never eyesight got, nor was ever guessed what for the
hearing?

27

No, but it was not these.
The jading and jar of the cart,
Time's tasking, it is fathers that asking for ease
Of the sodden-with-its-sorrowing heart,
Not danger, electrical horror; then further it finds
The appealing of the Passion is tenderer in prayer apart:
Other, I gather, in measure her mind's
Burden, in wind's burly and beat of endragonèd seas.

28

But how shall I . . . make me room there:
Reach me a . . . Fancy, come faster –
Strike you the sight of it? look at it loom there,
Thing that she . . . There then! the Master,
Ipse, the only one, Christ, King, Head:
He was to cure the extremity where he had cast her;
Do, deal, lord it with living and dead;
Let him ride, her pride, in his triumph, despatch and have done with
his doom there.

29

Ah! there was a heart right!
There was single eye!
Read the unshapeable shock night
And knew the who and the why;
Wording it how but by him that present and past,
Heaven and earth are word of, worded by? –
The Simon Peter of a soul! to the blast
Tarpeïan-fast, but a blown beacon of light.

30

Jesu, heart's light,
Jesu, maid's son,
What was the feast followed the night
Thou hadst glory of this nun? –
Feast of the one woman without stain.
For so conceivèd, so to conceive thee is done;
But here was heart-throe, birth of a brain,
Word, that heard and kept thee and uttered thee outright.

31

Well, she has thee for the pain, for the
Patience; but pity of the rest of them!
Heart, go and bleed at a bitterer vein for the
Comfortless unconfessed of them –
No not uncomforted: lovely-felicitous Providence
Finger of a tender of, O of a feathery delicacy, the breast of the
Maiden could obey so, be a bell to, ring of it, and
Startle the poor sheep back! is the shipwrack then a harvest, does
tempest carry the grain for thee?

32

I admire thee, master of the tides,
    Of the Yore-flood, of the year's fall;
  The recurb and the recovery of the gulf's sides,
      The girth of it and the wharf of it and the wall;
 Stanching, quenching ocean of a motionable mind;
  Ground of being, and granite of it: past all
    Grasp God, thronèd behind
Death with a sovereignty that heeds but hides, bodes but abides;

33

With a mercy that outrides
    The all of water, an ark
  For the listener; for the lingerer with a love glides
    Lower than death and the dark;
 A vein for the visiting of the past-prayer, pent in prison,
  The-last-breath penitent spirits – the uttermost mark
    Our passion-plungèd giant risen,
The Christ of the Father compassionate, fetched in the storm of his
  strides.

34

Now burn, new born to the world,
    Double-naturèd name,
  The heaven-flung, heart-fleshed, maiden-furled
    Miracle-in-Mary-of-flame,
 Mid-numberèd he in three of the thunder-throne!
 Not a dooms-day dazzle in his coming nor dark as he came;
    Kind, but royally reclaiming his own;
A released shower, let flash to the shire, not a lightning of fire
  hard-hurled.

35

Dame, at our door
Drowned, and among our shoals,
Remember us in the roads, the heaven-haven of the reward:
Our King back, Oh, upon English souls!
Let him easter in us, be a dayspring to the dimness of us, be a
crimson-cresseted east,
More brightening her, rare-dear Britain, as his reign rolls,
Pride, rose, prince, hero of us, high-priest,
Our hearts' charity's hearth's fire, our thoughts' chivalry's throng's
Lord.

The Windhover

To Christ our Lord

I caught this morning morning's minion, king—
dom of daylight's dauphin, dapple-dawn-drawn Falcon, in
his riding
Of the rolling level underneath him steady air, and striding
High there, how he rung upon the rein of a wimpling wing
In his ecstasy! then off, off forth on swing,
As a skate's heel sweeps smooth on a bow-bend: the hurl and
gliding
Rebuffed the big wind. My heart in hiding
Stirred for a bird, – the achieve of, the mastery of the thing!

Brute beauty and valour and act, oh, air, pride, plume, here
Buckle! AND the fire that breaks from thee then, a billion
Times told lovelier, more dangerous, O my chevalier!

No wonder of it: shéer plód makes plough down sillion
Shine, and blue-bleak embers, ah my dear,
Fall, gall themselves, and gash gold-vermilion.

Hurrahing in Harvest

Summer ends now; now, barbarous in beauty, the stooks rise
Around; up above, what wind-walks! what lovely
     behaviour
Of silk-sack clouds! has wilder, wilful-wavier
Meal-drift moulded ever and melted across skies?

I walk, I lift up, I lift up heart, eyes,
Down all that glory in the heavens to glean our Saviour;
And, éyes, heárt, what looks, what lips yet gave you a
Rapturous love's greeting of realer, of rounder replies?

And the azurous hung hills are his world-wielding shoulder
Majestic – as a stallion stalwart, very-violet-sweet! –
These things, these things were here and but the beholder
Wanting; which two when they once meet,
  The heart rears wings bold and bolder
And hurls for him, O half hurls earth for him off under his
     feet.

The May Magnificat

    May is Mary's month, and I
    Muse at that and wonder why:
        Her feasts follow reason,
        Dated due to season –

    Candlemas, Lady Day;
    But the Lady Month, May,
        Why fasten that upon her,
        With a feasting in her honour?

    Is it only its being brighter
    Than the most are must delight her?
        Is it opportunest
        And flowers finds soonest?

Ask of her, the mighty mother:
Her reply puts this other
    Question: What is Spring? –
    Growth in everything –

Flesh and fleece, fur and feather,
Grass and greenworld all together;
    Star-eyed strawberry-breasted
    Throstle above her nested

Cluster of bulge blue eggs thin
Forms and warms the life within;
    And bird and blossom swell
    In sod or sheath or shell.

All things rising, all things sizing
Mary sees, sympathising
    With that world of good,
    Nature's motherhood.

Their magnifying of each its kind
With delight calls to mind
    How she did in her stored
    Magnify the Lord.

Well but there was more than this:
Spring's universal bliss
    Much, had much to say
    To offering Mary May.

When drop-of-blood-and-foam-dapple
Bloom lights the orchard-apple
    And thicket and thorp are merry
    With silver-surfèd cherry

And azuring-over greybell makes
Wood banks and brakes wash wet like lakes
    And magic cuckoocall
    Caps, clears, and clinches all –

This ecstasy all through mothering earth
Tells Mary her mirth till Christ's birth
    To remember and exultation
    In God who was her salvation.

Duns Scotus's Oxford

Towery city and branchy between towers;
Cuckoo-echoing, bell-swarmèd, lark-charmèd, rook-racked,
  river-rounded;
The dapple-eared lily below thee; that country and town did
Once encounter in, here coped and poisèd powers;

Thou hast a base and brickish skirt there, sours
That neighbour-nature thy grey beauty is grounded
Best in; graceless growth, thou hast confounded
Rural rural keeping – folk, flocks, and flowers.

Yet ah! this air I gather and I release.
He lived on; these weeds and waters, these walls are what
He haunted who of all men most sways my spirits to peace;

Of realty the rarest-veinèd unraveller; a not
Rivalled insight, be rival Italy or Greece;
Who fired France for Mary without spot.

Felix Randal

Felix Randal the farrier, O is he dead then? my duty all ended,
Who have watched his mould of man, big-boned and hardy-handsome
Pining, pining, till time when reason rambled in it and some
Fatal four disorders, fleshed there, all contended?

Sickness broke him. Impatient, he cursed at first, but mended
Being anointed and all; though a heavenlier heart began some
Months earlier, since I had our sweet reprieve and ransom
Tendered to him. Ah well, God rest him all road ever he offended!

This seeing the sick endears them to us, us too it endears.
My tongue had taught thee comfort, touch had quenched thy tears,
Thy tears that touched my heart, child, Felix, poor Felix Randal;

How far from then forethought of, all thy more boisterous years,
When thou at the random grim forge, powerful amidst peers,
Didst fettle for the great grey drayhorse his bright and battering
  sandal!

'I wake and feel the fell of dark, not day'

I wake and feel the fell of dark, not day.
What hours, O what black hoürs we have spent
This night! what sights you, heart, saw; ways you went!
And more must, in yet longer light's delay.

With witness I speak this. But where I say
Hours I mean years, mean life. And my lament
Is cries countless, cries like dead letters sent
To dearest him that lives alas! away.

I am gall, I am heartburn. God's most deep decree
Bitter would have me taste: my taste was me;
Bones built in me, flesh filled, blood brimmed the curse.

Selfyeast of spirit a dull dough sours. I see
The lost are like this, and their scourge to be
As I am mine, their sweating selves; but worse.

'Thou art indeed just, Lord, if I contend'

*Justus quidem tu es, Domine, si disputem tecum; verumtamen
justa loquar ad te: Quare via impiorum prosperatur? &c.*

Thou art indeed just, Lord, if I contend
With thee; but, sir, so what I plead is just.
Why do sinners' ways prosper? and why must
Disappointment all I endeavour end?

Wert thou my enemy, O thou my friend,
How wouldst thou worse, I wonder, than thou dost
Defeat, thwart me? Oh, the sots and thralls of lust
Do in spare hours more thrive than I that spend,

Sir, life upon thy cause. See, banks and brakes
Now, leavèd how thick! lacèd they are again
With fretty chervil, look, and fresh wind shakes

Them; birds build – but not I build; no, but strain,
Time's eunuch, and not breed one work that wakes.
Mine, O thou lord of life, send my roots rain.

ROBERT BRIDGES
(1844–1930)

Johannes Milton, Senex

Scazons

Since I believe in God the Father Almighty,
Man's Maker and Judge, Overruler of Fortune,
'Twere strange should I praise anything and refuse Him praise,
Should love the creature forgetting the Crēator,
Nor unto Him ᵛin suff'ring and sorrow turn me:
Nay how could I withdraw me from ᵛHis embracing?

But since I have seen not, and cannot know Him,
Nor in my earthly temple apprehend rightly
His wisdom and the heav'nly purpose ēternal;
Therefore will I be bound to no studied system
Nor argument, nor with delusion enslave me,
Nor seek to pleáse Him in any foolish invention,
Which my spirit within me, that loveth beauty
And hateth evil, hath reprov'd as unworthy:

But I cherish my freedom in loving service,
Gratefully adoring for delight beyond asking
Or thinking, and in hours of anguish and darkness
Confiding always on ᵛHis excellent greatness.

W. B. YEATS
(1865–1939)

Calvary

PERSONS IN THE PLAY

Three Musicians (*their faces made up to resemble masks*)
Christ (*wearing a mask*)
Lazarus (*wearing a mask*)
Judas (*wearing a mask*)
Three Roman Soldiers (*their faces masked or made up to resemble masks*)

At the beginning of the play the First Musician comes to the front of the bare place, round three sides of which the audience are seated, with a folded cloth hanging from his joined hands. Two other Musicians come . . . one from either side, and unfold the cloth so that it shuts out the stage, and then fold it again, singing and moving rhythmically. They do the same at the end of the play, which enables the players to leave the stage unseen.

[*Song for the folding and unfolding of the cloth*]
First Musician.

> Motionless under the moon-beam,
> Up to his feathers in the stream;
> Although fish leap, the white heron
> Shivers in a dumbfounded dream.

Second Musician.

> God has not died for the white heron.

Third Musician.

> Although half famished he'll not dare
> Dip or do anything but stare
> Upon the glittering image of a heron,
> That now is lost and now is there.

Second Musician.

> God has not died for the white heron.

First Musician.

> But that the full is shortly gone
> And after that is crescent moon,
> It's certain that the moon-crazed heron
> Would be but fishes' diet soon.

Second Musician.
        God has not died for the white heron.
     [*The three Musicians are now seated by the drum, flute,
       and zither at the back of stage.*]
First Musician. The road to Calvary, and I beside it
  Upon an ancient stone. Good Friday's come,
  The day whereon Christ dreams His passion through.
  He climbs up hither but as a dreamer climbs.
  The cross that but exists because He dreams it
  Shortens His breath and wears away His strength.
  And now He stands amid a mocking crowd,
  Heavily breathing.
     [*A player with the mask of Christ and carrying a cross
       has entered and now stands leaning upon the cross.*]
               Those that are behind
  Climb on the shoulders of the men in front
  To shout their mockery: 'Work a miracle',
  Cries one, 'and save yourself'; another cries,
  'Call on your father now before your bones
  Have been picked bare by the great desert birds';
  Another cries, 'Call out with a loud voice
  And tell him that his son is cast away
  Amid the mockery of his enemies'.
                   [*Singing*]
        O, but the mockers' cry
        Makes my heart afraid,
        As though a flute of bone
        Taken from a heron's thigh,
        A heron crazed by the moon,
        Were cleverly, softly played.
                 [*Speaking*]
Who is this from whom the crowd has shrunk,
As though he had some look that terrified?
He has a deathly face, and yet he moves
Like a young foal that sees the hunt go by
And races in the field.
     [*A player with the mask of Lazarus has entered.*]
Lazarus.   He raised me up.
  I am the man that died and was raised up;
  I am called Lazarus.

Christng.   Seeing that you died,
    Lay in the tomb four days and were raised up,
    You will not mock at me.
Lazarus.   For four whole days
    I had been dead and I was lying still
    In an old comfortable mountain cavern
        When you came climbing there with a great crowd
    And dragged me to the light.
Christ.   I called your name:
    'Lazarus, come out', I said, and you came out
    Bound up in cloths, your face bound in a cloth.
Lazarus. You took my death, give me your death
        instead.
Christ. I gave you life.
Lazarus.   But death is what I ask.
    Alive I never could escape your love,
    And when I sickened towards my death I thought,
    'I'll to the desert, or chuckle in a corner,
    Mere ghost, a solitary thing.' I died
    And saw no more until I saw you stand
    In the opening of the tomb; 'Come out!' you called;
    You dragged me to the light as boys drag out
    A rabbit when they have have dug its hole away;
    And now with all the shouting at your heels
    You travel towards the death I am denied.
    And that is why I have hurried to this road
    And claimed your death.
Christ.   But I have conquered death,
    And all the dead shall be raised up again.
Lazarus. Then what I heard is true. I thought to die
    When my allotted years ran out again;
    And that, being gone, you could not hinder it;
    But now you will blind with light the solitude
    That death has made; you will disturb that corner
    Where I had thought I might lie safe for ever.
Christ. I do my Father's will.
Lazarus.   And not your own;
    And I was free four days, four days being dead.
    Climb up to Calvary, but turn your eyes
    From Lazarus that cannot find a tomb

Although he search all height and depth: make way,
Make way for Lazarus that must go search
Among the desert places where there is nothing
But howling wind and solitary birds.   [*He goes out.*]
First Musician. The crowd shrinks backward from the face that seems
Death-stricken and death-hungry still; and now
Martha, and those three Marys, and the rest
That live but in His love are gathered round Him.
He holds His right arm out, and on His arm
Their lips are pressed and their tears fall; and now
They cast them on the ground before His dirty
Blood-dabbled feet and clean them with their hair.

[*Sings*]

Take but His love away,
Their love becomes a feather
Of eagle, swan or gull,
Or a drowned heron's feather
Tossed hither and thither
Upon the bitter spray
And the moon at the full.

Christ. I felt their hair upon my feet a moment
And then they fled away – why have they fled?
Why has the street grown empty of a sudden
As though all fled in terror?
Judas [*who has just entered*].   I am Judas
That sold you for the thirty pieces of silver.
Christ. You were beside me every day, and saw
The dead raised up and blind men given their sight,
And all that I have said and taught you have known,
Yet doubt that I am God.
Judas.   I have not doubted;
I knew it from the first moment that I saw you;
I had no need of miracles to prove it.
Christ. And yet you have betrayed me.
Judas.   I have betrayed you
Because you seemed all-powerful.
Christ.   My Father
Even now, if I were but to whisper it,
Would break the world in His miraculous fury
To set me free.

Judas.   And is there not one man
   In the wide world that is not in your power?
Christ. My Father put all men into my hands.
Judas. That was the very thought that drove me wild.
   I could not bear to think you had but to whistle
   And I must do; but after that I thought,
   'Whatever man betrays Him will be free';
   And life grew bearable again. And now
   Is there a secret left I do not know,
   Knowing that if a man betrays a God
   He is the stronger of the two?
Christ.   But if
   'Twere the commandment of that God Himself,
   That God were still the stronger.
Judas.   When I planned it
   There was no live thing near me but a heron
   So full of itself that it seemed terrified.
Christ. But my betrayal was decreed that hour
   When the foundations of the world were laid.
Judas. It was decreed that somebody betray you –
   I'd thought of that – but not that I should do it,
   I the man Judas, born on such a day,
   In such a village, such and such his parents;
   Nor that I'd go with my old coat upon me
   To the High Priest, and chuckle to myself
   As people chuckle when alone, and do it
   For thirty pieces and no more, no less,
   And neither with a nod nor a sent message,
   But with a kiss upon your cheek. I did it,
   I, Judas, and no other man, and now
   You cannot even save me.
Christ.   Begone from me.
                  [*Three Roman Soldiers have entered.*]
First Roman Soldier. He has been chosen to hold up the
         cross.
            [*During what follows, Judas holds up the cross while
               Christ stands with His arms stretched out upon it.*]
Second Roman Soldier. We'll keep the rest away; they are too persistent;
   They are always wanting something.

Third Roman Soldier.　　　　Die in peace.
There's no one here but Judas and ourselves.
Christ. And who are you that ask your God for nothing?
Third Roman Soldier. We are the gamblers, and when you are dead
We'll settle who is to have that cloak of yours
By throwing dice.
Second Roman Soldier. Our dice were carved
Out of an old sheep's thigh at Ephesus.
First Roman Soldier. Although but one of us can win the cloak
That will not make us quarrel; what does it matter?
One day one loses and the next day wins.
Second Roman Soldier. Whatever happens is the best, we say,
So that it's unexpected.
Third Roman Soldier.　　　Had you sent
A crier through the world you had not found
More comfortable companions for a death-bed
Than three old gamblers that have asked for nothing.
First Roman Soldier. They say you're good and that you made the
world,
But it's no matter.
Second Roman Soldier. Come now; let us dance
The dance of the dice-throwers, for it may be
He cannot live much longer and has not seen it.
Third Roman Soldier. If he were but the God of dice he'd know it,
But he is not that God.
First Roman Soldier.　　　One thing is plain,
To know that he has nothing that we need
Must be a comfort to him.
Second Roman Soldier.　　　In the dance
We quarrel for a while, but settle it
By throwing dice, and after that, being friends,
Join hand to hand and wheel about the cross.

　　　　　　　　　　　　　　　　[They dance.]

Christ. My Father, why hast Thou forsaken Me?
　　　　[Song for the folding and unfolding of the cloth]
First Musician.
　　　Lonely the sea-bird lies at her rest,
　　　Blown like a dawn-blenched parcel of spray
　　　Upon the wind, or follows her prey
　　　Under a great wave's hollowing crest.

Second Musician.

    God has not appeared to the birds.

Third Musician.

    The ger-eagle has chosen his part

    In blue deep of the upper air

    Where one-eyed day can meet his stare;

    He is content with his savage heart.

Second Musician.

    God has not appeared to the birds.

First Musician.

    But where have last year's cygnets gone?

    The lake is empty; why do they fling

    White wing out beside white wing?

    What can a swan need but a swan?

Second Musician.

    God has not appeared to the birds.

ERNEST DOWSON
(1867–1900)

Extreme Unction

Upon the eyes, the lips, the feet,
    On all the passages of sense,
The atoning oil is spread with sweet
    Renewal of lost innocence.

The feet, that lately ran so fast
    To meet desire, are soothly sealed;
The eyes, that were so often cast
    On vanity, are touched and healed.

From troublous sights and sounds set free;
    In such a twilight hour of breath,
Shall one retrace his life, or see,
    Through shadows, the true face of death?

Vials of mercy! Sacring oils!
   I know not where nor when I come,
Nor through what wanderings and toils,
   To crave of you Viaticum.

Yet, when the walls of flesh grow weak,
   In such an hour, it well may be,
Through mist and darkness, light will break,
   And each anointed sense will see.

J. M. SYNGE
(1871–1909)

Prayer of the Old Woman, Villon's Mother

Mother of God that's Lady of the Heavens, take myself, the poor sinner, the way I'll be along with them that's chosen.

Let you say to your own Son that He'd have a right to forgive my share of sins, when it's the like He's done, many's the day, with big and famous sinners. I'm a poor aged woman, was never at school, and so no scholar with letters, but I've seen pictures in the Chapel with Paradise on one side, and harps and pipes in it, and the place on the other side, where sinners do be boiled in torment; the one gave me great joy, the other a great fright and scaring, let me have the good place, Mother of God, and it's in your faith I'll live always.

It's yourself that bore Jesus, that has no end or death, and He the Lord Almighty, that took our weakness and gave Himself to sorrows, a young and gentle man. It's Himself is our Lord surely, and it's in that faith I'll live always.

D. H. LAWRENCE
(1885–1930)

Fatality

No one, not even God, can put back a leaf on to a tree
once it has fallen off.

And no one, not God nor Christ nor any other
can put back a human life into connection with the living cosmos
once the connection has been broken
and the person has become finally self-centred.

Death alone, through the long processes of disintegration
can melt the detached life back
through the dark Hades at the roots of the tree
into the circulating sap, once more, of the tree of life.

Retort to Jesus

And whoever forces himself to love anybody
begets a murderer in his own body.

Pax

All that matters is to be at one with the living God
to be a creature in the house of the God of Life.

Like a cat asleep on a chair
at peace, in peace
and at one with the master of the house, with the mistress,
at home, at home in the house of the living,
sleeping on the hearth, and yawning before the fire.

Sleeping on the hearth of the living world
yawning at home before the fire of life
feeling the presence of the living God
like a great reassurance
a deep calm in the heart
a presence
as of the master sitting at the board
in his own and greater being,
in the house of life.

Lord's Prayer

For thine is the kingdom
the power, and the glory —

Hallowed be thy name, then
Thou who art nameless —

Give me, Oh give me
besides my daily bread
my kingdom, my power, and my glory.

All things that turn to thee
have their kingdom, their power, and their glory.

like the kingdom of the nightingale at twilight
whose power and glory I have often heard and felt.

Like the kingdom of the fox in the dark
yapping in his power and his glory
which is death to the goose.

Like the power and the glory of the goose in the mist
honking over the lake.

And I, a naked man, calling
calling to thee for my mana,
my kingdom, my power, and my glory.

D. H. LAWRENCE

'My name is Jesus'

My name is Jesus, I am Mary's son,
I am coming home,
My mother the Moon is dark.

Brother, Quetzalcoatl,
Hold back the wild hot sun.
Bind him with shadow while I pass.
Let me come home.

Quetzalcoatl Looks Down on Mexico

Jesus had gone far up the dark slope, when he looked back.
Quetzalcoatl, my brother! he called. Send me my images,
And the images of my mother, and the images of my saints.
Send me them by the swift way, the way of the sparks,
That I may hold them like memories in my arms when I go to sleep.

And Quetzalcoatl called back: I will do it.

Then he laughed, seeing the sun dart fiercely at him.
He put up his hand, and held back the sun with his shadow.

So he passed the yellow one, who lashed like a dragon in vain.
And having passed the yellow one, he saw the earth beneath.
And he saw Mexico lying like a dark woman with white breast-tips.

Wondering he stepped nearer, and looked at her,
At her trains, at her railways and her automobiles,
At her cities of stone and her huts of straw.
And he said: Surely this looks very curious!

He sat within the hollow of a cloud, and saw the men that worked in
    the fields, with foreign overseers.
He saw the men that were blind, reeling with aguardiente.
He saw the women that were not clean.
He saw the hearts of them all, that were black, and heavy, with a stone
    of anger at the bottom.

Surely, he said, this is a curious people I have found!

So leaning forward on his cloud, he said to himself:
I will call to them.
Hola! Hola! Mexicanos! Glance away a moment towards me.
Just turn your eyes this way, Mexicanos!

They turned not at all, they glanced not one his way.

Holala! Mexicanos! Holala!

They have gone stone deaf! he said.

So he blew down on them, to blow his breath in their faces.
But in the weight of their stupefaction, none of them knew.

Holala! What a pretty people!
All gone stupefied!

A falling star was running like a white dog over a plain.
He whistled to it loudly, twice, till it fell to his hand.
In his hand it lay and went dark.
It was the Stone of Change.

This is the stone of change! he said.

So he tossed it awhile in his hand, and played with it.
Then suddenly he spied the old lake, and he threw it in.
It fell in.
And two men looked up.

Holala! he said. *Mexicanos!*
Are there two of you awake?
So he laughed, and one heard him laughing.

Why are you laughing? asked the first man of Quetzalcoatl.

I hear the voice of my First Man ask me why I am laughing? *Holala,*
Mexicanos! It is funny!
To see them so glum and so lumpish!

Hey! First Man of my name! Hark here!
Here is my sign.
Get a place ready for me.

Send Jesus his images back, Mary and the saints and all.
Wash yourself, and rub oil in your skin.
On the seventh day, let every man wash himself, and put oil on his
    skin; let every woman.
Let him have no animal walk on his body, nor through the shadow of
    his hair. Say the same to the women.
Tell them they all are fools, that I'm laughing at them.

The first thing I did when I saw them, was to laugh at the sight of
    such fools.
Such lumps, such frogs with stones in their bellies.
Tell them they are like frogs with stones in their bellies, can't hop!
Tell them they must get the stones out of their bellies,

Get rid of their heaviness,
Their lumpishness,
Or I'll smother them all.

I'll shake the earth, and swallow them up, with their cities.
I'll send fire and ashes upon them, and smother them all.
I'll turn their blood like sour milk rotten with thunder,
They will bleed rotten blood, in pestilence.
Even their bones shall crumble.

Tell them so, First Man of my Name.

For the sun and the moon are alive, and watching with gleaming eyes.
And the earth is alive, and ready to shake off his fleas.
And the stars are ready with stones to throw in the faces of men.
And the air that blows good breath in the nostrils of people and beasts
Is ready to blow bad breath upon them, to perish them all.

The stars and the earth and the sun and the moon and the winds
Are about to dance the war dance round you, men!
When I say the word, they will start.
For sun and stars and earth and the very rains are weary
Of tossing and rolling the substance of life to your lips.
They are saying to one another: Let us make an end
Of those ill-smelling tribes of men, these frogs that can't jump,
These cocks that can't crow
These pigs that can't grunt
This flesh that smells
These words that are all flat
These money vermin.

These white men, and red men, and yellow men, and brown men, and
   black men
That are neither white, nor red, nor yellow, nor brown, nor black
But everyone of them dirtyish.
Let us have a spring cleaning in the world.

For men upon the body of the earth are like lice,
Devouring the earth into sores.
This is what stars and sun and earth and moon and winds and rain
Are discussing with one another; they are making ready to start.
So tell the men I am coming to,
To make themselves clean, inside and out.
To roll the grave-stone off their souls, from the cave of their bellies,
To prepare to be men.

Or else prepare for the other things.

ROBERT GRAVES
(b.1885)

In the Wilderness

He, of his gentleness,
Thirsting and hungering
Walked in the wilderness;
Soft words of grace he spoke
Unto lost desert-folk
That listened wondering.
He heard the bittern call
From ruined palace-wall,
Answered him brotherly;
He held communion
With the she-pelican
Of lonely piety.
Basilisk, cockatrice,
Flocked to his homilies,
With mail of dread device,
With monstrous barbèd stings,
With eager dragon-eyes;

Great bats on leathern wings
And old, blind, broken things
Mean in their miseries.
Then ever with him went,
Of all his wanderings
Comrade, with ragged coat,
Gaunt ribs – poor innocent–
Bleeding foot, burning throat,
The guileless young scapegoat:
For forty nights and days
Followed in Jesus' ways,
Sure guard behind him kept,
Tears like a lover wept.

EDWIN MUIR
(1887–1959)

The Incarnate One

The windless northern surge, the sea-gull's scream,
And Calvin's kirk crowning the barren brae.
I think of Giotto the Tuscan shepherd's dream,
Christ, man and creature in their inner day.
How could our race betray
The Image, and the Incarnate One unmake
Who chose this form and fashion for our sake?

The Word made flesh here is made word again,
A word made word in flourish and arrogant crook.
See there King Calvin with his iron pen,
And God three angry letters in a book,
And there the logical hook
On which the Mystery is impaled and bent
Into an ideological instrument.

There's better gospel in man's natural tongue,
And truer sight was theirs outside the Law
Who saw the far side of the Cross among
The archaic peoples in their ancient awe,
In ignorant wonder saw
The wooden cross-tree on the bare hillside,
Not knowing that there a God suffered and died.

The fleshless word, growing, will bring us down,
Pagan and Christian man alike will fall,
The auguries say, the white and black and brown,
The merry and sad, theorist, lover, all
Invisibly will fall:
Abstract calamity, save for those who can
Build their cold empire on the abstract man.

A soft breeze stirs and all my thoughts are blown
Far out to sea and lost. Yet I know well
The bloodless word will battle for its own
Invisibly in brain and nerve and cell.
The generations tell
Their personal tale: the One has far to go
Past the mirages and the murdering snow.

EDITH SITWELL
(1887–1964)

Still Falls the Rain

(The Raids, 1940. Night and Dawn)

Still falls the Rain –
Dark as the world of man, black as our loss –
Blind as the nineteen hundred and forty nails
Upon the Cross.

Still falls the Rain
With a sound like the pulse of the heart that is changed to the
    hammer-beat
In the Potters' Field, and the sound of the impious feet
On the Tomb:
        Still falls the Rain
In the Field of Blood where the small hopes breed and the human
    brain
Nurtures its greed, that worm with the brow of Cain.

Still falls the Rain
At the feet of the Starved Man hung upon the Cross.
Christ that each day, each night, nails there, have mercy on us –
On Dives and on Lazarus:
Under the Rain the sore and the gold are as one.

Still falls the Rain –
Still falls the Blood from the Starved Man's wounded Side
He bears in his Heart all wounds, – those of the light that died,
The last faint spark
In the self-murdered heart, the wounds of the sad uncomprehending
    dark,
The wounds of the baited bear, –
The blind and weeping bear whom the keepers beat
On his helpless flesh . . . the tears of the hunted hare.

Still falls the Rain –
Then – O Ile leape up to my God: who pulles me doune –
See, see where Christ's blood streames in the firmament:
It flows from the Brow we nailed upon the tree
Deep to the dying, to the thirsting heart
That holds the fires of the world, – dark-smirched with pain
As Caesar's laurel crown.

Then sounds the voice of One who like the heart of man
Was once a child who among beasts has lain –
'Still do I love, still shed my innocent light, my Blood, for thee.'

DAVID JONES
(1895–1974)

from *In Parenthesis*

PART 7

Every one of these, stood, separate, upright, above ground,
blinkt to the broad light
risen dry mouthed from the chalk
vivified from the Nullah without commotion
and to distinctly said words,
moved in open order and keeping admirable formation
and at the high-port position[1]★
walking in the morning on the flat roof of the world
and some walked delicately
sensible of their particular judgement.

Each one bearing in his body the whole apprehension of that innocent,
on the day he saw his brother's votive smoke diffuse and hang to soot
the fields of holocaust; neither approved nor ratified nor made
acceptable but lighted to everlasting partition.
Who under the green tree
had awareness of his dismembering, and deep-bowelled damage; for
whom the green tree bore scarlet memorial, and herb and arborage
waste.

Skin gone astrictive
                for fear gone out to meet half-way –
bare breast for –
to welcome – who gives a bugger for
the Dolorous Stroke.[2]

But sweet sister death has gone debauched today and stalks on this
high ground with strumpet confidence, makes no coy veiling of her
appetite but leers from you to me with all her parts discovered.
    By one and one the line gaps, where her fancy will – howsoever
they may howl for their virginity
she holds them – who impinge less on space
sink limply to a heap
nourish a lesser category of being

★ For notes, see end of poem.

like those other who fructify the land
like Tristram
Lamorak de Galis
Alisand le Orphelin
Beaumains who was youngest
or all of them in shaft-shade
at strait Thermopylae
or the sweet brothers Balin and Balan
embraced beneath their single monument.
   Jonathan my lovely one
on Gelboe mountain
and the young man Absalom.
White Hart transfixed in his dark lodge.
Peredur of steel arms
and he who with intention took grass of that field to be for
him the Species of Bread.
   Taillefer the maker,
and on the same day,
thirty thousand other ranks.
And in the country of Béarn – Oliver
and all the rest – so many without memento
beneath the tumuli on the high hills
and under the harvest places.[3]

But how intolerably bright the morning is where we who are alive and remain, walk lifted up, carried forward by an effective word.

---

1. *the high-port position*. Regulation position at which to hold rifle, with bayonet fixed, when moving toward the enemy. It was held high and slantingly across the body.
2. *Each one ... and arborage waste ... Dolorous Stroke.* Cf. Genesis iv; Malory, book xvii, ch. 5; Canon of the Mass, Prayer, 'Quam Oblationem', and Malory, book ii, ch. 15.
3. *shaft-shade.* Cf. Herodotus, book vii, *Polymnia*, Dieneces' speech.
   sweet brothers ... monument. Cf. Malory, book ii, ch. 19
   White Hart transfixed. Cf. *Richard II*, Act v, Sc. vi.
   Peredur of steel arms. Peredur. The *Percivale* of the romances called 'of steel arms' in the Triads, and by the Gododdin poet: 'Peredur with arms of steel ...' (he commemorates other warriors, and proceeds) '... though men might have slain them, they too were slayers, none returned to their homes.'
   with intention ... Species of Bread. In some battle of the Welsh, all reference to which escapes me, a whole army ate grass in token of the Body of the Lord. Also somewhere in the Malory, a single knight feeling himself at the point of death makes this same act.

Taillefer . . . other ranks. Cf. Wace, *Roman de Rou:* 'Then Taillefer, who sang right
   well, rode before the duke singing of Carlemaine and of Rollant, of Oliver and
   the vassals who died at Renchevals.'
country of Béarn . . . harvest places. Not that Roncesvalles is in the Béarn country, but I
   associate it with Béarn because, once, looking from a window in Salies-de-Béarn I
   could see a gap in the hills, which my hostess told me was indeed the pass where
   Roland fell.

from *The Anathemata*

Teste David cum Sibylla

We already and first of all discern him making this thing other. His
groping syntax, if we attend, already shapes:
   ADSCRIPTAM, RATAM, RATIONABILEM . . .[1]* and by preapplication
and for *them*, under modes and patterns altogether theirs, the holy and
venerable hands[2] lift up an efficacious sign.

These, at the sagging end and chapter's close, standing humbly before
the tables spread, in the apsidal houses, who intend life:
   between the sterile ornaments
under the pasteboard baldachins
as, in the young-time, in the sap-years:
   between the living floriations
under the leaping arches.

   (Ossific, trussed with ferric rods, the failing numina of column and
entablature, the genii of spire and triforium, like great rivals met when
all is done, nod recognition across the cramped repeats of their dead
selves.)

These rear-guard details in their quaint attire, heedless of incongruity,
unconscious that the flanks are turned and all connecting files
withdrawn or liquidated – that dead symbols litter to the base of the
cult-stone, that the stem by the palled stone is thirsty, that the stream
is very low.

* For notes, see end of poem.

The utile infiltration nowhere held
creeps vestibule
is already at the closed lattices,[3] is coming through each door.

The cult-man stands alone in Pellam's[4] land: more precariously than he knows he guards the *signa*: the pontifex among his house-treasures, (the twin-*urbes* his house is) he can fetch things new and old:[5] the tokens, the matrices, the institutes, the ancilia, the fertile ashes – the palladic foreshadowings: the things come down from heaven together with the kept memorials, the things lifted up and the venerated trinkets.

This man, so late in time, curiously surviving, shows courtesy to the objects when he moves among, handles or puts aside the name-bearing instruments, when he shows every day in his hand[6] the salted cake given for this *gens* to savour all the *gentes*.[7]

Within the railed tumulus[8]
he sings high and he sings low.

In a low voice
as one who speaks
where a few are, gathered in high-room
and one, gone out.

There's conspiracy here:
Here is birthday and anniversary, if there's continuity
here, there's a new beginning.
By intercalation of weeks
(since the pigeons were unfledged
and the lambs still young)
they've adjusted the term
till this appointed night
(Sherthursdaye bright)[9]
the night that falls
when she's first at the full
after the vernal turn
when in the Ram he runs.[10]

By the two that follow Aquarius[11]
toiling the dry meander:
through the byes
under the low porch

up the turning stair
to the high nave

      where the board is
to spread the board-cloth
under where the central staple is
for the ritual light.

In the high cave they prepare
        for guest to be the *hostia*.
They set the thwart-boards
and along:
      Two for the Gospel-makers[12]
      One for the other Son of Thunder
      One for the swordsman, at the right-board,[13] after;
to make him feel afloat. One for the man from Kerioth,[14]
seven for the rest in order.

They besom here and arrange this handy, tidy here, and furbish with
the green of the year the cross-beams and the gleaming board.

  They make all shipshape
      for she must be trim
          dressed and gaudeous
      all Bristol-fashion here
      for:

        Who d'you think is Master of her?

In the prepared high-room
he implements inside time and late in time under forms indelibly
marked by locale and incidence, deliberations made out of time, before
all oreogenesis

        on this hill
  at a time's turn
        not on any hill
  but on this hill.
[On this unabiding rock
        for one Great Summer
          lifted up
        by next Great Winter[15]
          down
  among the altitudes

with all help-heights
        down
as low as Parnassus
        (it's Ossa on Pelion now).
Seven templum'd montes
        under terra-marl.[16]
Sinai under.
        Where's Ark-hill?
Ask both the Idas.
And where:
        West horse-hills?
        Volcae-remnants' crag-*carneddau*?[17]
        Moel[18] of the Mothers?
        the many *colles Arthuri*?

All the efficacious asylums
in Wallia vel in Marchia Walliae,[19]
        ogofau[20] of, that cavern for
        Cronos, Owain, Arthur.
Terra Walliae!
        Buarth Meibion Arthur![21]
        Enclosure of the Children of Troy![22]

Nine-strata'd Hissarlik[23]
        a but forty-metre height
yet archetype of sung-heights.
Crux-mound at the node
gammadion'd castle.
Within the laughless Megaron
        the margaron[24]
beyond echelon'd Skaian
        the stone
        the fonted water
        the fronded wood.[25]

Little Hissarlik
        least of acclivities
yet
        high as Hector the Wall
        high as Helen the Moon
who, being lifted up
        draw the West to them.

Hissarlik, traversed Hissarlik
        mother of forts
        hill of cries
small walled-height
        that but 750 marching paces would circuit[26]
first revetted of anguish-heights[27]
        matrix for West-*oppida*
            for West-technic
            for West-saga
down
        under, sheet-darkt Hellespont?
        pack for the Cyclades?
And where, from the potent flotsam, florid she breached, with spume
on her spear-flukes,[28] the great fluked mammals blow? glaciation
cones her own Thebes?[29] loess drifts Leogate?

All *montes*
      with each dear made-height
et omnes colles
      down?
hautes eagle-heights under
low as Lambourn Down?
        As solitary tump, so massif?
Alp, as Bredon
      down?
obedient to the fiery stress
und icy counter-drag
      down, and
there shall be yet *more*
      storm-dark sea?[30]

Lord! what a morning yet may break
on this new-founded Oberland.]

At this unabiding Omphalos
      this other laughless rock
at the stone of division
      above the middle water-deeps[31]
at the turn of time
      not at any time, but
at this acceptable time.

From the year of
    the lord-out-of-Ur
about two millennia.
Two thousand lents again
    since the first barley mow.[32]
Twenty millennia (and what millennia more?)
Since he became
    man master-of-plastic.[33]

Who were his *gens*-men or had he no *Hausname* yet
no *nomen* for his *fecit*-mark
    the Master of the Venus?
whose man-hands god-handled the Willendorf stone
    before they unbound the last glaciation
for the Uhland Father to be-ribbon *die blaue Donau*
    with his Vanabride blue.[34]
O long before they lateen'd her Ister
or Romanitas manned her gender'd stream.

O Europa!
    how long and long and long and very long
again, before you'll maze the waltz-forms in gay Vindobona in the
ramshackle last phases; or god-shape the modal rhythms for nocturns
in Melk in the young-time;[35] or plot the Rhaetian limits in the Years of
the City.[36]
    But already he's at it
the form-making proto-maker
busy at the fecund image of her.
    Chthonic? why yes
but mother of us.

    Then it is these abundant *ubera*, here, under the species of worked
lime-rock, that gave suck to the lord? She that they already venerate
(what other could they?)
    her we declare?

Who else?[37]
    And see how they run, the juxtaposed forms, brighting the
vaults of Lascaux; how the linear is wedded to volume, how they do,
within, in an unbloody manner, under the forms of brown haematite
and black manganese on the graved lime-face, what is done, without,
    far on the windy tundra

302

at the kill
that the kindred may have life.
       O God!
O the Academies!

What ages since
his other marvel-day
      when times turned?
and *how* turned!
When
   (How?
   from early knocking stick or stane?)
the first New Fire wormed
   at the Easter of Technics.
What a holy Saturn's day!
O vere beata nox![38]

     A hundred thousand equinoxes
(less or more)
since they cupped the ritual stones
for the faithful departed.[39]

      What, from this one's cranial data, is like to have been
his kindred's psyche; in that they, along with the journey-food, don-
ated the votive horn? and with what *pietas* did they donate these
among the dead – the life-givers – and by what rubric?
Was their oral gloss from a Heidelberg gaffer or did they emend a
Piltdown use, was the girl from Lime Street a butty of theirs, or were
the eight Carmel fathers consanguine or of any affinity to those that
fathered them, that told what they had heard with their ears of those
german to them, before the palmy arbours began again to pine – and
at which of the boreal oscillations?
     And before them?
those who put on their coats to oblate the things set apart in an older
Great Cold.
     And who learned them
if not those whose fathers had received or aped the groping *disciplina*
of their cognates, or lost or found co-laterals, on the proto-routes or at
the lithic foci?

Tundra-wanderers?
or was there no tundra as yet, or not as yet again, to wander – but grew green the rashes over again? Or was all once again *informis*, that Cronos for the third time might see how his lemmings run and hear the cry of his tailless hare from south of the sixties, from into the forties?

For the phases and phase-groups
sway toward and fro within that belt of latitude.
There's where the world's a stage
for transformed scenes
with metamorphosed properties
for each shifted set.
Now naked as an imagined *belle sauvage*, or as is the actual Mirriam.[40]
Now shirted, kilted, cloaked, capped and shod, as were the five men of Jutland, discovered in their peaty cerements, or as the bear-coped Gilyak is, or was, the other day.
The mimes deploy:
anthropoid
anthropoi.
Who knows at what precise phase, or from what floriate green-room, the Master of Harlequinade, himself not made, maker of sequence and permutation in all things made, called us from our co-laterals out, to dance the Funeral Games of the Great Mammalia, as, long, long, long before, these danced out the Dinosaur?

Now, from the the draughty flats
the ageless cherubs
pout the Southerlies.
Now, Januarius brings in the millennial snow that makes the antlered mummers glow for many a hemera.
The *Vorzeit*-masque is on
that moves to the cosmic introit.
Col canto the piping for this turn.
Unmeasured, irregular in stress and interval, of interior rhythm, modal.
If tonic and final are fire
the dominant is ice
if fifth the fire
the cadence ice.

At these Nocturns the hebdomadary is apt to be vested for five
hundred thousand weeks.[41]
Intunes the Dog:
            Benedicite ignis . . .
Cantor Notus and Favonius with all their south-aisled numina:
            con flora cálida
            mit warmer Fauna
The Respond is with the Bear:
            Benedicite frigus . . .
Super-pellissed, stalled in crystallos, from the gospel-side, choir all the
boreal schola
            mit kalter Flora
            con fauna fría
Now, sewn fibre is superfluous where Thames falls into Rhine. Now
they would be trappers of every tined creature and make corners in
ulotrichous hide and establish their wool-cartels as south as Los
Millares. Where the stones shall speak of his cupola-makers:[42] but here
we speak of long, long before their time.
                    When is Tellus
to give her dear fosterling
                her adaptable, rational, elect
and plucked-out otherling
                a reasonable chance?
Not yet – but soon, very soon
                as lithic phases go.

So before then?
            Did the fathers of those
who forefathered them
            (if by genital or ideate begetting)
set apart, make other, oblate?

By what rote, if at all
        had they the suffrage:
        Ascribe to, ratify, approve
in the humid paradises
        of the Third Age?[43]
But who or what, before these?
        Had they so far to reach the ground?
and what of the pelvic inclination of their co-laterals, whose far
cognates went – on how many feet? – in the old time before *them*?

For all WHOSE WORKS FOLLOW THEM[44]
        among any of these or them
dona eis requiem.
     (He would lose, not any one
               from among them.
Of all those given him
       he would lose none.)

          By the uteral marks
that make the covering stone an artefact.
         By the penile ivory
and by the viatic meats.
          Dona ei requiem.
Who was he? Who?
Himself at the cave-mouth
          the last of the father-figures
to take the diriment stroke
         of the last gigantic leader of
thick-felled cave-fauna?
Whoever he was
      Dona ei requiem
sempiternam.
(He would not lose him
        ... *non perdidi*
ex eis quemquam.)[45]

         Before the melt-waters
had drumlin-dammed a high hill-water for the water-maid to lave her
maiden hair.

Before they morained Tal-y-llyn, cirqued a high hollow for Idwal,
brimmed a deep-dark basin for Peris the Hinge and for old Paternus.[46]

Long ages since they'd troughed, in solid Ordovician
his Bala bed for Tacitus.
Long, long ago they'd turned the flow about.
But had they as yet morained
       where holy Deva's entry is?
Or pebbled his mere, where
       still the Parthenos
she makes her devious exit?[47]

Before the Irish sea-borne sheet lay tattered on the gestatorial couch of
Camber the eponym
            lifted to every extremity of the sky
by pre-Cambrian oreos-heavers
            for him to dream
the Combroges' epode.[48]
In his high *sêt*[49] there.
            Higher than any of 'em
south of the Antonine limits.[50]
Above the sealed hypogéum
            where the contest was
over the great *mundus* of sepulture (there the *ver-tigérnus* was)
here lie dragons and old Pendragons
            very bleached.[51]
His uncomforming bed, as yet
            is by the muses kept.

And shall be, so these Welshmen say,[52] till the thick rotundities give,
and the bent flanks of space itself give way
         and the whitest of the Wanderers
falters in her transit
         at the Sibyl's *in favilla*-day.[53]

Before the drift
         was over the lime-face.
Sometime between the final and the penultimate débâcle.
         (Already Arcturus deploys his reconnoitering
chills in greater strength: soon his last *Putsch* on any scale.)
Before this all but proto-historic transmogrification of the land-face.
Just before they rigged the half-lit stage for dim-eyed Clio to step with
some small confidence the measures of her brief and lachrymal pavan.
Before, albescent, out of the day-starred neoarctic night the
Cis-Alclyde[54] pack again came sud of the Mull.
         Across the watersphere
over the atmosphere, preventing the crystal formations
ambient grew the wondrous New Cold:
         trauma and thauma, both.
This is how Cronos reads the rubric, *frangit per medium*, when he
breaks his ice like morsels, for the therapy and fertility of the
land-masses.[55]

Or before
     from Eden-dales, or torn from the becked fells
           transmontane
           transmarine
the barrier-making flood-gravels
the drumlined clays and the till-drift
        had bye-wayed and delta'd the mainway
for Tanat and Vyrnwy.
      Before the heaped detritus
had parted the nymphaean loves
      of naiad Sabrina and sibylline Dee.[56]
She must marl her clear cascade-locks in dawdling Stour's English bed
                    and she
must glen her parthenogenic waters a shorter cut by Gwenfrewi's
well, before she comes to Wirral.[57]
Before, trans-Solway
     and from over Manannan's *moroedd*, the last debris-freighted
floes echeloned solid from Monapia to Ynys Fôn[58]
      discharged on Arfon *colles*
what was cargoed-up on Grampius Mons.
      Off the 'strath' into tye *ystrad*
out of the 'carse' on to the *traeth*.[59]
Heaped amorphous
      out of Caledonia
into Cambria[60]
      bound for Snowdonia
transits Cumbria.
      Long, long, long before
(fifty thousands of winter calends?
fifty thousand calends of Maia before?)
      the Lord Cunedda[61]
conditor noster
      filius Æterni, son of Padarn Red Pexa,[62] son of Taci-
tus, came south over the same terrain and by way of the terrain-gaps
then modified or determined: for the *viae* are not independent of geol-
ogy: that his hobnailed[63] *foederati*, his twelve cantred-naming sons[64]
and himself, the loricated leader in his gaffer's purple, might scrape
from their issue *caligae* and mud of Forth into Conwy.

Clyde into Clwyd.

                                            Otadini

over Venedotia
            and even in Irish Demetia
a Cunedda's Hill.
            Combroges bore us:
tottering, experienced, crux-signed
                        old Romà
the yet efficient mid-wife of us.[65]

        Before the slow estuarine alchemies had coal-blacked the green dryad-ways over the fire-clayed seat-earth along all the utile seams from Taff to Tâf.[66]

Before the microgranites and the clay-bonded erratics wrenched from the diorites of Aldasa, or off the Goat Height in the firth-way, or from the Clota-sides or torn from either Dalriada,[67] with what was harrowed-out *in via*, up, from the long drowned out-crops, under, coalesced and southed by the North Channel.[68]
        As though the sea itself were sea-borne
and under weigh
        as if the whole Ivernian *mare*
directed from hyperboreal control-points by strategi of the axis were one complex of formations in depth, moving on a frontage widening with each lesser degree of latitude.

        Heading toward, right astride
to one degree beyond
        Ffraid Santes'[69] fire-track
where Brendan shall cry from his sea-horse
Mirabilis Deus in sanctis suis![70]

From before all time
        the New Light beams for them
and with eternal clarities
        infulsit and athwart
the fore-times:
        era, period, epoch, hemera.

Through all orogeny:
                group, system, series, zone.
Brighting at the five life-layers
                species, species, genera, families, order.
Piercing the eskered silt, discovering every stria, each score and macula, lighting all the fragile laminae of the shales.
However Calypso has shuffled the marked pack, veiling with early the late.
Through all unconformities and the sills without sequence, glorying all the under-dapple.
Lighting the Cretaceous and the Trias, for Tyrannosaurus must somehow lie down with herbivores, or, the poet lied, which is not allowed.
However violent the contortion or whatever the inversion of the folding.
Oblique through the fire-wrought cold rock dyked from convulsions under.
Through the slow sedimentations laid by his patient creature of water.
Which ever the direction of the strike, whether the hade is to the up-throw or the fault normal.
Through all metamorphs or whatever the pseudomorphoses.

As, down among the palaeo-zoe
                he brights his ichthyic sign
so brights he the middle-zone
                where the uterine forms
are some beginnings of his creature.
Brighter yet over the mammal'd Pliocene
                                        for these continuings
certainly must praise him:
                How else, in his good time
should the amorous Silvy
                to her sweetest dear
her fairest bosom have shown?[71]

                How else we?
                or he, himself?
whose name is called He-with-us
because he did not abhor the uterus.

Whereby these uberal forms
are to us most dear
and of all hills
the most august.

How else her iconography?
How other his liturgy?
Masters and doctors
of seven-breasted Roma
or of all sites that offer nurture
of which it is said
Hinc lucem et pocula sacra[72]
or you of Rhydychen[73]
that have the Lord for your light:
Answer me!
Brighting totally
the post-Pliocene
both Pleistocene and Recent.
An aureole here
for Europa's tundra-*beata*
who of duck's bone had made her needle-case.
And where the carboniferous floor
yields from among the elk-bones and the breccia
this separated one
the data of whose cause is known alone to *him*.

The *egregius*

young, toward the prime,
wearing the amulets of ivory and signed with the life-giving ochre.[74]

Strayed from among the nine and ninety
Aurignacian *beati*
that he has numbered
at his secret shearing
as things made over
by his Proserpine
to himself.[75]
When on a leafy morning
late in June
against the white wattles
he numbers his own.

As do they
               taught of the herdsman's *Ordinale*
and following the immemorial *numeri*
who say:
               Yan, tyan, tethera, methera, pimp
sethera, lethera, hovera, dovera, dick.[76]
               For whom he has notched
his crutched tally-stick
               not at: less one five twenties
               but
at *centum*[77]
               that follow the Lamb
from the Quaternary dawn.
               Numbered among his flock
that no man may number
               but whose works follow them.

Searching where the kitchen midden tells of the decline which with the
receding cold marked the recession of the Magdalenian splendours.
Yet there he brights fragmented protomorphs
where lies the rudimentary bowl.[78]

                                                                    How else

multifariam multisque modis[79]
               the splendour of forms yet to come?

How the dish
               that holds no coward's food?[80]
How the *calix*
               without which
               how *the* re-calling?
And there
               where, among the exactly faceted microliths[81]
               lie the bones
of the guardian and friend.
               How else Argos
the friend of Odysseus?
               Or who should tend
the sores of lazars?
(For anthropos is not always kind.)

How Ranter or True, Ringwood
or the pseudo-Gelert?[82]
How Spot, how Cerberus?
(For men can but proceed from what they know, nor is it for the mind
of this flesh to practise poiesis, *ex nihilo*.)
How the hound-bitches
of the stone kennels of Arthur
that quested the hog and the brood of the hog
from Pebidiog to Aber Gwy?
How the dog Toby? How the flew'd sweet thunder for dewy Ida?[83]

And over the submerged dryad-ways
intensively his ray searches

where the alluvium holds
the polished neoliths
and where the long mound inhumes
his neolithic loves
or the round-barrow keeps
the calcined bones
of these, his still more modern hallows
that handled the pitiless bronze.

(Pray for her by whom came war
for whose urn-burial
they made the cist four-square
on the bank of the Alaw.)[84]
And over the Cis-padane marls
searching the trapezoidal platforms:
for but for the Terramare *disciplina*
how should his Mantuan have sung
the Quadrilateral Plan?[85]

Upon all fore-times.
From before time
his perpetual light
shines upon them.
Upon all at once
upon each one
whom he invites, bids, us to recall
when we make the recalling of him
daily, at the Stone.

DAVID JONES

When the offerant
        our *servos*, so theirs whose life is changed
not taken away[86]
                    is directed to say
                        Memento etiam.
After which it is allowed him then to say
                        Nobis quoque.
That we too may be permitted some part with these like John is!
        as is Felicity.[87]
                    Through the same Lord
that gave the naiad her habitat
            which is his proto-sign.
How else from the weathered mantle-rock
and the dark humus spread
(where is exacted the night-labour
            where the essential and labouring worm
saps micro-workings all the dark day long[88]
                        for his creature of air)
should his barlies grow
                who said
I am your Bread?

1. See the Roman Mass, the Prayer of Consecration, beginning 'Which oblation do thou ... ascribe to, ratify, make reasonable ...'

2. Cf. the same, '... in sanctas ac venerabiles manus suas ...'

3. Cf. the derivation of the word chancel, from *cancelli*, lattice bars.

4. King Pellam in Malory's *Morte d'Arthur* is lord of the Waste Lands and the lord of the Two Lands.

5. Cf. 'Every scribe instructed in the kingdom of heaven is like to a man who is a householder, who bringeth forth out of his treasure new things and old.' See the Common of a Virgin Martyr, Mass 2, Gospel.

6. Cf. Middle-English poem: *Of a rose a lovly rose* 'Every day it schewit in prystes hond'.

7. *Mola salsa*, the cake of spelt and salt made by the Roman Vestals and used at the purification of sacrifices; and cf. Mark IX, 49–50, which indicates the same use of salt in Jewish rites.

8. 'tumulus' because the tumuli, the barrows on our downlands and hill-sites, were essentially burial places and because a Christian altar, by the requirements of Canon Law, and in observance of a use at least as old as the fourth century, should contain relics of the dead. Cf. at the beginning of Mass the priest kisses the altar, saying, '... by the merits of thy saints whose relics are here ...' and cf. the Offertory prayer *Suscipe sancta trinitas* in which the words occur 'and of these here' (*et istorum*). This prayer is very explicit; it says that the oblation is offered to the Trinity, in remembrance of the Passion, Resurrection and

314

Ascension and in honour of the Theotokos, of certain named saints and those whose relics lie under the particular altar at which the Mass is being celebrated, together with all the saints departed.

9. See *Le Morte d'Arthur*, xvii, 20, 'Everyman' edition; modernized spelling: 'the holy dish wherein I ate the lamb on Sher-Thursday'.

The textual authority on Malory's works, Professor Vinaver, gives 'on Estir Day' for Caxton's 'on sherthursdaye' and notes the latter as a corrupt variant. A French source is given as *le jour de Pasques*.

But as the words 'Thursday' and 'the holy dish' are, by gospel, rite, calendar and cultus, indissolubly connected, I regard Caxton's variant as most fortunate. Hence the use of 'sherthursdaye' here . . .

10. The conditions determining the exact time of the Passover were that the moon must be at the full, the vernal equinox past and the sun in Aries. The fixed date of the feast was the fourteenth day of the first month, Nisan; and if that date was due to fall before these conjunctions the necessary number of days were inserted into the calendar in order to postpone it. Subsidiary causes influencing this intercalation, such as the backwardness of the crops and the beasts, are also mentioned in the rabbinical writings. There was as yet no fixed calendar and adjustments were made each year on an empirical basis.

See Schürer, *Hist. of Jewish People*, Div. I, Vol. II, Appendix. 'The Jewish and Macedonian months compared with the Julian calendar.' (Eng. Trans. Edtn. 1890.)

11. Cf. the instructions given to Peter and John in the Passion according to Luke.

'As you go into the city there shall meet you a man carrying a pitcher of water: follow him into the house where he entereth in . . . And he will show you a large dining-room furnished: and there prepare.' (Trans. of Vulgate.)

The passage also partly reflects memories I have of walking in the lanes of Jerusalem, the excessive dryness and white dust, the low arched entries and stairs up into cool interior rooms.

12. Cf. song, *Green grow the rashes O*

'Four for the Gospel makers'.

Of the four evangelists, Matthew was present at the supper. John, one of the two 'Sons of Thunder', was also present. Whether this was the author of the Fourth Gospel has been much debated. Here the traditional identification is taken for granted.

13. 'the right-board' – starboard.

14. Kerioth, a village of Judea from which Judas came, hence 'the Iscariot'.

15. 'This is the Aristotelian theory of the Great Summer and the Great Winter, according to which the earth passes through a cycle of climatic change, each phase of which is linked with a corresponding change in the relative area of land and sea.'-Dawson, *Age of the Gods*, 1929. The author goes on to explain that this Greek guess as to the cosmic rhythm is largely verified by modern physical science.

16. Cf. the layout of a *templum* (space), temple, camp, city, etc., with which the city on the seven hills is associated, and the connection between this and the prehistoric settlements on the marls of the Po Valley – hence called the Terramara (marl-earth) Culture . . .

17. *Carneddau*, carn-neth-ei, neth as in nether, ei as in height, accent on middle syllable; thus rhyming with Volcae in the same line, and having some slight assonance with *Arthuri* below. *Carneddau* is the plural of *carnedd* a mound or cairn.

It was from *Volcae*, the name of a Celtic tribe, that the Teutonic word *Wealas*, 'the Welsh', derived. Just as the Romans got from the Illyrians the word 'Greeks' and applied it to all the Hellenes, so the Germans used the name of one Celtic tribe to designate other

315

Celts. Later it meant 'foreigners' and was so used by the English of the Celts in this country, but only of those Celts who had formed part of the Roman world. The Anglo-Saxons did not call the Scots or the Picts *Wealas*, though these were equally foreigners and Celts. So that *Bret-Wealas*, Brit-Welsh, might be said to mean 'British-Roman foreigners'.

18. *Moel*, pronounce moil, hill.

19. 'In Wales or in the March of Wales.' I write *Walliae* for 'of Wales', although in the thirteenth-century document quoted, this genitive is spelt *Wallie*. But I wish it to be pronounced *Walliae*, ae as i in wine, thus rhyming with the immediately following word *ogofau* (caves) and having assonance with Owain, which rhymes with wine.

20. *Ogofau*, caves, og-ov-ei, ei as in height. Plutarch, in *Of the Failing Oracles*, says that Cronos sleeps in a cave in Britain; and in Welsh folk-tradition, both Arthur and Owain (Owen of the Red Hand, Yvain de Galles in Froissart) have been assimilated into this tradition of a sleeping hero who shall come again.

21. *Buarth Meibion Arthur*, bee-arrth mei-be-yon (ei as in height) arr-thur; 'The Enclosure of the Children of Arthur'. This name, and such names as 'The Stones of the Children of Arthur' and 'The Mound of the Children of Owen', occur as the local traditional names for various stone circles and burial-chambers in what comprised the Principality of Wales and the March of Wales.

22. The legend that gave a Trojan origin to the Britons made Camber, a supposed great-grandson of Aeneas, the eponym of Cambria. Cf. among the last tragic diplomatic exchanges between the lord Llywelyn ap Gruffydd, *princeps Wallie*, and Friar John, Archbishop Pecham, where appeal is made to this supposed Trojan origin; cf. also the phrase 'the dregs of the Trojans' quoted by Henry of Knyghton with reference to the dead lord Llywelyn. For the continued popularity of this theme, cf. *Henry V*, V, 2. *Pist*. Base Trojan thou shalt die. *Flu*. You say very true, scauld knave, when God's will is.

23. It was in a strategic key-position, on the mound of Hissarlik ('place of forts'), some three to four miles from the Dardanelles, about forty metres above sea-level, that Troy stood. Nine successive cities have occupied the site.

24. I am associating the rock called Agelastos Petra, 'the laughless rock', at pre-Hellenic Eleusis (where the modelled cult-object in its stone cist within the cleft of the rock, represented the female generative physiognomy) with the Megaron-type buildings on Troy-rock where Helen was the pearl-to-be-sought within the traversed and echeloned defences of the city. But apart from this association we can accurately describe the hall of Priam as 'laughless', and certainly Helen was a margaron of great price.

25. Where Vergil (*Aeneid* II, 512–514) describes the palace of Priam he uses ancient material as to sacred tree and stone but puts them in a contemporary setting – a Roman *atrium* – so water is implied, for an atrium would have its sunk basin. By whatever means of fusion he hands down three of the permanent symbols for us to make use of.

26. Helen's Troy seems to have been circular and about 200 yards in diameter – so about 628 yards in circumference (= 753 military paces).

27. Troy was one of the first walled cities. We can therefore take it as archetypal of all defended sites, and the persistence and integral position of the story of Troy and of Helen in our Western tradition thus finds support in modern scientific archaeology; while our civilization remains the word 'Troy' will equate automatically with 'love and war'.

28. When I wrote this I had an idea that in some presentation of the nativity of the goddess, she is shown with a spear or fish-hook, but I can get no confirmation of this and therefore suppose I am mistaken. I will let it remain, because, after all, a fish-spear is not inappropriate to her, whether as sea-goddess or goddess of love.

29. Aphrodite was patroness of the city of Thebes.

30. Of the most extensive of all past glaciations – that of the Permo-Carboniferous age – it is said that the sheet-ice reached nearly as far as the Equator. I have no idea if at some remote geological time from now, there is any possibility of a similar glaciation. In the whole passage in square brackets I am merely employing such a possibility as a convenient allegory. There are freezings-up and convulsions of many kinds, there are 'ends' of all sorts of 'worlds', as we in our age have reason to understand. There are also new beginnings and freeings of the waters.

31. The great rock over which the temple of Jerusalem was built was regarded not only as the navel of the world but as separating the waters of the abyss under the earth from the celestial waters.

32. It is usually supposed that Abraham moved north-west up the Euphrates valley from 'Ur of the Chaldees' about 2,000 B.C. The cultivation of grain had begun in Mesopotamia at least by 4,000 B.C.

33. The first examples of visual art so far (1940) discovered date from about 20,000 B.C. There is evidence of artefacture, of a sort, twenty thousand and more years earlier still, e.g. flints and marked stones, but these are hardly 'visual art' in the accepted sense.

34. In Northern myth, Uhland is the abode of the gods of the atmosphere, the *Luftraum*. Vanabride is Freyja, a kind of Teutonic Venus. White cats draw her car across the blue sky and her myth seems in part confused with that of Frigg the wife of Odin. She is the most beautiful of the Vanir and half the departed (who die bravely) are hers.

35. The reference is to the Benedictine abbey of Melk, in Austria, which I am told was one of the great centres of church music.

36. Cf. the *Limes Raetiae*, which marked the limits of the civilized world in the Danube district.

37. The reference is to the first work of plastic art in-the-round known to us, the little limestone sculpture just over four inches high, of very ample proportions, known as 'the Venus of Willendorf'. It is dated, I believe, as contemporary with some of the recently discovered Lascaux cave-paintings, and is of the same Aurignacian culture of 20–25,000 B.C. If it is a 'Venus' it is very much a Venus Genetrix, for it emphasizes in a very emphatic manner the nutritive and generative physiognomy. It is rather the earliest example of a long sequence of mother-figures, earth-mothers and mother goddesses, that fuse in the Great-Mother of settled civilizations – not yet, by a long, long way, the Queen of Heaven, yet, nevertheless, with some of her attributes; in that it images the generative and the fruitful and the sustaining, at however primitive and elementary, or, if you will, 'animal' a level; though it is slovenly to use the word 'animal' of any art-form, for the making of such forms belongs only to man.

38. *O vere beata nox*, 'O truly blessed night'. See the *Exsultet* chanted by the deacon at the blessing of the Paschal Candle which is lighted from a fire of charcoal newly kindled by striking flint. This occurs once in the annual cycle, in the spring, on Easter Saturday. From the new fire so kindled the lamps and candles used during the ensuing twelve months are subsequently lit.

39. Although Neanderthal man of 40 to 60,000 B.C. appears not to be regarded by the anthropologists as a direct ancestor of ourselves, nevertheless it would seem to me that he must have been 'man', for his burial-sites show a religious care for the dead. At his places of interment the covering stones have revealed ritual markings; moreover food-offerings, weapons and possibly a life-symbol (a horn) have been found buried with him. Further, the hollow markings ('cup-marks') are similar to those which characterize the sacred stones of tens of thousands of years afterwards, in the New Stone Age culture which began, as far

as Western Europe is concerned, as recently as *c.* 5,000 B.C., or later, to continue among some primitive peoples to this day, in some parts of the world.

40. The Mirriam are a people of the Shendam Division of the Plateau Province of Nigeria. The men of this tribe are not totally naked, but the women in general are, except for ornaments of bamboo pith. I am indebted for this information to Capt A. L. Milroy, M.C. for many years a British official in that area.

41. Cf. the term Hebdomadarius, which is used of that member of a chapter or religious community whose office it is to lead in choir. His or her duties last a week.

42. The first cupolas or rounded vaults in Europe were made by men of the Megalithic culture in Southern Spain, in the first and second millennium B.C. We are, in our text, referring to conditions in the twentieth millennium B.C. or earlier.

43. 'It was no doubt in the ... Tertiary Age ... that the earliest forms of man first came into existence' ... .'Thus it was probably only after the expulsion of man from the Paradise of the Tertiary World ... that he made those great primitive discoveries of the use of clothing, of weapons and above all of fire, which rendered him independent of the changes of climate ...' Dawson, *Age of the Gods*, 1929.

44. See '... *opera enim illorum sequuntur illos*' in the Epistle for the Third Mass of All Souls' Day. *Apocalypse* xiv, 13. These *opera* are of course those that follow supernatural faith whereby the doers gain supernatural benefit. But I suppose it is permitted to use the same words analogously of those *opera* which we call artefacts, which man alone can cause to be.

The dictionary defines artefact as an artificial product, thus including the beaver's dam and the wren's nest. But I here confine my use of the word to those artefacts in which there is an element of the extra-utile and the gratuitous. If there is any evidence of this kind of artefacture then the artefacturer or artifex should be regarded as participating *directly* in the benefits of the Passion, because the extra-utile is *the* mark of man.

For which reason the description 'utility goods' if taken literally could refer only to the products of sub-man.

45. Quoted from the Good Friday Liturgy. '... I have not lost of them any single one.'

46. 'In places the irregularly eroded valley floors have been hollowed into true rock basins and are now occupied by lakes, though most of the lakes are at least in part dammed by morainic material.' *Brit. Reg. Geol. N. Wales*, p. 81. The lake of Idwal, well above the 1,200 contour, six miles N.W. of Capel Curig, occupies one such basin. The saint after whom Llanberis and Lake Peris are named has, for some reason, acquired the description 'cardinal of Rome'. A Peris son of Helig occurs in one genealogy.

Llyn Padarn means the Lake of Paternus: after Paternus 'of the red tunic', grandfather of Cunedda, or after Padarn, the sixth-century saint? I suppose the latter.

47. Bala Lake or Pimblemere is called in Welsh Llyn Tegid, the Lake of Tacitus. It may be noted that Tacitus was the name of Cunedda's great-grandfather. The basin is formed of solid rock but the S.W. end at least is thought to have been influenced by morainic deposits. At some remote geological period the outflow was southward, whereas now the Dee flows northward through the lake, but, says immemorial tradition, the two waters never mingle. Bala 'rhymes' with valour not with parlour.

48. The word Cymry, kum-ry, the Welsh people, derives from the old Celtic compound *combrox* 'a person of the same kind', plural Combroges; pronounce kum-bro-gees, g hard, accent on middle syllable.

49. *sêt* (Welsh ê *somewhat* resembles the a in 'cake'), seat, pew.

50. The earth wall built between Clyde and Forth by Quinctius Lollius Urbicus in the

reign of Antoninus Pius represented for a short while the outer *limes* of the empire in Britain.

51. The Welsh name for the peak of Snowdon is Moel yr Wyddfa, the Hill of the Burial Mound. Traditions of imprisoned dragons and buried heroes attach to the site; *ver-tigérnus*, a 'chief lord'. Cf. Vortigern.

52. When a Welsh poet of the eighteenth-century wished to express the final catastrophe he wrote 'Snowdon's peak is one with the plain', just as Isaias or John, had they been gentiles, would have written 'Olympus is brought low', or 'Ida is cast into the sea'.

An analogous sentiment is to be detected in the twelfth-century Welshman who told King Henry I that whatever policy he pursued, Welshness would endure until the dissolution of all things.

53. See the hymn by Thomas of Celano, *Dies Irae*.
'day on which the world dissolves into ashes (*in favilla*) as David and the Sibyl testify.'

54. Cis-Alclyde. The old name for the Rock of Dumbarton was Altclut, or Petra Cloithe, the Rock in the Clyde. It was from just south of the Clyde, from the Southern Uplands of Scotland, that the deposits were carried into the Midland Plain of England and into the Plain of Gwent and elsewhere in Wales. See note 68 below.

55. See the rubric directing the celebrant at the point of the Mass called the Fraction. 'He . . . takes the host and breaks it in half (*frangit per medium*) over the chalice.'
Cf. also Psalm CXLVII, 17, Bk of Com. Pr version. 'He casteth forth his ice like morsels: who is able to abide his frost?'

56. The courses of the rivers Tanat, Vyrnwy, Severn and Dee have all been affected by glacial action. The latter two flowed as one, but the Severn was later caused to flow east and mingle with the Stour while the Dee took its present course north through the border lands gathering to itself many associations and coming to be regarded as a sacred stream. Indeed some have interpreted its Welsh name, Dyfrdwy, as meaning the 'divine water'.

57. Gwenfrewi, in English, Winefred, whose sacred well gave the English name Holywell and the Welsh name Treffynnon (homestead+spring) to that site a mile-and-a-half only from where the estuary of the Dee divides the two nations.

58. Manannan mac Lir, in Welsh Manawydan mab Llyr, the sea god: *moroedd*, seas, mor-roithe. Monapia, the name of the Isle of Man in Pliny. Ynys Fôn, un-iss von, o as in vote, the Island of Mona, Anglesey.

59. The elements 'strath' and 'carse' in Scottish place-names have a correspondence with *ystrad*, us-trad (vale, flats) and *traeth*, ae as ah+eh (shore, estuary) in Welsh ones.

60. Caledonia is sometimes made to mean the Highlands, but here I use it as a synonym for Scotland and in particular for the Southern Uplands, because it was from this southern area that geological deposits of the Ice Age and certain legendary and historical deposits of the sub-Roman age came to Wales. For instance, in spite of medieval pseudo-history, 'King Cole' has no relationship with Colchester, but is the *Coil hen guotepauc* of Harleian MS. 3859 and is to be associated with the district of Kyle in Ayrshire. In 1912 in Camberwell a Miss Williams said to me, 'On my father's side I am descended from Coel Hên Godebog'. It is the boast of many old Welsh families.

61. Cunedda, kin-eth-ah, th as in nether, accent on middle syllable.

62. The grandfather of Cunedda is known in the Welsh genealogies as Padarn Beisrudd. *Beis* is a mutation of *peis*, a coat, petticoat or tunic, and is known to derive direct from the Latin *pexus, pexa*, descriptive of a woollen fabric that had not lost its nap, thence something new and well cared for, and as a metonym it came to be used of the garment called the *tunica*.

The Welsh word *rudd* meant crimson red.

These considerations tend to support the view, now held by historians, that the family of Cunedda had a tradition of holding office under the Roman imperium. 'Beisrudd' might possibly imply the *tunica* with the broad purple laticlave, associated with rank, or the all-purple *tunica* associated with military command, or with some other dyed garment of legatine significance.

63. The absence of archaeological evidence from the burial-places of sub-Roman Britain contrasts with the considerable evidence from the graves of the Saxon invaders. There is, however, one thing which archaeology has shown: a number of Britons of this period who died, or were buried, with their boots on, had hob-nails in their boots. We know also that the field-service boot (*caliga*) of the Roman army was similarly studded.

64. The *Historia Brittonum* gives the number of Cunedda's sons as twelve, other evidence supposes nine. Six of these gave their names to Welsh cantreds or to lesser divisions of land.

65. It is generally accepted that the man known to Welsh tradition as Cunedda Wledig was a Romanized Briton, almost certainly a Christian, and possibly associated with the office of Dux Britanniarum. Sometime before the year A.D. 400, he came, presumably under Roman auspices, from the district of the Otadini or Votadini in South Scotland, into Venedotia (N. Wales). His great-grandfather, his grandfather, his father and three of his nine(?) sons and one of his grandsons bore Roman names; two of which, Donatus and Marianus, are said to be certainly of Christian provenance. The rule which these men established in Wales, in the age of St Ambrose, was destined to evolve into a dynasty of native princes, which endured, in however precarious a fashion, for nine centuries.

Demetia (S.W. Wales) was held by Irish settlers. Nennius (A.D. 800) says that Cunedda cleared this area also, but this is denied by modern historians. Nevertheless there is, near Kidwelly, a hill called Allt Cunedda.

66. Symbolically speaking only, these two rivers can be said to bound, on the east and on the west, the South Wales coalfield. Taff rhymes with saff in saffron, but Tâf (tahv) rhymes with calve.

67. Pronounce dal-ree-adda, accent on ad. I follow the present Scottish pronunciation as told to me by a native of Dumbarton.

There was a kingdom of Dalriada on the Irish side also; indeed it was the invasions of the Dalriad Scots from Ireland that gave the names Scotland and Dalriada to parts of northern Britannia.

68. 'Contemporaneous with the glaciers of North Wales, ice sheets from the Clyde Valley and the Southern Uplands of Scotland, from the Lake District and from the heights of north-eastern Ireland descended and converged into the depression of the Irish Sea. From this area of congestion the combined flows moved southward under great pressure, part escaping directly by way of St George's Channel, but part thrust against the land mass of North Wales.' Bernard Smith and T. Neville George in *Brit. Reg. Geol. N. Wales*, pp. 77-8.

69. Ffraid Santes, St Bride, Brigit. *Ffraid* rhymes approx. with bride and *Santes* approx. with aunt + ess. Cf. the association of Brigit with fire-rites; and cf. St Bride's Bay, Pembs, an area of water covered by the ice-sheets.

70. The glaciation reached to about 51 deg. North Lat., thus extending just beyond the waters between South Wales and Ireland, which very many millennia later were to become associated with the marvel-voyages of the Celtic ascetics; such as the navigation-saint, Brendan, who in the legend rides the narrow channel on a marine creature and hails Fin-

bar, mounted on David's swimming horse, with the words 'God is marvellous in his saints'.

71. Cf. *On a Time the Amorous Silvy*, verse 2.

> 'With that her fairest bosom showing,
> Op'ning her lips, rich perfumes blowing,
> She said, Now kiss me and be going,
> My sweetest dear!'

John Attey. *The First Booke of Ayres Of Four Parts, With Tableture for the Lute*, 1622.

72. 'From this place light and a sacred potion.'

73. Pronounce rhid-uch-en, accent on middle syllable; from *rhyd*, ford, and *ychen*, oxen; *ch* as in Scottish *loch*.

74. For the uncovering of the bones of the earliest known South Wallian at the oldest burial-site in Britain we are indebted to the Rev. William Buckland, Reader in Geology in the University of Oxford, who made his discovery in 1822, and called it the Red Lady. These remains were in association with those of mammoth and elk and other fauna of Palaeolithic times. It is now established that the skeleton was that of a man about twenty-five years old. He had been buried with rites, in a cerement of powdered red oxide of iron, signifying life; with rods of ivory and wearing ornaments of the same 'incorruptible' substance. When this man's body was committed to the Paviland lime-rock in Gower ten miles or so south-west of Swansea, we can presume that some of his continental contemporaries were engaged upon such works as those which the little French boys and their dog stumbled upon in the Lascaux caves in 1940. Works which have since proved a reassurance to us all, that man, already, 20 to 40,000 years ago, whatever his limitations or capabilities was capable of superb artistry. In some respects we have not again equalled that artistry, let alone surpassed it.

75. Mr Jackson Knight writes: 'Proserpina, queen of the dead, was thought to mark for death all who died, by cutting a lock of their hair as hair is cut from animals to mark them for sacrifice'. Proserpine, that brings with her the spring, stands for death in general, so then for that particular death, indeed particularly for that death which is 'shown forth' and 'recalled' in the eucharist. Further, in the rite of the fourth-century Egyptian bishop, Serapion, the eucharist is regarded as a recalling of all the dead: 'We entreat also on behalf of all who have fallen asleep, of which this (i.e. this action) is the recalling'. Here 'all who have fallen asleep' refers to the departed members of the Christian community in Egypt and throughout the world, because no institution can, in its public formulas, presume the membership of any except those who have professed such membership. But over and above these few there are those many, of all times and places, whose lives and deaths have been made acceptable by the same Death on the Hill of which every Christian breaking of bread is an epiphany and a recalling.

With regard to the Upper Palaeolithic South Welshman buried in Paviland, it would seem that Theology allows us to regard him among the blessed by forbidding us to assert the contrary.

76. This particular variant of the sheep-score is used here because it happens to be the only one I know. It is from Lancashire. As with all the variants from different parts of England it is a corruption of the ordinary Welsh cardinal numbers. It is sometimes questioned whether these immemorial English uses have come down direct from the Celtic-speaking population of previous to the Anglo-Saxon invasions, or whether they derive from later contacts with the Welsh sheep-trade. For many reasons the latter seems extremely unlikely. Moreover, the association of sheep with Wales is relatively modern,

being in part due to Cistercian enterprise in the thirteenth century, and as late as Queen Anne the typical Welsh stock was cattle rather than sheep.

77. Various local traditions prevail as to the marking of the tally. In parts of Wales a notch is made in the stick for every ten sheep counted and in parts of the Lake District the hand is raised for every twenty and the tally notched for every hundred.

One Welsh way of saying 'ninety-nine' is 'except one, five twenties' (*amyn un pum ugain*). This is used in the Welsh gospel where St Luke reports our Lord as saying, in terms of the hill-people from whom he came: 'What man of you, having an hundred sheep, if he lose one, etc.' He was addressing Aramaean canonists, but he spoke as though to Powell Chapel Farm, Lewis the Vision or Watkins Tal Sarn.

78. Rather oddly, the first beginnings of anything like pottery are found among the depressed peoples who lived after the decline of the Palaeolithic cultures and before the rise of the Neolithic.

79. See the Epistle for the Third Mass of Christmas Day, Heb. I, 1. '. . . at sundry times and in divers manners'.

80. In Welsh mythology, when Arthur goes to raid the Celtic hades one of the spoils he has to recover is a vessel from which no coward can eat or drink.

81. To the same Mesolithic epoch of the first beginnings of pottery belongs also the first domestication of the dog. This was during a low ebb of prehistoric culture, yet the pygmy weapon-heads are famous: 'their microliths, although often measuring no more than half an inch long, are yet meticulously trimmed' write J. and C. Hawkes in *Prehistoric Britain*.

82. I use the mutated form, Gelert, because this is familiar and customary; the radical form is Celert and is the name of a man, presumably a sixth-century saint. The hound-association at Beddgelert is said to be not older than the Romantic Revival of the eighteenth-nineteenth centuries. There are, however, tales of devoted Welsh hounds of early date (Cf. Giraldus) from which the Gelert *motif* may stem.

83. Cf. the names of certain of the megaliths of South Wales: 'The Stone of the Greyhound Bitch', 'The Kennel of the Greyhound Bitch', 'The Stone of the Children of Arthur', 'The Enclosure of Arthur', etc.

If the hunt of the boar Trwyth by the men and dogs of Arthur described in the tale of *Culhwch* is read with one eye on the Ordnance Survey's map, the Distribution of the Megaliths (sheets 7), the possibility of some connection between the itinerary of this great mythological hunt and the sites of the megaliths may suggest itself. Pebidiog is the south-west extremity of Wales where the hog and his pigs came in from Ireland. Aber Gwy (gooy) means Mouth of the Wye, where the hog escaped into the Severn estuary, to be overtaken in Cornwall and to be driven into the Atlantic. Cf. also *Mids. N.D.* IV, 1.

84. Cf. the *mabinogi* of Branwen daughter of Llyr in *The Mobinogion*, Gwyn and Thomas Jones trans. *Everyman* edtn 1949.

'Alas, son of God, said she, . . . two good islands have been laid waste because of me . . . and with that her heart broke. And a four-sided grave was made for her and she was buried there on the bank of the Alaw.'

In 1813 an Anglesey farmer requiring stone for repairs is said to have uncovered a mound by the River Alaw and to have found a square cist containing a funerary urn. This is said to have occurred on a site traditionally known as 'Bronwen's Island'. Alaw rhymes with vow, accent on 'Al'.

85. Cf. the opinion of scholars that the rectilineal layout of camps and cities characteristic of Rome and the Latin civilization was derived from the Bronze Age agriculturalists of the Po Valley who constructed their solid pile settlements with great care

for alignment and consistent orientation, with intersecting streets, the whole forming a trapezoid. See page 301 above.

86. 'See the preface in the Mass for All Souls' Day and for all Masses of the departed '... Tuis enim fidelibus, Domine, vita mutatur non tollitur'. 'For thy faithful, O Lord, life is changed not taken away.'

87. The commemoration of the dead in the Latin rite follows the consecration and begins: 'Remember them, O Lord, thy servants'. This prayer for the departed is followed immediately by: 'To us also, sinners, grant some part ... with John, etc., Felicity, etc., ... into whose company admit us ... through Christ our Lord'. The prayer concludes with a kind of recalling of the fruits of the land ('hallow, quicken and bless these and give them to us') without which no sacrament could be.

88. Darwin, in *The Formation of Vegetable Mould through the Action of Worms*, Ch. I, says in effect that worms do their 'day-labour light deny'd' in two senses, in that they work only by night and are blind, yet are far from being insensitive to light.

General Note to Section I. The findings of the physical sciences are necessarily mutable and change with fresh evidence or with fresh interpretation of the same evidence. This is an important point to remember with regard to the whole of this section of my text where I employ ideas based on more or less current interpretations of archaeological and anthropological data. Such interpretations, of whatever degree of probability, remain hypothetical. The layman can but employ for his own purposes the pattern available during his lifetime. The poet in *c.* 1200 could make good use of a current supposition that a hill in Palestine was the centre of the world. The poet of the seventeenth-century could make use of the notion of gravitational pull. The abiding truth behind those two notions would now, in both cases (I am told), be differently expressed. But the poet, of whatever century, is concerned only with how he can use a current notion to express a permanent mythus.

from *The Hunt*

... When the free and the bond and the mountain mares and the fettled horses and the four-penny curs and the hounds of status in the wide, jewelled collars

        when all the shining Arya[1] rode

with the diademed leader

        who directs the toil

        whose face is furrowed

with the weight of the enterprise

   the lord of the conspicious scars whose visage is fouled with the hog-spittle whose cheeks are fretted with the grime of the hunt-toil:

        if his forehead is radiant

like the smooth hill in the lateral light
        it is corrugated
like the defences of the hill
        because of his care for the land
and for the men of the land.

If his eyes are narrowed for the stress of the hunt and because of the hog they are moist for the ruin and for love of the recumbent bodies that strew the ruin.

If his embroidered habit is clearly from a palace wardrobe it is mired and rent and his bruised limbs gleam from between the rents, by reason of the excessive fury of his riding when he rode the close thicket as though it were an open launde

        (indeed, was it he riding the forest-ride
or was the tangled forest riding?)

for the thorns and flowers of the forest and the bright elm-shoots and the twisted tanglewood of stamen and stem clung and meshed him and starred him with variety

and the green tendrils gartered him and briary-loops galloon him with splinter-spike and broken blossom twining his royal needlework
        and ruby petal-points counter
the countless points of his wounds

and from his lifted cranium where the priced tresses dragged with sweat stray his straight brow-furrows under the twisted diadem
        to the numbered bones
of his scarred feet
        and from the saturated forelock
of his maned mare
        to her streaming flanks
and in broken festoons for her quivering fetlocks
he was caparison'd in the flora
        of the woodlands of Britain
and like a stricken numen of the woods
        he rode
with the trophies of the woods
        upon him
who rode
        for the healing of the woods
and because of the hog.

Like the breast of the cock-thrush that is torn in the hedge-war when bright on the native mottle the deeper mottling is and brighting

the diversity of textures and crystal-bright on the delicate fret the clear
dew-drops gleam: so was his dappling and his dreadful variety
    the speckled lord of Prydain
in his twice-embroidered coat
    the bleeding man in the green
and if through the trellis of green
    and between the rents of the needlework
the whiteness of his body shone
    so did his dark wounds glisten.

 And if his eyes, from their scrutiny of the hog-track and from
considering the hog, turned to consider the men of the host (so that
the eyes of the men of the host met his eyes) it would be difficult to
speak of so extreme a metamorphosis.
    When they paused at the check
when they drew breath.
 And the sweat of the men of the host and of the horses salted the
dew of the forest-floor and the hard-breathing of the many men and of
the many dogs and of the horses woke the fauna-cry of the Great
Forest[2] and shook the silent flora.
    And the extremity of anger
alternating with sorrow
    on the furrowed faces
of the Arya
    transmogrified the calm face
of the morning
    as when the change-wind stirs
and the colours change in the boding thunder-calm
    because this was the Day
of the Passion of the Men of Britain
    when they hunted the Hog
life for life.

 1. The word Arya means the nobles or high-men, and has nothing whatever to do with
race. Among the Sumerians, Chinese, Mongols and the Hamitic tribes of Africa, wherever
there was a warrior-culture and the cult of the sky-god, the tribal king or chieftain tended
to personify that god, and be addressed by the same title. As noted by Mr Christopher
Dawson in *The Age of the Gods*, in the case of the Etruscans a whole mixed people are
known to history as 'the Lords', merely because their female cult-figure was Turan, The
Lady, and their male cult-figure Maristuran, Mars the Lord.

2. The initial letters are in capitals because the reference is not only to a large tract of forest-land but to a district name, Forest Fawr, an upland area of Breconshire which formed part of the itinerary taken by the boar, Trwyth, and Arthur's hunt.

Note: This fragment is part of an incomplete attempt based on the native Welsh early medieval prose-tale, Culhwch ac Olwen, in which the predominant theme becomes the great hunt across the whole of southern Wales of the boar Trwyth by all the war-bands of the Island led by Arthur.

T. S. ELIOT
(1888–1965)

from *Landscapes*

III. Usk

Do not suddenly break the branch, or
Hope to find
The white hart behind the white well.
Glance aside, not for lance, do not spell
Old enchantments. Let them sleep.
'Gently dip, but not too deep',
Lift your eyes
Where the roads dip and where the roads rise
Seek only there
Where the grey light meets the green air
The hermit's chapel, the pilgrim's prayer.

Little Gidding

I

Midwinter spring is its own season
Sempiternal though sodden towards sundown,
Suspended in time, between pole and tropic.
When the short day is brightest, with frost and fire,
The brief sun flames the ice, on pond and ditches,
In windless cold that is the heart's heat,
Reflecting in a watery mirror
A glare that is blindness in the early afternoon.
And glow more intense than blaze of branch, or brazier,
Stirs the dumb spirit: no wind, but pentecostal fire
In the dark time of the year. Between melting and freezing
The soul's sap quivers. There is no earth smell
Or smell of living thing. This is the spring time
But not in time's covenant. Now the hedgerow
Is blanched for an hour with transitory blossom
Of snow, a bloom more sudden
Than that of summer, neither budding nor fading,
Not in the scheme of generation.
Where is the summer, the unimaginable
Zero summer?

          If you came this way,
Taking the route you would be likely to take
From the place you would be likely to come from,
If you came this way in may time, you would find the hedges
White again, in May, with voluptuary sweetness.
It would be the same at the end of the journey,
If you came at night like a broken king,
If you came by day not knowing what you came for,
It would be the same, when you leave the rough road
And turn behind the pig-sty to the dull façade
And the tombstone. And what you thought you came for
Is only a shell, a husk of meaning
From which the purpose breaks only when it is fulfilled
If at all. Either you had no purpose

Or the purpose is beyond the end you figured
And is altered in fulfilment. There are other places
Which also are the world's end, some at the sea jaws,
Or over a dark lake, in a desert or a city –
But this is the nearest, in place and time,
Now and in England.

        If you came this way,
Taking any route, starting from anywhere,
At any time or at any season,
It would always be the same: you would have to put off
Sense and notion. You are not here to verify,
Instruct yourself, or inform curiosity
Or carry report. You are here to kneel
Where prayer has been valid. And prayer is more
Than an order of words, the conscious occupation
Of the praying mind, or the sound of the voice praying.
And what the dead had no speech for, when living,
They can tell you, being dead: the communication
Of the dead is tongued with fire beyond the language of the living.
Here, the intersection of the timeless moment
Is England and nowhere. Never and always.

II

        Ash on an old man's sleeve
        Is all the ash the burnt roses leave.
        Dust in the air suspended
        Marks the place where a story ended.
        Dust inbreathed was a house –
        The wall, the wainscot and the mouse.
        The death of hope and despair,
           This is the death of air.

There are flood and drouth
Over the eyes and in the mouth,
Dead water and dead sand
Contending for the upper hand.
The parched eviscerate soil
Gapes at the vanity of toil,
Laughs without mirth.
    This is the death of earth.

Water and fire succeed
The town, the pasture and the weed.
Water and fire deride
The sacrifice that we denied.
Water and fire shall rot
The marred foundations we forgot,
Of sanctuary and choir.
    This is the death of water and fire.

In the uncertain hour before the morning
  Near the ending of interminable night
  At the recurrent end of the unending
After the dark dove with the flickering tongue
  Had passed below the horizon of his homing
  While the dead leaves still rattled on like tin
Over the asphalt where no other sound was
  Between three districts whence the smoke arose
  I met one walking, loitering and hurried
As if blown towards me like the metal leaves
  Before the urban dawn wind unresisting.
  And as I fixed upon the down-turned face
That pointed scrutiny with which we challenge
  The first-met stranger in the waning dusk
  I caught the sudden look of some dead master
Whom I had known, forgotten, half recalled
  Both one and many; in the brown baked features
  The eyes of a familiar compound ghost
Both intimate and unidentifiable.
  So I assumed a double part, and cried
  And heard another's voice cry: 'What! are *you* here?'

Although we were not. I was still the same,
  Knowing myself yet being someone other –
  And he a face still forming; yet the words sufficed
To compel the recognition they preceded.
  And so, compliant to the common wind,
  Too strange to each other for misunderstanding,
In concord at this intersection time
  Of meeting nowhere, no before and after,
  We trod the pavement in a dead patrol.
I said: 'The wonder that I feel is easy,
  Yet ease is cause of wonder. Therefore speak:
  I may not comprehend, may not remember.'
And he: 'I am not eager to rehearse
  My thoughts and theory which you have forgotten.
  These things have served their purpose: let them be.
So with your own, and pray they be forgiven
  By others, as I pray you to forgive
  Both bad and good. Last season's fruit is eaten
And the fullfed beast shall kick the empty pail.
  For last year's words belong to last year's language
  And next year's words await another voice.
But, as the passage now presents no hindrance
  To the spirit unappeased and peregrine
  Between two worlds become much like each other,
So I find words I never thought to speak
  In streets I never thought I should revisit
  When I left my body on a distant shore.
Since our concern was speech, and speech impelled us
  To purify the dialect of the tribe
  And urge the mind to aftersight and foresight,
Let me disclose the gifts reserved for age
  To set a crown upon your lifetime's effort.
  First, the cold friction of expiring sense
Without enchantment, offering no promise
  But bitter tastelessness of shadow fruit
  As body and soul begin to fall asunder.
Second, the conscious impotence of rage
  At human folly, and the laceration
  Of laughter at what ceases to amuse.

And last, the rending pain of re-enactment
    Of all that you have done, and been; the shame
    Of motives late revealed, and the awareness
Of things ill done and done to others' harm
    Which once you took for exercise of virtue.
    Then fools' approval stings, and honour stains.
From wrong to wrong the exasperated spirit
    Proceeds, unless restored by that refining fire
    Where you must move in measure, like a dancer.'
The day was breaking. In the disfigured street
    He left me, with a kind of valediction,
    And faded on the blowing of the horn.

III

There are three conditions which often look alike
Yet differ completely, flourish in the same hedgerow:
Attachment to self and to things and to persons, detachment
From self and from things and from persons; and, growing between
    them, indifference
Which resembles the others as death resembles life,
Being between two lives – unflowering, between
The live and the dead nettle. This is the use of memory:
For liberation – not less of love but expanding
Of love beyond desire, and so liberation
From the future as well as the past. Thus, love of a country
Begins as attachment to our own field of action
And comes to find that action of little importance
Though never indifferent. History may be servitude,
History may be freedom. See, now they vanish,
The faces and places, with the self which, as it could, loved them,
To become renewed, transfigured, in another pattern.
Sin is Behovely, but
All shall be well, and
All manner of thing shall be well.
If I think, again, of this place,
And of people, not wholly commendable,
Of no immediate kin or kindness,
But some of peculiar genius,
All touched by a common genius,

United in the strife which divided them;
If I think of a king at nightfall,
Of three men, and more, on the scaffold
And a few who died forgotten
In other places, here and abroad,
And of one who died blind and quiet,
Why should we celebrate
These dead men more than the dying?
It is not to ring the bell backward
Nor is it an incantation
To summon the spectre of a Rose.
We cannot revive old factions
We cannot restore old policies
Or follow an antique drum.
These men, and those who opposed them
And those whom they opposed
Accept the constitution of silence
And are folded in a single party.
Whatever we inherit from the fortunate
We have taken from the defeated
What they had to leave us – a symbol:
A symbol perfected in death.
And all shall be well and
All manner of thing shall be well
By the purification of the motive
In the ground of our beseeching.

IV

The dove descending breaks the air
With flame of incandescent terror
Of which the tongues declare
The one discharge from sin and error.
The only hope, or else despair
    Lies in the choice of pyre or pyre –
    To be redeemed from fire by fire.

Who then devised the torment? Love.
Love is the unfamiliar Name
Behind the hands that wove
The intolerable shirt of flame
Which human power cannot remove.
    We only live, only suspire
    Consumed by either fire or fire.

v

What we call the beginning is often the end
And to make an end is to make a beginning.
The end is where we start from. And every phrase
And sentence that is right (where every word is at home,
Taking its place to support the others,
The word neither diffident nor ostentatious,
An easy commerce of the old and the new,
The common word exact without vulgarity,
The formal word precise but not pedantic,
The complete consort dancing together)
Every phrase and every sentence is an end and a beginning,
Every poem an epitaph. And any action
Is a step to the block, to the fire, down the sea's throat
Or to an illegible stone: and that is where we start.
We die with the dying:
See, they depart, and we go with them.
We are born with the dead:
See, they return, and bring us with them.
The moment of the rose and the moment of the yew-tree
Are of equal duration. A people without history
Is not redeemed from time, for history is a pattern
Of timeless moments. So, while the light fails
On a winter's afternoon, in a secluded chapel
History is now and England.

With the drawing of this Love and the voice of this Calling
We shall not cease from exploration
And the end of all our exploring
Will be to arrive where we started
And know the place for the first time.
Through the unknown, remembered gate
When the last of earth left to discover
Is that which was the beginning;
At the source of the longest river
The voice of the hidden waterfall
And the children in the apple-tree
Not known, because not looked for
But heard, half-heard, in the stillness
Between two waves of the sea.
Quick now, here, now, always –
A condition of complete simplicity
(Costing not less than everything)
And all shall be well and
All manner of thing shall be well
When the tongues of flame are in-folded
Into the crowned knot of fire
And the fire and the rose are one.

ROY CAMPBELL
(1902–1957)

*St John of the Cross: Songs of the soul in rapture at having arrived at
the height of perfection, which is union with God by the road of
spiritual negation*

Upon a gloomy night,
With all my cares to loving ardours flushed,
(O venture of delight!)
With nobody in sight
I went abroad when all my house was hushed.

In safety, in disguise,
In darkness up the secret stair I crept,
(O happy enterprise!)
Concealed from other eyes
When all my house at length in silence slept.

Upon that lucky night
In secrecy, inscrutable to sight,
I went without discerning
And with no other light
Except for that which in my heart was burning.

It lit and led me through
More certain than the light of noonday clear
To where One waited near
Whose presence well I knew,
There where no other presence might appear.

Oh night that was my guide!
Oh darkness dearer than the morning's pride,
Oh night that joined the lover
To the beloved bride
Transfiguring them each into the other.

Within my flowering breast
Which only for himself entire I save
He sank into his rest
And all my gifts I gave
Lulled by the airs with which the cedars wave.

Over the ramparts fanned
While the fresh wind was fluttering his tresses,
With his serenest hand
My neck he wounded, and
Suspended every sense with its caresses.

Lost to myself I stayed
My face upon my lover having laid
From all endeavour ceasing:
And all my cares releasing
Threw them amongst the lilies there to fade.

St John of the Cross: Song of the soul that is glad to know God by faith

How well I know that fountain's rushing flow
Although by night

Its deathless spring is hidden. Even so
Full well I guess from whence its sources flow
Though it be night.

Its origin (since it has none) none knows:
But that all origin from it arose
Although by night.

I know there is no other thing so fair
And earth and heaven drink refreshment there
Although by night.

Full well I know its depth no man can sound
And that no ford to cross it can be found
Though it be night.

Its clarity unclouded still shall be:
Out of it comes the light by which we see
Though it be night.

Flush with its banks the stream so proudly swells;
I know it waters nations, heavens, and hells
Though it be night.

The current that is nourished by this source
I know to be omnipotent in force
Although by night.

JOHN BETJEMAN
(1906 – 1984)

Sunday Morning, King's, Cambridge

File into yellow candle light, fair choristers of King's
  Lost in the shadowy silence of canopied Renaissance stalls
In blazing glass above the dark glow skies and thrones and wings
  Blue, ruby, gold and green between the whiteness of the walls
And with what rich precision the stonework soars and springs
  To fountain out a spreading vault – a shower that never falls.

The white of windy Cambridge courts, the cobbles brown and dry,
  The gold of plaster Gothic with ivy overgrown,
The apple-red, the silver fronts, the wide green flats and high,
  The yellowing elm-trees circled out on islands of their own –
Oh, here behold all colours change that catch the flying sky
  To waves of pearly light that heave along the shafted stone.

In far East Anglian churches, the clasped hands lying long
  Recumbent on sepulchral slabs or effigied in brass
Buttress with prayer this vaulted roof so white and light and strong
  And countless congregations as the generations pass
Join choir and great crowned organ case, in centuries of song
  To praise Eternity contained in Time and coloured glass.

W. H. AUDEN
(1907–1973)

Law Like Love

    Law, say the gardeners, is the sun,
    Law is the one
    All gardeners obey
    To-morrow, yesterday, to-day.

Law is the wisdom of the old,
The impotent grandfathers feebly scold;
The grandchildren put out a treble tongue,
Law is the senses of the young.

Law, says the priest with a priestly look,
Expounding to an unpriestly people,
Law is the words in my priestly book,
Law is my pulpit and my steeple.
Law, says the judge as he looks down his nose,
Speaking clearly and most severely,
Law is as I've told you before,
Law is as you know I suppose,
Law is but let me explain it once more,
Law is The Law.

Yet law-abiding scholars write:
Law is neither wrong nor right,
Law is only crimes
Punished by places and by times,
Law is the clothes men wear
Anytime, anywhere,
Law is Good morning and Good night.

Others say, Law is our Fate;
Others say, Law is our State;
Others say, others say
Law is no more,
Law has gone away.

And always the loud angry crowd,
Very angry and very loud,
Law is We,
And always the soft idiot softly Me.

If we, dear, know we know no more
Than they about the Law,
If I no more than you
Know what we should and should not do
Except that all agree
Gladly or miserably
That the Law is
And that all know this,
If therefore thinking it absurd
To identify Law with some other word,
Unlike so many men
I cannot say Law is again,
No more than they can we suppress
The universal wish to guess
Or slip out of our own position
Into an unconcerned condition.
Although I can at least confine
Your vanity and mine
To stating timidly
A timid similarity,
We shall boast anyway:
Like love I say.

Like love we don't know where or why,
Like love we can't compel or fly,
Like love we often weep,
Like love we seldom keep.

September 1939

The Shield of Achilles

She looked over his shoulder
    For vines and olive trees,
Marble well-governed cities
    And ships upon untamed seas,
But there on the shining metal
    His hands had put instead
An artificial wilderness
    And a sky like lead.

A plain without a feature, bare and brown,
    No blade of grass, no sign of neighbourhood,
Nothing to eat and nowhere to sit down,
    Yet, congregated on its blankness, stood
    An unintelligible multitude,
A million eyes, a million boots in line,
Without expression, waiting for a sign.

Out of the air a voice without a face
    Proved by statistics that some cause was just
In tones as dry and level as the place:
    No one was cheered and nothing was discussed;
    Column by column in a cloud of dust
They marched away enduring a belief
Whose logic brought them, somewhere else, to grief

She looked over his shoulder
    For ritual pieties,
White flower-garlanded heifers,
    Libation and sacrifice,
But there on the shining metal
    Where the altar should have been,
She saw by his flickering forge-light
    Quite another scene.

Barbed wire enclosed an arbitrary spot
   Where bored officials lounged (one cracked a joke)
And sentries sweated for the day was hot:
   A crowd of ordinary decent folk
   Watched from without and neither moved nor spoke
As three pale figures were led forth and bound
To three posts driven upright in the ground.

The mass and majesty of this world, all
   That carries weight and always weighs the same
Lay in the hands of others; they were small
   And could not hope for help and no help came:
   What their foes liked to do was done, their shame
Was all the worst could wish; they lost their pride
And died as men before their bodies died.

      She looked over his shoulder
        For athletes at their games,
      Men and women in a dance
        Moving their sweet limbs
      Quick, quick, to music,
        But there on the shining shield
      His hands had set no dancing-floor
        But a weed-choked field.

A ragged urchin, aimless and alone,
   Loitered about that vacancy; a bird
Flew up to safety from his well-aimed stone:
   That girls are raped, that two boys knife a third,
   Were axioms to him, who'd never heard
Of any world where promises were kept,
Or one could weep because another wept.

      The thin-lipped armourer,
        Hephaestos, hobbled away,
      Thetis of the shining breasts
        Cried out in dismay
      At what the god had wrought
        To please her son, the strong
      Iron-hearted man-slaying Achilles
        Who would not live long.

Precious Five

Be patient, solemn nose,
Serve in a world of prose
The present moment well,
Nor surlily contrast
Its brash ill-mannered smell
With grand scents of the past.
That calm enchanted wood,
That grave world where you stood
So gravely at its middle,
Its oracle and riddle,
Has all been altered; now
In anxious times you serve
As bridge from mouth to brow,
An asymmetric curve
Thrust outward from a face
Time-conscious into space,
Whose oddness may provoke
To a mind-saving joke
A mind that would it were
An apathetic sphere:
Point, then, for honour's sake
Up the storm-beaten slope
From memory to hope
The way you cannot take.

Be modest, lively ears,
Spoiled darlings of a stage
Where any caper cheers
The paranoiac mind
Of this undisciplined
And concert-going age,
So lacking in conviction
It cannot take pure fiction,
And what it wants from you
Are rumours partly true;
Before you catch its sickness
Submit your lucky quickness

And levity to rule,
Go back again to school,
Drudge patiently until
No whisper is too much
And your precision such
At any sound that all
Seem natural, not one
Fantastic or banal,
And then do what you will:
Dance with angelic grace,
In ecstasy and fun,
The luck you cannot place.

Be civil, hands; on you
Although you cannot read
Is written what you do
And blows you struck so blindly
In temper or in greed,
Your tricks of long ago,
Eyes, kindly or unkindly,
Unknown to you will know.
Revere those hairy wrists
And leg-of-mutton fists
Which pulverized the trolls
And carved deep Donts in stone,
Great hands which under knolls
Are now disjointed bone,
But what has been has been;
A tight arthritic claw
Or aldermanic paw
Waving about in praise
Of those homeric days
Is impious and obscene:
Grow, hands, into those living
Hands which true hands should be
By making and by giving
To hands you cannot see.

Look, naked eyes, look straight
At all eyes but your own
Lest in a tête-a-tête
Of glances double-crossed,
Both knowing and both known,
Your nakedness be lost;
Rove curiously about
But look from inside out,
Compare two eyes you meet
By dozens on the street,
One shameless, one ashamed,
Too lifeless to be blamed,
With eyes met now and then
Looking from living men,
Which in petrarchan fashion
Play opposite the heart,
Their humour to her passion,
Her nature to their art,
For mutual undeceiving;
True seeing is believing
(What sight can never prove)
There is a world to see:
Look outward, eyes, and love
Those eyes you cannot be.

Praise, tongue, the Earthly Muse
By number and by name
In any style you choose,
For nimble tongues and lame
Have both found favour; praise
Her port and sudden ways,
Now fish-wife and now queen,
Her reason and unreason:
Though freed from that machine,
Praise Her revolving wheel
Of appetite and season
In honour of Another,
The old self you become
At any drink or meal,

That animal of taste,
And of his twin, your brother,
Unlettered, savage, dumb,
Down there below the waist:
Although your style be fumbling,
Half stutter and half song,
Give thanks however bumbling,
Telling for Her dear sake
To whom all styles belong
The truth She cannot make.

Be happy, precious five,
So long as I'm alive
Nor try to ask me what
You should be happy for;
Think, if it helps, of love
Or alcohol or gold,
But do as you are told.
I could (which you cannot)
Find reasons fast enough
To face the sky and roar
In anger and despair
At what is going on,
Demanding that it name
Whoever is to blame:
The sky would only wait
Till all my breath was gone
And then reiterate
As if I wasn't there
That singular command
I do not understand,
Bless what there is for being,
Which has to be obeyed, for
What else am I made for,
Agreeing or disagreeing?

STEVIE SMITH
(1902–1971)

Scorpion

'This night shall thy soul be required of thee'
My soul is never required of *me*
It always has to be somebody else of course
Will my soul be required of me tonight perhaps?

(I often wonder what it will be like
To have one's soul required of one
But all I can think of is the Out-Patients' Department –
'Are you Mrs Briggs, dear?'
No, I am Scorpion.)

I should like my soul to be required of me, so as
To waft over grass till it comes to the blue sea
I am very fond of grass, I always have been, but there must
Be no cow, person or house to be seen.

Sea and *grass* must be quite empty
Other souls can find somewhere *else*.

O Lord God please come
And require the soul of thy Scorpion

Scorpion so wishes to be gone.

LOUIS MACNEICE
(1907–1963)

Whit Monday

Their feet on London, their heads in the grey clouds,
The Bank (if you call it a holiday) Holiday crowds
Stroll from street to street, cocking an eye
For where the angel used to be in the sky;
But the Happy Future is a thing of the past and the street
Echoes to nothing but their dawdling feet.
The Lord's my shepherd – familiar words of myth
Stand up better to bombs than a granite monolith,
Perhaps there is something in them. *I'll not want* –
Not when I'm dead. *He makes me down to lie* –
Death my christening and fire my font –
The quiet (Thames or Don's or Salween's) *waters by*.

Goodbye to London

Having left the great mean city, I make
Shift to pretend I am finally quit of her
Though that cannot be so long as I work.
  Nevertheless let the petals fall
  Fast from the flower of cities all.

When I first met her to my child's ear
She was an ocean of drums and tumbrils
And in my nostrils horsepiss and petrol.
  Nevertheless let the petals fall
  Fast from the flower of cities all.

Next to my peering teens she was foreign
Names over winking doors, a kaleidoscope
Of wine and ice, of eyes and emeralds.
  Nevertheless let the petals fall
  Fast from the flower of cities all.

347

Later as a place to live in and love in
I jockeyed her fogs and quoted Johnson:
To be tired of this is to tire of life.
   Nevertheless let the petals fall
   Fast from the flower of cities all.

Then came the headshrinking war, the city
Closed in too, the people were fewer
But closer too, we were back in the womb.
   Nevertheless let the petals fall
   Fast from the flower of cities all.

From which reborn into anticlimax
We endured much litter and apathy hoping
The phoenix would rise, for so they had promised.
   Nevertheless let the petals fall
   Fast from the flower of cities all.

And nobody rose, only some meaningless
Buildings and the people once more were strangers
At home with no one, sibling or friend.
   Which is why now the petals fall
   Fast from the flower of cities all.

Apple Blossom

   The first blossom was the best blossom
   For the child who never had seen an orchard;
   For the youth whom whisky had led astray
   The morning after was the first day.

   The first apple was the best apple
   For Adam before he heard the sentence;
   When the flaming sword endorsed the Fall
   The trees were his to plant for all.

The first ocean was the best ocean
For the child from streets of doubt and litter;
For the youth for whom the skies unfurled
His first love was his first world.

But the first verdict seemed the worst verdict
When Adam and Eve were expelled from Eden;
Yet when the bitter gates clanged to
The sky beyond was just as blue.

For the next ocean is the first ocean
And the last ocean is the first ocean
And, however often the sun may rise,
A new thing dawns upon our eyes.

For the last blossom is the first blossom
And the first blossom is the best blossom
And when from Eden we take our way
The morning after is the first day.

Belfast

The hard cold fire of the northerner
Frozen into his blood from the fire in his basalt
Glares from behind the mica of his eyes
And the salt carrion water brings him wealth.

Down there at the end of the melancholy lough
Against the lurid sky over the stained water
Where hammers clang murderously on the girders
Like crucifixes the gantries stand.

And in the marble stores rubber gloves like polyps
Cluster; celluloid, painted ware, glaring
Metal patents, parchment lampshades, harsh
Attempts at buyable beauty.

In the porch of the chapel before the garish Virgin
A shawled factory-woman as if shipwrecked there
Lies a bunch of limbs glimpsed in the cave of gloom
By us who walk in the street so buoyantly and glib.

Over which country of cowled and haunted faces
The sun goes down with a banging of Orange drums
While the male kind murders each its woman
To whose prayer for oblivion answers no Madonna.

DYLAN THOMAS
(1914–1953)

Do Not Go Gentle Into That Good Night

Do not go gentle into that good night,
Old age should burn and rave at close of day;
Rage, rage against the dying of the light.

Though wise men at their end know dark is right,
Because their words had forked no lightning they
Do not go gentle into that good night.

Good men, the last wave by, crying how bright
Their frail deeds might have danced in a green bay,
Rage, rage against the dying of the light.

Wild men who caught and sang the sun in flight,
And learn, too late, they grieved it on its way,
Do not go gentle into that good night.

Grave men, near death, who see with blinding sight
Blind eyes could blaze like meteors and be gay,
Rage, rage against the dying of the light.

And you, my father, there on the sad height,
Curse, bless, me now with your fierce tears, I pray.
Do not go gentle into that good night.
Rage, rage against the dying of the light.

THEODORE ROETHKE
(1908–1963)

In a Dark Time

In a dark time, the eye begins to see,
I meet my shadow in the deepening shade;
I hear my echo in the echoing wood –
A lord of nature weeping to a tree.
I live between the heron and the wren,
Beasts of the hill and serpents of the den.

What's madness but nobility of soul
At odds with circumstance? The day's on fire!
I know the purity of pure despair,
My shadow pinned against a sweating wall.
That place among the rocks – is it a cave,
Or winding path? The edge is what I have.

A steady storm of correspondences!
A night flowing with birds, a ragged moon,
And in broad day the midnight come again!
A man goes far to find out what he is –
Death of the self in a long, tearless night,
All natural shapes blazing unnatural light.

Dark, dark my light, and darker my desire.
My soul, like some heat-maddened summer fly,
Keeps buzzing at the sill. Which I is *I*?
A fallen man, I climb out of my fear.
The mind enters itself, and God the mind,
And one is One, free in the tearing wind.

The Marrow

I

The wind from off the sea says nothing new.
The mist above me sings with its small flies.
From a burnt pine the sharp speech of a crow
Tells me my drinking breeds a will to die.
What's the worst portion in this mortal life?
A pensive mistress, and a yelping wife.

II

One white face shimmers brighter than the sun
When contemplation dazzles all I see;
One look too close can take my soul away.
Brooding on God, I may become a man.
Pain wanders through my bones like a lost fire;
What burns me now? Desire, desire, desire.

III

Godhead above my God, are you there still?
To sleep is all my life. In sleep's half-death,
My body alters, altering the soul
That once could melt the dark with its small breath.
Lord, hear me out, and hear me out this day:
From me to Thee's a long and terrible way.

IV

I was flung back from suffering and love
When light divided on a storm-tossed tree.
Yea, I have slain my will, and still I live;
I would be near; I shut my eyes to see;
I bleed my bones, their marrow to bestow
Upon that God who knows what I would know.

The Right Thing

Let others probe the mystery if they can.
Time-harried prisoners of *Shall* and *Will* –
The right thing happens to the happy man.

The bird flies out, the bird flies back again;
The hill becomes the valley, and is still;
Let others delve that mystery if they can.

God bless the roots! – Body and soul are one!
The small become the great, the great the small;
The right thing happens to the happy man.

Child of the dark, he can out leap the sun,
His being single, and that being all:
The right thing happens to the happy man.

Or he sits still, a solid figure when
The self-destructive shake the common wall;
Takes to himself what mystery he can,

And, praising change as the slow night comes on,
Wills what he would, surrendering his will
Till mystery is no more: No more he can.
The right thing happens to the happy man.

R. S. THOMAS
(*b.*1913)

The Country Clergy

I see them working in old rectories
By the sun's light, by candlelight,
Venerable men, their black cloth
A little dusty, a little green
With holy mildew. And yet their skulls,
Ripening over so many prayers,

Toppled into the same grave
With oafs and yokels. They left no books,
Memorial to their lonely thought
In grey parishes; rather they wrote
On men's hearts and in the minds
Of young children sublime words
Too soon forgotten. God in his time
Or out of time will correct this.

Ann Griffith

So God spoke to her,
she the poor girl from the village
without learning. 'Play me,'
he said, 'on the white keys
of your body. I have seen you dance
for the bridegrooms that were not
to be, while I waited for you
under the ripening boughs of
the myrtle. These people know me
only in the thin hymns of
the mind, in the arid sermons
and prayers. I am the live God,
nailed fast to the old tree
of a nation by its unreal
tears. I thirst, I thirst
for the spring water. Draw it up
for me from your heart's well and I will change
it to wine upon your unkissed lips.'

C. H. SISSON
(b.1914)

In Autumn

The sap is going out of my fingers
And the tune that my father used to drum
Comes readily to them.

Nothing that I could plead to young beauty
Could secure that my cold hand would be forgiven
Or the tears I cannot shed.

Well might Augustine pray that the ebb be not too fast
Holm-oak and myrtle and the treacherous bay-tree
Could not comfort him.

So turn me home towards God, and my last sunlight
Fall on no child of woman but on ash and chestnut
When the leaf falls.

DAVID GASCOYNE
(b.1916)

Tenebrae

'*It is finished.*' The last nail
Has consummated the inhuman pattern, and the veil
Is torn. God's wounds are numbered.
All is now withdrawn: void yawns
The rock-hewn tomb. There is no more
Regeneration in the stricken sun,
The hope of faith no more,
No height no depth no sign
And no more history.

Thus may it be: and worse.
And may we know Thy perfect darkness.
And may we into Hell descend with Thee.

Ecce Homo

Whose is this horrifying face,
This putrid flesh, discoloured, flayed,
Fed on by flies, scorched by the sun?
Whose are these hollow red-filmed eyes
And thorn-spiked head and spear-stuck side?
Behold the Man: He is Man's Son.

Forget the legend, tear the decent veil
That cowardice or interest devised
To make their mortal enemy a friend,
To hide the bitter truth all His wounds tell,
Lest the great scandal be no more disguised:
He is in agony till the world's end,

And we must never sleep during that time!
He is suspended on the cross-tree now
And we are onlookers at the crime,
Callous contemporaries of the slow
Torture of God. Here is the hill
Made ghastly by His spattered blood.

Whereon He hangs and suffers still:
See, the centurions wearing riding-boots,
Black shirts and badges and peaked caps,
Greet one another with raised-arm salutes;
They have cold eyes, unsmiling lips;
Yet these His brothers know not what they do.

And on his either side hang dead
A labourer and a factory hand,
Or one is maybe a lynched Jew
And one a Negro or a Red,
Coolie or Ethiopian, Irishman,
Spaniard or German democrat.

Behind his lolling head the sky
Glares like a fiery cataract
Red with the murders of two thousand years
Committed in His name and by
Crusaders, Christian warriors
Defending faith and property.

Amid the plain between His transfixed hands.
Exuding darkness as indelible
As guilty stains, fanned by funereal
And lurid airs, besieged by drifting sands
And clefted landslides our about-to-be
Bombed and abandoned cities stand.

He who wept for Jerusalem
Now sees His prophecy extend
Across the greatest cities of the world,
A guilty panic reason cannot stem
Rising to raze them all as He foretold;
And He must watch this drama to the end.

Though often named, He is unknown
To the dark kingdoms at His feet
Where everything disparages His words,
And each man bears the common guilt alone
And goes blindfolded to his fate,
And fear and greed are sovereign lords.

The turning point of history
Must come. Yet the complacent and the proud
And who exploit and kill, may be denied –
Christ of Revolution and of Poetry –
The resurrection and the life
Wrought by your spirit's blood.

Involved in their own sophistry
The black priest and the upright man
Faced by subversive truth shall be struck dumb,
Christ of Revolution and of Poetry,
While the rejected and condemned become
Agents of the divine.

Not from a monstrance silver-wrought
But from the tree of human pain
Redeem our sterile misery,
Christ of Revolution and of Poetry,
That man's long journey through the night
May not have been in vain.

ROBERT LOWELL
(1917–1977)

The Quaker Graveyard in Nantucket

(For Warren Winslow, Dead at Sea)

Let man have dominion over the fishes of the sea and the fowls of the
air and the beasts and the whole earth, and every creeping creature that
moveth upon the earth.

I

A brackish reach of shoal off Madaket, –
The sea was still breaking violently and night
Had steamed into our North Atlantic Fleet,
When the drowned sailor clutched the drag-net. Light
Flashed from his matted head and marble feet,
He grappled at the net
With the coiled, hurdling muscles of his thighs:
The corpse was bloodless, a botch of reds and whites,
Its open, staring eyes
Were lustreless dead-lights
Or cabin-windows on a stranded hulk
Heavy with sand. We weight the body, close
Its eyes and heave it seaward whence it came,
Where the heel-headed dogfish barks its nose
On Ahab's void and forehead; and the name
Is blocked in yellow chalk.
Sailors, who pitch this portent at the sea

Where dreadnaughts shall confess
Its hell-bent deity,
When you are powerless
To sandbag this Atlantic bulwark, faced
By the earth-shaker, green, unwearied, chaste
In his steel scales: ask for no Orphean lute
To pluck life back. The guns of the steeled fleet
Recoil and then repeat
The hoarse salute.

II

Whenever winds are moving and their breath
Heaves at the roped-in bulwarks of this pier,
The terns and sea-gulls tremble at your death
In these home waters. Sailors, can you hear
The Pequod's sea wings, beating landward, fall
Headlong and break on our Atlantic wall
Off 'Sconset, where the yawing S-boats splash
The bellbuoy, with ballooning spinnakers,
As the entangled, screeching mainsheet clears
The blocks: off Madaket, where lubbers lash
The heavy surf and throw their long lead squids
For blue-fish? Sea-gulls blink their heavy lids
Seaward. The winds' wings beat upon the stones,
Cousin, and scream for you and the claws rush
At the sea's throat and wring it in the slush
Of this old Quaker graveyard where the bones
Cry out in the long night for the hurt beast
Bobbing by Ahab's whaleboats in the East.

III

All you recovered from Poseidon died
With you, my cousin, and the harrowed brine
Is fruitless on the blue beard of the god,
Stretching beyond us to the castles in Spain,
Nantucket's westward haven. To Cape Cod
Guns, cradled on the tide,
Blast the eelgrass about a waterlock
Of bilge and backwash, roil the salt and sand
Lashing earth's scaffold, rock
Our warships in the hand
Of the great God, where time's contrition blues
Whatever it was these Quaker sailors lost
In the mad scramble of their lives. They died
When time was open-eyed,
Wooden and childish; only bones abide
There, in the nowhere, where their boats were tossed

Sky-high, where mariners had fabled news
Of IS, the whited monster. What it cost
Them is their secret. In the sperm whale's slick
I see the Quakers drown and hear their cry:
'If God himself had not been on our side,
If God himself had not been on our side,
When the Atlantic rose against us, why,
Then it had swallowed us up quick.'

IV

This is the end of the whaleroad and the whale
Who spewed Nantucket bones on the thrashed swell
And stirred the troubled waters to whirlpools
To send the Pequod packing off to hell:
This is the end of them, three-quarters fools,
Snatching at straws to sail
Seaward and seaward on the turntail whale,
Spouting out blood and water as it rolls,
Sick as a dog to these Atlantic shoals:
Clamavimus, O depths. Let the sea-gulls wail

For water, for the deep where the high tide
Mutters to its hurt self, mutters and ebbs.
Waves wallow in their wash, go out and out,
Leave only the death-rattle of the crabs,
The beach increasing, its enormous snout
Sucking the ocean's side.
This is the end of running on the waves;
We are poured out like water. Who will dance
The mast-lashed master of Leviathans
Up from this field of Quakers in their unstoned graves?

V

When the whale's viscera go and the roll
Of its corruption overruns this world
Beyond tree-swept Nantucket and Wood's Hole
And Martha's Vineyard, Sailor, will your sword
Whistle and fall and sink into the fat?
In the great ash-pit of Jehoshaphat

The bones cry for the blood of the white whale,
The fat flukes arch and whack about its ears,
The death-lance churns into the sanctuary, tears
The gun-blue swingle, heaving like a flail,
And hacks the coiling life out: it works and drags
And rips the sperm-whale's midriff into rags,
Gobbets of blubber spill to wind and weather,
Sailor, and gulls go round the stoven timbers
Where the morning stars sing out together
And thunder shakes the white surf and dismembers
The red flag hammered in the mast-head. Hide,
Our steel, Jonah Messiah, in Thy side.

VI

OUR LADY OF WALSINGHAM

There once the penitents took off their shoes
And then walked barefoot the remaining mile;
And the small trees, a stream and hedgerows file
Slowly along the munching English lane,
Like cows to the old shrine, until you lose
Track of your dragging pain.
The stream flows down under the druid tree,
Shiloah's whirlpools gurgle and make glad
The castle of God. Sailor, you were glad
And whistled Sion by that stream. But see:

Our Lady, too small for her canopy,
Sits near the altar. There's no comeliness
At all or charm in that expressionless
Face with its heavy eyelids. As before,
This face, for centuries a memory,
Non est species, neque decor,
Expressionless, expresses God: it goes
Past castled Sion. She knows what God knows,
Not Calvary's Cross nor crib at Bethlehem
Now, and the world shall come to Walsingham.

VII

The empty winds are creaking and the oak
Splatters and splatters on the cenotaph,
The boughs are trembling and a gaff
Bobs on the untimely stroke
Of the greased wash exploding on a shoal-bell
In the old mouth of the Atlantic. It's well;
Atlantic, you are fouled with the blue sailors,
Sea-monsters, upward angel, downward fish:
Unmarried and corroding, spare of flesh,
Mart once of supercilious, wing'd clippers,
Atlantic, where your bell-trap guts its spoil
You could cut the brackish winds with a knife
Here in Nantucket, and cast up the time
When the Lord God formed man from the sea's slime
And breathed into his face the breath of life,
And blue-lung'd combers lumbered to the kill.
The Lord survives the rainbow of His will.

CHARLES CAUSLEY
(b.1917)

I Am the Great Sun

From a Normandy crucifix of 1632

I am the great sun, but you do not see me,
    I am your husband, but you turn away.
I am the captive, but you do not free me,
    I am the captain you will not obey.

I am the truth, but you will not believe me,
    I am the city where you will not stay,
I am your wife, your child, but you will leave me,
    I am that God to whom you will not pray.

I am your counsel, but you do not hear me,
  I am the lover whom you will betray,
I am the victor, but you do not cheer me,
  I am the holy dove whom you will slay.

I am your life, but if you will not name me,
Seal up your soul with tears, and never blame me.

Sailor's Carol

Lord, the snowful sky
  In this pale December
Fingers my clear eye
  Lest seeing, I remember

Not the naked baby
  Weeping in the stable
Nor the singing boys
  All round my table,

Not the dizzy star
  Bursting on the pane
Nor the leopard sun
  Pawing the rain.

Only the deep garden
  Where green lilies grow,
The sailors rolling
  In the sea's blue snow.

Timothy Winters

Timothy Winters comes to school
With eyes as wide as a football pool,
Ears like bombs and teeth like splinters:
A blitz of a boy is Timothy Winters.

His belly is white, his neck is dark,
And his hair is an exclamation mark.
His clothes are enough to scare a crow
And through his britches the blue winds blow.

When teacher talks he won't hear a word
And he shoots down dead the arithmetic-bird,
He licks the pattern off his plate
And he's not even heard of the Welfare State.

Timothy Winters has bloody feet
And he lives in a house on Suez Street,
He sleeps in a sack on the kitchen floor
And they say there aren't boys like him any more.

Old Man Winters likes his beer
And his missus ran off with a bombardier,
Grandma sits in the grate with a gin
And Timothy's dosed with an aspirin.

The Welfare Worker lies awake
But the law's as tricky as a ten-foot snake,
So Timothy Winters drinks his cup
And slowly goes on growing up.

At Morning Prayers the Master helves
For children less fortunate than ourselves,
And the loudest response in the room is when
Timothy Winters roars 'Amen!'

So come one angel, come on ten:
Timothy Winters says 'Amen
Amen amen amen amen.'
Timothy Winters, Lord.
                    Amen.

King's College Chapel

When to the music of Byrd or Tallis,
   The ruffed boys singing in the blackened stalls,
The candles lighting the small bones on their faces,
   The Tudors stiff in marble on the walls,

There comes to evensong Elizabeth or Henry,
   Rich with brocade, pearl, golden lilies, at the altar,
The scarlet lions leaping on their bosoms,
   Pale royal hands fingering the crackling psalter,

Henry is thinking of his lute and of backgammon,
   Elizabeth follows the waving song, the mystery,
Proud in her red wig and green jewelled favours;
   They sit in their white lawn sleeves, as cool as history.

JOHN HEATH-STUBBS
(b. 1918)

from *Artorius*

      The raft drifted
Further and further from the shore,
Over the darkening waves. Then she began to sing,
Her voice booming over the waters:

   'We send you, body of a notable man,
   By the waste paths of the sea,
   The salt, unharvested element,

   'To the polity of the fish,
   To the furtiveness of the crab,
   To the tentacle of the squid,

   'To the red ruler of the tornado,
   To the green ruler of the undersea,
   To the black ruler of the dead,

'To the three-headed dog,
To the sharp-toothed Scylla –
Cuttle fish, and sea-bitch.

'O Lord, who said to the deep:
"So far, and no further!"
Deliver Thy darling from the tooth of the shark.

'O Christ descending
To the profound, redeem him
From the belly of the fish.

'O Spirit, brooding on tohu-bohu, save
From the embrace of the sea-morgan,
From Tiamat, the formless –

'Dove, bearing your olive leaf
Through the rains of the new year,
Breathe into the nostrils of the drowned.

'Star of the Sea,
In intercession gleam
Over the black waters.

'And our vows follow him,
Like petrels flittering
Over the crests and troughs of the waves.

'To the verdict and oblivion of the sea,
Artorius, we consign
Your actions, your defeat.'

PHILIP LARKIN
(*b.* 1922)

The Explosion

On the day of the explosion
Shadows pointed towards the pithead:
In the sun the slagheap slept.

Down the lane came men in pitboots
Coughing oath-edged talk and pipe-smoke,
Shouldering off the freshened silence.

One chased after rabbits; lost them;
Came back with a nest of lark's eggs;
Showed them; lodged them in the grasses.

So they passed in beards and moleskins,
Fathers, brothers, nicknames, laughter,
Through the tall gates standing open.

At noon, there came a tremor; cows
Stopped chewing for a second; sun,
Scarfed as in a heat-haze, dimmed.

The dead go on before us, they
Are sitting in God's house in comfort,
We shall see them face to face –

Plain as lettering in the chapels
It was said, and for a second
Wives saw men of the explosion

Larger than in life they managed –
Gold as on a coin, or walking
Somehow from the sun towards them,

One showing the eggs unbroken.

Days

What are days for?
Days are where we live.
They come, they wake us
Time and time over.
They are to be happy in:
Where can we live but days?

Ah, solving that question
Brings the priest and the doctor
In their long coats
Running over the fields.

Water

If I were called in
To construct a religion
I should make use of water.

Going to church
Would entail a fording
To dry, different clothes;

My liturgy would employ
Images of sousing,
A furious devout drench,

And I should raise in the east
A glass of water
Where any-angled light
Would congregate endlessly.

JOHN ORMOND
(*b.* 1923)

Cathedral Builders

They climbed on sketchy ladders towards God,
With winch and pulley hoisted hewn rock into heaven,
Inhabited sky with hammers, defied gravity,
Deified stone, took up God's house to meet Him,

And came down to their suppers and small beer;
Every night slept, lay with their smelly wives,
Quarrelled and cuffed the children, lied,
Spat, sang, were happy or unhappy,

And every day took to the ladders again;
Impeded the rights of way of another summer's
Swallows, grew greyer, shakier, became less inclined
To fix a neighbour's roof of a fine evening,

Saw naves sprout arches, clerestories soar,
Cursed the loud fancy glaziers for their luck,
Somehow escaped the plague, got rheumatism,
Decided it was time to give it up,

To leave the spire to others; stood in the crowd
Well back from the vestments at the consecration,
Envied the fat bishop his warm boots,
Cocked up a squint eye and said, 'I bloody did that.'

ELIZABETH JENNINGS
(b. 1926)

Teresa of Avila

Spain. The wild dust, the whipped corn, earth easy for footsteps, shallow to starving seeds. High sky at night like walls. Silences surrounding Avila.

She, teased by questions, aching for reassurance. Calm in confession before incredulous priests. Then back – to the pure illumination, the profound personal prayer, the four waters.

Water from the well first, drawn up painfully. Clinking of pails. Dry lips at the well-head. Parched grass bending. And the dry heart too – waiting for prayer.

Then the water-wheel, turning smoothly. Somebody helping unseen. A keen hand put out, gently sliding the wheel. Then water and the aghast spirit refreshed and quenched.

Not this only. Other waters also, clear from a spring or a pool. Pouring from a fountain like child's play – but the child is elsewhere. And she, kneeling, cooling her spirit at the water, comes nearer, nearer.

Then the entire cleansing, utterly from nowhere. No wind ruffled it, no shadows slid across it. Her mind met it, her will approved. And all beyonds, backwaters, dry words of old prayers were lost in it. The water was only itself.

And she knelt there, waited for shadows to cross the light which the water made, waited for familiar childhood illuminations (the lamp by the bed, the candle in church, sun beckoned by horizons) – but this light was none of these, was only how the water looked, how the will turned and was still. Even the image of light itself withdrew, and the dry dust on the winds of Spain outside her halted. Moments spread not into hours but stood still. No dove brought the tokens of peace. She was the peace that her prayer had promised. And the silences suffered no shadows.

Works of Art

So often it appears like an escape,
That cool, wide world where even shadows are
Ordered and relegated to a shape
Not too intrusive and yet not too spare.
How easy it has seemed to wander deep
Into this world and find a shelter there.

Yet always it surprises. Nervous hands
Which make the first rough sketch in any art,
Leave their own tension, and the statue stands,
The poem lies with trouble at its heart.
And every fashioned object makes demands
Though we feel uncommitted at the start.

Yeats said that gaiety explained it all,
That Hamlet, Lear were gay, and so are we.
He did not look back to a happy Fall
Where man stood lost, ashamed beneath a tree.
There was no art within that garden wall
Until we chose our dangerous liberty.

And now all making has the bitter-sweet
Taste of frustration yet of something done.
We want more order than we ever meet
And art keeps driving us most hopefully on.
Yet coolness is derived from all that heat,
And shadows draw attention to the sun.

from *The Sonnets of Michelangelo*
LXXV

I wish, God, for some end I do not will.
Between the fire and heart a veil of ice
Puts out the fire. My pen will not move well,
So that the sheet on which I'm working lies.

I pay you mere lip-service, then I grieve;
Love does not reach my heart, I do not know
How to admit that grace which would relieve
My state and crush the arrogance I show.

Oh tear away that veil, God, break that wall
Which with its strength refuses to let in
The sun whose light has vanished from the world.

Send down the promised light to bless and hold
Your lovely bride. So may I seek for all
I need in you, both end there and begin.

GEOFFREY HILL

GEOFFREY HILL
(*b.* 1932)

Genesis

I

Against the burly air I strode,
Where the tight ocean heaves its load,
Crying the miracles of God.

And first I brought the sea to bear
Upon the dead weight of the land;
And the waves flourished at my prayer,
The rivers spawned their sand.

And where the streams were salt and full
The tough pig-headed salmon strove,
Curbing the ebb and the tide's pull,
To reach the steady hills above.

II

The second day I stood and saw
The osprey plunge with triggered claw,
Feathering blood along the shore,
To lay the living sinew bare.

And the third day I cried: 'Beware
The soft-voiced owl, the ferret's smile,
The hawk's deliberate stoop in air,
Cold eyes, and bodies hooped in steel,
Forever bent upon the kill.'

III

And I renounced, on the fourth day,
This fierce and unregenerate clay,

Building as a huge myth for man
The watery Leviathan,

And made the glove-winged albatross
Scour the ashes of the sea
Where Capricorn and Zero cross,
A brooding immortality –
Such as the charmed phoenix has
In the unwithering tree.

IV

The phoenix burns as cold as frost;
And, like a legendary ghost,
The phantom-bird goes wild and lost,
Upon a pointless ocean tossed.

So, the fifth day, I turned again
To flesh and blood and the blood's pain.

V

On the sixth day, as I rode
In haste about the works of God,
With spurs I plucked the horse's blood.

By blood we live, the hot, the cold,
To ravage and redeem the world:
There is no bloodless myth will hold.

And by Christ's blood are men made free
Though in close shrouds their bodies lie
Under the rough pelt of the sea;

Though Earth has rolled beneath her weight
The bones that cannot bear the light.

ANONYMOUS

Go Down Moses

1

When Israel was in Egypt land,
Let my people go,
Oppressed so hard they could not stand,
Let my people go.
  Go down, Moses,
  Way-down in Egypt land,
  Tell old Pharaoh
  To let my people go.

2

'Thus spoke the Lord' bold Moses said,
'Let my people go,
If not, I'll smite your first-born dead,
Let my people go.' *(Chorus)*

3

'Your foes shall not before you stand,
Let my people go,
And you'll possess fair Canaan's land,
Let my people go.' *(Chorus)*

4

'You'll not get lost in the wilderness,
Let my people go,
With a lighted candle in your breast,
Let my people go.' *(Chorus)*

NICHOLAS KILMER
(b. 1941)
from *Petrarch*

In my first gentle days
I saw born and grow like grass
That wild desire that made my illness.
Because my singing makes the wound less violent,
I will sing how I lived in liberty, looked down upon;
While love lived in me, looked down upon;
How my neglect offended him;
What I have suffered on this account.

I have made myself an example to many.
I apologize for repeating injuries
Whose words have by now worked into the walls
Of these valleys, scrawled with broken chalk.

I have been sad. Memory does not help
Me as it used to. If this be true, blame
The sacrifice first, and the thinking that worries the wound.
I have become one single idea, fashioned of anguish.
I forget myself.
I am a cold rim around an inhabitant I have not
Been introduced to.

I say that from the day of the first mark
Love gave me, so many years have gone
My face is changed with age; thinking has closed
My heart and varnished it to an impermeable brilliance.
My pain for this reason has not slackened.
Tears will not break the surface, nor bathe
My sleep. And my sorrow being invisible,
I have thought it a miracle that sadness could show in others.

What I am, what I was.
Life praises end: the day praises its evening.
The cruel being of whom I speak felt
His blade had pierced no further than the cloth,
And took a powerful lady into his following,
Against whom strength never served me, nor talent,
Asking pardon.
Both changed me into what I am,
Made of a living man a green laurel,
Evergreen.

When I first realized
The transfiguration of my person,
I saw made of my hair the branch
I had once hoped to weave a crown with;
The feet I stood on, moved, ran,
As every limb follows the soul's direction,
Become two roots over the face of proud water,
Both arms branches.

So I was stilled with terror:
Terrified no less, covered with white feathers.
My hope had climbed to the lightning's reach
And was struck dead.
I found myself alone, hopeless and weeping;
I walked day and night, searching on either side
Into the water.

My tongue has never been silent since,
While I was able to speak, of this terrible fall.
And I took the sound and color of a swan.

I wandered this bank
Wanting to speak; but singing always
Calling for mercy with a foreign voice.
Nor could I sing with sufficient charm or care
To humble her heart out of its cruelty.
If memory is pain, then painful
The wound itself in feeling:
But there is worse to say of her delicate harm,
And I must speak, though she is beyond speaking.

She stood looking at me – let me
Tell you this – opened my chest,
Still with the look that took my balance,
And grasped my heart in her hand,
Saying to me, 'Don't talk about it.'

Then I saw her again, her face changed
To the point where I didn't know her,
And told her everything: told her the truth,
Terrified as I was. She turned on me
And I recognized her.
I became stone, troubled with life at the deep heart.

She spoke, her face so moved
Fear shook the stone I was, hearing her.
'I may not be what you think.'
I prayed my wound to quicken me.
Life would allow me weeping;
The cultivation of a living grief, less painful.

I don't know how: my feet began moving.
I am walking still. I say little of what is in my mind.
There is not much time in the day between death and life;
So I say only the marvelous things,
Reserving my ill will to myself,
Reserving blame.
Death was clenched around my heart,
Nor, by silence, could I escape his hand,
Nor bring my aid to force under attack.
My living speech kept from me,
What I wrote then was written only: I am not mine.
If I die, the blame is yours.

I thought to make a fool of myself to find mercy.
My hope made me bold. But sometimes humility
Stifles disdain, sometimes enflames it.
I understood this later, in a long period when
I was wrapped in darkness. Because my prayer
Put the light out. Being in her shadow
I could see neither her shadow, nor the trace of her passing.
I lay down on the grass like a drunk who sleeps in the street.

Then, cursing the lost light, I let everything go,
Let my tears fall as they willed.
I felt myself wandering as snow in sunlight
Wanders into water; and was a fountain
At the foot of a beech tree.
For some time I made damp runnels.
Who ever heard of a man becoming a fountain?
I am that man. I am aware of what I am saying.

The soul that God has shaped
Receptive to no other's grace
Keeps its master's patience.
Therefore it will forgive those with broken hearts
Who come for mercy, eventually,
However many their offenses.
And if she waited so long, looking on Him,
So that my guilt would be better known to me, more feared,
My repentance was at fault. I raised another sin
To shield the first.

                But she, moved with pity at this second,
Deigned to look at me, and recognized my sin
And punishment coequal; kindly
Reduced me to the man I had been.
Wisdom is distrust of the world.
For as I prayed there it was not finished.
My nerves and sinews calcified, my voice
Was driven from me, and I became that voice,
Calling on death familiarly by my first name.

I remember myself a wandering wounded spirit
Haunting caves and odd empty places.
I cried my desire unchecked for years,
Until the end of this evil came over me
And I slid back into my earthy shape;
I suppose because I could feel more pain there.

And moving my body now, still with desire,
One day, hunting – I used to hunt –
I opened trees enough to find her,
Glancing sun, wild naked, stretched in cold water.
I stood and watched while shame took over her body.
I wanted only to stand staring, not the shame.
Revenge – or she wishing to hide herself – hurled
An arc of water into my face; my whole being
Shook with it, came apart, turned animal
Stag, bayed from forest to forest, alone.
I can hear the dogs while I write this.

I was never a cloud of gold.
God makes His love where He wills.
I am sparked flame, I am the ugly bird whose huge wings raise her.
Pleasure fades from my heart. All other figures.
I am standing alone in the shadow of that first laurel.

MORE ABOUT PENGUINS, PELICANS
AND PUFFINS

For further information about books available from Penguins please write to Dept EP, Penguin Books Ltd, Harmondsworth, Middlesex UB7 0DA.

In the U.S.A.: For a complete list of books available from Penguins in the United States write to Dept DG, Penguin Books, 299 Murray Hill Parkway, East Rutherford, New Jersey 07073.

In Canada: For a complete list of books available from Penguins in Canada write to Penguin Books Canada Ltd, 2801 John Street, Markham, Ontario L3R 1B4.

In Australia: For a complete list of books available from Penguins in Australia write to the Marketing Department, Penguin Books Australia Ltd, P.O. Box 257, Ringwood, Victoria 3134.

In New Zealand: For a complete list of books available from Penguins in New Zealand write to the Marketing Department, Penguin Books (N.Z.) Ltd, Private Bag, Takapuna, Auckland 9.

In India: For a complete list of books available from Penguins in India write to Penguin Overseas Ltd, 706 Eros Apartments, 56 Nehru Place, New Delhi 110019.

PENGUIN POETRY

☐ *The Penguin Book of American Verse*
   Ed. Geoffrey Moore   £5.95

'A representative anthology which will give pleasure to the general reader and at the same time presents a full range of American poetry of all periods' – *The Times Literary Supplement*

☐ *Selected Poems* **Pasternak**   £2.50

Translated from the Russian by Jon Stallworthy and Peter France. 'These translations from *My Sister Life* and the other famous collections are the best we have, faithful to the originals, and true poems in their own right' – *The Times*

☐ *The Penguin Book of Bird Poetry*
   Ed. Peggy Munsterberg   £3.95

'Beautifully produced and intelligently compiled. Peggy Munsterberg has done a fine job. Her anthology will please lovers of birds and of poetry alike' – *The Times Literary Supplement*

☐ *The Complete Poems* **Jonathan Swift**   £9.95

A new, authoritative edition of the poems of this great satirist, pamphleteer and author of *Gulliver's Travels*. With an introduction, notes and a biographical dictionary of Swift's contemporaries by the editor, Pat Smith.

☐ *London in Verse* **Ed. Christopher Logue**   £2.95

Nursery-rhymes, street cries, Shakespeare and Spike Milligan trace a route through the streets, sights and characters of London in this lively anthology, which has a linking commentary and illustrations chosen by Christopher Logue. 'A rare and delightful book' – *Country Life*

☐ *The Penguin Book of Spanish Civil War Verse*
   Ed. Valentine Cunningham   £4.50

Poetry and prose making up 'an outstanding piece of historical reconstruction . . . a human document of absorbing interest' – *The Times Literary Supplement*

PENGUIN POETRY

☐ *The Penguin Book of Women Poets*
Ed. Cosman, Keefe and Weaver £3.95

From Sappho and Li Ching-chao to Emily Dickinson and Anna Akhmatova, this acclaimed anthology spans 3,500 years and forty literary traditions; it also includes a biographical/textual note on each poet.

☐ *Selected Poems* **William Carlos Williams** £2.95

Poems extracted by Williams from small-town American life, 'as a physician works upon a patient, upon the thing before him, in the particular to discover the universal'. Edited and introduced by Charles Tomlinson.

☐ *The Memory of War* and *Children in Exile*
James Fenton £2.25

Including 'A German Requiem' and several pieces on the Vietnam War, this collection of Fenton's poems 1968–83 is a major literary event. 'He is a magician-materialist . . . the most talented poet of his generation' – Peter Porter in the *Observer*

☐ *Poems of Science*
Ed. John Heath-Stubbs and Phillips Salman £4.95

This unusual anthology traces our changing perceptions of the universe through the eyes of the poets, from Spenser and Shakespeare to Dannie Abse and John Updike.

☐ *East Anglia in Verse* **Ed. Angus Wilson** £2.95

The sea, flat wheat fields and remote villages of East Anglia have inspired poets as diverse as John Betjeman, Thomas Hood, Edward Lear and Horace Walpole. Containing theirs and many other poems, this is a collection 'full of small marvels' – *Guardian*

☐ *Selected Poems* **Lorca** £2.50

With music, drama, the gypsy mythology, and the Andalusian folk-songs of his childhood, Lorca rediscovered and infused new life into the Spanish poetic traditions. This volume contains poems, plus excerpts from his plays, chosen and translated by J. L. Gili.

PENGUIN POETRY

☐ *Contemporary American Poetry* **Ed. Donald Hall**   £2.50

Robert Lowell, Richard Wilbur, Denise Levertov, Frank O'Hara, Dudley Randall, Sylvia Plath and Anne Sexton are among the thirty-nine poets represented in this virtuoso collection.

☐ *New Volume*
Adrian Henri, Roger McGough and Brian Patten   £1.50

A new anthology from three of the most popular poets writing today. This Penguin also contains some poems originally published in their bestselling volume: *The Mersey Sound*.

☐ *Paterson* **William Carlos Williams**   £2.95

Part autobiography, part the story of the New Jersey city near which Williams lived, *Paterson* is among the greatest long poems in modern American literature.

These books should be available at all good bookshops or newsagents, but if you live in the UK or the Republic of Ireland and have difficulty in getting to a bookshop, they can be ordered by post. Please indicate the titles required and fill in the form below.

NAME _____ BLOCK CAPITALS

ADDRESS _____

_____

_____

Enclose a cheque or postal order payable to The Penguin Bookshop to cover the total price of books ordered, plus 50p for postage. Readers in the Republic of Ireland should send £IR equivalent to the sterling prices, plus 67p for postage. Send to: The Penguin Bookshop, 54/56 Bridlesmith Gate, Nottingham, NG1 2GP.

You can also order by phoning (0602) 599295, and quoting your Barclaycard or Access number.

Every effort is made to ensure the accuracy of the price and availability of books at the time of going to press, but it is sometimes necessary to increase prices and in these circumstances retail prices may be shown on the covers of books which may differ from the prices shown in this list or elsewhere. This list is not an offer to supply any book.

This order service is only available to residents in the UK and the Republic of Ireland.